Chocolate
Kisses

Chocolate Kisses

Margaret Brownley
Raine Cantrell
Alexis Harrington
Sue Rich

St. Martin's Paperbacks

CHOCOLATE KISSES

"Rocky Road" copyright © 1997 by Margaret Brownley.
"Miss Delwin's Delights" copyright © 1997 by Theresa Di Benedetto.
"The Taste of Remembrance" copyright © 1997 by Alexis Harrington.
"Sweet Creations" copyright © 1997 by Sue Rich.
Excerpt from *Deep as the Rivers* copyright © 1997 by Shirl Henke.

ISBN: 0-312-96111-1

Printed in the United States of America

St. Martin's Paperbacks edition / February 1997

10 9 8 7 6 5

Contents

ROCKY ROAD

Margaret Brownley

❧ *Chapter 1* ❧

*O*f all the blasted luck! Josh Travis couldn't believe his eyes. Now he had no choice but to cut the damned thing off!

He stepped away from the red velvet barber chair, scissors held midair, took a deep breath, and considered how best to break the news to his unsuspecting customer.

Blissfully unaware that anything was wrong, Leland J. Crummer III continued his long-winded commentary on national affairs as if it were his God-given duty. Under normal circumstances, Josh wouldn't allow such political hogwash to go unchallenged, but at the moment it seemed more important to protect his hide from his hot-tempered customer than to defend President Wilson.

Crummer was clearly egging Josh on, and looked disappointed when Josh failed to take the bait. Crummer obviously had no idea that half of the long sweeping mustache he considered his pride and joy was missing one of its handles.

No, indeed, it was definitely not the time to inform the man that his political opinions were an abominable disgrace.

"Mark my words," Crummer continued. "The biggest mistake this country ever made was turning its back on Teddy Roosevelt and his Bull Moose Party."

"You could be right," Josh said, biting his tongue. The man was dead wrong, but Josh would correct him at a later date, perhaps in a year or two after the hairy handlebar had grown back.

Dammit! He couldn't believe. The whole left side of the mustache, gone! Never had he been so careless, though he'd once poured axel grease on a customer's head, instead of pomade. But that was years earlier, when he was still an apprentice.

If it hadn't been for that fool Mrs. Ryefield, the owner of the Sweet Dreams Confectionery, none of this would have happened. Imagine sending the heart-shaped box of Rocky Road chocolates he'd ordered special for Miss Laura Baker to Miss Winklemeyer instead.

How could such a mistake occur? Miss Winklemeyer of all people! The town's old maid schoolmarm.

He only hoped Mrs. Ryefield retrieved the chocolates before Miss Winklemeyer read the poem he'd spent half the night composing. If the flowery words he'd penned didn't put a blush on the spinster's prim face or take some starch out of her corset, nothing would! Just thinking of the poem and how he'd poured his heart out filled him with horror. How foolish of him to write his feelings down on paper. What in the world had possessed him? If Miss Winklemeyer read his ramblings before Mrs. Ryefield managed to retrieve the chocolates, he'd be the laughingstock of the town. Of the county!

What a day this had been. Starting with his decision to send his poem to Laura Baker along with a box of chocolates and ending with Crummer's mustache, the day had been one disaster after another.

He peered out his window and stared down the length of the brick paved street known as Main. The largest of the town's brick gothic buildings housed the telegraph and postal office. Stonewell Pines Bank was on the right-hand side, next to the two-story parlor furniture and undertaking store known as Franco's.

A dark green awning with yellow stripes marked the Sweet Dreams Confectionery, located at the other end of the block across from Horace's Hardware Store.

Where was she? Mrs. Ryefield had promised to stop by his barber shop just as soon as she had straightened out the mess. That was over two hours ago! No wonder he couldn't keep his mind on his work.

"Dang it, Josh, what's taking you so long?"

Josh drew his gaze away from the window. "Eh, well, I was thinking perhaps you might want a more modern look."

"Modern?" It was clear by the way Crummer's eyebrows rose to his hairline, he wanted no such thing. Despite the popularity and affordability of Model T Fords, he still owned a horse and carriage, insisted upon using gas light instead of electricity and steadfastly refused to avail himself of the telephone. "How do you mean, modern?" He made it sound as if Josh had suggested robbing the bank.

"Mustaches are no longer in style. Perhaps we could shave yours off and . . ."

"Absolutely not! The ladies like my mustache." He winked. "They said it tickles. So if you've finished, I'll take my leave." He stood up, flipped a coin onto the counter, slid his hat over his old-fashioned shingle cut hair and sauntered out of the shop without so much as a glance in the mirror.

Josh knew it would only be a matter of time before Crummer came storming back to demand a refund and probably Josh's head. It was one more thing to worry about, second only to the box of chocolates that had been sent to the wrong house.

It was late afternoon before Josh spotted Mrs. Ryefield leaving her shop. Dressed in a rather gaudy hobble skirt and a ridiculous hat that was all points and angles, she took her own sweet time walking the short distance from her shop to his. He wouldn't have minded so much had she not paused in front of the window of Randall's dry goods store, and stopped to admire Mrs. Cambridge's new baby girl.

By the time she finally reached Josh's shop, he was sorely out of patience. Josh hoped she had good news, but one never could tell. She had a perpetual frown and an annoying habit of beating around the bush.

"Well? Did you get the box of chocolates from Miss Winklemeyer?"

"The trouble with you, Josh, is that you worry too much."

"Did you or didn't you? A simple yes or no will do."

"Do calm down. It's not as big a problem as you might suppose."

Josh glared at her from beneath a knitted brow. "You didn't get the chocolates."

"It was a little difficult to do. You see Miss Winklemeyer is out of town. Peter . . ." She pressed an open palm on her chest and held her head back as if in agony. For a moment Josh feared one of her sharp pointed hat pins had worked its way into her scalp. Just as he was about to yank her hat off her head, the pained expression left her face. "The poor sweet boy feels terrible about the mix-up."

"He should," Josh said, not feeling particularly charitable at the moment. It was Peter's fault that the box of rocky road chocolates with his poem had gone to the wrong woman. If Crummer did, indeed, return with a shotgun in hand, Josh would personally hold the delivery boy responsible. "You said she's out of town."

"Yes, that's why Peter left the chocolates with Miss Winklemeyer's housekeeper."

This was the best news he'd heard all day. "Then she hasn't seen the poem . . . eh, chocolates."

"Not yet. Unfortunately, the housekeeper had already left by the time I arrived. But don't you worry about a thing. I understand Miss Winklemeyer is due to return tomorrow. In which case, I shall personally explain the mix-up, myself."

He hated the thought of having to wait until the following day before the problem was resolved.

"Don't worry about a thing," Mrs. Ryefield continued. "As soon as I retrieve the box of chocolates, I shall personally deliver them to their rightful owner, Laura Baker. Trust me, no one will be the wiser."

"I certainly hope you're right, Mrs. Ryefield." He was relieved, of course, that no one had read his poem. Still, he didn't like knowing that a poem as personal as the one he'd written for Laura was still at the schoolteacher's house. God knows what might happen if Miss Winklemeyer returned home and read it before the candy store owner had a chance to explain the mix-up.

"Of course I'm right." Mrs. Ryefield patted his arm in a way that made him wonder if he had more to worry about than she'd led him to believe. "You just go back to work and let me worry about the chocolates."

After Mrs. Ryefield had left, Travis carefully washed and dried the dozen or so china shaving mugs stacked by the sink, placing each one on the shelf to the right of the pot-bellied stove and making certain the names of his customers faced outward. He then swept the floor, stacked the dog-eared copies of the *Police Gazette* in a neat pile, counted out his money and hauled the six-foot tall wooden barber pole inside for the night.

The red, white, and blue pillar normally turned all day on a single winding. The pole wasn't turning and he suddenly remembered why. He'd been so busy thinking about Laura Baker and the poem he'd spent half the night composing, he'd completely forgotten to wind the clock works inside.

He closed up shop and drove his Model T Ford to Mrs. Clatterway's boarding house just outside of town. He rented the room above the carriage house. The room was light and airy and provided more privacy than the main house. The reasonable rates and home-cooked meals made Mrs. Clatterway's strict rules tolerable, but lately, he found himself longing for a home of his own, and dreamed of having a wife and children.

He'd sent away for the building plans offered free in the Sears and Roebucks mail-order catalog. It was a magnificently designed house, with a wraparound porch, an enormous kitchen, a huge pantry and enough bedrooms to raise a large family. He fully expected to have enough money saved by the end of the year to build the house.

Now he wondered if he'd been a bit too optimistic in making his plans. It was entirely possible that Laura Baker wouldn't want any part of him after reading his poem. *If* she read his poem.

Despite his misgivings, he had no reason to think Mrs. Ryefield wouldn't keep her word. She said she would straighten out the mess and she would! So what was he worried about?

Lord almighty, what wasn't he worried about? What if Laura Baker read his letter and hated it? What if she wanted nothing more to do with him?

It had taken him all of six months to muster enough nerve to send the box of rocky road chocolates to Laura in the first place. Six months. Now this!

Perhaps writing that his "heart took flight in her presence" was a trifle bit presumptuous of him. Why he'd hardly spoken three sentences to her since she and her family had moved to Stonewell Pines, Oregon from Philadelphia last fall.

If it hadn't been for Laura's brother, Logan, Josh might never have come up with the idea in the first place. Logan had come in for his monthly haircut and just happened to mention how he sometimes sneaked into Laura's room to snitch her favorite chocolates. That's how Josh knew to send her rocky road.

The chocolates were perfect. He wished he could say the same for the poem. But now that he thought about it, the words that had, in the wee hours of the morning, seemed brilliant, struck him as embarrassingly inept. What a bunch of sentimental, flowery, not to mention meaningless, gibberish! Not that he hadn't tried. He'd spent hours composing the poem, checking Nuttall's Standard Dictionary and perusing through Mrs. Clatterway's vast collection of poetry books for inspiration. *The rose is known for its beauty but it pales next to thee.*

He groaned and placed the palm of his hand on his forehead. What in the world possessed him to use the word *thee?* And what about the rest of the poem? The part about her spirit dancing to the music of the stars?

The more he thought about what he'd written, the more

depressed and miserable he was. Hands clasped behind his back, he paced about his room in an effort to calm himself. Laura can't see that poem! Not ever! Maybe, just maybe Mrs. Ryefield's delivery boy had done him a favor.

He raced down the stairs of the carriage house and cut across the lawn to the main house. He had to talk to Mrs. Ryefield before she delivered the chocolates to Laura.

The wall telephone was in the hallway next to the stairwell. He lifted the handset from its cradle and cranked. Stonewell Pines had but one telephone operator. Her name was Miss Baxter and she was the most irritating busybody, know-it-all Josh had the misfortune of knowing.

Miss Baxter was far more interested in her social life than she was in servicing the town's switchboard. Some said she had more gentlemen callers than the chicken house on Redford Street and judging by the number of times Josh was unable to get the uppity switchboard operator to handle his calls, he believed it.

"Mercy me, Josh, this is your second telephone call this week. If the whole town takes to using the telephone any time they darn well please, I'll have to give up my social life altogether."

Josh was tempted to tell her his opinion of her social life, but thought better of it. "Please connect me with Mrs. Ryefield."

"Mrs. Ryefield is visiting her sister and won't be back till morning."

Josh couldn't believe his ears. Why wasn't he told this? What if Miss Winklemeyer arrived home before Mrs. Ryefield returned from her sister's? Why the schoolmarm might read the note and . . . why the poor woman would be shocked and . . . his life would be in ruins!

"Cancel my call and you better not count this one!"

"It counts," Miss Baxter replied.

"But I didn't talk to anyone."

"You talked to me."

He slammed the handset in place, and tried to think. He had nothing to worry about. If worse came to worse and Miss

Winklemeyer happened to find his chocolates and read his poem, it wouldn't be the end of the world. It would only be the end of his life in Stonewell Pines.

He paced about in a circle. This was no time to panic. She was a schoolmarm. She'd probably read a lot of drivel in her time. Though drivel hardly described the embarrassingly inane passages he'd written. Suffering catfish, what had ever possessed him to put his feelings down on paper? He'd never been one to express his feelings in the past. Matters of the heart should be kept inside and from now on, that's exactly where he intended to keep them!

The more he thought about the poem he'd written, the more he dreaded the idea of it being read by anyone, including Laura.

He'd been a bit too hasty in his earlier contention; it *was* time to panic. And since Mrs. Ryefield had left him no choice, he would have to break into Miss Winklemeyer's house and fetch the box of rocky road chocolates himself, along with that confounded poem.

❧ *Chapter 2* ❧

*M*iss Winklemeyer lived alone in a small white clapboard house outside of town on Appleton Lane. She was known for her magnificent rose gardens and her delicious fresh peach pies, but her reputation as a schoolteacher was legendary.

She had personally seen to it that every child in Stonewell Pines over the age of nine could read fluently from their McGuffey Readers, recite their multiplication tables and write a proper essay. Any child failing to meet Miss Winklemeyer's high standards could expect to receive a personal visit, followed by long hours of intensive tutoring.

Josh had heard some call her a witch, though he supposed she was only doing her job. Still, he didn't want *her* reading anything he wrote, espccially his poetry! For all he knew, she'd come banging on his door, wanting to tutor him. He didn't know her, of course, not personally. But he recalled she wore dour gray or black clothes like she was in mourning or something. She also kept her hair in a rigid tight bun. She came to town only on rare occasions and, then, quickly darted in and out of various businesses with a purposeful air that made one think twice before getting in her way. She never stopped to gossip with any of the townsfolk, though she talked to every child. Come to think of it, the only time he'd ever seen her smile was when she was keeping company with a child.

He turned his late model Model T onto Appleton Lane and drove slowly over the narrow dirt road. Not wanting to be seen by Miss Winklemeyer's neighbors, he parked beneath a willow tree a block away and walked the distance to the house.

He had waited until after dark before leaving the boarding house. Electricity was not yet available this far south of Main Street and the residents still relied on gas to light their homes. Here and there a yellow glow shone from an open window, but mainly he depended on the silvery light of the full moon to guide him.

His senses alert, he was aware of every sound. He jumped when an owl swooped by in eerie white silence, and his heart nearly stopped at the sound of rustling leaves from a nearby bush. He froze in his tracks and held his breath until at last he decided the rustling sound had been either a rabbit or rodent darting to safety, maybe both.

Though the night was cool, his forehead was damp with perspiration by the time he reached the white picket fence guarding Miss Winklemeyer's property. The gate made a strange grating sound as he pushed against it, and his heart took to hammering against his rib cage. Lord almighty, if he didn't know it before, he knew it now; he wasn't cut out to break into other people's houses.

He circled the outside of the house slowly, checking each window in turn. At the back of the house, he found a half open window. Someone should tell Miss Winklemeyer to take more care in locking up the house in her absence.

Glancing around anxiously, his nervousness increased with each passing minute. May the good Lord look the other way, just this once.

After tonight, he wouldn't have the nerve to look Miss Winklemeyer in the eye.

Anxious to get the distasteful task over with as soon as possible, he lifted his leg onto the wooden sill, and ducked his head beneath the raised sash. He grabbed onto the side of the window frame and heaved himself into the house.

Inside, he stood perfectly still, trying to get his bearings.

He couldn't see much, but the room held the delicate scent of roses with just a hint of lavender. Obviously, he was in the schoolmarm's bedroom.

A thin thread of moonlight allowed him to walk from the window to the hall door without tripping over the furniture. He could make out the outline of the four-poster bed, but not much more.

He ran his hands down the door's smooth oak finish until he felt the cold hard feel of the brass knob. The hinge made a loud rasping sound as he pulled the door toward him. Since the house was empty, he made no effort to control the sound, but the noise was nonetheless nerve-racking and his knees practically gave out beneath him.

The hallway was pitch black, making it necessary to feel his way into the parlor. He walked into something and the soft ticking sound told him it was a tall grandfather clock. The clock struck the hour and he practically jumped out of his skin. He banged his elbow against the wall and a sharp pain shot down his arm.

"Ouch!" He held his arm, bending up and down at the waist, and cursed aloud. At last the pain subsided and he backed against a hat rack. "Dang it all!" he cried aloud. No one would ever guess that the prim and proper Miss Winklemeyer lived in a booby trap.

At last he reached what he assumed was the parlor. A stream of moonlight filtered through the curtained windows, but it was difficult to make sense of the dark shapes and deep shadows at the back of the room.

He guessed the housekeeper had placed the chocolates on a table somewhere, possibly by the front door. But where? He reached in his pocket for his box of lucifers and ran a matchstick across the flint. He held the flickering match in front of him and moved across the room, checking each table and bookshelf in turn. It appeared Miss Winklemeyer owned half the books in town.

The match quickly burned to his fingertips and he blew it out. He was ready to light another match when he heard a noise from behind. He stood perfectly still, but his bones took to shaking like a Model T Ford on a rough gravel road.

For the longest while, he didn't dare move. If the truth were known, he couldn't have moved had he wanted to. Convinced, finally, he'd imagined the sound or that Miss Winklemeyer perhaps owned a cat, he fumbled with his matches once more. This time he didn't imagine the soft shuffling sound behind him. He spun on his heel. "Who's there?"

That was the last he remembered.

Amelia Winklemeyer sank into her favorite upholstered chair, too tired to drag herself to bed. What a day this had been. What a night! After traveling four hours on an overcrowded train, she had arrived home exhausted. She'd taken a hot bath, heated herself a bowl of chicken soup and had gone straight to bed.

No sooner had she'd fallen asleep, than she'd been awakened by a sound at her bedroom window. Never had she been so afraid in all her born days! If she lived to be a hundred, she would never forget the strange metallic taste of fear that filled her mouth as she watched an intruder enter her bedroom through the open window.

How she managed to keep from crying out, she'd never know. Instead, she'd laid perfectly still, praying that her loud beating heart wouldn't give her away. She knew it was a man, though she had no idea who he was at the time. He'd moved across her bedroom like he had every right to be there! Why he didn't even try to be quiet. The nerve of him!

How she ever got the courage to climb out of bed and follow him out to the hall, she'd never know. She had decided a weapon would come in handy, and had grabbed the first object available, a leather-bound copy of the *Fanny Farmer Cookbook* left on the hall table.

It wasn't much of a weapon, but luck was on her side, or so it seemed at the time. After she'd clobbered the intruder with the cookbook, he'd jumped back and slipped on the braided rag carpet. She'd heard a thud as he hit his head on the rough edge of the brick hearth. He was knocked out, cold.

Even the sheriff had expressed surprise that a woman

barely five-feet-three could knock out a man as tall as Josh Travis.

Good Lord, what was Mr. Travis doing in my house? Prior to seeing him stretched out on her parlor floor, she knew him only by sight. She probably hadn't said more than a dozen or so words to him in all the years she'd lived in Stonewell Pines. All she could remember saying to him was a polite good morning or good evening on occasion as they passed each other on the street.

He had a reputation for being an honest and hard-working businessman and, until tonight, she had no reason to believe otherwise. So what in heaven's name would make a respected pillar of the community suddenly skulk around in other people's houses?

As she sat exhausted in her chair, her head resting against the spotless white antimacassar, she leveled her gaze across the room to the odd-shaped red box on the fine polished oak end table next to the divan couch.

"What in the world . . . ?" Surely she was imagining things. She sat upright and after assuring herself that something out of the ordinary was, indeed, gracing her table, she reluctantly left the comfort of her chair to take a closer look. It *was* a candy box. A large heart-shaped candy box tied with a shiny red satin bow.

Never before had anyone sent her a box of chocolates. She couldn't for the life of her imagine who would send her one now.

Her heart fluttering excitedly, she fingered the beautiful red box. Her fingers froze on the shiny bow as a disturbing thought occurred to her. Did the chocolates have anything to do with Josh Travis? The man she'd knocked out cold and who had been unceremoniously hauled off to jail the moment he came to?

No sooner had the thought occurred to her when she immediately discounted it. Mr. Travis wouldn't break into her house to leave her chocolates. Would he?

With shaking hands, she tore open the envelope. A letter

was written in a bold handwriting that was masculine in shape and form.

It was more of a poem than a letter, its exalted style praising her eyes and hair and even, *my goodness*, her neck. After reading about the "crowning glory of golden sunlight" she self-consciously touched the prim bun at her nape and read the rest.

> *Your eyes are the pride*
> *of the blue purple*
> *cornflower,*
> *Your lips pink*
> *as the dew-kissed*
> *rose,*
> *You wear the color of Heaven's garden.*

"Oh, my." But it was the next lines that brought tears to her eyes.

> *Your spirit dances*
> *to the music of the*
> *stars;*
> *Your heart sings*
> *the anthem of the*
> *universe.*

Dances? Sings? How in the world would anyone know this about her? She'd never attended a dance in her life, though Lord knows she wanted to, especially after seeing that famous dancing pair, the Castles, perform in Chicago. She did sing, on occasion, as she worked in her garden and, lately, she'd even tried out a dance step or two, pretending the rake was a dancing partner.

Unless someone had been spying on her, which she seriously doubted, no one could possibly know how she spent her private moments. Nor was it possible for anyone to guess her innermost thoughts.

Shivering, she glanced around the empty room in an effort

to assure herself that no stranger lurked behind the furniture. At the age of twenty-five, she still had girlish dreams and that wasn't exactly something she wanted others to know. It was foolish to dream of falling in love at her age!

Feeling strangely exposed, as if her heart and soul were on display for everyone to see, she drew the poem to her chest and caught sight of her reflection in the beveled glass mirror over the fireplace. Though she generally allowed herself no more than a cursory glance in the mirror before she left for school each morning, tonight she studied herself at length, desperate to see the woman in the poem, the woman who danced and sang and wore the colors of Heaven's garden.

She never thought herself pretty, of course, but the word "plain" hardly seemed to fit, either. Her eyes were far too big, her cheeks too high for plain. She was definitely distinctive-looking, she decided, though whether that was good or bad, she didn't know.

Never had she spent much time on her appearance and for good reason; she never wanted to call attention to herself. It was the only way she could protect herself. Her father had been orphaned at three, badly scarred in a fire at the age of five, and had been sent to prison at twelve for a murder he hadn't committed. Though he was later proven innocent, the town continued to treat him like an outcast until his death, and never forgave him for marrying the mayor's pretty daughter.

Amelia still recalled the constant whispers in her childhood. She was the oldest child and people pointed and stared at her whenever she appeared in public. She eventually learned that if she dressed in drab clothes, wore her hair tucked inside her bonnets, spoke softly and conducted herself in a subdued manner, people seemed less inclined to notice her. She soon became known as the "mousey one" and that's how she liked it. Anything was better than being called the "killer's daughter."

And, until recently, she had been perfectly content to live her quiet, unassuming life and dress in her nondescript way.

Then something strange happened. One day, while taking care of her weekly errands, she found herself standing in front of Maizie's Fashions, staring at the beautiful gowns in the window and longing to try one on. Not that she wanted to call attention to herself. She was simply curious as to what she'd look like in the pretty summery rainbow-colored chiffon dress displayed in the window.

She'd never have the nerve to try on such a gown, of course. It was just another one of her wild dreams. Besides, the Rules of Propriety for Teachers didn't allow for feminine whims or anything that might draw attention away from one's duties as a teacher. Some of the other teachers complained about the rigid rules, but she never had, never even thought much about them, until now.

The school required her to wear the same unadorned dresses in basic gray, brown or black she'd always worn and, until recently, this suited her just fine. Still, she tried to imagine what would happen if she showed up at school in a bright-colored dress with pretty ruffles and ribbons and maybe even lace. Wouldn't that give the school board something to think about!

Oh, but she would never wear such a dress. Of course she wouldn't. The need to fade into the background was too deeply ingrained.

How very odd that Mr. Travis didn't seem to notice how mousey she was. It was almost as if he described the woman she longed to be, and not the woman she actually was.

Crowning glory, indeed! Why her hair was too tightly contained to qualify as a crowning glory. As for the part about golden sunlight. . . . She turned her head from side to side, letting the light from the gas lamp play across each shiny strand. Maybe . . .

She pulled out the hairpins and tortoise combs holding her bun in place. Her hair tumbled down her back in a mass of golden curls, almost to her waist. Gathering her hair in one hand, she pulled it over her shoulder so that she could better examine it. She supposed it did, indeed, look like sunlight, but how in the world would anyone have known that? She always wore a hat or sunbonnet in public and never wore her hair loose except when she washed or brushed it.

She turned away from the mirror. What was the matter with her? She was a schoolmarm, not one of those professional beauties who graced the pages of fashion magazines. No one cared what she looked like. No one! The poem was nothing but someone's idea of a joke.

She reached for the letter and scanned it quickly for a signature. The poem was signed on the second sheet in neat, precise and ultimately bold handwriting. *Respectfully, Josh Travis.*

"Oh, dear." Feeling faint, she dropped down on the divan and read the poem again. And again. "Oh, dear, dear, dear." She pulled a lace handkerchief out of her sleeve and dabbed the corner of her eyes. Never had she felt so flattered. So exposed. So perfectly dreadful.

Poor Mr. Travis. Why all he was trying to do was leave her a box of chocolates and how did she show her gratitude? By hitting him over the head with her Fanny Farmer Cookbook, that's how!

She felt worse than awful, she felt sick. Especially now that she'd read—practically memorized, more like it—his dear sweet words of affection. *My heart takes flight . . .* A warm flush washed over her each time she read that particular passage. She knew his barbershop overlooked Main Street but never in her wildest dreams had she imagined him watching her run her errands. That means he must have seen her staring in the window of Maizie's Fashions. Instead of feeling horrified at the thought of someone singling her out, she was, quite frankly, intrigued.

"Oh, Mr. Travis," she sighed. She conjured up a vision of him as he had looked earlier, sitting on the floor of her parlor. He'd held his head, looking dazed. Even so, it was hard not to notice his handsome square face and the startling color of his eyes. Why, she would swear they were blue as the irises that grew in her backyard. And because she felt as if she'd been given a privileged look into his heart, she whispered his given name "Josh."

She had no idea he harbored such feelings, but he hardly seemed the kind to play tricks. She'd practically ignored him all these years and to think that all the while, he'd been pining away with love.

Dear God, would he ever forgive me. The Lord knows he would be perfectly in his right if he never spoke to her again. Dismayed by the thought, she rose to her feet, her legs shaking. Somehow she had to make amends.

She grabbed her cape off the peg by the door and wrapped it around her shoulders. She then walked the short distance to Dr. Albert's house to use his telephone. He'd always said she could use his telephone in an emergency. Well, if ever there was an emergency, this was it.

She was relieved to see the lights still on in the doctor's residence, but he seemed surprised to see her. The top of his head was more shiny than usual, and the fringe of pure white hair more unruly. "I heard you had some trouble tonight. Are you sure it was Josh Travis who broke into your house?"

"It was Josh, all right."

Dr. Albert clucked his tongue and shook his head. "Unbelievable. I delivered that boy myself and he was a fine robust baby!" The doctor made it sound as if Josh had been born only yesterday rather than twenty-eight years ago. "I've never delivered anyone but the finest citizens! My reputation has always been impeccable." He looked so upset, Amelia felt sorry for him.

"Your reputation is safe," she hurriedly assured him. "Josh broke into my house, but there are extenuating circumstances." She explained how she'd found a box of rocky road chocolates in her parlor from Josh. Knowing that Josh had gone to the trouble of finding out her favorite chocolates made her regret having rendered him unconscious. "That's why I have to call the sheriff and tell him I want to drop the charges."

The doctor nodded and nudged her toward the telephone. "If the sheriff gives you any trouble, tell him I personally delivered Josh myself. He knows I stand behind all my deliveries."

The sheriff listened to Amelia's story, and had it not been for the busybody telephone operator, Miss Baxter, who kept interrupting the conversation to give her biased opinions, Amelia was positive she would have had Josh out of jail in a blink of an eye.

"It sounds fishy to me," Miss Baxter insisted. "I never heard of anyone breaking into someone's house just to leave chocolates."

Amelia's temper flared. "Well, he did."

The sheriff cleared his voice. "No matter what his reasons, the fact remains he still broke into your house."

"But I'm sure it was only because he was too shy to give me the chocolates in person."

The doctor whispered, "Tell him what I told you."

Miss Baxter laughed in her ear. "Anyone who makes as many telephone calls as Josh Travis is not shy!"

"You don't know him." Amelia wondered what Miss Baxter would think if she knew Josh wrote poetry.

"And I suppose you do?"

"Ladies, ladies," the sheriff said, his voice thin with exasperation. "Now, Miss Winklemeyer, I know you mean well and I think it's very generous of you to give Josh the benefit of the doubt, but under the circumstances—"

"Please, sheriff. Dr. Albert says he'll personally vouch for Mr. Travis."

The sheriff was silent for a moment. "Dr. Albert, eh? Well, if you're sure you don't want to press charges."

"I'm positive," Amelia said.

"Do you have any objection, Miss Baxter?"

"None." The operator sniffed. "As long as he doesn't try to place more than his fair share of telephone calls."

Amelia hung up the telephone, feeling considerably better. She turned to her host. "Thank you for letting me use your telephone."

Dr. Albert nodded. "Does this mean that Josh is courting you?"

Amelia blushed. She'd never had so much as a beau and now, suddenly, by virtue of Josh's intimate ode, she was practically betrothed. It was hard to believe, but the etiquette of courtship was quite clear. A poem such as Josh wrote was a clear intent of marriage. Of course, the doctor had no knowledge of the poem and Amelia had no intention of revealing its contents to anyone. Not yet. "We hardly know each other," she said evasively.

"And you won't know each other that well even after years of marriage," the doctor said, alluding to his own twenty-five-year marriage. "It's what keeps life interesting." He winked. "You tell that young man of yours I have a standing invitation to the wedding of every baby I've ever delivered."

The very next day, Amelia stared at herself in the beveled glass mirror that stood in the corner of her bedroom. Never had she remembered feeling quite this nervous. Though social custom was clear as to how to accept or decline a man's romantic overtures, Amelia had no idea what to do in her particular case. What does a woman do when a man she hardly knows bares his heart and soul by way of a poem?

Dressed in a ready-made hobble skirt and silk shirtwaist she'd purchased the previous day from Maizie's Fashions and Millinery, she adjusted her brand new hat and rehearsed her speech. The shirtwaist was the exact same blue as her eyes, the skirt a shade darker. Maizie had been absolutely astonished when Amelia walked in and asked to try on the outfit in the window. Astonishment hardly described the expression on the shopkeeper's face when Amelia left the top button of the shirtwaist undone so as to show off the neck that Josh had so generously described as long and graceful.

Word had traveled through town like wildfire and by the time Amelia had made her purchases and finished her other errands, people were actually stopping to gawk at her as she walked toward her horse and buggy. Strangely enough, Amelia didn't mind. The curious eyes of the townsfolk didn't bother her nowhere near as much as they had when she was but a child. It truly shocked and amazed her that she no longer cared what anyone else thought. Now that she knew how Josh Travis felt about her, that's all she could think about.

The mother of one of Amelia's students had made it her business to stop by the classroom to inform Amelia what others were saying about her.

"Some people have nothing better to do but gossip," Mrs. Hoppersmith had said, looking unbearably self-righteous. "Why a fine schoolteacher like yourself would never think of exposing her neck."

Amelia had listened politely before turning to write the week's spelling words on the blackboard. She was tempted to thank Mrs. Hoppersmith for her concern and be done with it, but then she realized how tired she was at having to do everything a certain way because she was a schoolteacher. She'd often dreamed of bucking convention and kicking up her heels—even if it meant drawing attention to herself— but until she read Josh's poem, she never thought she'd actually have the nerve.

It had touched her deeply that Josh had seen through the prim, almost prudish facade of hers erected years earlier as a defense. But nothing surprised her more than discovering that her carefully nurtured facade suddenly seemed more like prison bars than a protective shell.

Surprise hardly described how she felt. She was shaken to the very core, to the very essence of her being, and standing in front of Mrs. Hoppersmith, she had been tempted—no, more than that, determined—to let the woman Josh and only Josh had guessed existed escape for all the world to see.

Amelia waited until she had finished writing the last of the words on the blackboard. She then slowly, methodically laid the chalk on the wooden lip and turned.

"I can assure you, Mrs. Hoppersmith, that whether or not I choose to expose my neck has nothing to do with my teaching ability." It wasn't much, but it was a start.

Now, she stood in her bedroom and recalled the appalled look on Mrs. Hoppersmith's face. She smiled to herself and leaned closer to the mirror. Mrs. Hoppersmith should see her now.

Maizie had shown her how to apply face powder and lip rouge and Amelia had to admit she liked the results. The powder added a delicate soft, almost porcelain look to her complexion. The rouge made her lips look fuller and as pink and dewy as Josh had described them in his poem. Why glory be, she hardly recognized herself. Her heart thudded with excitement. The woman staring back from the mirror was identical to the woman described in Josh's poem and, strangely enough, it was the way she'd always imagined herself in her dreams. Just wait till Josh saw her now!

❧ *Chapter 3* ❧

A knock sounded on Josh's apartment door. "Are you all right, Mr. Travis?"

Recognizing his landlady's voice, Josh opened the door. A bandage was still wrapped about his head and whenever he moved too quickly, he was overcome with dizziness. The doctor had said he'd suffered a slight concussion from hitting his head on the edge of the hearth, but otherwise nothing really hurt but his pride.

He wouldn't be surprised if the whole confounded town was talking about the poem he wrote to Laura. It was bad enough having to spend time in jail, but knowing he was the object of ridicule was the worst possible fate.

"You have a visitor," Mrs. Clatterway said. "She's waiting in the parlor."

She? Mrs. Clatterway had strict rules about where her boarders could entertain guests and it appeared that not even a head injury was reason enough to allow a visitor to his room. This meant he'd have to walk down all twenty-four stairs and trek the distance to the main house. The thought made his head throb.

She lowered her voice. "It's that old maid schoolmarm."

Josh's groan turned into a choking cough. What in tarnation was Miss Winklemeyer doing visiting him? Wasn't it enough she'd tried to kill him? Naturally, he was grateful she'd dropped the charges, but even so, he didn't want to face her. Especially now that she'd no doubt read the poem meant for Laura.

"My word, Mr. Travis. You look ghastly. Shall I tell your visitor you're indisposed?"

It was a tempting offer but he declined it. "That won't be necessary." Perhaps if Miss Winklemeyer saw the sad shape he was in, she'd take pity on him and cut her visit short. In any case, he intended to demand she return his poem and not reveal its contents to anyone. The chocolate she could keep!

Walking like a man with a bad hangover, he followed his landlady down the stairs, stopping halfway due to dizziness. His head ached with every shuffling step he took. Though combing his hair was too painful, he had earlier managed to shave and change into fresh clothes. He wore bright red suspenders and the sleeves of his fresh boiled shirt was held in place with bright red garters.

The woman rose to her feet as he walked into the room. "Mr. Travis."

He stopped and wondered what kind of game Mrs. Clatterway was playing. The woman in the parlor wasn't Miss Winklemeyer. It was . . . good Lord! He blinked his eyes in disbelief. The fashionably dressed woman in front of him *was* Miss Winklemeyer and she looked . . . different. Beautiful!

For a moment, all he could do was stare. Her stylish blue outfit revealed a soft-rounded bosom and a tiny waist he'd not noticed the night before when she stood over him and managed, despite her small frame, to look as menacing as a grizzly.

Her shirtwaist was unbuttoned at the neck, revealing a neck as long and graceful as the one he'd described in his poem. She wore a gored skirt that flared gracefully from her womanly hips. Her jaunty hat was decorated with silk forget-me-nots and taffeta ribbons that matched the exact color of her pretty blue eyes.

But it was her delicate features that made him hold his breath. No longer did she look stern and serious. Instead, her face was soft with concern as she stared at his bandaged head, her dewy lips pursed together in something akin to a half-kiss.

"Is your head . . . ?"

Unable to tear his eyes away from her, he shook his head without thinking and winced at the pain. Miss Winklemeyer's eyes widened with alarm.

He brushed away her concern with a raised hand. "It's all right. . . . It's just a slight concussion. The doctor said I'll be as good as new in a day or two." Still staring and unable to do a damned thing about it, he extended his arm in the direction of the divan. "Please . . . have a seat."

She sat down again, this time in the center of the divan and folded her hands primly on her lap. The placement of her hands and the way she sat stiff-backed and proper-like was all that remained of the schoolmarm's former self. Confused by the amazing transformation, but no less intrigued, he sat on an upholstered chair and completely forgot about his sore head.

He couldn't stop staring at her, nor could he think of a single intelligent thing to say.

He was greatly relieved when at last she sat forward to speak. "I want to apologize," she said softly, her cheeks slightly flushed. She had a musical voice, whispery as a summer's breeze. He wondered why he'd never really noticed her until today. And why in Heaven's name had he never noticed the lovely blue of her eyes? Or, for that matter, the lush thickness of her lashes?

She was considerably younger than he'd previously thought, no more than twenty-four or twenty-five at the most. Now that he saw her in the full light of day, he realized her hair was remarkably similar to the hair he'd described in his poem. The fact that he was comparing Miss Winklemeyer with his poem struck him as odd and he was almost convinced he was dreaming—or that the concussion was more serious than the doctors had led him to believe.

"I didn't mean to hurt you, Mr. Travis. I thought you were a prowler."

Still puzzled by the dramatic change in her appearance, and dazzled by the warm smile she gave him, his face grew warm. Any moment now, she was bound to change back into her usual prim self and express shock and disapproval at his poem. He intended to fake a dizzy spell the moment she did. "That's understandable."

"I never imagined you were simply trying to leave a gift for me."

He stared at her, not sure he'd heard right. "A gift?"

She lowered her head, but he could see the sweetest smile teasing her lips. "I was referring to the chocolates. Why Mr. Travis, you are a clever man. How did you know I have a weakness for rocky road chocolates?"

"Really? I mean . . ." Great thunder, she thought the chocolates were meant for her. "You do?"

"And your—" Her face grew red as a beet. "Your poem was—" Suddenly her eyes glistened with tears. Astonished that the young and previously formidable schoolmarm was crying over something he'd written filled him with dismay. He knew the poem was dreadful, but he had no idea it was *that* bad. He searched his pockets until he located a freshly laundered handkerchief. "I never had any formal training in poetry," he explained by way of an apology.

She took his handkerchief from him, smiling through her tears. "That's amazing," she said. "I never read anything so beautiful in my life."

Josh was so astonished, he could hardly think what to say. Under the circumstances, it seemed impolite to tell her the poem was meant for Laura Baker. "You don't think it was poorly written?"

"Not at all"

"Or offensive?"

"Heavens, no!"

She seemed sincere for which he was profoundly grateful, though no less puzzled. "You being a teacher, I thought you might find my attempts at poetry rather dull and mundane."

She dabbed at her eyes. "Not at all. Your poem made me look at myself in a whole new way. That's what good poetry does, you know. It makes us see things or think things we would not otherwise see or think.''

He studied her, not sure he'd heard right. Did she actually think his poem had merit? ''But you must have thought me forward. I mean, we hardly know each other.''

''That's what I want to talk to you about.'' She lifted her chin in a way that made him ache with the need to protect her. He knew, then, at that moment, he would never have the heart to tell her the truth. Whatever the consequences, he would let her continue to think the poem had been written just for her.

She returned his handkerchief, pulling her hand away quickly when their fingers touched. ''I don't think we should hurry into anything.''

His mouth went dry. He cleared his throat and ran a finger around his collar. ''I quite agree.''

''And then, of course, I'm still obligated to fulfill my contract with the school district.''

He frowned. ''Your contract.''

''The school board is very strict as to how a teacher should conduct her social life.''

''So I've heard,'' he said, though he had no idea what the school board had to do with him.

A look of relief crossed her face. ''Then it's all right with you if we don't become betrothed right away?''

Something the size of a boot caught in Josh's throat. He couldn't breathe and when he tried to clear his lungs, his throat closed altogether in a sudden coughing fit.

Her eyes widened in dismay. ''Oh, dear. Are you all right?''

When it seemed as if he would never stop coughing, he rose from his chair, fought off a sudden dizzy spell and reached for the decanter of sherry on the sideboard. ''Yes,'' he croaked, sounding like a frog. Not trusting his legs to hold him upward, he draped himself over the sideboard, fumbled with the stopper and poured himself a drink and gulped it down.

Taking a moment to regain his composure, he turned to

face her. She was standing only a few feet away and he wondered if the delicate fragrance of roses was perfume or if she naturally carried the scent of her garden with her.

His throat cleared and he no longer felt dizzy, but now he was having heart palpitations. "It's a bit warm in here."

She looked surprised and glanced at the moving curtains that indicated the window was open and took her place on the divan again, watching him as if she expected him to keel over at any moment.

Not wanting her to think he was a hypochondriac or anything, he forced a cheerfulness in his voice. "Would you care for some sherry?"

"No, thank you," she replied. "The school board . . ." She stopped herself, and a slow smile curved her pretty mouth. "Why, Mr. Travis, I believe I would like some sherry, after all."

"Very well, then." He poured her a glass and handed it to her.

"Thank you." He watched her lift the glass to her lips and take the smallest possible sip. "Oh, my." She sat back with her fingertips on her lips. "That's strong, isn't it?"

Actually, he suspected that Mrs. Clatterway made a practice of watering down the sherry, but he made no comment.

Miss Winklemeyer set the nearly full glass on the table in front of the divan and continued where she had left off. "As I was saying, I think we need to get to know one another."

He refilled his glass, took another bracing gulp and forced himself to relax. It was too soon to panic. Getting to know someone could take months. *Years!*

She moistened her lips with the tip of her tongue. "I would have to give up teaching."

"G-give up teaching? Why?"

"The school board strictly forbids teachers to marry."

"Is that so?" *Praise the Lord!* "Well, then it's out of the question. What kind of selfish cad would I be to ask you to give up something you obviously love just to marry me?"

"Why Mr. Travis." Her eyes filled with tears for a second time. "You're the most considerate man I've ever met. Why, most men wouldn't hesitate to ask a woman to give up a teaching post and a lot more for the sake of marriage."

"You can rest assured, I'm not one of them," Josh said.

"But of course, if there's no other way for us to get married . . ."

"Nonsense! I won't hear of it."

She looked uncertain. Obviously, she sensed something was wrong and he wished he could put her mind at ease. If only he could think of a way to tell her the truth without hurting her. Marriage! By God, he hardly knew her.

"You aren't having second thoughts, are you?"

"I'm just thinking about what's right for you and the children," he explained. "You have a reputation as being an excellent teacher."

She looked relieved. "I thought perhaps you were having second thoughts because I knocked you out. I wouldn't want you to think I'm a violent person."

He rubbed his chin. "The thought never crossed my mind." *She was pushy, perhaps, but not violent.*

"I could hardly blame you if it did. I never gave anyone a concussion before. You were the first one."

"I suppose I should be honored then." He cleared his throat. "Eh . . . Miss Winklemeyer."

"Under the circumstances, it seems you should call me by my given name, Amelia."

"Amelia."

"Would it be all right if I call you Josh?"

"Yes, of course."

"Josh," she said softly, and smiled.

He smiled back and for a moment they gazed at each other like two lost friends meeting after a very long absence. Suddenly aware he was staring, he glanced down at the glass in his hand, swirling the sherry about before drinking it down. How in tarnation did he get himself in such a pickle? He set the empty glass on the sideboard and took another deep breath. "Miss Winklemeyer . . . ."

"Amelia."

"Amelia. I have to be honest."

Her eyes grew more luminous. "I wouldn't want you to be any less."

"I'm not ready for anything . . . I mean . . . you know, serious."

Her fingers curled into a ball as she held her hand to her chest. "You can't imagine how relieved I am to hear you say that. I was so afraid you would want us to marry right away."

"I . . . I . . . I'm . . . not right away." He was stammering like a fool. He mopped his forehead with his handkerchief. "Some people say it takes . . . years—yes, years—to get to know each other."

"Oh, I would never keep you waiting that long and I don't care what the school board says!" She gave a determined nod of her head. "Besides . . ." She lowered her head and he could no longer see her face. "I feel I already know you to some extent."

He realized this was a worse mess than he'd first supposed. Maybe it *was* time to panic. "K-K-Know me how?" He was stalling for time, but anything was better than having to tell her the truth. How he hated the thought of hurting her. She seemed to have a kind heart and none of this was her fault. If he ever got his hands on that fool delivery boy, Peter, he'd not be responsible for his actions.

"I know that you're very intellectual."

No one had ever called him intellectual, but it pleased him that she thought it of him, even if it was a slight exaggeration.

"I do believe I saw a hint of Browning in your writing," she said. "I like a man who appreciates poetry."

Heat rose to his face. "I'm afraid my humble attempts to imitate Browning leave much to be desired. Some of the descriptions were perhaps a bit too flowery."

She smiled, blushing prettily. "No one ever said such nice things about me before."

"Really?" Lord, he could think of all sorts of nice things to say to her. This surprised him since he was usually a man of few words.

"And that part about my spirit dancing to the music of the stars—" She bit her lip and he feared she was going to get all teary-eyed again. "How did you know?"

He gazed at her soft-rounded face not knowing what to say. Up until a day or so ago, he was hardly aware of this woman. Now, suddenly he felt as if he'd known her for a lifetime. It was the damnedest thing. "Do you dance to the music of the stars?" he asked, though he was willing to bet she did.

"As a child, I used to go outside at night after everyone was asleep, and dance barefooted beneath the night sky."

"Really?" He couldn't believe his ears. "I used to sneak outside at night and stand on the hill behind my house. There, I'd wave an imaginary baton at the sky, pretending I was the conductor and the stars were the musicians in a symphony orchestra and . . ." Surprised to find himself sharing such private memories, he fell silent. He recalled the many times he'd been punished for his fanciful notions. He was only ten when he'd vowed to keep his ideas to himself. Until that moment, that's exactly what he'd done.

"Oh, please don't stop," she pleaded.

He looked into her eyes and felt like he was swimming in a big blue sea. "Do you still like to dance?"

Her cheeks turned pink like a ripening peach. "The school board restricts me from going to dances, of course, but sometimes at night, when no one is looking—" She lowered her lashes and he felt a sense of loss because he couldn't see her expression.

Looking suddenly embarrassed, she quickly rose to her feet and fumbled as she put on her gloves. "I'm glad we had this little talk. I feel so much better now, don't you?"

He felt like a cheat and a fraud. The sooner he told her the truth about the rocky road chocolates, the better. "Miss Winklemeyer . . . Amelia."

"What is it, Josh?" she asked when he hesitated.

"T-t-t-hank you f-f-for—" He was doing it again, stuttering like a fool. He took a deep breath. "Thank you for not laughing at my poem. It was terrible. The worst possible garbage. I don't know what got into me.''

''It wasn't terrible, Josh. All the things I said earlier are true. No one but you ever saw the person I am inside. No one! I'd almost forgotten myself. I'll always be grateful to you for reminding me.''

He took in a deep breath. She was giving him credit he didn't deserve and he felt like a heel.

She wrapped her gloved fingers around his arm and he was helpless to do anything but swim aimlessly in the depths of her eyes. ''Thank you.''

She turned and quickly left the parlor and her quick little steps tapped across the wood floor of the entryway before the door opened and closed.

He crossed to the window, lifted the lace curtain and watched her drive off in her horse and buggy before making a beeline for the telephone. ''Please put me through to Horace.'' He was so upset, he could hardly get the words out.

Miss Baxter made a funny snorting sound. ''Don't you try to disguise your voice, Josh Travis. I know it's you and this is the third call you've made this week.''

Josh tightened his hold on the handset. He was sick and tired of arguing with the persnickety operator every time he wanted to make a simple telephone call. ''It's an emergency,'' he said, biting back his irritation. Horace was his best friend. They grew up together and knew each other's deepest secrets. If Horace couldn't help him, nobody could.

Miss Baxter didn't seem the least bit impressed. ''That's what everyone says.''

''I mean it, Miss Baxter. It's worse than an emergency. It's a matter of life and death.''

Miss Baxter sighed. ''It better be, Josh Travis, or you'll never make a call in this town again!''

❧ *Chapter 4* ❧

"*P*ssst!"

Josh jumped at the sound, his heart racing like a galloping pony, and spun around, but it was too dark to see. "Horace? Is that you?" He was standing on the corner of Third and Main.

"No, it's me, Leland Crummer III."

"Dammit, Crummer, you scared the life out of me. What are you doing here?"

"I need to talk to you. I have a problem."

"I can't talk now, I'm waiting for Horace."

"But you're the only one who can help me. You're an expert."

"An expert on what?"

"Mustaches."

Recalling suddenly how he'd cut off Crummer's mustache by mistake, Josh held his breath expecting the worse. For all he knew Crummer was pointing a pistol at him. He narrowed his eyes, but it was too dark to know for certain.

Crummer moved closer. "I got up this morning and went through my usual morning routine and when I looked in the mirror, it was gone."

"Gone?"

"My mustache. Or at least half of it was gone."

Feeling a twinge of guilt, Josh tried to think of something to say by way of apology. He should have told Crummer immediately what he'd done. "There's a perfectly logical explanation—"

"I certainly hope so. You . . . you don't suppose it's serious, do you?"

"Great guns, Crummer, you lost a mustache. How serious could that be?"

"What if my eyebrows fall out? Or my hair?"

"That's not going to happen,"

"How can you be certain?"

"I'm an expert, remember?"

"Yes, yes, yes, but you won't mind checking my hair tomorrow, will you? Please, Josh, just to be on the safe side."

"All right, if it'll make you feel better." Josh was anxious to get rid of the man so that he could concentrate on his own problems.

"Thank you." Crummer grabbed Josh's hand and shook it gratefully and Josh felt another twinge of guilt. "I can't tell you how much this means to me. It'll be hard enough going to the Spring Ball without my mustache. But to go bald would be disastrous. I'll see you tomorrow." No sooner had Crummer left than Horace drove up in his Buick Roadster.

Josh climbed into the companion seat. "It's about time. I told you this was important."

"And I told you I'd come as soon as I took Mary-Anne home. What's so dog-gone urgent that couldn't wait till tomorrow? I had to cancel my plans to take Christina to the ice cream parlor."

Josh shook his head and sighed. He'd never been able to understand what women saw in Horace. "Do you remember me telling you I was going to start courting Laura Baker, if she'd have me?"

"She turned you down, eh? Well, don't let it bother you. There's plenty more fish in the sea."

"She didn't turn me down."

"Oh?" Horace sounded surprised. "So what's the problem?"

"I arranged for a box of her favorite rocky road chocolates to be sent to her with a . . . eh . . . letter." He'd die rather than admit to writing a poem, even to his best friend.

"You can't go wrong with chocolates and letters. Women love that kind of thing."

"The problem is the chocolates were sent to Miss Winklemeyer by mistake."

Horace tapped his fingers on the steering wheel. "So that's why the old maid schoolmarm knocked you out."

Josh groaned. "You heard about that?"

"Everyone's heard about it. That's all Mary-Anne could talk about earlier. Didn't you explain that the chocolates were meant for someone else?"

"No, actually, I didn't."

"Why not?"

"I couldn't think of a way of telling her without hurting her feelings. She was really very nice about it. She said she didn't expect us to rush into marriage or anything."

"Marriage!" Horace made the word sound like a death sentence. "This is worse than I thought."

"That's why you've got to help me."

"Me? What can I do?"

"I thought perhaps if you called on her and made her think you're interested, she'd be less likely to . . . you know . . ."

"Settle for you," Horace finished.

Josh wouldn't have worded it quite that way, but Horace had the general idea. "I don't know that she's ever had a beau." With the school board's rules being as strict as they were, she probably didn't socialize that much, if at all.

"Don't worry. Once the old maid sees what she's missing, she'll forget about marrying you. I guarantee it."

Josh frowned. Old maid wasn't exactly the way he'd describe the woman who had paid him a visit at his boarding house earlier. It still astounded him that he'd hardly noticed her until now. He wondered if Horace had even noticed her big blue eyes and feminine curves. "So you'll do this for me?"

"Of course I'll do it," Horace said. "Anything for a friend."

"I can't tell you how much this means to me." Josh rubbed his chin, wishing he felt better about the whole thing. "You will treat her like a lady, won't you?"

"You know me."

Josh knew him only too well. That's what worried him. "Miss Winklemeyer is a very kind-hearted and gentle person."

Horace laughed. "Gentle? Is that why she knocked you out?"

"A woman can be gentle and still know how to take care of herself."

"So what are you worried about?"

Josh tried to relax. He wasn't worried about a thing—not a thing. It was all going to work out. Of course it was. "You don't have to take her anywhere special. Maybe for a drive or an ice cream soda." Surely the school board wouldn't have any trouble with that, especially if Horace got her home before nightfall.

"For a friend, I'll do anything."

Grateful that Horace would agree so readily, Josh grinned. "I'll make this up to you, Horace, I swear."

"Forget about it," Horace said magnanimously. "Now that the problem's solved, what do you say we go to the nickelodeon?"

The following morning, Crummer was waiting outside the barbershop when Josh arrived. Crummer held a newspaper in front of his face to hide his mustache, then dashed inside the barbershop the minute Josh unlocked the door.

"What did I tell you?" Crummer said. He dropped the newspaper to reveal his half-mustache, then quickly hid his face again. "What am I going to do?"

"It'll grow back," Josh assured him, wishing there was something he could do to make things right. "Meanwhile, I think it'll be less noticeable if we cut the whole thing off."

"But my hair. What about my hair?"

Josh made a show of checking Crummer's scalp. "Your hair's fine, but it's hopelessly old-fashioned, especially now the mustache has to come off."

"What about my eyebrows? I'm almost positive one hair fell out this morning while I was getting dressed."

"Your eyebrows are fine. Now calm down while I shave off the other half of your mustache and trim your hair. Trust me, you'll look like a new man."

Crummer looked a hundred times better without his floppy mustache, but the more modern business haircut made him look surprisingly sophisticated. "See? What did I tell you?" Josh held up a hand mirror, but Crummer refused to look. Instead, he pulled his felt hat down and lifted the collar of his coat up and darted outside before anyone had a chance to see him.

No sooner had Crummer left when Horace walked in, looking like the canary who'd swallowed the cat. "I was brilliant!" he said. He flicked an imaginary piece of lint off his checked suit jacket and straightened his bowler hat. "Absolutely brilliant."

Josh finished sweeping the floor and stood the broom in the corner. "And modest as always."

Horace never missed an opportunity to jump on a compliment, whether or not one was intended. "You know me, I've never been much for bragging. Anyway, Miss Winklemeyer fell for me just like that." He snapped his fingers to indicate.

Josh knitted his brows together. "What do you mean fell for you?"

Horace discounted the question with a wave of his hand. "Must you take everything so literal?"

"You said she fell for you."

"All right, I'll spell it out for you. She agreed to go to the Spring Ball with me."

"The Spring Ball?" Josh couldn't believe his ears. "But I thought we agreed you were only going to take her for a drive or ice cream."

"Trust me, this is a much better idea."

"But . . . but . . . what about the school board? School-teachers aren't allowed to dance."

Horace lifted his shoulders. "I pointed this out to her, but she said you made her realize something about herself that she'd ignored for too long."

Josh blinked. "I did?" He was beginning to get an uneasy feeling. "What was that?"

"She didn't say." Horace thought for a moment and laughed. "You won't believe this, but she was worried that *you* might be hurt if she went out with me."

Josh felt another twinge of conscience. "She was worried about me?"

"Yeah." Horace's laughter turned into loud guffaws. "Doesn't that take the cake?"

Not sure what Horace found so funny, Josh tried to make sense out of the mess. "Was it really that easy? I mean she agreed to go with you just like that?"

"At first she was a bit hesitant," Horace admitted. "She said she'd never been to a dance before. But I explained that you had already asked Laura Baker. When I told her how miserable you were at the thought of her sitting home alone, she accepted my invitation without another thought."

"That's wonderful," Josh said, though his voice lacked enthusiasm. What would happen if the school board found out? He'd hate to be responsible for Amelia losing her teaching post.

"Thanks to me, your problems are over." Whistling to himself, Horace struck a match to his cigar and walked out the front door and down Main.

Josh busied himself preparing for his next customer, but his mind was not on his work. What in blazes had he said in his poem that made Amelia decide to go to the dance with Horace? He was so lost in his thoughts, he hadn't noticed Wally Newberry sitting in the barber chair until he spoke.

"How's everything with you?" Wally asked.

"Everything's just dandy," Josh muttered. He honed a straight-edged razor on a canvas strop, then flipped the strop over to finish the job on the leather side before he recalled that Wally was here for his monthly haircut, not a shave.

He exchanged the razor for the hair clippers and trimming comb, and tried to convince himself everything was going as planned. He was taking Laura Baker to the Spring Ball and Horace was taking Amelia Winklemeyer.

So what the devil was he worried about?

The following day, Mrs. Clatterway tapped on Josh's door, lifting her voice as she knocked. "Mr. Travis, there's a young lady downstairs who wishes to see you."

Josh sat with his feet on the desk, reading the newspaper. Hearing he had a visitor, he let his feet drop to the floor and hastened to open the door. "Is it the same one who came to see me the other day?" he asked, trying to imagine why Amelia would come calling a second time.

"Oh, no, Mr. Travis. It's someone else." She clucked her tongue like a mother hen. "I don't know what the world is coming to. In my day, a young lady would never think of calling on a gentleman."

Josh tried to ignore the curiosity on his landlady's face as he followed her downstairs, across the lawn and into the main house. Casting a disapproving look over her shoulder, Mrs. Clatterway left him to enter the parlor alone.

Laura Baker was sitting on the divan looking all red-faced and teary-eyed.

"Laura? What in the world . . . ?"

"Don't you touch me, Josh Travis. I've never been so humiliated in my entire life. You asked *me* to the Spring Ball and you sent chocolates to that—"

"You know about the chocolates?"

"Everyone knows about the chocolates. And they were *my* favorites." She let out a series of loud sobs, which brought some of the other boarders rushing into the room. "It's the talk of the town."

Josh waved the others away, and sat by her side. He hated to see her so upset. "Don't cry, Laura. It's all a terrible mistake."

A dubious look crossed her face, but at least the infernal

sobbing stopped. "What do you mean, a mistake?"

Josh patiently explained how the chocolates had ended up in Miss Winklemeyer's house. "I didn't want to hurt her feelings so I let her think the chocolates were meant for her."

Laura pressed her fingers over her mouth and watched him with red-rimmed eyes. "Oh, Josh, you're right. The poor old maid would be heartbroken if she knew the truth."

"She's not a poor old maid," he said irritably, then immediately regretted snapping at her. "She's very kind-hearted," he explained.

"I'm sure that's true." Laura lifted a lace handkerchief to her nose and blew daintily. "I don't think the school board would employ anyone who was any less."

"You're not angry with me, are you?"

"Well . . ." She fluttered her eyelashes and kept him waiting for the longest while before setting his mind at rest. "I could never be angry at you for long."

"And you're still going to the Spring Ball with me?"

She smiled. "Of course I am."

He sighed in relief. Happy days. The last of his troubles were over.

❧ Chapter 5 ❧

*L*aura Baker looked pretty as a picture the night of the Spring Ball. Dressed in a white empire-style gown trimmed in blue, her hair was a mass of golden curls tied back with a blue satin ribbon.

Josh picked her up in his Model T that had been washed and polished until it shone, his stomach clenched tight. He'd hardly slept the last three nights worrying about what would happen when he came face-to-face with Amelia Winkle-meyer. Would she tell Laura about that blasted poem? What if Horace failed to make her realize she didn't have to marry the first man to come along? *What if she refuses to give up the ridiculous notion I want to marry her?*

Laura tried her best to engage him in conversation during the short drive from her house to the dance. "Oh, look, a full moon."

"Yes."

"I can't remember it being so warm the night of the Spring Dance. Do you suppose we're going to have an early summer?"

"Yes."

"You do?"

"No."

She glanced his way. "Do you know how to dance that new dance, the tango?"

"Of course not!"

"You don't have to snap my head off," Laura said, sulking. "It's only a dance."

"It's not just a dance and you know it." It had already been banned in several cities, including Boston. Even if the tango hadn't caused such a stir, he thought the hot-blooded dance was too wild for his taste.

Laura obviously didn't agree with him, but he found it hard to concentrate on what she was saying. He felt guilty for not being better company, but he couldn't help it. He pulled up behind the barn and glanced around for Horace's car, spotting it parked next to the orchard. So Horace was already at the dance. That meant Amelia was there, too.

He ran a finger along his stiff collar before hopping over the side of his car. Straightening his bowtie, he walked around to open the door for Laura. A black cat ran across his path, startling him.

"Mercy me, Josh. I don't know what's the matter with you tonight. You're as nervous as a puppy in a thunderstorm."

"It's not often that a man gets to escort such a beautiful woman to the Spring Dance," he said.

She giggled. "Oh, Josh. You say the nicest things."

He tucked her small hand in the crook of his elbow, told himself for the hundredth time that Amelia Winklemeyer was too much of a lady to say or do anything to embarrass either one of them, and led Laura to the double doors leading inside the barn.

The Spring Ball was held at the old Kimble Barn outside of town. It was the social event of the year. The barn had been whitewashed and scrubbed for the occasion. Fresh sawdust had been sprinkled on the dirt floor and paper streamers hung from the rafters. Music was provided by Hal King and his Fiddlers Three.

He spotted Amelia at once, though she stood at the far side of the barn in deep conversation with Horace. She didn't look like a schoolmarm. Hell, she didn't even look like a spinster.

She looked beautiful and he didn't miss the fact that he wasn't the only one in the room to notice.

The faint pink color in her cheek matched the rose-colored gown she wore. And what a gown it was. The soft chiffon fabric floated around her like a cloud, the shirred Empire waist flaring into a draped overskirt. A scooped neckline dipped daringly to reveal the soft rise of her breasts and he wasn't the only man in the room who noticed. Not by any means. His heart beat fast and his breath grew ragged.

Had she lost her cotton-picking mind? No schoolteacher in her right mind should wear such a dress in public!

"Don't you agree, Josh?" Laura said, tapping him on the arm with the tip of a folded fan.

He glanced at Laura and the group of people who were Laura's friends. To his embarrassment, he realized he hadn't the slightest idea what anyone was talking about. "Yes," he said heartily, though the look on Laura's face said he fooled no one.

Out of guilt, he tried to concentrate on the conversation, but Laura and her friends seemed content to discuss the most mundane things. His head fairly ached from all the talk about who was wearing what and which couple took a liking to each other, though his ears did perk up whenever someone mentioned Amelia's name.

"Mercy me! Is that Miss Winklemeyer?"

"No. It can't be!"

While the women expressed their shock verbally, their escorts were content to simply stare. One of Josh's customers leaned over and whispered, "If that's a schoolteacher, school sure ain't what it used to be."

Wally Newberry walked over to Josh, shaking his head. "Something strange is going on around here."

"How do you mean, strange?" Josh asked.

"First Crummer and now Miss Winklemeyer."

"What are you saying?"

"I can't believe you haven't noticed. Take Crummer, for example." Wally pointed to where Crummer, stood, surrounded by a group of women, who seemed to be hanging on to his every word. "You know how old-fashioned he is. Now, suddenly, he's purchased himself an automobile and he's talking about converting to electricity."

Josh shook his head in disbelief. "No!"

"And that's not all. He's even wearing one of those bracelet watches."

"I believe they're called wristwatches," Josh said.

"Whatever you call them, you'll never catch me wearing one." Wally lowered his voice. "He said he caught some sort of disease that made his mustache fall off and suddenly women started chasing him. Do you suppose the disease did something to his brain? I'm telling you, he's not the same person."

"I doubt it's because of any disease."

"How can you be sure? And how would you explain Miss Winklemeyer's sudden change? Look at her! She's not the same person. I'm telling you, something's not right. Do you suppose something's wrong with the water? I noticed an odd taste lately."

"Nothing's wrong with the water."

"If it's not the water, then what's making everyone act so strange? And how do you explain Crummer's mustache disease."

"I'm telling you it's not the water," Josh repeated.

"I intend to call the water department, first thing Monday morning. Just to be on the safe side." Wally moved toward the refreshment table where he proceeded to sniff the punch bowl suspiciously.

Sighing to himself, Josh rejoined Laura and her friends, but it was hard to keep his gaze from wandering around the room—*across* the room.

Amelia hadn't moved, nor for that matter had Horace. Didn't they know they were supposed to talk to *other* people? Why would a couple attend a dance and only talk to each other?

"What do you think, Josh?" Laura asked, breaking into his thoughts.

"I think they should talk to someone else," he blurted out without thinking.

Everyone in Laura's circle stared at him. Finally, a newly married woman, whose name he vaguely remembered was Dorothy, spoke up. "By talking to someone else, do you mean another doctor?"

"Of course he means a doctor," Laura said, though she looked less certain than she sounded. "I suppose it can't hurt to get a second opinion."

"But if I'm not expecting, what on earth could be wrong with me?"

Everyone stared at Dorothy's swelling waistline that no amount of gathered fabric could hide and she burst into tears.

"Nothing's wrong," Laura said and the others quickly agreed.

"Of course, the doctor was right in his diagnosis."

"What else but a baby would make you look so fat?"

Despite all the attempts to make her feel better, Dorothy kept crying.

For his part, Josh felt terrible for having spoiled the poor woman's evening and he finally managed to talk Hal Mason, the animal doctor, into giving his professional opinion.

"It's a baby," Hal said and everyone breathed a sigh of relief.

For the next hour, Josh watched Horace act like a fool. Horace spent his time whispering in Amelia's ear, waiting on her hand and foot and laughing like a hyena. Thinking the man was acting a bit too forward, Josh staked himself against the back wall so he could better watch out for Amelia's welfare.

Now that he could better see Amelia's face, he realized, by George, she was laughing, too! Not just laughing, but *laughing!*

Josh frowned. He'd known Horace for a good many years and he never thought Horace *that* amusing!

"Well mercy me," the woman known as Cynthia Kopeck cried out. She and her escort had just arrived. "Is that Miss Winklemeyer over there?"

"Isn't it shocking?" Dorothy agreed. "How in the world can she teach phonics dressed like that?"

"I doubt that she dresses like that in the classroom," Josh said, his ill temper increasing by the moment.

"I should hope not," Cynthia said.

Josh was almost relieved when the conversation returned to Dorothy's condition, though it didn't seem possible that an unborn infant could cause so much comment. Bored to tears, Josh leaned over and whispered in Laura's ear. "Would you excuse me for a moment?"

Before Laura had a chance to respond, he threaded his way through the crowded room to Horace's side.

Amelia smiled up at him, her face radiant. "Why, Josh. How nice to see you."

She acted like she hadn't noticed him staring at her from across the room. "You're looking mighty pretty tonight, Amelia." Even if the dress was lacking some essential fabric at the neckline.

She smiled up at him with her big liquid eyes and Josh's heart literally did a somersault.

Horace frowned at Josh. "Do you want something?"

"Not particularly. I only came over to pay my respects."

"How very kind of you," Amelia said. "I hope you're not worried about me. Horace explained everything." Next to her Horace placed a possessive hand on the back of her chair.

"Did he now?" Josh asked.

"Yes," Amelia replied. "He told me you'd already asked Laura Baker to the dance."

"That's true."

"I'm sure you probably thought I'd turn you down, being a schoolteacher and all."

"I know how strict the *school board* is," Josh said, emphasizing the words for Horace's benefit. He glanced over at Laura, who was still conversing with her friends and didn't seem to notice his absence. He should return to his table, but something held him back. Horace's roving fingers for one, which were toying with the bow at the back of Amelia's gown. It was Josh's idea that Horace ask Amelia out, but fiddling with her dress was not part of the bargain.

"May I talk to you a moment in private?" Josh asked, giving Horace a meaningful look. If Horace refused to take a hint, then Josh had no choice but to spell out the ground rules.

Horace didn't look especially pleased at the idea of leaving Amelia's side, but he shrugged his shoulders, stood and followed Josh over to the punch bowl. "What do you want, Josh? Can't you see I'm busy?"

"Oh, you're busy all right and I don't like it. What's the matter with you? Miss Winklemeyer is a schoolteacher."

"And I own a hardware store. So what's your point?"

"My point is, the school board has strict rules as to what a schoolteacher can and cannot do and sitting in public being mauled by a man is definitely not allowed."

Horace looked insulted. "I wasn't mauling her. Besides, what they don't know won't hurt them. Anything else?"

Josh realized he wasn't getting anywhere and switched tactics. "Listen, Horace. I trusted you. You know she's very vulnerable right now."

"Vulnerable? How do you figure that?"

"She thinks I want to marry her."

"That puts her judgment in question, but I don't think it makes her especially vulnerable."

Josh's patience snapped. "Listen to me. I don't want you taking advantage of her, do you hear me?"

"What's it to you anyway? You're interested in Laura Baker."

"But I feel responsible for Amelia. If it wasn't for those chocolates and that damned po . . . eh letter, she'd be home right now, safe from the likes of you."

"Are you suggesting . . . ?"

"I'm not suggesting anything . . ."

"Oh, there you are." Laura looked from Josh to Horace, a look of uncertainty on her face. "I thought perhaps you might like to dance."

"That's a wonderful idea," Horace called over his shoulders as he headed back to his table.

Josh had no choice but to follow Laura onto the dance floor, but he vowed to keep his eye on Amelia and if Horace tried anything, Josh wouldn't hesitate to take matters into his own hands.

The fiddlers played a medley of popular tunes until the barn shook with the sound of stomping feet. "Change partners!" King Cole cried out and laughter rose above the resin screams of the fiddles while woman whirled from one partner to the next. The music stopped and everyone applauded.

Charley "Ragtime" Richardson stepped forward, and shocked the crowd by playing the hot-blooded rhythm of a tango. A gasp swept across the room and young women, horrified at the thought of dancing to the erotic new dance craze, scurried from the dance floor, their escorts chasing after them.

"Oh, do stay and dance with me," Laura pleaded. "I'll show you how to do it."

"It's the tango," Josh said.

Laura giggled. "I know."

"Your father trusted me and I'm not about to let him down." He took Laura by the hand and pulled her off the dance floor.

Suddenly aware of the shocked look on the faces of those around him, he turned toward the dance floor. Only one couple remained and damned if it wasn't Horace and Amelia, moving with sultry steps across the floor, their faces touching. Josh couldn't have been more shocked had Amelia taken off her clothes.

The two made a stunning couple as they made their way across the floor, their movements slow and sensuous like two tigers on the prowl.

Josh didn't want to believe what was happening. Amelia was a schoolteacher, for Pete's sake. What was she doing putting that kind of passion into a dance? And when had

Horace become such a tango expert? Look at him. Slinking around like a male cat in heat.

Josh knew he had to do something to put a stop to this nonsense. Fast!

❧ *Chapter 6* ❧

$\mathcal{T}$he air practically sizzled with the pulsing throb of Latin music. Desperate, Josh took Laura by the hand and practically dragged her onto the dance floor. "Josh, what are you doing? You said—"

"The hell with what I said." He took her hand and held it at arms' length before it occurred to him he had no idea how to tango. "What in hell do I do next?"

"You put your cheek next to mine and we walk forward like a panther in a jungle." An elephant crossing a swamp was more like it, but Laura didn't seem to notice. "That's it," she said gaily. "Now make a snapping turn and start back." It was while he was in the midst of the snapping turn that Josh noticed Amelia and Horace doing some rather steamy turns of their own.

"Perfect!" Laura cried excitedly, her cheeks flushed. "Keep your movements sharp and crisp."

"Change partners," Charley "Ragtime" called out and suddenly Josh's heart filled the "jungle" with the sound of a frantic drum.

Amelia pulled away from Horace and turned to face Josh. When he made no move toward her she lifted her hand. "Josh?"

He stepped forward and took her offered hand. It felt ever so warm and delicate in his and trembled to his touch. He extended his arm and pressed his cheek next to hers. "Ready?"

"Ready," she said breathlessly. They moved with slinking motions across the dance floor, turned quickly and started back again. Suddenly, it seemed like it was only the two of them in that room and for all he knew, no one else existed.

No longer feeling self-conscious, Josh forgot about trying to get the steps right and concentrated on the softness of her skin next to his cheek, on the subtle fragrance of roses in her hair, on the secretive smile she gave him when they made their snapping turn—a smile that made him long to know all the secrets of her heart.

All too soon the music stopped. Next to him, Horace dipped Laura until she almost touched the floor. Josh, not wanting to be outdone, followed his lead.

The crowd went wild, the thunderous applause nearly drowning out the music. He lifted Amelia upright and she laughed gaily, her eyes sparkling.

"Why, Josh Travis, you're full of surprises. Not only are you a fine poet, you're a fine dancer."

It was a gross exaggeration, of course, but he was pleased and touched. No one had ever said such things to him before.

The tempo of the music changed to a less scandalous fox-trot and other couples began crowding the dance floor. Josh fully intended to ask Amelia to dance with him again, but Horace had already whisked her away and Laura had taken her place.

"I thought you said you didn't know how to tango," she said accusingly.

"I'm a fast learner," he said, drawing her into his arms. His gaze traveled to the far side of the barn. Horace was hovering over Amelia like a bridegroom on a honeymoon.

"Ow, you stepped on my toes," Laura complained.

"What?"

She pulled away from him. "Josh Travis! If you don't want to be with me, I wish you'd just say so!"

Other couples glanced their way. His face red, he tried to calm her down. "Don't be ridiculous, Laura. Of course I want to be with you."

"Well you have a funny way of showing it. You've hardly said a word to me all night."

"I didn't come to talk," Josh said defensively. "I came to dance." He slipped his hand around her waist and drew her close, determined to make up to her for his lack of attentiveness.

Josh tried to concentrate fully on Laura for the rest of the evening, he really did. But no matter how hard he tried, he simply couldn't ignore Amelia. He felt responsible for her. Lord almighty, just wait until the school board got wind of her dancing the tango! And it was all Horace's fault.

Who did Horace think he was? Holding Amelia so close. She was a schoolteacher, for goodness' sakes. Responsible for the minds of Stonewell Pines's impressionable youth.

Suddenly, and for no reason that Josh could figure out, Laura pulled away and flounced off the dance floor. "Laura?" Puzzled, he chased after her, catching up to her outside the barn, away from the glare of lights and blaring music. "What's the matter with you?"

"What's the matter with me? You're the one who's been acting strange all night."

"I've never acted strange in my life."

"You keep staring at that schoolteacher."

"I wasn't staring at her. I'm simply concerned. You should be concerned, too. She's with Horace and you know what a womanizer he is."

"From what I can see, she's quite capable of taking care of herself."

His heart thudded. "What do you mean by taking care of herself? Did Horace try something?"

"Ooooooh."

"Come on, Laura, that's a girl. I'm only doing my civic duty."

Laura didn't look the least bit impressed. "I had no idea you were so civic-minded."

"Trust me, Laura. There're a lot of things you don't know about me. Now come on, that's a girl." It took some doing, but Josh finally managed to sweet-talk Laura into going back inside.

Later, after Laura and her girlfriends excused themselves to powder their noses, which was the new expression bandied around by the fairer sex, Josh used the opportunity to corner Amelia and Horace.

Amelia was laughing, her cheeks flushed and her eyes sparkling. The instant she spotted Josh, the laughter died on her pretty pink lips and it was as if something sizzled between them like summer lightning. "I had no idea you and Horace were so good on the dance floor."

Neither did Josh. "Tell me, where did *you* learn to tango?"

She blushed, but looked pleased by the compliment. "Actually, I have Horace to thank for making me look good. We practiced every night this week."

"Did you, now?" Josh said evenly.

"Yes, and I happened to see the Castles perform the tango when I was in Chicago visiting my sister."

Horace glowered at Josh. "The last I heard, you were opposed to the tango."

"Really?" Amelia asked.

"Not all tangos," Josh said. "Just the French ones."

"I thought the tango came from Argentina," Amelia said, looking confused.

"Yes, well you know the French. They'll put a twist on anything and claim it as their own."

Amelia laughed. "You're so clever."

"Yes, isn't he?" Horace said, unsmiling.

Ignoring his *former* best friend, Josh never took his eyes off her face. "May I have a word with you privately, Amelia?"

"Of course, Josh." She turned to Horace. "You don't mind, do you?"

Horace kissed her hand, but he didn't look happy. "Just hurry back."

Josh led Amelia outside, away from the crowd. It was a beautiful clear night with a full moon that danced upon the golden highlights of Amelia's hair. Josh hesitated, measuring her. "I hope you don't mind my speaking openly."

"Please do," Amelia said.

"Horace is rather . . . don't get me wrong, but he is, you know . . . around women."

"You're not saying he's shy, are you?"

"Shy? Oh, no, nothing like that."

"I didn't think so." She thought for a moment. "So what, exactly, are you saying?"

"He's . . . the opposite of shy."

She thought for a moment. "Oh, you mean he's outgoing. Friendly?"

"You're close." He tried to think of a polite way of saying Horace is a low-down womanizing cad. "Amelia, I . . ." She pursed her lips thoughtfully and he had an almost overwhelming urge to kiss them.

"What is it, Josh? You look so serious."

He shoved his hands into his pockets in frustration. "Be careful."

"But—"

Afraid if he stayed any longer, he would give in to his impulse and kiss her, he turned, held the barn door open for her, then followed her inside.

Horace intercepted them. "Ah, it's about time." He held out his hand to Amelia and bowed. "I believe there're playing our song."

Josh watched in frowning contemplation as Horace led Amelia to the dance floor. He didn't like the idea of Horace and Amelia sharing a favorite anything, let alone a song. Gritting his teeth, Josh walked over to the refreshment table to join Laura and her friends.

Wally stuck a cup of punch under Josh's nose. "Do you smell anything funny?"

"No, why?"

"Why? Look around you, Josh. Hardly anyone's acting normal. Not even you. The tango, for God's sakes. I'm telling you, it's got to be the water."

Wally hurried off to discourage everyone from drinking

the punch. Meanwhile, Josh noticed Horace helping Amelia with her cape. It didn't take a crystal ball to guess what Horace had on his mind. "Let's go, Laura."

Laura looked at him funny, but didn't say anything until they were outside. She sighed as she looked up at the sky. "What a beautiful night. Did you ever see such a full moon in your life?"

Josh looked up at the sky in disgust. It was a full moon, all right, a damned lover's moon. It was the kind of moon that Horace would use to best advantage. Josh grimaced in disgust. Even nature was conspiring against him.

Laura waited in the car while Josh cranked the motor. He then climbed behind the driver's seat and took the old road out of town.

"Where are we going?" Laura asked.

"It's such a pretty night, I thought we'd take the long way around." It was the long way, all right, clear past Amelia Winklemeyer's house, but of course Laura would have no way of knowing this.

Josh turned up Appleton Lane and it was just as he'd predicted. Horace's shiny black Buick was parked in front of Amelia's house. A light shone from the window of Amelia's parlor. What in heaven's name was Amelia Winklemeyer doing entertaining a womanizing scoundrel like Horace at this hour of night?

The man was up to no good, Josh was sure of it.

Next to him, Laura sighed, oblivious to the fact that the virtue of one of Stonewell Pines's finest schoolteachers was at stake. Laura apparently didn't have a civic bone in her body. "I don't want the night to end."

Josh grunted and swung a U-turn so he could drive past Amelia's house for a second look. This time, Horace had better be leaving.

☙ *Chapter 7* ☙

*A*melia's head was still spinning from the excitement of her first Spring Ball. What a wonderful, utterly glorious night. It was disappointing, of course, that Josh had made a prior commitment to Laura. But he really was a dear and he had tried his best to make amends. Heavens, he kept stopping by her table to see how she was doing. What more could she ask for?

Lordy be! She'd never forget the look on his face when he first saw her doing the tango with Horace! On everyone's face!

Though she couldn't name the expression on Josh's face when he danced with her, it made her feel all shivery with pleasure. She still felt the fire on her face where he'd rested his cheek. Still felt the heat of his hand on hers.

Just thinking about the warm lights in his eyes made her cheeks grow hot. She smiled to herself then suddenly remembered her guest. "Would you like some tea, Horace?"

Horace had been flipping through the vast collection of wax cylinder records she kept next to the graphophone. "That's most hospitable of you."

"Make yourself comfortable. I won't be long."

Upon reaching the privacy of her kitchen, she picked up the hem of her gown and moved her feet to the tempo of the music that still rang in her ears. Amelia had enjoyed the evening far more than she had ever imagined. What in Heaven's name was so wicked about dancing?

She shuddered to think what would happen when the school board heard about her behavior! The way word traveled in Stonewell Pines, she was surprised the board members weren't pounding on her door at that very moment. She sighed and reached for the teakettle.

Tonight had been a dream come true and she wasn't going to let anyone ruin it for her.

At twenty-five, she had all but given up the thought of marriage. Who would ever think that out of the clear blue sky, that nice barber, Josh Travis, would give her a heart-shaped box of rocky road chocolates? That and the beautiful love poem had made her realize how narrow and rigidly focused her life had become. It was a wonderful, beautiful world out there and with Josh at her side, she intended to embrace life to its fullest.

Her heart pounded every time she recalled his words to her. To think that he preferred her to that pretty Laura Baker didn't seem possible. But it was absolutely true. Why mercy sakes alive, he hadn't stopped staring at her all evening long. The reason she knew this, of course, was because she hadn't been able to keep her eyes off him, either, though she certainly hoped she had managed to be a bit more discreet than Josh.

How handsome he looked in his fine wool suit and fancy bowtie. She hummed to herself as she prepared tea for her guest, imitating the passionate rhythm of the tango until at last she found herself panther-stepping across the kitchen, mop in hand, her eyes closed as she imagined herself in Josh's arms. When she came to the kitchen table, she made a quick turn, swinging the mop around and knocking one of her best china cups clear across the room. It fell to the floor with a shattering crash.

Much to her embarrassment, she found Horace watching her from the doorway, a silly grin on his face.

"I sure do like the way you swing your hips when you dance, Amelia."

"I wish you wouldn't sneak up on me like that, Horace!" she said, feeling foolish. She exchanged the mop for the broom and busied herself sweeping up the broken pieces. She then arranged cups and saucers on a tray.

"I wasn't sneaking up on you, Amelia. I just wanted to know what was taking you so long. I didn't mean to embarrass you none. But you do have a mighty nice way of moving certain parts."

She didn't like the way he was looking at her. Not one bit. Perhaps she had made a mistake inviting him into the house. Still, he had behaved like such a gentleman all evening and he *was* Josh's friend. In any case, she intended to make certain there was no misunderstanding. "It's not proper to talk about a lady's anatomy," she scolded in the voice usually reserved for her most wayward students. "Especially since Josh and I have an understanding."

Horace leaned against the doorjamb. "If I spoke out of turn, I hope you'll find it in your heart to forgive me."

She dropped a teaspoon on the floor and he stooped to pick it up. He handed her the spoon like he was handing her a single rose and this time there was no mistaking the look on his face.

"Thank you, Horace," she said, her mouth dry. She had never had a beau and now suddenly it appeared she had two!

"Would you like to go for a drive tomorrow afternoon?" he asked. "We could take a picnic lunch."

"Tomorrow? Well I—"

"Oh, please say you will. The wild flowers are in bloom and I hear tell the colors are magnificent."

He seemed so earnest that she didn't have the heart to say a flat-out no, especially since he was the first man to ask her out for a drive. "As I said earlier, Josh and I have decided to get to know each other better."

"That's why I suggested this drive. I've known Josh all my life. Who better than me to help you get to know him?"

She blushed with embarrassment. Mercy, what had gotten into her? Horace hadn't been flirting with her. He was simply trying to be friendly and he was absolutely right; what better way to get to know Josh than through his best friend. "It would be my pleasure to take a drive with you."

Laura folded her arms across her chest and flung herself against the back of her seat in a huff. "What's the matter with you, Josh Travis?"

Josh steered the motorcar so as not to clip Horace's rear fender. The fool man parked as if he owned the road. "What makes you think anything's the matter with me?"

"You've been driving up and down this same street for the last half hour."

"I told you, it's the best place in town to see the stars. There's too much light closer to town. Since everyone's been converting to electricity it's near impossible to see the night sky. Oh, look, over there, a shooting star." He slowed down and swung another U-turn. "Tell me, Laura, have you ever danced to the music of the stars?"

"Don't be ridiculous, Josh. The stars don't make music."

He drove past Horace's Buick once again. For two cents he was ready to get out of his car and . . .

"I've seen enough of the night sky." Laura sounded downright petulant. "Besides, it's getting late. I think you better take me home."

It was late all right, and that scoundrel Horace still hadn't left Amelia's house.

"Josh!"

"Oh, all right." He swung a U-turn and pressed his foot on the gas pedal, pushing his Model T as fast as it would go, and took every possible shortcut on his way back to town. He even went so far as to drive through a narrow alley.

"Good Heavens, Josh!" she cried out as he zipped around a corner and over a curb. "Must you drive so fast?"

He pulled up in front of her house with squealing tires, deposited her onto the front porch, pecked her on the cheek and raced back to his car. Just before climbing behind the steering wheel, he remembered to say good night, but she'd already rushed into the house, slamming the door behind her.

Retracing his route, he drove the distance back to Amelia's street in record time.

Horace's motor car was gone and the lights were turned off in Amelia's house. Josh slumped against his steering wheel in relief. "It's about time," he muttered. Now that the schoolteacher's virtue was no longer in danger of being compromised, Josh swung another U-turn and drove home, satisfied that he had done his civic duty.

The Monday following the barn dance, Horace walked the short distance from his hardware store to Josh's barbershop and flopped into the barber chair.

Josh was still steaming over Horace's behavior the night of the dance, but he tried not to let it show. He dutifully lathered Horace's face and decided not to mention Amelia's name. The less said the better. But Horace had to go and ruin everything by dropping a little bombshell.

Josh slammed the cup of warm shaving soap onto the counter and leaned over the chair until his nose was practically in Horace's face. "What do you mean you took Amelia for a drive?"

Horace's eyes crossed as he stared nervously at the razor which was moving back and forth like a snake about to bite. "Take it easy with that thing."

"Don't change the subject."

"I don't know why you're so riled up. I thought you wanted me to take her off your hands."

"I did . . . I do. But I don't want any child deprived of a good education because you've compromised the best teacher in Stonewell Pines."

"Relax, Josh. Amelia's in good hands. Another week or two and she won't even remember your name."

Amelia wasn't quite sure what to make of Josh Travis. He'd broken into her house to leave an extravagant box of chocolates, along with a poem containing the sweetest words in the world, and then he didn't so much as pay her a social call. A week had gone by since the night of the dance and nothing.

Not that he didn't have ample opportunities to ask her out. She was always bumping into him lately. It was the strangest thing. She never much noticed him before and now, it seemed, she couldn't go anywhere without running into him.

She ran into him at the library, and the bakery. They bumped into each other at Joseph Teller's Dry Goods Store and the post office. Why she even ran into him as she and Horace were leaving the ice cream parlor. He always stopped to talk to her and seemed genuinely concerned for her welfare, but he made no attempt to ask her out. How in Heaven's name were they supposed to get to know each other if they only saw each other for a few minutes at a time?

Well, Josh Travis. Enough is enough! One box of chocolates and a poem does not constitute a proper courtship! It was time to take matters into her own hands.

The knock came just as Josh had returned to his room at the end of the day, exhausted. "Mr. Travis, you have a visitor," Mrs. Clatterway said, her voice thick with disapproval. "A *lady* visitor."

Moments later, he walked into the parlor to find Amelia Winklemeyer waiting for him. She wore a pretty yellow taffeta dress with a short jaunty jacket. A yellow butterfly bow and a cluster of velvet flowers decorated her straw braid hat. She looked as pretty and summery as an English tea garden.

Amelia gave a polite nod. "Josh."

"Amelia."

"I thought perhaps you and I should have a little talk."

Certain she was about to bring up the marriage issue again, he tried to think of how to tell her the truth. Finding himself staring at her or, more accurately, staring at her lips, he tore his gaze away and concentrated on the floral pattern of the wool rug beneath her feet.

"The poem you sent me was the most . . ." He glanced up and she continued. "I really believed you meant what you said."

"That poem—" How could he possibly tell her that what he wrote was nothing but a bunch of meaningless words, written to impress someone else who, it turned out, he had no real desire to impress. "The poem doesn't do you justice."

Her eyes opened wide and he found himself sinking into their velvety soft depths. Something suddenly occurred to him. Something so amazing, so utterly unbelievable that it momentarily took his breath away. "By thunder!" he exclaimed.

Startled she jumped, her hand on her chest. "Whatever is the matter?"

"Your eyes are the color of cornflowers!" He bent forward to get a closer look. "It's incredible. Come over here." He took her hand and pulled her next to the window where he turned to cup her face in his hands. "It's incredible. Even the purple hue is right."

She looked startled at first, then embarrassed, but her face softened. "I don't understand why you're so surprised. It's exactly what you said in your poem."

"Yes, I know, but . . ." Still holding her lovely face in his hands, he noticed something else. "And your lips . . . When you hold them like that, they really do look like a dew-kissed rose."

Her lips parted at the precise moment he lowered his head and covered her mouth with his own. He drew back and looked deep into her eyes then kissed her again.

This time, she surprised him by wrapping her arms around his neck and kissing him back. *Oh, heavenly days.* Not only did she have luscious soft lips, she knew how to use them.

He slipped his arms around her waist and pulled her closer, then slowly and thoroughly ravished her lips. Never before had he kissed lips like hers. So soft and yielding at first, then passionate and hot. And when he slid his tongue inside her mouth, she actually—

"Well, I never!" At the sound of Laura Baker's voice, Josh and Amelia jumped apart.

Laura stood at the entryway next to Mrs. Clatterway. It

was difficult to say which of the two looked the most out-
raged and shocked, but his landlady recovered first. "Mr.
Travis! May I remind you that the parlor is meant for polite
conversation."

"Believe me, Mrs. Clatterway, all my conversations are
polite."

Mrs. Clatterway leveled a disapproving glance at Amelia
before walking away.

Laura was more to the point. "Josh Travis! I saw you
kissing her and don't you dare say you weren't!"

Since Josh could hardly deny her accusations, he couldn't
think of anything to say.

Laura stamped her foot. "I think it's time we told her."

"Laura, let's talk about this—"

Laura ignored him and triumph gleamed in her eyes as she
blurted out the awful truth. "The rocky road chocolates were
meant for me!"

It was obvious Amelia didn't believe a word Laura said.
"Then why did Josh deliver them to my house?"

"I'll explain," Josh said, glaring at Laura, but once she
had begun, there was no stopping her.

"The chocolates were meant for me, not you," Laura said,
ignoring the looks he was giving her. "They were delivered
to you by mistake. That's why Josh broke into your house.
He was trying to retrieve *my* chocolates."

A terrible silence followed Laura's outburst, a silence so
intense it was painful to the ears.

As if standing from afar, he watched, helplessly, as the
color slowly drained from Amelia's face. Looking astound-
ingly calm, she turned from Laura to Josh. "Is this true,
Josh?"

"I'm afraid so," he said, though he wished with all his
heart it wasn't. Never had he felt so miserable in his life.

"And the poem?" Amelia persisted. "Was that meant for
Laura, too?"

"What poem?" Laura asked.

Both women stared at him, waiting. Josh let his hands drop
to his side. "The poem was a mistake."

"I see." Amelia not only looked pale, she appeared almost frighteningly calm. Josh decided there was something to be said for female hysterics. At least a man knew where he stood. With Amelia, he couldn't be certain.

"I guess the joke's on me, then, isn't it?" Without another word, she swept past him, through the entry hall and out the front door.

Laura looked as if she was having second thoughts about what she'd done. "She had to know the truth," she said. "Please don't look at me like that, Josh. You know I'm right."

"It was my job to tell her, not yours," Josh said, his voice distant. He was more furious at himself than at Laura. He should have been honest with Amelia from the start. God, would she ever forgive him?

He stalked out of the parlor, hoping to catch Amelia before she left.

"Josh, please don't go!" Laura called after him, but he kept walking.

✌ *Chapter 8* ✌

*A*melia ripped up Josh's poem and threw the pieces into the fire. Flames licked each scrap of paper in turn, curling the edges before consuming it. It might as well have been her heart that went up in smoke. It was that painful.

What a fool she'd been. To even think that a man like Josh Travis would be interested in the likes of her.

Just because he looked at her like no man had ever looked at her—and kissed her like no man had ever kissed her—was no reason to fill her head with foolish notions. She was a schoolteacher, plain and simple. She was not and never could be the woman in that poem, no matter how many pretty gowns she wore or how many tangos she danced.

Someone knocked on the door. For the longest while, she stood frozen in place, and tried to stay calm. The knock came again and, this time, it was more persistent.

Why was Josh doing this to her? He had followed her home from his boarding house yesterday and had spent the rest of the day pounding on her door. It was nearly ten by the time he finally gave up and went home. Now, it sounded like he was back again. Why didn't he just leave her alone?

Enough was enough! She didn't need him feeling sorry for her. She took a deep breath, held her head up high and practically ripped the door off its hinges.

Only it wasn't Josh standing on her doorstep, it was three members of the school board. ''What an unexpected ah . . .

surprise," she said, forcing a smile. "Do come in."

Mr. Comstock, Mr. Dodd and Miss Oxley made no attempt at polite conversation as they followed her into her parlor in a perfect straight line like a family of ducks.

"Please, sit down," she said, and the three sat on the couch in perfect unison.

Smiling nervously, she sat down opposite them. "Would you care for some tea?"

"That won't be necessary," Mr. Comstock said. "We are here to discuss a serious matter." A tall thin man with a long narrow face and flyaway ears, he looked amazingly like a donkey.

"Most serious," Miss Oxley parroted, her fleshy jowls shaking with emphasis.

"I should say," Mr. Dodd agreed, the gold chain of his watch stretching across his barrel-shaped middle.

Mr. Comstock looked like a judge about to serve out a death sentence. "As you know, Miss Winklemeyer, you signed a contract." He pulled a sheet of paper from a leather portfolio. "If you will permit me to read a portion of the agreement you signed." He cleared his voice and began. "I, Miss Amelia Winklemeyer, promise to uphold the following rules: Number one: I will not marry during the term of my contract." He looked at her sternly. "Number two: I agree to be home between eight P.M. and six A.M. unless I am at a school function. Three: I will not loiter downtown in ice cream stores. Four: I will not dance, nor dress in bright colors." He glanced up at her. "Do you wish me to go on, Miss Winklemeyer?"

"That won't be necessary," she replied. "I remember the rules quite well."

He replaced the sheet and folded his hands on his lap. "In that case, we can proceed. It has come to our attention that you were seen, how should I say it . . . ?"

"Out after eight," Miss Oxley said with a sniff. "And wearing blue. *Bright* blue."

"And pink," added Mr. Dodd. "The dress you wore to the Spring Ball was reportedly pink."

Miss Oxley made a strange snorting sound. "How many times must I tell you? It wasn't pink, it was rose."

"The rule doesn't differentiate between bright colors," Mr. Comstock pointed out.

Miss Oxley puckered her mouth before adding, "You forgot to mention that teachers are not allowed to keep company with men."

"One thing at a time," Mr. Comstock pleaded.

Mr. Dodd leaned forward. "Personally, I think that dancing is a much more serious offense than loitering in the ice cream parlor."

"She wasn't just dancing," Miss Oxley said. "She was doing the tango." As if the mere word was too much for her, Miss Oxley fanned herself with her gloves. "What a sad day this is."

"Very sad," Mr. Dodd agreed.

Mr. Comstock gave an impatient shrug. "The rules of the school board are very clear concerning the conduct of our teachers."

"Extremely clear," Miss Oxley agreed.

Mr. Comstock appeared relieved that everyone was in agreement. "Have you got anything to say on your own behalf?"

They made it sound like she'd broken all the rules, which, of course, wasn't true. "I didn't get married," she said. After the humiliation of thinking herself practically engaged, she had no intention of going through anything like that again. "Nor did I dye my hair or smoke cigarettes." She did take a sip of sherry and had let Josh kiss her, but she wasn't about to admit to either.

The board members didn't look the least bit impressed and the dark looks they gave her was full of censure. She almost wished she *had* dyed her hair and maybe even taken up smoking.

Taking a deep breath, she decided her best bet was to apologize and throw herself at their mercy. She had previously been a model teacher. That had to count for something. It wasn't until Josh had broken into her house that she started acting crazy. She decided to plead for leniency.

"I would like to apologize for my actions," she began. "You see, something rather extraordinary happened to me. I received a box of rocky road chocolates out of the clear blue sky and . . ." Feeling embarrassed at having to admit how foolish she'd behaved, she hesitated. That's when she noticed a piece of paper containing a part of Josh's poem had drifted to the side of the fireplace, away from the flames. It was the part that contained the phrase *your spirit dances to the music of the stars.*

Suddenly, she couldn't do what the board expected her to do. Or say what they wanted her to say. She drew her gaze away from the fireplace and regarded each board member in turn.

"It's true I danced the tango," she said. "I also went to the ice cream parlor and wore bright colors. But it's also true that I taught class these last few days with more vigor and enthusiasm than I have felt in a very long time."

The three board members drew back, clearly aghast. Mr. Comstock stuck his monocle in his eye and stared at her. "What are you saying, Miss Winklemeyer?"

"I'm saying that the restrictions you put on a teacher's social life does not make her a better teacher. My personal experience leads me to believe that such unfair rules do more harm than good."

Miss Oxley's chins quivered. "Surely you're not suggesting that you're a better teacher because you did the . . . oh, dear, I can't say it."

Amelia said it for her. "The tango." She thought for a minute before replying. "What I'm saying is that a teacher needs the freedom to experience life in all its glory. To feel pleasure and joy, and more than anything, love." A lump rose in her throat as she recalled Josh's sweet warm kisses and she bit back the tears that threatened her composure.

"Dear me," Mr. Comstock exclaimed. "Next you'll be suggesting that teachers be allowed to marry."

"And why shouldn't a teacher marry?" Amelia asked, not for herself, but for others. It was too late for her. Now that she knew how Josh had lied to her, she'd never trust another man as long as she lived. But that wasn't the point. The point was that the school board was tainting *her* classroom with their old-fashioned ideas and she intended to put a stop to it!

Mr. Comstock looked at the other two board members for direction, but none was forthcoming. "I believe we'll have to make a full report to the board." He rose to his feet. "You'll be hearing from us."

"Indeed you will," Miss Oxley said, rising next to him.

"Most definitely," Mr. Dodd said, taking his place at the end of the line, behind the other two.

Amelia followed the trio to the door, resisting the urge to hurry them along. Oh, dear, what was she going to do? She'd never felt so miserable in her life. One minute she thought herself practically engaged and the next minute, nothing. After today, it was entirely possible she wouldn't even have her teaching post. It was hard to believe. None of this would have happened had that box of rocky road chocolates not been delivered to her house by mistake.

Josh had never felt so miserable in his life. Amelia refused to see him, Laura wasn't talking to him, Miss Clatterway had raised his rent for misusing her parlor, and Miss Baxter insisted he'd used up his entire allotment of telephone calls for the next six months. Added to all this was the water matter. Wally had managed to convince city officials a water problem existed. Members of the city counsel had stopped by the barbershop to question Josh.

"It's not the water," Josh had explained, much to the mayor's relief. "My trouble all began with Mrs. Ryefield's rocky road chocolates." The water was given a clean bill, but the Sweet Dreams Confectionary underwent a thorough inspection. Now, even Mrs. Ryefield was mad at him.

With half the town not talking to him, he was surprised when Mrs. Clatterway knocked at his door to announce a visitor.

Thinking Amelia had a change of heart, he practically

killed himself racing across the room. He ripped the door open with such force, Mrs. Clatterway gasped in surprise. "Is it a lady caller?"

His landlady leveled her gray eyes at him. "Not this time." Her tone of voice implied it was lucky for him that it wasn't.

Horace waited in the parlor, looking amazingly unscathed by the mess he had helped to create.

"What are you doing here?" Josh demanded. It seemed like every time Horace showed up, his own troubles took a turn for the worse.

"I think I have a solution to your problem."

"What problem would that be, Horace? The fact that neither Amelia nor Laura will talk to me? Or the fact that my reputation is in ruins?"

"Sit down and relax, my friend. I'm about to solve all your problems."

Josh sat down, more out of dread than curiosity. That smirking smile on Horace's face couldn't possibly mean good news.

"I wanted you to be the first one to know. I've asked Amelia to marry me."

Josh jumped to his feet, almost knocking over the end table in his haste. "You did what?"

Horace's smile grew broader. "I told you I was about to solve your problems. As soon as Laura hears that Amelia is betrothed to me, she'll forgive you."

"You're betrothed?" His voice rose several octaves.

"Not yet. Amelia said she has to think about it and she has to work out some problems with the school, but what woman in her right mind would turn down an offer of marriage?"

Josh held his head and groaned. The woman he loved was about to marry someone else and there wasn't a thing in the world he could do about it.

He dropped his hands and stared at his palms. What was he thinking? The woman he loved? Amelia? Impossible!

"So what do you say?" Horace asked.

Josh hadn't heard a word Horace said after he'd dropped that little bombshell about asking Amelia to marry him. "What?"

"Will you be my best man or won't you?"

"No, I won't be your best man because there isn't going to be a wedding. Do you hear me?" With that he dashed out the front door and headed for his car.

Never had Josh driven his Model T Ford so fast. He drove so fast that his teeth chattered as he rattled along Third Street and followed Main Street to the old Mill Road. Lord if they didn't do something about the roads around here, he wouldn't have any teeth left. He then swung a sharp turn onto Appleton Lane.

Amelia opened the door at his knock, but it was obvious by the look of surprise on her face, she was expecting someone else. "Go away. I told you a hundred times, I don't want to talk to you!"

She tried closing the door in his face, but he was too quick for her. With a well-placed foot, he managed to push his way inside. "You don't have to talk. Just listen."

"I'm not interested in anything you have to say."

"You might be surprised."

"Don't tell me. You sent Laura Baker a box of chocolates—or was it flowers this time? And they've gone astray." She glanced around. "As you can plainly see, there are no chocolates or flowers here. Now please go."

"Amelia, listen to me . . ."

"No, you listen to me, Josh Travis. I've never been so humiliated in my entire life. First you let me think you sent the chocolates and poem to me. Then you force your best friend to take me to the Spring Dance . . ."

"I did no such thing!"

"Don't lie to me, Josh. Horace told me everything. He quoted you as saying I was a dried-up spinster who would jump at the chance to go out with any man."

Josh was truly aghast. *I'll kill him, I swear I will.* "I never called you a dried-up anything, Amelia, you've got to believe me. I . . . I love you.''

She covered her mouth and looked at him with tear-filled eyes. ''How can you say such a thing? After what you wrote in that poem to Laura . . .''

''I know it's hard to believe. I can't even believe it myself, but it's true. I have no idea how it happened. That's why you can't marry Horace.''

''I'll marry whomever I please.''

''But don't you see? He's a womanizer. He'll bring you nothing but heartache.''

''He's been nothing but kind and good to me. A perfect gentleman.''

Horace a gentleman. That had to be a first. ''But Horace doesn't love you, Amelia. I do.''

''I know you're only trying to be kind, but can't you see, you're only making matters worse?'' She turned her back to him. ''Go, Josh. Please go.''

He spun her around to face him. ''I'm not going until we straighten this out.''

''There's nothing to straighten out, Josh. Whether or not I marry Horace is my business.''

He released her and backed away. It was obvious by the stubborn look on her face that nothing he said was going to change her mind. With a muttered curse, he stormed out of the house, slamming the door shut behind him.

He drove straight to the Cross-Eyed Rooster Saloon on Main Street. He never before felt the need to drown his sorrows, until today. As luck would have it, Horace was at the bar looking unbearably pleased with himself.

Pointedly ignoring him, Josh ordered a whiskey from the bartender. He could hear Horace's voice as he bragged about his latest conquest. ''Let me tell you, men, beneath Amelia Winklemeyer's prudish facade beats the heart of a passionate woman.''

Red lights flared in front of Josh's eyes. He couldn't see straight, let alone think straight. Without warning, he whirled about, grabbed Horace by the collar and punched him in the jaw.

A startled look crossed Horace's face as he stumbled backward against the bar, but he made a quick recovery and flew at Josh in a rage. "Why you—"

The other patrons circled around as the two men attacked each other with shouted insults and flying fists.

"I won't let you marry her!" Josh said as he rammed into Horace.

"Oh, no?" Horace shouted back. "Try and stop me!"

The headline in the morning's paper stopped Josh cold when he opened up the door to his apartment. BRAWL FOUGHT OVER SCHOOLMARM.

Never had Josh felt worse in his life. His misery had little if anything to do with Horace's well-placed punches, though every bone and muscle in his body ached and one eye was swollen shut.

Blast the luck. The newspaper reporter was evidently trying to score points with the editor and had left no stone unturned. He'd interviewed Peter, the delivery boy; Josh's landlady; the telephone operator and the city counsel. If that wasn't enough, the reporter had somehow managed to round up quotes from half of Josh's customers. It appeared that everyone and his brother had an opinion about the unlikely triangle.

Josh never felt so humiliated in his life, but he felt even worse for Amelia. She must be mortified at having the whole affair aired in public.

She didn't look mortified when she swept into his barbershop later that day; she looked hopping mad.

Hands on her hips, she planted herself by the barber chair opposite Josh who was shaving Wally. Before Josh had a chance to apologize for the newspaper, she lashed out at him. "Thanks to you, I no longer have a way to support myself!"

"What are you talking about?"

"The school board has decided to put me on suspension."

"Suspension. Whatever for? Everyone knows you're the best teacher in Stonewell Pines."

"And they took that into full consideration when they decided not to suspend me for doing the tango."

"That's good news," Josh began. "But I thought you said—"

"They rescinded their decision because of this!" She flung a copy of the morning newspaper into his face.

"That's terrible. They can't do that."

"They can do whatever they want. They said it was unseemly for men to fight over a schoolteacher. You've ruined my reputation!"

"I was trying to save you from that fool man, Horace. If you marry him, you'll be making the biggest mistake of your life."

"It's my life and I can do anything I please!"

Sitting between the feuding pair, Wally shifted uneasily in his seat. Josh was brandishing the straight-edged razor only inches above Wally's face.

"If it's not the water, it's gotta be the air," Wally mumbled, holding his breath so as not to breathe in too much.

"Just stay out of my life, Josh Travis. I don't want to ever see or hear from you again!" She turned and stormed out of the shop.

"Don't worry, you won't!" he called after her, though he knew darn well he was simply blowing off steam. He had every intention of spending the rest of his life with Amelia, just as soon as he figured out how.

❧ *Chapter 9* ❧

For the remainder of the week, Josh was impossible to live with. He solicited advice from each customer who had the misfortune of needing a haircut or shave. Not a hair was clipped nor a whisker shaved without its owner being subjected to Josh's tale of woe. "What am I going to do? She won't talk to me. She won't listen to anything I have to say."

Not one customer had anything of value to offer, though several tried to get Josh's mind off his problems by discussing politics. A few, like old man Hendrix, grew irritated. "I'm mighty tired of hearing about your love problems, Travis. If I wanted to hear about all that love garbage, I'd have my hair cut at Miss Patricia Stevens's Beauty Salon."

At night, Josh followed Mrs. Clatterway around the boarding house, asking her advice. "You're a woman. Pretend you're Amelia Winklemeyer. What would make you forgive me?"

Mrs. Clatterway shook her head. "I don't know. Maybe if I thought you loved me . . ."

"But I told her I did."

"Sometimes saying it isn't enough. You have to prove it with your actions."

"Prove it, how?"

When Mrs. Clatterway offered no further suggestions, he picked up the phone and poured out his heart to the telephone operator. But did Miss Baxter take pity on him? She did not!

She kept interrupting to tell him he'd already used up his fair share of calls.

"All right," she relented at last. "I'll let you make one call, Josh, and that'll be the end of it for the rest of the year."

"I don't want to make a call. I want to talk to you."

"Talking to the operator is not an option."

"I'm finished talking. What I want is some advice. Come on, Miss Baxter. You're a woman. If you were Amelia, what would make you believe I really loved you?"

Miss Baxter sighed. "All right, you say you love Miss Winklemeyer, but she won't listen."

"That's right."

"She probably thinks you're fickle."

"Fickle?"

"Think about it. You thought you loved Laura Baker, and look how long that lasted. Before her there was Mary-Jo and Elizabeth-Anne. You drove me crazy with all the calls you made to her!"

"But this is different. I never got into a fist fight over any other woman. And I can't ever remember having lost sleep before. I'm telling you, what I feel for Amelia is the real thing and I've got to do something, fast. Horace will make her miserable. Why the man has no scruples when it comes to women. He's been known to court two or three at a time." Suddenly Josh had an idea. "Miss Baxter, you're an angel." He made a kissing sound over the line and hung up.

The following morning, he walked into Mrs. Ryefield's Sweet Dreams Confectionery and ordered a box of chocolates sent to every eligible woman in Stonewell Pines except for Amelia.

The total came to twenty-one boxes, which cost him dearly. But if his plan worked, it would be worth every penny. If nothing else, his purchase put him back in Mrs. Ryefield's good graces.

He signed each card with Horace's name and left the sweet shop whistling to himself. All that was left to do was wait.

By three o'clock that afternoon all hell broke loose. Telephone calls began to pour in, jamming the town's single switchboard and forcing poor Miss Baxter to cancel her "social" engagements for the entire night.

Having heard this from one of his customers, Josh stood at the window of his barber shop and watched the parade of grim-faced fathers, dressed in dark suits and bowler hats, storm into Horace's hardware to issue stern warnings.

But it wasn't until nearly five o'clock that afternoon that he knew for certain his plan to make Horace look like a two-timing womanizer had been an unequivocal success. For that's when Amelia rode her horse and buggy into town and, picking up the hem of her skirt, barreled into Horace's dry goods store, slamming the door shut behind her. In little more that a minute and a half, she stormed back outside and, looking neither left nor right, drove away.

Satisfied that Horace was now out of the picture, Josh closed up his shop, hopped into his Model T and drove the distance to Appleton Road.

He wasn't too surprised that she wouldn't let him in, but he'd hoped for a chance to explain himself. "Amelia. It's me, Josh. I need to talk to you."

No matter how much he pounded on the door or pleaded with her, she refused to open up.

Disheartened, he drove home, his heart feeling as if it had been replaced by a heavy lead weight. For the third night in a row, he poured out his heart to his landlady.

Mrs. Clatterway shook her gray head and adjusted her spectacles. "Now let me see if I have the story straight. You sent a box of rocky road chocolates to Laura Baker."

"That's what started this whole mess," Josh said miserably.

"And now you've sent a box of chocolates to every eligible woman in Stonewell Pines."

"Except for Amelia, of course."

Mrs. Clatterway's forehead creased as she tried to sort through all the facts. "That's the part I don't understand. You're in love with Miss Winklemeyer, yet she's the only woman you've not sent chocolates to, except by accident."

Josh thought about this for a moment. Lord almighty, his

landlady was absolutely right. "Mrs. Clatterway, you're brilliant!" He pecked her parched painted cheek and raced to his room.

He searched his desk for paper and pen and a bottle of ink. He would write Amelia a poem that would win her heart. It was such a simple idea, he didn't understand why he hadn't thought of it before.

His heart pumping with excitement, he dipped the nib into the ink and began to write. *Your eyes are the color of* . . . He closed his eyes and conjured up a vision of Amelia that quickened his pulse. Her face looked so clear to him, he could almost imagine she was in the room. Her eyes were the color of cornflowers, but he wanted to say something more, something more unique, more literary. He jabbed his pen in its holder and paced the floor. Blue as the sky. Blue as a bluejay. Blue as a . . .

Not even Shakespeare was of any help. He scanned every book on his shelf. Longfellow, Burns, Browning. What kind of poets were they? Not one of them had succeeded in describing a woman as beautiful as Amelia.

He struggled with his poem until the wee hours of the morning and still he had nothing to show for his efforts. He closed his eyes, holding on to the vision of her like a precious gem. She really did have eyes the color of cornflowers and her lips really did look like a dew-touched rose.

That's when inspiration hit. The words started coming fast, now, flowing from his pen as if dictated by some magical force. Faster and faster he wrote, until he filled two sheets of paper.

When his poem said everything he wanted it to, he addressed it to Amelia so this time there would be no mistaking who it was meant for. He then signed his name, folded the poem in thirds and placed it in an envelope.

Tomorrow, he would arrange for Mrs. Ryefield to send Amelia a box of rocky road chocolates, along with his poem. And this time, nothing better go wrong.

The box of rocky road chocolates felt like a brick when it came down hard on his head. He'd been leaning over the barber chair shaving Crummer when suddenly, wham! Right on the noggin. First he saw stars and then he saw Amelia's flashing cornflower blue eyes.

"What did you do that for?" he asked, his senses reeling.

"You know darn well why!" She shook his poem in his face. "How dare you put my name on the poem you wrote for Laura Baker!"

"I wrote that poem for you, no one else."

"Don't lie, Josh. It's the same one you wrote before you even knew me. To the word!"

"I'm not lying." He grabbed the poem from her and stabbed at the bold handwriting with his finger. "Read it, Amelia."

"I did read it."

"Then you know that not a single word describes Laura. I didn't get the color of her hair right, nor her eyes, and I sure in hell didn't get anything else right, either."

A look of bewilderment crossed Amelia's face. "But I don't understand,"

"I don't either," said Crummer, looking up from his chair, but neither Josh nor Amelia paid him the least bit of attention.

"I didn't understand it either until last night. I was trying to write a poem especially for you and I found myself writing the very same words I'd written before. That's when I realized the most amazing thing; the poem I wrote described the woman of my dreams, the woman I always hoped to meet. It was never meant for Laura."

"But you wrote the poem before we even knew each other."

"I know."

"Before I let myself do the things I always wanted to do. Like tango and let my hair down and . . ."

"I know."

"None of this makes sense."

"Yes, it does. Don't you see? I wrote the poem before I knew you and yet, it describes you perfectly. That can only mean one thing. *You* are the woman of my dreams. No one else. You're the woman I always hoped to meet. The one who dances to the music of the stars.''

"But what about the cornflowers?" she stammered.

He thought for a moment. That puzzled him, too. How could he have described Amelia's eye color so perfectly when he'd never really noticed them prior to writing the poem? Then he remembered something. "My grandmother used to grow cornflowers when I was a little boy and I've always associated them with love and kindness and everything that was good in the world."

Amelia's eyes grew soft. "Really?"

"Really?" Crummer repeated.

"Really. I guess it only makes sense. I gave the girl of my dreams eyes the color of love." Josh touched his hand to her cheek and gazed at her tenderly. "I love you." He leaned toward her and she leaned toward him and together they formed a bridge over the barber chair as their lips touched.

"I love you, Josh Travis."

"In that case, would you do me the honor of agreeing to be my tango partner from this day forward?"

"Are you asking her to marry you?" Crummer asked.

Josh grinned. "That's exactly what I'm doing."

Amelia smiled back, her face radiant. "In that case, I accept."

Josh wrapped his arms around her and kissed her again, this time holding nothing back.

Crummer was forced to slouch down in the barber chair to keep from getting crushed. But he didn't mind; he didn't mind one bit. He was too busy collecting the rocky road chocolates that had fallen on to his lap.

After replacing each piece carefully into the heart-shaped box, Crummer then ducked out of the barber chair and wiped the lather from his chin with a Turkish towel. He sighed happily as he gazed at the happy couple who had obviously forgotten he was even in the shop.

Crummer didn't take offense. Quite the contrary. He couldn't be happier. He smiled to himself as he glanced in the mirror and straightened his bowtie. He couldn't believe how his life had changed since that rare disease had caused his mustache to fall off. Who knows? Maybe Lady Luck was about to strike again.

If he wasn't mistaken, that pretty Laura Baker would be needing a shoulder to cry on. Yes, indeed, a shoulder and maybe even a sympathetic ear. He tucked the box of rocky road chocolates beneath his arm and strolled out of Josh Travis's barber shop, whistling.

Miss Delwin's Delights

Raine Cantrell

❧ *Chapter 1* ❧

*K*it Sidell was a man on a mission. The most sought-after bachelor in Denison had lost a bet which fueled him to make an absolutely outrageous one in return.

A flock of wild geese honking above him on their way south seemed to mock his attempt to find a position in the saddle to avoid the gusts of October wind. He'd already been caught by a wicked gust that snaked its way between his sheepskin-lined jacket and his shirt. Old man Acheson, who carried the largest stock of glass in town, had been right to warn folks to fix up their windows—it was getting colder.

Kit swore. His head felt like the dance drums drifting over the border from the Indian Territory.

His early ride this morning was all his cousin's fault. If Jasper hadn't changed his mind about attending the county convention in Sherman, Kit would never have been in town after Jasper caught the train. No trip to town meant he wouldn't have stopped at the Palace Beer Hall to sample a new barrel of six-year-old whiskey.

No whiskey, no challenge to Jamie McCarthy—the bane of his life from the time they both learned to walk—to play a few games on the new billiard table. No game, no bet, equaled no loss and no mission when a sane man would be sleeping off his excesses.

Kit swore again. "Damn, how could I let McCarthy goad me into that stupid bet?" If nothing else came of this, he would swear off drinking anything stronger than his sister's lemonade.

For at least two months, he amended.

"What possessed me?" His chestnut stallion pricked up his ears. "Hell, you wouldn't know the answer," Kit muttered.

His thoughts turned black. Of all the luscious, available females in town, why had *her* name come up?

Bridie Delwin.

"An' make no mistake, horse, I wasn't that drunk. Her name came tripping off my tongue like I said it once a day."

Bridie?

Dear God in heaven, what had he done?

The chestnut tossed his head as if reminding Kit what he had put at risk.

"I won't lose this bet. I can't lose the best thoroughbred racehorse in the state."

The stallion picked up his pace. Kit couldn't decide if the animal agreed with him, or was warning him that he had better not lose. Kit's thoughts veered from his mission to the memory of seeing High Man for the first time.

North into Indian territory the Cherokees held horse races. Men with the same fever for fine horseflesh, good whiskey and gambling were an irresistible combination that drew Kit time and again.

One look at the stallion and Kit made an offer before the horse raced. The Tennessee-bred horse was everything he had been looking for in a stud for his growing stable.

Heavy bets and steady winning helped him meet the high price demanded for the horse. Kit gladly paid. Two thousand dollars poorer, minus the stallion he had been riding, saw High Man wear his saddle in the race. The horse won and kept on winning.

Kit knew he had gotten the best of the deal. And no one ever dared to accuse him of letting grass take seed when he went after something he wanted.

But this had happened five years ago, when he was twenty-two, still a little wet behind the ears.

He was a twenty-seven-year-old man now, with no excuse for what he had done.

How could he have bet the pride of his stable that he could court, then get Bridie Delwin to accept his proposal of marriage?

If that hadn't been bad enough, he had been goaded on by Jamie's demand that a time limit be set.

"After all," Jamie had drawled, "even water wore down rock when it had time enough."

Thirty days.

He had thirty days to make good or High Man went to Jamie. Damn the weasel-smart, slicker'n-a-clay-hill-after-a-rainstorm bastard.

Jamie was an envy-laden sidewinder. But that had been true of Jamie and his friendship since the days of spitting, tree climbing, rock throwing and pissing contests they had had as boys.

Growing up had not changed much. They still found ways to challenge each other. All with the subtlety of one of Miss Mae's gals hiding her wares.

Kit could be thankful that no one else knew about the bet. But he knew, and he had given his word of honor.

"An idiot, horse, that's what you got for an owner." How could he forget that for five years he had avoided Jamie's attempts to sucker him into betting High Man?

Jamie had wanted his horse the first time he had seen him.

The opposite held true for Kit and Bridie. He had never teased her or chased her while they were in school. Never once tried to steal a kiss. Never once asked her to dance at the church socials. But then, he recalled, she had stopped coming to them a long time ago.

Oh, he was polite and tipped his hat if he chanced to cross her path in town or at church. She was usually wrapped in a shabby cloak, walking head down, the wide sweep of her bonnet hiding her face. Truth to tell, he couldn't remember the last time he had seen her face or heard more than three words from her.

Timid and plain always came to mind if her name was mentioned.

A scowl creased his face. A few months ago he had offered to carry her bundles to the buckboard. She had shook her head so hard refusing his help that he had a notion her bonnet would fly off. He remembered her barely mumbled thank you as she fled. And he remembered thinking at the time that Bridie was running scared of him as if he had asked her to do something sinful.

As if he would. Annoyance crept into his thoughts. There wasn't one feature to recall. Not her hair or eye color. Not shape or height. Only a vague sense that he had missed something.

Not that it mattered. He had never, even once, had a thought to courting her.

Truth was, and this had remained Kit's secret, he was hankering after the women who baked the delicious desserts for the Planter's house.

He urged his stallion across a stream, his thoughts occupied with his fondness for sweet things. Wednesday nights the hotel had pecan pie. He always had three slices. Friday night's offering was Chocolate Clouds. A man might die happy after eating four or five. He tried his best to get into town on Monday nights, too, despite his sister's nagging. An eight-inch-high piece of chocolate cake flavored with pecans and bourbon set a man to thinking about other smooth, delicious and silky things.

His mouth watered. Kit frowned. He had tried his best to convince Jack Lea, the proprietor of the hotel, to reveal who did the baking. Jack claimed that if he told, the woman would sell to the Alamo Hotel, his biggest competitor. Not even for the size of Kit's bribe would Jack risk losing what drew more cowboys into eating at his place than the food.

Kit wasn't about to give up. In the past few months he had narrowed down the most likely candidates to widow Marylee Hanna and the mighty flirtatious Sedalia Chadick.

Twice now, he had accepted supper invitations to the Chadicks' ranch. He couldn't accept another without declaring his attentions. He was tempted. Both times, Sedalia had served him a chocolate cake every bit as good as the one at the hotel. Not as high, but just as smooth, sweet and silky.

Then, Chocolate Clouds had shown up in MaryLee's box lunch that he bid upon at the last church social. It was a good thing the men in his family didn't run to fat, for she had let him eat all six of the delightful dessert.

Despite all his charm—he'd been told it was considerable by enough women to believe them—he couldn't get either woman to admit she was baking for the hotel.

His daddy always said that Kit was like a bloodhound when he went after something. He'd find a way to overcome the woman's scruples. And when he did, he just might marry the lady who had baked her way into his heart.

Just thinking about those sweets was almost as good as remembering a rousing night of good sex.

He jerked ramrod straight in the saddle, yanking the reins and causing the chestnut to toss his head in annoyance for the abrupt move.

Thank the good Lord he had not bet that he would actually marry Bridie.

If ever the Lord and man had fashioned a woman who would *not* excite a cowboy off a trail drive to lusty thoughts, that woman was Bridie Delwin.

He would bet—and only with himself this time—that she had never been kissed.

By a man, that is.

A man who liked his females as hot as a working forge, with more curves than the Red River, and knew how to give as good as she could take.

Kit, without modesty, admitted to having his share of such women. He had never gone without a willing female from the time he was old enough to understand the difference between a whispered no-come-convince-me-to-yes, and a flat-out no.

Not that he had heard too many of those. His sister Alva,

being the oldest, said women fell over themselves admiring the combination of green eyes, thick black lashes with hair to match and a cocky devil's grin. Kit enjoyed the attention. Only a fool wouldn't. But he knew it was merely luck that the Lord had taken the best of his folks and wrapped it up handsomely in him.

He wondered if Bridie had ever noticed. He couldn't recall her ever looking directly at him. She had to be the most timid creature walking the land.

Now for the rest of her . . . no! He had to stop right there or he'd hightail it back home.

Despite the chill, Kit broke out in a cold sweat. He had to go on. There was no choice. Patting the stallion's neck, he mumbled an apology. He wasn't going to lose his horse. Bridie would be courted.

A quick glance showed him that he had ridden the three miles southeast of town and crossed onto Delwin land. He drew rein in a thick stand of pecan timber. The one-hundred-foot trees towered above him. Guilt ate at him for what he was about to begin. He reached high to touch one of the clusters of thin-shelled nuts hidden among the yellowing leaves. Another sign of winter coming.

Bridie would blossom under his attention.

Thirty days.

His mamma had been fond of telling him that the Lord would always help him overcome his difficulties. Kit knew if ever he had needed divine guidance, he needed it now.

Delay wasn't winning him any bets. He rode forth to meet his fate.

What was the stud of the county doing on her land?

Bridie Delwin clung to the tree limb and stared in disbelief at the man who kept his horse to a walk through her woods not thirty feet from her.

Kit Sidell had never called on her. And it was the middle of the week. No one came calling in the middle of the week. What could he want?

She shimmied back along the limb until her boot hit the

crook of the tree. She was shaking so badly that she dropped the long pole she had been using to knock down the ripe pecans. Inching her way up to a sitting position, Bridie wrapped her arms around her middle.

The fifteen-foot height hadn't robbed her of breath or caused her heart to pound at a furious rate. Lordy! It really was Kit heading for her house. A strangled moan escaped her lips. The most sought-after bachelor in town had come to call.

On her. Her stomach churned at the thought. Why?

Did she really care to know the reason? If she could gather her courage, she could go after him and feast her eyes upon him. Bridie licked her suddenly dry lips.

But she no longer stared at Kit's receding back. She glanced down at herself. She couldn't let him see her. She couldn't let anyone see her. She would expire right on the spot.

No, that wasn't true. She couldn't die. Wouldn't.

She could just stay right there, hidden in the tree, ignore Kit, swallow the curiosity that burned its way through her and spend the next month of Sundays calling herself all kinds of a fool for missing the chance to see him.

Her gaze drifted down to the old mended sheet she was using to gather her pecan harvest. When in need, use what's at hand. Papa had been fond of quoting that to her.

Minutes later, having conquered her trembling, Bridie stacked the nuts at the base of the tree, then made her way through the forest toward her house.

Reminding herself that this was her land helped her find backbone and steadied her breathing. She warned herself with every step that this time she would look directly at his face. She would even find a way to unstick her lips and tongue and talk to him.

Brazen. That's what she would be. Then, when he'd gone, she would hightail it into the house and cry for lost opportunities and for missing the line where the Lord had handed out feminine wiles, a flirtatious manner, a body that men tripped over their own feet to admire, and the knowledge to use them to capture the elusive Kit.

Not that the man didn't have enough women chasing after him. From her first day at school she had understood that Kit belonged to all the pretty girls.

Now it was the pretty women. She knew what MaryLee and Sedalia were up to, asking her to bake goodies to tempt Kit and passing them off as their own. Like either woman needed more ammunition than what they were blessed with. And Janny Sue McCarthy wasn't any better. She had come around for months, pretending to be a friend, while all the time she was trying to steal her recipes.

A smile teased Bridie's lips. She bit back a laugh. She had fixed Janny Sue. Leaving out an ingredient here and adding a few there, had showed Janny Sue that she didn't have the talent to bake an upside down cake.

The smile disappeared. Bridie admitted that she missed having female company. Fox sly though it was.

She smelled the wood smoke from her chimney and slowed her pace.

Where was she rushing? Who was she fooling? She didn't have one thing that Kit wanted.

Memories charged forth. Bridie froze. She had learned her school lessons well, and those that had taken place beyond the classroom. Nothing had changed in the years that slipped away, lonely day by lonely day.

Squaring her shoulders, Bridie tightened her grip on the sheet. She was ready to confront the devil if need be.

Kit called her a timid mouse of a woman. When other men were around, a knowing laugh always followed. She had had her fill of sly remarks. She was twenty-five years old and tired of dreaming, of hoping and praying for the moon.

The sheet she had draped over herself for cover fell behind her. Dragging it forth with one hand, Bridie stepped into the clearing. The realization that she had arrived in time to stop Kit from entering the house forced her to shout.

"Lost your way? 'Cause I can't figure why else you'd be standing one foot in and one foot out of my kitchen."

The husky taunting voice had Kit spinning around. He lost his breath somewhere between word one and the last. His brows felt like they were climbing to his hairline. He shook his head. He closed his eyes, only to open them and stare. This couldn't be Bridie Delwin.

Could not be.

⋙ *Chapter 2* ⋘

*B*ridie Delwin *was* a woman. An Eve. The kind of woman old Reverend Tobias preached would lead a man to sin. Hot damn, lead him away!

Kit stared at the figure-hugging breeches, the likes of which he had never seen on any female. Blood rushed, pooled and heated his body. He was in lust. For the sake of a man's sanity—his—he should look away before he lost his eyesight staring at the button-gaping, faded blue shirt she wore.

Bridie yearned to retreat into the woods. She had never seen such an intent look on any man's face. Not when he was looking at her. She couldn't name it, but it frightened her. Moments later honesty forced the admission that the look on Kit's handsome face excited her, too.

Remember, you have backbone. Before her newly found backbone melted into a puddle, she propped one hand on her hip and used the other to flip back the lone braid whose end brushed the top of her thigh. They were moves she had witnessed countless times made by other women when they had flirted with Kit. Likely they used them on other men, too, but she never had cared.

"Well?" she prompted in a husky voice.

"B-Bridie?" Kit cleared his throat. He didn't want to talk to her, just look his fill. He whipped off his hat just remembering his manners, then stood like a block of wood on the shadowed back porch of her neat little frame house.

"You must be here for a reason." But Bridie couldn't figure it out.

"Right. I am."

What had she done? Had her appearance so shocked him that he could not tell her?

"You'd better leave."

Kit didn't hear her. Why hadn't he noticed that her hair, dappled in sunlight and shadow where she stood at the edge of the wood, was the same color as his chestnut stallion? Just as thick and long as the horse's tail. A man could have dreams about that braid, how he'd hold it, slowly unwind it and wrap it around his . . . Kit broke his thought.

He spied the cloth she held. It appeared to be a sheet.

What was Bridie doing dragging a sheet from the woods? Suspicion sent a scowl over his features. He knew what use he would put a sheet, shady woods and a willing female to. But this was Bridie-the-timid-Delwin. No mistake. She had admitted as much.

Innocent Bridie didn't know what went on between a man and a most desirable female. How could she? He'd have heard if anyone found Bridie desirable. But this reasoning didn't stop him from casting a narrow-eyed, searching glance around the yard. Her horse was in the barn. Alone. In the small fenced pasture next to the barn, a cow chewed her cud with her calf cuddled close by. Chickens pecked the dirt in their pen. No one had answered his knock.

Staring at Bridie again, he watched her shift her weight. Impatient, was she? He'd just bet she was anxious to get back to what she had been doing.

"Who's here with you?" Not a question, but a demand. A downright, forceful, possessive sounding one, too. Kit wasn't sure if he or Bridie was more surprised by it. Her lips parted on a strangled sound.

"Well, Bridie?"

He threatened her with the scowl marring his features. Tension rolled off his tall, lanky body. Bridie didn't understand why he asked such a foolish question. She looked for a sign of blood. He must be wounded and fevered out of his head.

"Are you hurt? Is that why you're here?"

"No." Well, Kit amended, that wasn't quite true. He wasn't hurting when he rode up, but he was sure hurting now.

"If the leaves weren't turning, Kit, I'd believe you had too much sun. Asking me who's here? You know there is no one but me since my daddy died."

"Then what are you doing with that sheet?"

She looked down, having forgotten she still held on to the cloth. "I was gathering pecans when I saw you ride up."

"Nuts?" He felt like seven kinds of fool.

"That's right, Kit, pecans are nuts."

It was her Miss Maples now-do-we-understand-class voice. Kit usually grew annoyed when he heard it. Not today. It explained why she dressed in those outrageous breeches. No, he couldn't look any longer. And he didn't understand why a calm rolled over him learning the sheet was for gathering nuts. What the devil was happening to him? She had him at a loss for words.

He shoved his hands into the pockets of his jacket, needing to do something with them. He rocked back on his boot heels and couldn't drag his gaze from her.

Bridie gripped the sheet with both hands. Her nerves were in an awful state. Her stomach churned again, her knees shook, and she couldn't draw a full breath. Lord, but he was handsome. She wished he would smile. Kit had a wonderful smile that made her mouth want to turn up its corners too. She'd die for a peek of that cocky grin, the one MaryLee claimed made her want to find the nearest dark corner. Bridie couldn't imagine the connection, but it was a sight to make her heart beat faster.

She took a step back. It was a fine, brave thing to tell herself that she had backbone. Fine to tell herself she could be as brazen as she liked. Acting as if it were true was harder.

She had something else to worry about. Kit still stood close to the kitchen door. She didn't want him to look inside.

Yet, a funny feeling that they could go on for hours chasing words around made her summon courage.

"You've never said why you're here."

"I've come calling."

"Calling? For what?" Her eyes tracked the moves of his strong-looking hands as he set his hat back on his head. Long fingers held the front and back edge of the brim to adjust the slant. She was sorry he covered up his thick, curly, black hair. When she had sat behind him in school, she had ached to touch it. Just once. Just to see if it really felt like Janny Sue's mamma's silk shawl.

"You've got to leave. I have work to do."

Kit stepped to the edge of the porch. Things had gotten off to a bad start. Hell! How was he supposed to court a woman who blindsided him?

"I'm not calling for a thing, Bridie. I've come to call on you." There, he'd said his piece, as honest as he could make it. But he wished she would stop squirming. He had not, after all, looked his fill. One second he had to admire the curve of her hip, or the length of shapely legs, and in the next, his gaze was drawn back to the gaping spot in the middle of her shirt where something white and frilly peeked enticingly.

She was biting her lip when he repeated his reason for being here. The thought crossed his mind that he should pay a visit to Doc Walker. He might need spectacles. He could, and would swear, that the last time he had seen Bridie, she had no more curves than a piece of barn siding. If he weren't so in lust with that feminine, curvaceous body, he would be furious that she had fooled him all these years.

"Go on home, Kit. You must be drunk. I've got no time for your foolishness."

Bridie didn't wait to see his reaction to her dismissal. She hightailed it into the woods, ignoring the tears streaming down her cheeks. Calling on her? Not likely. Not even in her dreams had she gone that far. Of all the cruel, insensitive things that had been done to her over the years, this was the meanest.

"I'll be back, Bridie. Tonight. Right after supper."

The wind carried his garbled shout to Bridie. Sobbing, she ran deeper into the woods. She didn't understand what he said, and made no attempt to. If she had, she wouldn't have believed him.

Distance from Bridie eased the sexual tension that had gripped Kit. She aroused his hunting instinct by fleeing. Pure temptation beckoned to chase after her, but he didn't believe she was ready for what would happen when he caught her. Yet the thought of chasing Bridie disturbed him. He blamed that and her curt dismissal for still feeling a bite of temper.

For the first time Kit didn't feel soothed as he rode over the rich, black prairie, farm and timber lands that comprised the four thousand acres he called home.

What had been his grandfather's log cabin was now a sprawling two-story farmhouse where smoke spiraled above the shade trees from three chimneys. His sister Alva hated being cold and kept the fires burning throughout the house especially when her husband Tom was away. Tom, a blood, bone, and heart farmer had traveled to Houston to see the first Texas rice crop. With a yellow fever quarantine over most of the south there wasn't enough rice in Texas. Kit had agreed with Tom to investigate the chance of their growing rice, for the yield promised to be sixty bushels to an acre. Kit was not a man to turn down a chance to make more money. Tom had four imps to provide for, dowries for the two girls, and land and a house for the two boys.

Several leggy colts raced along the pasture fence, showing off to their sire. High Man ignored them, but Kit felt a swell of pride for the young animals and the mares resting near the spring-fed pond.

Nearer the stable, Kit's appearance set the hounds yapping for attention. Kit wished Bridie had been half as welcoming. He greeted men by name, but the sight of a ghostly gray mare hitched by the corral set his temper on boil and intensified his thoughts about Bridie and the bet. Usually Kit saw to High Man's grooming, but he cast the reins at one of the grooms employed to care for his racehorses, issuing orders in a terse voice for the stallion's care.

The very last person he wanted to see was Jamie McCarthy. His nemesis sat at the kitchen table. While his sister folded laundry, Jamie struggled to stop Kit's year-old niece from grabbing what she could from the table.

"Kit! Where were you? I worried when you left so early."

"Business, Alva." Kit scooped the baby from Jamie's arms. He tickled her, loving her giggles and chubby arms hugging him. Over her curly head, he glowered at Jamie. "What the hell are you doing here?"

"Don't swear in front of Laurel. She's picking up too many of your habits, Kit."

"Sorry, lamb," he whispered, nuzzling the baby's soft cheek. She grabbed his nose, bouncing up and down with a demand that he play horsey.

"Not now, love." Kit, never losing his patience, stopped her from using his collar-length hair to climb on his shoulder. Another demand for horsey had him snatch a cookie from the plate on the table. "Have this instead." Her smile matched his. "Ah, you little heartbreaker, you're getting more like your sister Katie every day."

He caught Alva's frown over the cookie, but she didn't say a word. They had fought over the other three children being spoiled with sweets at any hour of the day.

"Smile, sister. What's an uncle for?"

"A single one makes me a target of every marriage-minded female." Alva shook out a pillowcase with a vigor that made the cloth snap then folded it for the ironing pile. "Isn't that right, Jamie? Your sister must tell you the very same. Both of you should be married with children of your own."

"Ouch." Kit tried to appear contrite. He knew his sister was constantly pestered by requests to be in his company and Jamie had the same problem. But sympathy didn't eliminate his anger at his friend. "Finished socializing, Jamie?"

Jamie merely smiled. "Seems Kit's in one of his black moods, Miz Alva." Jamie met Kit's warning look with a smirk. "Must've been mighty important business to take a man from his bed so early on a chilly morning. Ain't that so, Kit?"

Kit couldn't resist the taunt. "You should know. You're here."

"So I am." Jamie sipped his coffee. "Just couldn't sleep. Kept thinking about protecting my—" Kit's growl made him recall that the bet was a private one. "Investment, yeah, that's what I'm doing. So how did your . . . er . . . business go?"

"Smooth as this little lamb's bottom. What else did you expect?" Little fingers, sticky with oatmeal and molasses, found their way to Kit's cheeks, along with another demand for him to play horsey.

"Sweetheart, like all women, you're learning to have a one-track mind when you want something. Here, go spread crumbs on your mamma. I've got to see Jamie out."

"Kit! What's wrong with you? That's rude." Alva had to drop the union suit she was folding to take hold of her daughter. "Did you leave your manners in the barn with your horse?"

"No, sister, and Alva, you're not mamma. Don't take me to task in my house. Old Jamie here isn't company. Out," he ordered, taking the coffee cup from Jamie and putting it in the dry sink.

"Forgive him, Jamie. My brother—"

"No need to apologize, Miz Alva. I know Kit don't mean to act like he's been soaking up Yankee manners along with their whiskey." But as he spoke, he rose from his chair. There was a time to push Kit and a time to back off.

"That's enough, James Michael. The war's long over." Feeling her hair slip free, Alva untangled her daughter's fingers from her hair. She plucked a few hair pins from a crumb-filled palm. "Just you wait, Christopher Robert. I'll get even for this. Come, love, mamma'll wash you."

Kit shared a knowing look with Jamie. Alva always used people's full names when she got into a snit.

Jamie smoothed down straw-shaded hair that curled to his

shoulders. He tucked his chair back in place, then went to the back door. Hat in hand, he turned to face Alva.

"Thank you for the coffee and the company. A man sure appreciates something hot on a cold morning." His grin spread to a taunting, devilish smile aimed at Kit. "Ain't that right?"

"Lord knows, boy, I sure did." Locking his fingers together to stop from throttling his friend, Kit stretched his arms over his head. "Yep," he added, licking his lips, "something hot and sweet sets a man up for whatever comes his way."

The slow drawl, coated with masculine satisfaction, and challenge to dare dispute his words, wiped the smile from Jamie's face.

Kit swallowed a lump of guilt for the lie. He blessed heaven no one knew about the bet but Jamie. And Jamie was not going to tell a soul. He could follow Jamie's thinking process from stupefied expression to dawning knowledge that Kit knew more about Bridie Delwin then he'd let on when they made the bet. Smiling, Kit placed his hand on Jamie's shoulder and urged him out the door.

"Hold up, you two. What's going on? And don't tell me it's nothing," Alva warned. She looked at the two friends, both handsome in their own way, of similar height and build and identical innocent expressions. "Go on, tell me. I've seen this rooster-crowing game before."

"This ain't no game, Miz Alva."

"Sure the hell isn't," Kit confirmed.

The edge in her brother's voice made Alva leave it alone. She shifted her baby's weight to one hip. "Before you leave, Jamie, I want to know if we can count on you to come Friday night?" His blank look had her explain. "For the cakewalk? At the church hall? For shame, Jamie, how could you forget? We need every bachelor and widower to come. How else can we raise money for our needy brethren in New Orleans?"

"What's your sister talking about?"

"Don't you read the *Daily News*? Ah, Jamie, there's yellow fever all over the state. Over three thousand have died.

Last year, Mrs. Davis, came up with the idea of a cakewalk to raise money for new school books, and—''

''I wasn't here.''

''No, you were in Kansas buying cattle. Anyway,'' Kit continued, ''the ladies got together to hold a cakewalk to raise money for the needy. You'll have fun, Jamie, and it's for a good cause.'' Kit smiled at the memory.

''Can I trust him, Miz Alva?''

''No, don't answer that. Would I fool you? All the bachelors and widowers pay ten cents admission and get a number. They play music and we all do a few fancy dance steps. When the music stops, the man whose number is called wins some lady's fancy cake. If you smile real nice at Mrs. Davis and pay another ten cents, they'll let you dance again. Just think of all those sweet goodies to eat.''

Jamie rocked back on his heels. ''Why can't we just pay ten cents and dance with the ladies?''

'' 'Cause that's not how it's done,'' Alva said. ''Back before the war, Mrs. Davis's family and friends gave a prize cake to the slave who strutted the best. Nowadays, it's a good way to match up single folks.'' She wore an expectant look as Jamie thought it over.

Kit took the decision from him. ''He'll come. Jamie loves to show off his dancing for the prettiest gals and the best baking in the county.''

''Heck, Kit, you ain't so bad.''

''Not as good as you. But what the hell, Jamie, we all know what I'm better at. Now say goodbye.''

Once outside, Kit pushed Jamie up against the stone base of the house. All camaraderie disappeared. ''What the devil got into you coming around this morning? Don't you trust me?''

''Now, calm down, Kit. It's just like I said. Couldn't sleep for thinking how I was going to protect my interest. And I wanted to see High Man. I'm mighty fond of that horse and can hardly wait till he's mine.''

''You'll wait,'' Kit snarled. ''You'll wait till cattle ranchers welcome sheep on their lands. I'm winning our bet.''

Jamie's expression turned sullen. "Hell, I should of guessed I'd lose my money if what you said about Bridie being that hot and sweet is true."

"You calling me a liar, boy?"

Jamie blocked Kit's swing. "Calm down. I'm not exactly calling you a liar. It's hard to believe. If she's so all fired hot for you, how come she ain't chasing after you like Sedalia and MaryLee? My sister, too."

"Bridie's a lady." Another lie, but backed by the feeling that it was true.

"Tell you what, Kit. Why don't you bring Bridie to this social Friday night? Yeah. I've got a right to see the progress you're making in your courting. How else can I know what's going on?"

Kit swallowed the protest springing to his lips. He lowered his arm and stepped back. Jamie had a valid point. They hadn't worked out all the details of their bet. Jamie couldn't come with him, couldn't sneak around and spy on him when he went calling on Bridie. Kit would beat him to a pulp if he did. But how the hell was he going to get Bridie to come? She never attended the socials.

"Gonna do it?"

"Sure. No problem, Jamie. I'll bring Bridie to the cakewalk." Kit nodded absently to Jamie's parting remark that he couldn't wait until Friday night.

Hell and damnation! His lies brought him into a satan's coil. He'd have to lie again. There was no way Bridie was going to the social if he asked her.

If he asked her?

Where had that stray bit come from? Why wouldn't he ask her?

'Cause everyone would know you were courting the most unlikely female for the role of wife?

Kit examined the unasked-for reason that a nagging little voice supplied. There was some truth in it, but memory supplied a better reason. Bridie, dappled in sunlight and shadow, fawn shy. His mind supplied another peek at the button-gaping shirt, figure-hugging breeches and that long chestnut hair. Glorious, arousing, and a true challenge.

He'd be hung for a sheep rancher before he would let Jamie see Bridie the way he had. None of the rabble-rousing bachelors were going to get a chance to feast their eyes on Bridie.

Appeased by the decision that painted him less black than his guilt had, Kit sauntered back into the house. He was aware of a smug, possessive streak running through him. Bridie was his secret. At least for a while. He'd do his damnedest to protect her while he won his bet.

But he'd sure like to discover how she had managed all these years to hide that lust-provoking body.

Lies. Guess he and Bridie had them in common. But he had a feeling he'd be telling whopper-sized ones in the near future.

He took Laurel from his sister to free her to finish her chores. He matched his niece's impish smile. "Lamb, you and I are gonna use all the black Irish charm we got from grandmama to get our own way."

After all, he'd bet on it.

❧ *Chapter 3* ❧

*B*ridie would have loved to indulge herself with a bath every night, but after evening chores she was so tired that she made do with a pan of hot water.

Tonight she needed the soothing balm of soaking sore muscles in the tub. Kit's visit had stolen the pleasure from her day.

It was a labor to draw buckets of water from the well outside, heat some in the large cast-iron cooking pots, and then, when she soaked until the water cooled, she had to lug the buckets outside until the round wooden tub that doubled for washing laundry was emptied.

She blamed Kit for upsetting her. She had worked far longer gathering pecans than she had intended to do today. And she had cried most of the time she was climbing up and down the trees. Immersing herself in baking a dozen pies for Mr. Lea usually made her happy, but Kit's surprise visit had stolen that joy, too.

Why had he come?

She couldn't believe for a minute that he really had intentions of calling on her. She wouldn't fool herself into thinking she had anything that Kit wanted.

Bridie added a few cloves and a piece of cinnamon to the simmering water. Within moments, the kitchen smelled of rich, spicy scents.

If she could afford it, she would buy perfume. But it

wasn't on her must-have list. She liked the warm, spicy aroma. And she didn't need to worry that anyone ever came close enough to know what scent she used.

Every penny she earned from baking for the hotel went into special jars in the pantry. The house roof had to be replaced. There was one for the doctor's bill, and one for feed. There was the undertaker to pay for her father's funeral, another for the cost of her baking goods, and her dream jar.

She shook her head. There was no more than a few dollars in that one. But someday she would have enough to have water piped into the house, and a new stove. Then she would turn one of the upstairs bedrooms into a fancy bathroom like the hotel had. A real porcelain bathtub, cistern water closet and a washstand all enclosed with carved mahogany. And she would have French-milled soap scented with roses, thick and soft towels and all the perfume she could want.

Someday . . .

Bridie mixed the hot water with cold from the buckets. She got into the tub, knees scrunched to her chin, and shivered as cool drafts swept over her bare back and shoulders.

Why had Kit really come to see her?

And why was she still thinking about him?

It would be far better to add a few more long-held wishes to her dream jar.

She could buy silks, cashmeres, gloves, hosiery, and handkerchiefs at Mr. Goldsoll's. And off she would go to Madam Raynal's to be fitted for new underpinnings and gowns. And why stop there. A trip to Uhlig's for new boots and shoes, Mrs. Everheart's for a hat or two or three.

And pick up a large bottle of Green's August Flower, a little voice suggested. *They claim it cures dizziness of the head among other ailments. You are surely suffering from this.*

Bridie thought it must be true.

She had had a chance to spend time alone with Kit and chased him off.

Perhaps she could spare a dollar to buy the tonic.

She had to stop thinking about him.

She just had to.

About the same time in Denison, Kit told himself he had to leave the Planters House once he finished his second slice of pecan pie.

Ah, the sacrifices a man had to make in the name of honor.

He had to begin his courting of Bridie in earnest this evening.

He just had to.

When Megan, the charming Irish lass who always waited on him, approached the table with a tray of fresh coffee and another slice of pie, Kit reluctantly refused it.

Megan was heard to remark that poor Mr. Sidell must be grievously ill.

Kit was forced to ignore her assumption.

But when he rode down Main Street, he kept glancing at the saloons where he could stop and spend an evening with congenial company.

Jim Nelms would welcome him at the Cattle Exchange, even if Kit usually won when they played poker. He could stop at the Grand Southern Saloon or the Bank Exchange.

The place he would not think about stopping at was the Palace Beer Hall.

Not that the place itself was at fault for his stupidity, but odds were that Jamie was there.

At the corner of Main and Burnet avenues, Jack Gallager, owner of the Eclipse Stable, hailed him.

"I was just on my way to join you at the hotel. Know you're usually there. Just like everyone knows how fond you are of those pies."

"I've discovered that a man's got to have some control over his excesses, Jack, or they'll lead him down the road to ruin."

"Amen to that."

"Why did you want to see me?"

Jack hitched his thumbs under his suspenders. "Kit, them puppies of Shadow's are ready to be weaned. Now, you know my Gayle's a right accommodating woman about most things, but she's giving me grief over getting rid of the litter. Need to know if you still want four."

"Sure. And I'll hear Alma's carrying on about spoiling her children till kingdom come. But you're not to worry, Jack. I'll come get them tomorrow."

"That's what I like about you, Kit. You're a true man of your word. You wouldn't be knowing of anyone that's got a soft spot for a runt of the litter, would you? Kind of hate to put the little critter by. Should of done it when it was born, but that Shadow's a big favorite of mine. She always gives me a litter of good pups."

"Wish I could help you, Jack. No one wants the runt. They usually turn out sickly and . . ." Mentally, Kit pulled up short. A runt? Someone with a soft spot?

"Jack, I can help you, after all."

Bridie was seated at the kitchen table. She had just finished the last of her hot cocoa and licked her lips. The reworked recipe for her mother's Angel Sighs would use less sugar with the addition of sorghum. A savings of more than a few pennies.

She rubbed the back of her neck and put her pencil down. Now she had another way to use up the pecans. If she had enough money she could hire help to harvest them, then sell the excess.

Lord, but she was mighty tired. And her bare feet hooked on the chair rungs were cold.

She set her cup in a pan of water in the dry sink, banked the kitchen stove and checked that the back door was locked. Taking up the kerosene lamp she went out into the hall.

She had taken no more than a few steps when someone tapped on the front door. She couldn't even see a shadow past the gathered white lace curtain covering the glass square in the upper half of the door.

The sound was repeated, only it wasn't soft tapping, but hard knocking. Whoever it was could see the light of the lamp she held.

Bridie slowly moved forward. She couldn't imagine who would be calling at this hour.

Bridie, standing even with the arched opening to the parlor, glanced at her father's shotgun hanging over the fire-place.

She wasn't exactly frightened, but she wasn't a fool. A woman living alone had to be careful.

The knocking ceased, but before she could breathe a sigh of relief, she heard a funny sound.

There it was again. The door was thick enough so that it wasn't quite clear, but it didn't sound like a human voice.

But animals don't knock on doors, Bridie.

Outside, Kit shifted from one foot to the other. He lifted the puppy out of his warm jacket and held it up nose to nose with his.

"Cry a little louder, you ungrateful runt, or we'll both chill our tails off out here."

His suggestion earned him a thorough licking. Kit had one arm clamped to his side so the puppy wouldn't fall when he put him back inside his jacket.

He peered through the glass. Bridie was there all right. No one else was holding the lamp. But why didn't she come to the door? He had told her he was coming to call on her tonight.

"Bridie? Bridie, answer the door. It's cold out here."

"Kit Sidell?"

He didn't appreciate the raised pitch of alarm in her voice. But he had gotten her attention. He listened with satisfaction to the key turning in the lock.

"What are you doing here, Kit?"

What would he do if he were honest and told her the truth? What was he thinking of? Women didn't want honesty, they liked being cajoled and seduced.

But Kit took a look at Bridie, thinking about the pecan pie he had abandoned, and realized that Bridie was obviously not expecting him.

The Bridie he knew, or had thought he did, would never open the door wearing a flannel robe two sizes too big that she clutched at the throat. She had been ready, all right. But for bed minus any company.

The kerosene lamp she held cast a creamy glow on her

skin. The panicked look in her eyes—why had he never noticed her eyes were full of color, as purple as violets?—told
Kit he hadn't misjudged the situation.

Bridie wasn't dressed to entice him.

"I told you this morning I was coming back to call on
you. Aren't you going to invite me in?"

"Now?" She snuck a quick peek at his face. Lord, help
her, but those green eyes of his stole her breath. "You . . .
er . . . you just can't come in. Are you drunk?" She leaned
forward and almost dropped the glass chimney off the lamp.

"Sober as Reverend Tobias." My, but Bridie blushed like
a pretty pink rose. The puppy began squirming. He pressed
his cold, wet nose under Kit's arm.

"Damn you!"

"I beg your pardon, Kit Sidell, but what gives you the
right to curse at me? Go on, get."

He wedged his boot between door and jamb before she
could slam it closed.

"I wasn't cursing. And I didn't mean that for you. I
brought you a courting present."

Bridie bit her lip. He sounded sober and serious. She was
in a quandary. No man had ever called on her. What was
she supposed to do? It was late, well, for her it was, and
they would be alone in the house.

Besides, his foot held the door open.

Even as she made up her mind to let him come as far as
the parlor, Kit was lifting the puppy out of his jacket.

"She needs a home. Runt of the litter. Good dog. From
the size of her paws she'll be a terrific watchdog for you."

"For me?"

Kit held the pup by the scruff of her neck. "Take her. She
needs someone to cuddle her."

The coal-black pup's whimpers tore at Bridie's heart. She
was handing Kit the lamp and taking the dog from him in
one second flat.

"Oh, you sweet little love." Thick black fur, floppy ears
and a tongue that wouldn't stop washing her cheek made
Bridie fall in love. She nestled the puppy against her heart

and with her head bent to whisper sweet nothings, she turned for the kitchen.

Kit just stared at her. How could she forget he was there? It was ridiculous for him to feel jealous of her complete attention to the puppy. After all, he had brought the little runt to her. But he was jealous. And getting worried. Twice she turned from him. And this time, a critter was his competition.

And while he was at it, he might as well admit that he wouldn't mind hearing that sexy, husky voice of Bridie's whisper sweet darling in his ear.

"Aren't you forgetting something?" Kit asked her in a testy voice.

She glanced over her shoulder at him. Big, violet eyes shining, a smile that was downright bewitching, had Kit stand still and wish it was all for him.

"Forgive me, Kit," she said shyly. "Thank you. I don't know what else to say. I've never had so nice a present, and never one from a man before now. Is she really mine to keep?"

Kit experienced the strangest feeling. He was in her hallway, holding the lamp, but he had stepped back in time, too. *"Is it really mine to keep?"* Big violet eyes, lips trembling, and thin, small hands holding the Valentine's Day card. No, it wasn't a card, but a wood carving he'd made.

There was no dizzy sensation, no room tilting and swirling around him, but he felt as if he were back in the one-room schoolhouse again.

He'd been fourteen, chafing because his parents made him finish out one more year of school. And angry. He remembered how angry he was with their spinster schoolteacher, Miss Maples.

She made everyone write their names on small pieces of paper and then put them into crocks. Two, he recalled, one for the boys and one for the girls. At recess, she called them inside one at a time to go up and pick someone's name out and make them a Valentine's Day card.

Being the tallest in class, and the oldest, he'd gone in last. When he saw Bridie's name, he tried to bribe all the other

boys to change with him. Mostly, he argued with Jamie.
Everyone, including Miss Maples, knew he was sweet on
Tessa Hopping. And because of what that spinster did, Jamie
was going to be the one to give his girl a Valentine.

It was all so crystal clear, it could be happening now.
When he had handed Miss Maples the wooden heart he'd
carved, he told her—with all respect and politeness, or his
daddy would have his hide—"that it was the dang dumbest
idea she had 'cause some girls, like skinny, shy Bridie, were
gonna get to thinking that these tokens really meant something."

She had tilted her head full of faded blond hair and smiled
sadly at him. "That's what I hope. Every girl needs to
dream."

He had stomped out of the room, took Tessa's hand and
went around back of the schoolhouse where Miss Maples
had caught them kissing.

"Kit? Kit, please answer me. Are you all right?"

He shook his head and drew back from where his thoughts
had taken him.

It was an effort of will for Bridie to look directly at his
face, and even more, to look into his eyes. She had the
strangest feeling that he appeared to be trapped. It was gone
in a flash. She told herself she had imagined it.

"Won't you say something, Kit?"

"You sleep upstairs?"

The abrupt question, his rough voice and the feeling that
he had suddenly grown in stature to tower over her made
Bridie shrink back from him.

"Do you?" he demanded.

"Where I sleep is—" Bridie's mouth remained open, but
no sound came out. Kit was running up the stairs.

"You come back here! Don't you dare go into my bedroom! Don't you dare," she ended in a whisper. The pup's
cold wet nose pressed against her neck. Bridie scooped up
the trailing ends of her father's old robe and went after Kit.

❧ *Chapter 4* ❧

$\mathcal{K}$it stopped at the open doorway and somehow knew this was Bridie's bedroom. The cooler air hit his face like a slap. He held the lamp high but couldn't dispel the shadows in the corners.

Neat, clean and stark. Kit's rapid assessment. From the plain wooden bedstead with it's faded quilt to the simply caned rocking chair near the lace-curtained window to the bureau with a scrap of ribbon tied around dried blue bonnets to the wavy glass of the mirror.

"It was stupid to think she kept it," he muttered.

"What are you doing in here?" Bridie's voice shook with outrage.

"A man can tell a lot about a woman by her bedroom."

"I'll bet you've been in enough bedrooms to qualify as an authority." Bridie clapped her hand over her mouth.

Were those her words?

Had she truly said them to him? To Kit? Bridie backed up the few steps of the narrow hall and leaned against the closed door to what had been her parents' bedroom.

Kit slowly turned around. "My, my, Bridie, you continue to surprise me. Don't you know that's the quickest way to keep a man dangling after you?"

"No." The word was muffled. Bridie lowered her hand. She couldn't look up at his face. She shook her head.

"Take my word for it as gospel truth."

"Why did you . . . what are you looking—"

"It's just what I said. I wanted to know something more about you." Kit had to look away from her. He couldn't explain to her what had sent him racing up the stairs into her bedroom.

He couldn't even begin to explain it to himself.

But he knew one thing—if ever a woman needed to be held, it was Bridie. She appeared ready to collapse into a boneless puddle.

He stepped over the threshold and was no more than an arm's reach away from her. Kit drew a deep breath. He hadn't realized a faint, spicy smell had been tantalizing him. Another breath confirmed the scent was Bridie's. And a glance at her flushed face told him the heat of her body intensified the scent lingering on her skin.

His gaze targeted the flesh revealed by the puppy having snuggled her way beneath the shawl collar of Bridie's robe.

The lamp shook in his hand. Kit looked down at it. What was happening to him? He wasn't a green kid. How could being near to her have his body reacting like he was unsure of himself?

"You'd better leave, Kit." Bridie lifted the puppy and gazed with regret at coal-black eyes. "Go away, Kit, and take your puppy with you."

One of them had to take the step closer to make the exchange of lamp and pup. Bridie wasn't moving.

Kit wanted to, but he wanted his hands free when he did.

"You can't return a gift, Bridie. I won't take her back. I can't. I promised Jack Gallager that I had a good home for her. I've already got four of the litter coming to my house tomorrow."

How could a man sound so sincere and have green eyes filled with temptation that lured and promised all sorts of wicked things that had nothing to do with his words?

Bridie didn't know. She didn't think she would ever know that secret. All she could do was to cuddle the pup and wish that he would leave.

She wasn't afraid of Kit. Only of what he made her feel.

The shift of his weight drew her gaze down to the squeaking floor board. As natural as breathing her gaze followed the polished leather of his boots up the long length of his legs. Kit had firmly muscled thighs. Oh Lord, she shouldn't be looking, shouldn't be thinking of such things. But those thighs were the mark of a horseman. His buckskin jacket hung open, creating a narrow hand's-width view of his gray shirt.

While she stared, she noticed how rapidly he was breathing. Bridie swallowed past the lump in her throat. The movement of his string tie fascinated her.

"Bridie? Bridie, are you all right?"

"No."

"No? Why? What's wrong?"

Her eyes held a vague look when she lifted them to his. Kit smiled, and saw the color of her eyes deepen to rich, dark purple. She'd look just like that when he kissed her.

And from thought, came action.

"Kit?" His name squeaked past dry lips in alarm for the sudden intensity on his face.

Just a simple little kiss. He'd keep holding the lamp and she'd have the puppy. Nothing was getting out of hand. He wouldn't think about how close that bed was. After all, he had experience in these matters.

No big deal. He wasn't fourteen.

Kit breathed through his teeth. He could handle this. Bridie, for goodness sake, wasn't the sort of woman to threaten a man's sanity with curiosity.

Remember that. Be calm, too. Don't frighten her.

He'd be calm. No problem for a man of his experience.

Only he felt the heat of her through his clothes.

Cloth. There was a sobering thought. Sobering? Was he losing his mind?

Cloth was all they had between them.

He could smell her now, clean, clear soap, and that heated hint of spice.

Petal soft. Trembling. Full and rich and sweet tasting with a touch of chocolate. He *was* losing his mind.

She didn't close her eyes. She didn't know how to angle her head for the perfect meeting of lips to lips. She even forgot to breathe.

Again. He had to taste her again. Whisper-soft touches. He loved drawing out the pleasure for a woman and for himself.

But he had to warn himself again to hang on to that calm. He drew back. A grin of sheer male satisfaction creased his lips. Bridie's eyes were rich, dark purple, almost black.

He watched with fascination the way the barest tip of her tongue slowly explored her bottom lip from corner to corner. He wouldn't mind doing a little of the same kind of exploring himself.

But that experience he kept reminding himself that he had kicked in and warned him off. A little taste to tease and tantalize went a long way.

Trouble was, Kit wasn't sure who had been teased and tantalized by whom.

"Bridie?" he asked, drawing another deep breath and deciding that the spices he smelled were warm, dark, exotic ones. "Do you bake?"

"What?" She attempted to focus on what he had asked her. Feeling a little dazed, and a whole lot confused by the purely melting sensations that turned her insides soft as pudding, she wasn't sure it worked.

"You're coming to the cakewalk Friday night. Bake something sweet. I'll come by around seven with the buggy to pick you up."

Kit set the lamp on the floor. His gaze traveled up her flannel robe as slowly as he stood straight again. Her braid reached past her hip. The tied tail end was caught between her body and the door behind her. He regretfully declined the urge to kiss her again.

Distance was what he needed.

"Bridie, wear your prettiest dress. There's always dancing afterward."

He was halfway down the staircase when she snapped out of her daze.

At least her voice did. She wanted very much to run after him, but she was afraid if she left the support of the solid wood behind her, her knees would buckle.

"You wait. I can't."

"Sure you can," he said, turning to look at her. Kit grinned. "Every woman knows how to bake something, even biscuits. And it's high time you started socializing with your neighbors."

"You're my neighbor. The only one. And . . . and what you just did wasn't any kind of socializing."

"Trust me, Bridie." A tinge of exasperation covered his guilt. "We've just got started being as social as a man and woman can get."

Social? Is that what he called it? She thought he had kissed her.

"I can't go. You can't come into my home and tell me—"

"Seven, Bridie. Be ready. I'm a mighty impatient man."

She heard the door close. The words wouldn't go away. Her head was reeling. She pressed the warm little body of the puppy against her racing heart and took several long, deep breaths.

He had kissed her. Kit Sidell had kissed Bridie Delwin.

She wanted to whimper like the puppy.

Somehow Bridie managed to walk into her room. "Little sweetheart," she whispered to the dog, "he really did kiss me. I have had my very first kiss from the only man I ever wanted to kiss."

Bridie heard the wonder in her voice. It echoed the feeling inside her.

She took a folded shawl from the seat of the rocker and wrapped it around the puppy. She put the bundle on the foot of her bed and moved to stand in front of her mirror.

She couldn't see a thing.

The lamp. She needed light. With that same dazzled, dazed expression on her face she managed to retrieve the lamp. Better. With shaking fingertips she reached upward but she couldn't touch her mouth.

She had no experience in the ways of men and women. Did everyone have these fluttery sensations? She drew another deep breath to settle her jolted nerves.

Kit Sidell had kissed her.

Bridie sort of floated toward the bed, dropped the robe on the floor and turned back the quilt. She didn't even feel the cool drafts swirling around her bare feet and ankles. But she wanted to lie down. She had to think about this. She wanted to dream about it.

One hand stole beneath her pillow and closed over the small wooden heart. Her fingertip traced the small letters that spelled out the word valentine.

For the past thirteen years she had fallen asleep holding this heart. But she never let herself dream of the boy who had given it to her.

He hadn't really wanted her to be his valentine.

But for a little while, a few precious minutes, she had felt a magical wonder that only a twelve-year-old girl on the verge of womanhood could ever feel.

Such a long, long time to wait for a dream to come.

Bridie closed her eyes. The puppy wormed her way beneath the quilt to cuddle close to her heart.

Toasty warm, Bridie dreamed.

❧ *Chapter 5* ❧

*Y*ips and a cold puppy nose brought Bridie awake before cock's crow. She let the dog out, stoked the fire in the stove and put coffee on before she went upstairs.

A minute inspection of the sleepy-eyed woman in the mirror revealed no visible changes. If it were not for the presence of the puppy, she would believe she had dreamed what happened last night.

She dressed hurriedly and made her bed. She stared at the wooden heart before she tucked it and her memory of last night out of sight.

Work waited for her.

She milked the cow and fed the animals by lantern light. When she went looking for the puppy she found her rolling in the stove ashes she had spread on her garden plot.

"You look like cinders yourself, little one," she said as the puppy scampered toward her. "Cinders. I rather like that for your name." She picked up the little dog, smiling at the tail wagging that set her little rump swaying from side to side. "Warm milk for you and coffee for me."

Bridie had her first morning caller before the dew had dried on the grass. She had just come into the kitchen with a jug of buttermilk for the chocolate decadence cakes she had to bake when she heard someone knocking on the front door.

The puppy was sound asleep in the laundry basket near the stove.

"We need to work on your being a watchdog."

She wiped her hands on her apron, and smoothed back her hair as she went to answer the knocking.

Bridie had no trouble with her breathing, so she didn't fear it was Kit who had come to see her. But she certainly didn't expect to find his sister Alma when she opened the door.

"Bridie, please forgive me for calling on you so early, but I've a round of calls to make and you were first on my list."

"List?"

"Bridie, we're having a cakewalk to raise money to help people who have lost family to yellow fever in New Orleans. Now I know you'll want to donate some baked goods to the cause. Friday night at the church hall. And Bridie, this time I want you to come, too."

"But I—"

"Bridie, I've no time to argue or to listen to your excuses. And it's high time you came out of mourning."

"Alma, this is a worthy cause and I will bake something, but I won't come."

"And why not, pray tell? It's not right for a young woman—"

"Alma, please. I'm a woman grown and I know my own mind. You'll have your donation. Now, you must excuse me for I have chores waiting."

Bridie started to close the door when Alma stopped her.

"Do you want me to stop by and pick it up? Or I could send Kit over."

"No," she answered quickly. "I'll drop it off at the church hall Friday afternoon."

Alma had to be satisfied with that, but as she climbed up on her buggy's seat, she cast a look back at the closed door. There had to be some way to bring Bridie out of her shy shell. As she lifted the reins and headed down the dirt road, she wondered if she should enlist her brother's aid. Kit could charm a butterfly into landing in the palm of his hand to drink sugar water. He could certainly charm Bridie.

Bridie was thinking about Kit, too. Not of his charm but of the similar won't-take-no-for-an-answer trait he shared with his sister.

She wished she could have said yes that she would be happy to come to the cakewalk. But not only didn't she have something pretty to wear, she didn't know how to dance.

And there would be dancing afterward. Both Marylee and Sedalia had said that once the cakes had been won by the bachelors and widowers, the married ladies served punch and start pushing couples together as soon as the fiddlers began playing.

Dawdling over what couldn't be wasn't getting her cakes baked. Bridie pushed the whole matter out of her mind.

She had dried currants soaking in bourbon while she rolled out the lumps of sugar she had shaved off the loaf. While the pecan meats blanched, she grated nutmegs. The three pounds of butter were soft and creamy as she began adding flour. The big crockery bowl would hold enough finished cake mix to bake twenty-four layers. Twenty-four eggs had to be beaten in two at a time to make the cakes light. Mace, cloves, and candied orange and lemon peels added spice to the mix.

Bridie was about halfway through adding in the eggs when once again she heard someone knocking at the front door. Her arm ached from stirring, but she hated to leave the mix.

The pounding grew louder, and something urgent about it sent her out of the kitchen.

Sedalia Chadick was a vision in soft blue wool. Bonnet and cape matched her skirt.

"Thank goodness, Bridie. I thought you weren't home." She didn't give Bridie a chance to refuse her entry but simply pushed her way inside the hall.

"And good morning to you, too, Sedalia."

"Bridie, I haven't time to be polite. You've got to bake me one of your chocolate cakes. I need it to bring to the cakewalk."

"I told you the last time—"

"You don't understand," she wailed.

"I don't want to. I'm not baking for you." Bridie had never more resented Sedalia's perfection that made her feel so poor.

"Bridie, I'm begging you." Sedalia clutched one of Bridie's arms. "You don't understand what this could mean to me. But I'll share my secret with you, Bridie. Kit's on the verge of making a proposal. He's got such a sweet tooth and loves those chocolate cakes. I must have one."

She released Bridie's arm, ignoring her refusal and fumbled with the drawstring of her reticule. "Here. I'll pay you three dollars this time."

"Sedalia, take your bonnet off. It's affecting your hearing. I said no."

She dug into her purse once more. "Five dollars."

Bridie could feel herself waver. It was more than Mr. Lea paid her per cake. When she thought of Sedalia using her baked goods to bait the trap and marry Kit, she had to refuse.

"I'm sorry, Sedalia. I wish I could help you out, but I can't."

"All I've got with me is ten dollars. It's yours."

"Wait right here." Bridie ran back to the kitchen and snatched up a small sack of pecans. She returned and handed them over to a stunned and disbelieving Sedalia.

"There. You can go home and bake a nice pecan pie."

"How can you be so cruel, Bridie? What have I ever done to make you turn mean on me?"

Bridie looked her right in the eye. "Sedalia, you want to trap a man into marriage on a lie. I'm trying to save you from yourself. What would you do after you're married to Kit? Come here again and again. And what if he wonders how come he never sees you do the baking?"

"After I have his ring on my finger it wouldn't matter. But I'll never forgive you for this, Bridie. Never."

"Thanks for stopping by," Bridie called out before she closed the door and leaned against it.

He's on the verge of a proposal.

That low-down, rotten parish stallion! How dare he come

around calling on her? Giving her a puppy? Kissing her?

Oh, she'd like to bake a very special chocolate cake for Kit Sidell. One he'd never forget.

And you promised his sister you'd bring something to the church hall.

And so she would.

But if Bridie thought she could continue her baking without any more interruptions, she was wrong. Not an hour went by before Marylee came to call.

Marylee arrived in her buggy and she asked for help with the laundry basket. Bridie couldn't summon an ounce of welcome, but she was curious to see what Marylee would offer.

She wasn't wrong about the woman's intent. She, too, wanted a chocolate cake, but Marylee had a bribe that was better than money. She had a basket full of cast-off gowns, skirts and pretty shirtwaists.

"Papa just insisted that I have a whole new wardrobe for winter. I thought you might like to have these, Bridie. I know how things are with you. Working all the time, never having any fun. And all I want is one itsy, bitsy little chocolate cake from you."

"Oh, is Kit Sidell on the verge of proposing to you, too?" Bridie asked with a sweet smile. The man was a danger to himself and every female under the age of thirty.

"Why how did you ever guess?"

"I didn't, Marylee. Sedalia was here on the very same mission early this morning."

"That . . . that—"

"Don't matter to me what you all call each other. As far as I'm concerned you both can have Kit Sidell and welcome to him. But I'm not baiting your trap any more than I'd bait hers."

"Bridie Delwin, what's gotten into you? You've never said no before. What difference can it make to you what I do, or even Sedalia does, to get Kit to propose?"

"Not a snap."

"Then why won't you help me?"

" 'Cause I promised Alma I'd be bringing one of my

cakes for her to have as a prize, that's why.'' Bridie clamped her hands onto the edge of her apron. What did she just say? How could she do such a thing?

Marylee couldn't have looked more surprised than if Bridie had announced she was going to marry Kit. "You can't mean that?''

"I do. And what's more, I might take a pie along, too. But I'll be as fair to you as I was to Sedalia. Wait here.''

Once more she ran into the kitchen and grabbed a small sack of pecans. "Now, Marylee, you don't forget that these nuts need to be shelled before you bake them.''

Bridie didn't give her a choice about taking them. She pushed the sack into her arms.

"I don't know what's come over you, Bridie. You used to be so nice.''

"Well a birthday's come and gone. It's high time I started worrying about me.''

"That's a selfish way of being. You know Kit's partial to me. I told you so.''

Bridie had to bite her lip to keep from blurting out that he had come calling on her. She stood with her arms crossed over her chest and tried for a stern look.

"Is there anything that would get you to change your mind?''

"You get him to propose and I'll bake your wedding cake. Get along now, Marylee. You've got pie to bake.'' Bridie pushed the laundry basket over the threshold. "Don't forget this. I'm sure the church sewing circle would be glad to have them.''

This time when she closed the door, she was vocal about what she thought of Kit. "Bounder. No-account. Slicker than a snake-oil drummer. He's got sawdust between his ears even if he does kiss like heaven.''

She wasn't sure if she was more angry with him or herself. But wherever the anger came from, it helped her beat in the remaining eggs and cocoa in no time.

She mumbled as she worked filling the cake pans and setting them carefully in the oven. Cinders sat up in the laundry basket, adding a yip in every now and then.

Bridie couldn't tell if the puppy was supporting her or defending Kit. By the time she had the chocolate melted for frosting, creamed the butter and began whipping egg whites, she made her decision. She was not going to add a pinch of this and dash of that so that Kit would be thinking about his body in ways he'd never imagined.

She would donate the most decadent chocolate cake she had ever baked.

Once the cakes had cooled, Bridie began slicing the layers. But one cake she held in reserve. She assembled the others for the hotel, and placed each one in round thin wood cheese boxes. Mr. Bibbs, who owned the Family Grocery on Main Street, was ready to throw them away. Bridie had washed them with lye soap and dried them in the sun to remove the strong odor of cheese. They made perfect carrying boxes for the cakes, even if the frosting on the sides had to be repaired. A jar of frosting always arrived with her cakes for the hotel cook to fix them.

Before she left to deliver her goods, she carefully sliced the last cake into almost paper-thin layers. Each sat on a plate and she sprinkled bourbon over the tops. More blanched pecans sat soaking up the liquor in a bowl.

She had to hurry to hitch up the wagon, for her callers had her running late. A thick layer of straw in the wagon bed cushioned the boxed cakes for the drive into town. At the last moment she decided to take Cinders with her, for there was no telling what mischief the puppy could get into if left alone.

The day was brisk, even colder to Bridie after being in the hot kitchen all morning. But the cold air helped to clear the cobwebs from a night spent dreaming impossible dreams, and a morning's dose of truth.

She took the long way around town to avoid being seen going to the back of the hotel. And for the first time, she wondered why she wanted it kept secret.

Pride, Bridie.

And she couldn't argue with that.

Mr. Lea was upset that she shorted him one cake, but

Bridie promised she would bring him two extra pecan pies next time. She collected her empty boxes, and refused all his pleas that she increase the amounts of baked goods that she sold him.

"I'll up the price, Miss Delwin. Folks is coming from far and wide. Your desserts are getting famous and my hotel right along with them."

Rather than being pleased, Bridie bristled. Men! All they thought about was putting temptation in a good woman's way.

But she needed more money to get debts paid. "I'll think about it."

Bridie usually left her bill-paying round until Friday, but she needed to stop at the grocery. To resist any temptation she kept her eyes straight ahead on the spot between her horse's ears. She wouldn't look at the store windows, especially not at Madam Raynal's or Mrs. Everheart's windows.

Cinders slept curled in the old horse blanket she put near her feet. She drew up before the grocery, set the pole brake and tied off the reins. The freedom of wearing her britches the last few days made her clumsy in the long skirt.

Bridie was shocked to find two strong hands at her waist helping her down. When she turned, she saw it was Jamie McCarthy.

"Thank you," she mumbled and hurried past him into the store. Mr. Bibbs was behind the counter, waiting on a customer. Bridie saw that he had a new wheel of cheese set out. She'd have another box, for he always saved them for her. Bridie picked out one tin of cocoa. She would stop tomorrow at the Alamo Grocery for another, then on Monday to the Corner Grocery. She didn't like shopping at Henry Merritt's because he always asked questions about every purchase. And men talked of how women gossiped.

She stopped at the board where Mr. Bibbs posted the back page of the *Denison Daily News*. There was a nasty farewell to the editor of the *Herald* who had closed up shop. A notice of the Ladies' Aid meeting at Mrs. Gilmore's, Mr. Ledrick's announcement that new carpets had arrived and were cheaply priced for superior stock and railroad news. Bridie skimmed these, and the notices of who was staying in town, mostly army personnel.

What did attract her attention was the small ad that Kansas City sugar cured dried beef had arrived at Wood & Company. Mr. Lea served it at the hotel, and she had tasted it. But it was not a purchase for her budget this month. Yeidel's was adding pure old apple and peach brandies. She added that to her list. The hardware store of McCarthy & Company on Third Street, which belonged to Jamie's family, had new cake pans, French coffee pots, pudding pans. If Bridie was to increase Mr. Lea's order, she would have to buy more pans. Another expense to figure.

Seeing that Mr. Bibb was alone at the counter, Bridie took her few purchases to him. After he had totaled it up, she added five dollars toward her account. She smiled and thanked him for saving the box for her.

Outside, Bridie had the unpleasant surprise of seeing Jamie leaning against the side of her wagon. He took advantage by taking the box from her and placing it on the seat, but blocked her way.

Jamie had been one of her worse tormentors. He'd pulled her braids, stuck the ends in his ink well, and called her Birdie, among other things. He had teased her unmercifully that there was a knothole in the outhouse so that she had refused to use it for a month of recesses. He wasn't the only one, put he'd been the ringleader urging others to steal her copy book, put snakes and frogs in her desk, and in her lunch basket. Kit, she recalled, was too often surrounded by the girls vying for his attention.

Bridie drew the edges of her old jacket together and tried to step around him.

"I waited for you. I want to know if you're coming to the cakewalk."

"I don't know that's business of yours, Jamie. Now let me by."

"Kit said he's bringing you. I got a vested interest in knowing if it's true."

Bridie looked up at him, for he was as tall as Kit and she supposed at a distance could be judged to have the same build and handsomeness. And she didn't like the way Jamie looked her over as if she were something he was thinking of buying.

"What you and Kit do don't matter a hill of beans to me."

Jamie stepped forward, crowding her against the roof post. "Now, don't you get all high and mighty with me. I asked you real nice. Seems to me you've been holding out on all us single men if what Kit says is true."

Bridie was so shocked she couldn't utter a sound. Kit had told him. Of all her youthful sufferings, this had to be the worst. She fought the tears stinging her eyes and wished she used a buggy whip. She wouldn't hesitate to use it.

"Get out of my way, Jamie McCarthy. And don't you ever, ever dare speak to me again." Hours of whipping batters had given strength to her arms. Bridie shoved him aside. She didn't think she had moved him by her push as much as by the sheer surprise that she did it.

She climbed on the wagon seat, then looked down at him. "And you tell that devil's-stud-of-the-country friend of yours that if he dares step on my land I'll have a shotgun waiting."

She fumbled untying the reins, and released the pole brake only to hear his reply.

"Kit ain't gonna like losing his bet. You'll need more than that to keep him away."

"Bet? What bet?"

Jamie had to look away. He'd done it now. If Kit found out that he had let the cat out of the bag, there'd be hell to pay. And he'd lose his chance to have High Man.

"You got my tongue all twisted, Bridie. He bet he'd have the cake, then a dance with all the prettiest gals around."

"But that wouldn't include me, would it, Jamie?"

❧ *Chapter 6* ❧

*B*ridie didn't cry on the way home. She couldn't even curse Kit. She had learned one more lesson. Next time she would trust her inner feelings that Kit was up to no good.

She didn't for a minute believe that Jamie had told her the truth. Even if it was a brag the likes of which Kit would make. There was something more.

A bet. About her. How could Kit, a man so handsomely packaged, have such a wicked turn of mind? She had never done anything to harm him. Why would he deliberately seek her out to hurt?

She put up the horse when she reached home. She mashed the boiled egg yolks left from the frosting, and mixed it with bread and warm milk for Cinders. If she hadn't already loved the puppy, she would take her right back to Mr. Gallager.

Bridie lost heart to finish her fancy cake. But ingrained practicality refused to allow her to waste it. She didn't bother to drain the pecans but crushed them right along with the bourbon they had soaked in. She sprinkled them on each layer.

She hadn't eaten anything since morning and the liquor's fumes went straight to her head. The frosting had been left sitting too long and it was stiff and dry. With the bottle handy, she poured in a small amount of bourbon and worked it in. She wouldn't think about what Jamie said. But that frosting got a beating that additional liquor helped to make creamy smooth. Foolishly, Bridie tasted it. Not a little finger lick, but a whole wooden spoon full.

"A little thinner or I won't have enough," she muttered and tilted the bottle over the bowl again.

Bridie didn't know if she had any tolerance for liquor. She never drank any, but within minutes of the throat-burning, eye-watering mouthful going down, she had another taste.

Warmth slid inside her with all the comfort of eating hot porridge on a cold winter's morning.

By the time she placed the last liquor-soaked layer on top there was no frosting left. Bridie wasn't feeling any pain as she viewed her four-layer creation through blurry eyes.

"Cinders, any man eating this cake is gonna need gallons and gallons of coffee to sober him up. His head'll feel like he stuck it in a hot oven. Just like mine," she added with a moan.

"Liar, liar, set your tongue on fire." The childish taunt was anything but to Bridie. She hoped that Kit won her cake, won it and ate every crumb and nut by himself. She hoped he'd make a fool of himself, too. Let everyone have a laugh at his expense for a change.

Having such spiteful thoughts didn't sit well with her. The tears came, and kept on coming as she stumbled her way through evening chores. By the time she returned to the house a haze settled on her and she felt like she was floating.

She played tug-of-war over a rag with the puppy, grinning and laughing far more than her antics called for, but Bridie had never felt so free and cared so little. Supper time came and went without notice. She struggled to remember something she had to do, but even that was beyond her.

Bridie pulled herself up by using the table for support. She stared at the clutter on the table. If she didn't find a way to clean it all, she'd have ants visiting by morning.

She kept tripping over her own feet and the puppy still wanting to play. The kettle whistled and spouted steam, adding heat to an already overhot room that had her stripped down to her camisole and drawers. She kept pushing herself to clean everything even when the happy daze disappeared and her head ached.

Bridie, clutching the wooden valentine to her heart, was close to passing out. She had a last thought before she gave way. She couldn't be angry with Kit. He had given her dreams with taste, scent, touch and sight of him that no imagings could. And no one would steal that from her.

Kit had spent the day with his early-returning brother-in-law. By suppertime he was chafing to get away from all the side-long glances Alma and Tom exchanged. He was pleased with Tom's report of how well the first rice crop yielded, but even that excitement had palled.

Kit had to be honest with himself. He wanted to see Bridie.

"Tom, we'll talk more tomorrow. Right now, my sister's aiming to clobber me if I don't let you two get on with her proper homecoming now that your brood's asleep."

"If you're going to town, Kit—"

"Alma, I'm a grown man. Don't be asking where I'm going an' don't be asking what I'll be doing, or when I'm coming back."

But Alma had forgotten to ask Kit her favor in the excitement of having Tom home early. She left Tom in the parlor and went after her brother.

"Kit, please wait. I want you to do something for me." The fact that he stood hat in hand and quiet was all the encouragement she needed. "Kit, I want Bridie to come to the social tomorrow night. I couldn't convince her, but I thought if you stopped by and asked . . ." Alma's voice trailed off, for Kit was scowling at her. "Did I say—"

"You said enough. What did Jamie tell you?"

"Jamie? What has he got to do with my asking you to call on Bridie? Kit, you can be so charming. Please. Do this for me. That young woman is so shy and she shouldn't be alone all the time."

"Sure." It was the easiest and quickest way for him to escape. Kit almost ran to the stable. He didn't want her to know what a possessive feeling came over him when Alma mentioned Bridie. Thank goodness that Tom was home. He'd keep her mind from questioning his slip about Jamie.

He ordered one of the geldings saddled for he wouldn't risk riding High Man in the dark. And when the groom took too long, Kit sent him away and finished saddling the horse himself.

It was barely eight o'clock. He'd have a good long visit with Bridie tonight.

But when Kit arrived at Bridie's after riding at a pace no sane man would have, he found the house dark. Another man would have left, certainly after receiving no response to his repeated knocking, but not Kit. He kept thinking about Bridie being alone, maybe sick or hurt, and no one would ever know.

He shouted her name, he went to the side of the house and tossed pebbles at her bedroom window. He earned nothing for his effort. The squeaky sound was so faint that at first he thought he imagined it. But no, there it was again, a bit louder. He was almost around to the back of the house when the sound registered as water being pumped.

And he stood stock still at the sight that greeted him.

Bridie—and that luscious, rounded form could be no one else—was bent over with head beneath the stream of water she pumped. He could not make sense of her mutterings, nor could he move. There wasn't much moonlight, but what there was showed pristine white drawers clinging to flesh that had to be chilled to the bone. She came up sputtering, that glorious length of chestnut hair cloaking her skimpily clad body.

"Never, never again," she groaned, and bent over once more.

"Bridie!" He strode forward when it appeared she didn't hear him.

Now Bridie had been outside trying to clear cobwebs and the nausea that sent her running from her bed for more than a few minutes. The ground around the pump was a muddy puddle.

Kit came skidding into it, too late to stop his momentum but he had enough sense to grab hold of Bridie and roll as he went down. She landed with her back to his chest, her legs straddling his.

It was cold. Wet. And crazy. But Kit discovered that his body liked Bridie's too much. It preened like every male in creation did when seeking its mate. And there wasn't a damn thing he could do about it.

He remembered last night, and all the effort he made to hang on to his calm. He also remembered that they had had cloth separating their bodies. The minute his hands lifted to her hips, a message went speeding along his nerve ends. The heated throb of his blood would have rivaled, then surpassed, the moment High Man won a race. The sheer cloth was no barrier at all.

And he couldn't seem to think past that fact.

Bridie was trying to figure out what had happened. One moment she had been pumping water over her aching head, the next her legs seemed to give way. But instead of cold, wet mud, her bottom was cushioned by hard heat.

"I swear I'll never touch the devil's drink again."

Bridie lowered her arms and found her fingertips barely grazed the ground. She blinked and stared, rubbed her eyes and stared again at the dark cloth knee raising in front of her. The awareness of what she was sitting on, and whose knee it was, hit her like the first icy splash from the well.

"Oh, my Lord!"

"No. It's me, Kit."

Cold, stone sober Bridie demanded that he let her go.

"Bridie, I don't think I can. I don't believe it is within my power to move at the moment. I might die."

"Christopher Sidell, you let me go or I'll do the dying."

"You don't seem to understand that—"

"You're holding my . . . touching my . . ." Bridie gave up and wailed.

"Bridie, honey, don't cry. I'll get up. I'll let you go. See? My hands are flat on mud. You just need to use a little care when you— Bridie! That's my—"

"Preening peacock!" she yelled and rolled over into the mud. It was a race who scrambled to their feet first. But

Bridie wanted nothing to do with him. He tore off his jacket and attempted to wrap her in its fleecy warmth, but she threw it back at him.

"Stop it, you little hellcat! I'm trying to keep you from getting sick. What possessed you to come out here and dunk yourself with cold water?" Kit reached out to grab her as she slipped, but his muddy hand slid along her arm and down she went.

"Don't call me names. Don't come near me." With every order Bridie scrambled backward. She was chilled to the bone, and more than thirteen years of misery over this one man was threatening to erupt.

"At least let me help you into the house."

"Oh, no. You're not going to fool me like that again. Let you inside and I might as well invite the devil to supper."

Kit struggled to dig deep for some of the charm that his sister had reminded him he had. Yelling hadn't worked. Pleading wasn't doing him a bit of good. With her hair all tangled over her face she couldn't see his smile as she managed to stand by clinging to the post of the small overhang's roof.

Her nipples were dark and puckered with cold, clearly revealed by the thin muddy cloth.

Perhaps it was better that Bridie couldn't see his smile, or the look in his eyes. Aroused as he was, Kit also was aware that Bridie was vulnerable right now. Not just physically but emotionally. But he'd be damned if he could leave her without knowing what had set her off. Last night she had come to him sweet as spun sugar and melted against him. He was hungry for another taste.

Bridie hauled herself up the back step, but Kit's voice stopped her when she reached for the door.

"You can't leave me out here drenched in mud, Bridie. I'd catch my death if I tried to ride home like this."

"I don't trust you, Kit. But you're right. I won't be responsible for having you sick. The women in this county would likely lynch me. Come as far as the kitchen. Not one step more."

Bridie ran upstairs, and in seconds ran back down. She stood in the doorway and tossed a pair of her father's pants and a shirt at him. And disappeared as quickly.

Kit shucked down quicker than a calf roper threw a loop. He didn't want Bridie to have an excuse to throw him out. But he faced another problem. Her father had been a short, stocky man. Kit felt like he was back wearing knee britches again. The shirt cuffs hung by his elbows and his shoulders strained the seams. He couldn't button the shirt.

He stoked the fire in the stove and put up coffee. A little hunting in the pantry gave him rags to clean his boots. He had a feeling he'd have more than enough time to spit polish them before Bridie showed her face.

He moved a chair near the stove and hung his clothes there to dry. The mud would brush off easier that way. The puppy whined and in need of both company and comfort, he held her on his lap, petting her and whispering questions that only Bridie could answer. He didn't spare more than a curious look at the old cheese box turned upside down in the middle of the table.

He waited.

And upstairs, Bridie knew it. She had hoped that he would change and leave. The aroma of fresh coffee came wafting up to her. She wouldn't put it past Kit to stand below and fan the scent her way. She slipped her feet into thick wool socks. She would never get warm unless she stood by the stove. Over the heavy flannel nightgown she put on the robe, then a shawl. She squeezed out her hair and tied it back with a ribbon, but she could feel the grainy bits of mud that clung to the ends. She was nervous as a pea in a hot skillet or as her mamma had been fond of saying, she had a bad case of the all-overs. The fact remained that she didn't want to see Kit.

But she wasn't about to hide in her own home and wallow in self-pity.

Bridie wouldn't dare call it disappointment that swept through her when she didn't immediately see Kit in the kitchen, but it came close. The room was toasty warm and a glance at the empty wood box revealed the reason. She leaned to one side and found Kit. Her socks didn't make any noise so he wasn't aware that she stood there in the doorway.

The lamplight draped him in golden shadows except for his hair, that glistened like a raven's wing in the sunlight. His eyes were closed. He sat next to the laundry basket with one hand over the top. From the movement she guessed he was petting Cinders.

Bridie moved without thought into the room and stopped once again. The open shirt revealed a wedge of dark, curling chest hair. The sight held her gaze. Reminding herself that she was furious with him didn't do a bit of good. He took her breath away. He should have appeared ridiculous with his bare feet, too short pants and too small shirt, but all she felt was the force of his masculine presence.

"There's hot coffee, Bridie."

"Made yourself right at home, I see."

"Oh I heat up right quick just being near you, Bridie. I made the coffee for you."

"Don't be giving me any of your charm-the-husk-off-corn lines. I don't want to hear them."

His drawl had been lazy, but his move to stand was anything but. "Sit down. I'll serve you. The way you're shaking you're liable to spill it all over yourself."

Bridie sat. Not on his suggestion, but because she was shaking. It hadn't a blessed thing to do with being cold. If Kit thought he heated up right quick near her, Bridie could have started a fire all by herself.

The feeling confused her. She blamed it on the kiss they shared. Some defense had weakened once he touched his lips to hers. She didn't like it a bit.

He set the cup of coffee in front of her and watched the way she wrapped her hands around the cup. "Don't you think you owe me some explanation for tearing into me? After last night—"

"Last night, Mr. Sidell, I had a memory lapse and took a walk down the path to sin. I will thank you not to ever mention my shameful behavior again."

Oh, my, Bridie, you're getting as good with lies as he is.
If they get rid of him, I shall do a suitable penitence.
She stiffened at the touch of his hand on her hair.

"You're wrapped up tighter than an armadillo. You can't
believe I'd attack you, Bridie."

"Are you asking or telling me? 'Cause if you're asking,
I—"

"Never mind." Kit kept his hands on the chair back, but
couldn't stop himself from leaning over her shoulder. "You
gonna hide all night? Can't you look at me?" A deep breath
brought the scent of something that Bridie not only shouldn't
have, but couldn't possibly be, in her kitchen. Bourbon? No.

"Would you mind sitting down? It's hard to breathe in
here." The soft, breathless note in her voice didn't sound
firm at all. Bridie shook her head. Her body had gone over
to the enemy. Could her mind be far behind?

"That's the nicest thing you've said to me since I got here.
And to show you that I mean no harm, I'll sit right here."

"Right here" was Kit's hooking the chair and bringing it
alongside hers. She wished she could curl up in a ball like
an armadillo, and while she wished, she prayed for the thick
hide of one.

Bridie discovered that Kit didn't need to kiss her to bring
her to a knee-shaking, stomach-churning, heart-pounding
state. All he had to do was breathe the same air near her.

She had to take charge or the man would have her melting
like a lump of chocolate in a few minutes.

Bridie took a deep breath. "Mistake," her body all but
screamed at her. She stared down at the cooling coffee. The
man must have doused himself with half a bottle of bay rum
and drank its equal in bourbon. Bourbon? That wasn't coming from Kit but the cake beneath the box. *Kit's partial to
chocolate cake.* One of his marriage-minded fillies said that
to her this morning. She had thought about telling that Jamie
slipped and told about their bet. Now an idea came that held
such brilliant illumination, Bridie thought she had lit every
lamp and candle in the house.

But did she have the courage to go through with it?

And that traitorous body of hers whispered warmly, yes.

Bridie didn't think she could count on that source for any courage but one that would have herself hopping into Kit's lap.

Lips moistened, eyelashes fluttering, Bridie turned to look at him. She found his wonderful smile that made her want to kiss it from his lips so she could have it for her own waiting. More like a trap, she sharply reminded herself.

"Bridie," he whispered in a husky voice, "if you keep on looking at me like you are, darlin', I'm not gonna be responsible for what happens."

"And how do I look at you?"

"Like a violet-eyed innocent too curious about men and—"

"Don't." She couldn't do this. Flirting with a man of Kit's experience took more skill than she could gain in a month of Sundays.

"Bridie?" Kit stroked her rigid back. "Won't you tell me what's wrong? Did something happen today? Someone come around and bother you? 'Cause if they did, I'll have a word—"

"No. No, nothing like that. And please stop touching me. I feel as fragile as my mamma's best china dish sitting on the edge of the shelf."

"Okay. No hands. See how agreeable I can be?"

She snuck a peek. His grin invited her to share. What his eyes were telling her, was another matter. She could drown in the forest-green color.

"Bridie, you're doing it again."

"What?" She blinked and looked away.

"You're telling me not to touch you, but your beautiful eyes are inviting me to do more than just touch."

Bridie was warm. That instantly. Heat climbed from her toes curled over the rung of the chair straight up to her hairline and didn't miss one body part in between.

"I know you're an innocent woman, Bridie. I had hoped that you would give me—I mean us—a little time to get to know each other better. That's why I've coming calling on you.''

She couldn't help herself. She looked directly into his eyes. ''If you're lying to me, Kit Sidell, may the devil take your soul on the road to hell.''

She knew. Kit didn't know how Bridie could have found out about the bet, but he knew women. Bridie had a burr under her, and from the gleam in her eyes, she wasn't going to be patient with him.

He thought of last night and the sweet, giving taste of her. Truth was, he had kept thinking about it all day long. And he was very sure that if he leaned a bit closer, he could share that little bit of heaven with her again.

But guilt reared its ugly head. And Kit knew he was definitely between a rock and a hard place. Tell her the truth and he lost his horse. Lie to her and he'd lose the chance to find out what it was about Bridie that drew him. For he had made the determination last night as he rode home that it was more than lust.

He had the damnedest urge to protect her, and he gave in to it.

But not before he leaned close and stole a brief kiss.

By the time Bridie collected herself, he had his boots on and was already putting on his jacket. He gathered up his clothes and winked at her.

''That's an answer?'' she called out.

''The only one you're gonna get tonight.''

The man needed a keeper.

She needed a keeper.

And wouldn't it be nice, a little voice whispered, *if you could keep each other?*

❧ *Chapter 7* ❧

*B*ridie awoke to the rumble of wagon wheels coming down the lane to the house. By the time she dressed and ran downstairs a rich male baritone greeted the lovely streaks of color lighting the sky.

She was treated to the sight of Kit unloading wood from a wagon, singing about the daring young men on "The Flying Trapeze." He tipped his hat when he saw her, smiled his scoundrel's smile and went on working.

Bridie let Cinders out—the puppy was sure to run to him and give her an excuse to get closer—but Cinders didn't quite understand her role. She ran off to the bushes. Bridie took the coffeepot to the pump.

"Mind telling me what you're doing here this morning, Kit?"

"Being neighborly. Noticed your wood pile was low."

"I can't pay for that wood."

He looked over to see the determined set of her chin, the flare of pride in her eyes and every line of her body. He was a mite disappointed not to be treated to the sight of Bridie in britches again, but he took heart from the fact that she hadn't come out toting a shotgun.

"Ain't asked you to."

Bridie worked the pump over his rendition of "The Blue Tail Fly." She was so busy staring at the smooth, muscled flow of his tall lean body that the water was running over her. She jumped back, but the hem of her brown skirt was soaked.

"I'll make you breakfast," she called out.

"Already ate. You don't owe me anything, Bridie. Like I said, I'm just being a good neighbor."

She finally went inside wondering where her gumption was. She swore she'd have nothing more to do with him and here she stood, moon-eyed and grinning, because the day was beautifully born with Kit's songs and his smile and his—

Bridie put a stop to her gushing thoughts. He'd have her as silly as those other women chasing after him if she didn't watch herself.

But in the spirit of being neighborly, she could bring him a cup of coffee. There was just enough wood left to fill one stove well. She had the perfect excuse to go near him. And discovered that she had lingered in her daydreams longer than she thought, for Kit was putting the last load of wood in the shed.

He climbed up on the wagon seat. "Don't forget. I'm coming by at seven."

"I'm not going, Kit."

"Seven."

She didn't want to watch him leave, but she stood there until the cold snaking its way up her skirt and through her shirtwaist made her move. The man must be deaf as well as stubborn. She should go into town and buy him a vial of Humphrey's Homeopathic Specific No. 28 or Parker's Ginger Tonic. Both claimed to cure as many ills as Hart's Discovery or Coleman's Concentrated White Sulphur Spring Water. And while she was at it, she'd purchase two bottles of Green's August Flower for herself. Surely it was a physical illness that stopped one protest from passing her lips where Kit was concerned.

Her nervous disorder continued through the day. She couldn't eat, worked her way through chores with a decided lack of strength and even Cinder's antics of scattering the hens in the yard couldn't bring a smile. But she did hitch up

the wagon near suppertime, early enough that she could go
to the church hall without being seen.

Seven o'clock on the dot, Kit pulled the buggy to a halt
in front of Bridie's house. He found what he expected—the
house dark, Bridie refusing to answer the door, refusing to
acknowledge him at all. If it wasn't for a good cause, he
would plant himself in her front yard, but he drove off with
the promise that he'd be back later.

Bridie twitched the lace curtain on the parlor window in
place. She had no one but herself to blame for this misery
stealing over her. She wished she could blame her cold bath
last night for the achy head, watering eyes, and throat-closing
lump, but she never caught cold.

But in the back of her mind, the small part that remained
sane and empty of thoughts about Kit and desire, she kept
remembering Jamie's words. Why would he lie to her? He
would not and that was a fact. Kit had bet she would come
to the cakewalk with him. She would be teased and laughed
at, and she couldn't knowingly put herself in that position.

She would ignore him from this moment on.

Kit was doing some ignoring of his own. Jamie's smirk
when he arrived without Bridie. Marylee's attempts to tell
him which pie was hers, and Sedalia's repeated remarks
about her perfect pecan pie. He ignored his sister's disappointment about Bridie, put up with her accusation that he
hadn't really tried.

He had two thoughts in mind. Leaving as soon as he could
to get back to Bridie, and winning the four-layer chocolate
cake that rested on one end of an overladen table. Alma
didn't know who baked it. Mrs. McCarthy and Janny Sue
made the same claim. He went to each of the women on the
church committee and came away frustrated that he wasn't
going to track down a confirmation of the ghostly baker. The
church hall was crowded with neighbors in their Sunday best.
The ladies' committee had not only made the rounds of out-
lying ranches and farms, but spent considerable time putting
up bunting and donated silk flowers around the walls. Three

fiddles tuned up, two harmonicas, and a banjo player waited to begin.

Talk and laughter waited at every turn as Kit worked his way to where Mrs. Davis stood near the fiddle players. He was in his element, joking with men who offered sips from the jugs stashed in wagons outside, serious talk and offers of help to those who were short-handed, or had illness in the family. The women, married and single alike, all received a smile, a word, and more than one sigh followed his passing.

But Kit was only half paying attention. He set himself to use his considerable charm, and a five-dollar donation, to make sure that Mrs. Davis called his number among the first men to dance, along with her promise that the prize chocolate cake was his. He made sure she marked it down on her card.

With the prize of the rich dessert in sight, Kit thought of smooth, delicious, and silky things and found those thoughts heightened when images of Bridie appeared.

Mrs. Davis shouted for space to be cleared and single men and widowers pinned the slips of paper with their numbers on jacket lapels. Most men had kept the papers received with the ten cents admission, hidden in pockets until they could work their way close to the lady of their choice. Kit had used the ploy himself of asking for a lady's help to pin it in place. Those few seconds in the hands of a smart man allowed a whispered compliment, the promise of a dance, and a walk outside to cool off. Of course, once the crowd's attention was on the dancers, one of the married men would slip out and return with a jug to spike up the ladies' punch and insure the need for a walk.

For some unexplainable reason, he flirted with no one and pinned his paper in place himself.

The numbers were called of ten of the men, and Kit hid a scowl when he found Jamie next to him. There was no time for talk as the music to "Turkey in the Straw" began. Here was another chance to show off for the lady of choice. Most of the single women were in the first circle of onlookers. Jamie had positioned himself to dance with Sedalia, and Kit thought it was due to the lady's encouragement.

With his thumbs hooked inside his belt, Kit kicked up his heels, his shuffle picked up from the traveling minstrel shows. He soon realized that Jamie and he kept in step, and the other men faded from sight. Their moves were fast and smooth. Kit thought they probably looked like a pair of rutting bucks, all but butting heads on the dance floor.

They twirled and turned, boots stomping in time to the lively music as they made their way around the circle, then back again to face each other. Kit was a good dancer, but Jamie was better. Even if his friend was promising payment to come with every glaring look.

The music ended abruptly, and everyone clapped as each man took a bow. Kit waited impatiently for the numbers to be called. He had already spied a basket for his prize under the skirted table. Alma would make sure it was returned to its owner. All he had to do was find a moment to slip away.

One pairing of pie and man didn't surprise him. Jamie won Sedalia's pie. Kit unfortunately was looking at Marylee when his prize and number were called. If looks could kill he'd have died on the spot.

Most of the men had already put their slips of paper near their cakes and pies. The second set was being called out on the floor, and Kit used that to make his getaway.

Jamie waited right by the door.

"So where's Bridie?"

"She couldn't come." Kit held the basket with both hands so as not to tip the cake. But he'd risk it, if Jamie didn't move out of his way.

"I suspect she wouldn't come is more like the truth."

"And how," Kit asked in a soft, too, too soft voice, "would you know what Bridie's thoughts are?"

"Saw her in town. She didn't sound like a woman happy to be courted by you. She—"

"If you messed up my chances with Bridie 'cause of your loose tongue, I'll tie it in a knot, friend or no friend, bet or no bet. Now get the hell out of my way."

"Hold on, Kit—"

"No. You hold on. I've got twenty-seven days to go. And I'll win all the way around.".

"Oh, Jamie, there you are," Sedalia said from behind Kit.

And anger drove Kit's response. "Watch yourself while walking out with him, Sedalia. He'll get you near the farthest wagon and claim he's got a pebble in his boot. By the time you figure out what he's up to, you'll either be kissing him back or slapping his face. Have a good evening, you hear."

Bridie had the parlor lamp lit. A fire was burning in the fireplace and she sat with her mending, straining to hear the sound of buggy wheels on the lane. She lost count of how many times she had put aside her work and gone to the window.

The little wooden clock that her mother had brought from her home in Rhode Island chimed nine times. Bridie glanced from the clock's face to Cinders curled on the rug before the hearth. The pup's body twitched as if her dreams were of valiant deeds where she raced to whatever waited for her. She folded her mending and put it on top of her sewing basket.

Kit wasn't coming. She had been more than foolish to bathe, and put on her best black skirt and a blue gingham blouse. She had thought about the bet. She had thought about how being with Kit made her feel. But he wasn't here to know what she had decided. She had believed she wasn't wallowing in self-pity, and yet that is exactly what she had been doing. Shy or not, she would have been the envy of every single woman at the social when she walked in on Kit's arm. And if there had been teasing or laughter at her expense, she had a bone-deep feeling that Kit would have defended her.

It was just too late to understand she would steal what time she could with him. Whether Kit knew it or not, he had breached her safe little lonely world.

She was reaching for the poker to bank the fire when she heard the sound she had been waiting for all night. The crunch of wheels on the lane were accompanied by a rich baritone voice singing "Oh, Susanna."

Bridie turned up the lamp. She retied the ribbon at the base of her neck that held her loose hair from her face. The puppy stretched and yawned, revealing tiny white teeth, and Bridie ran to scoop her up and put her in her bed in the kitchen.

She rushed back to the door just as Kit knocked.

"I've come to call—"

"Come in, Kit. We need to talk."

He held up the napkin-covered basket. "I've brought along the prize I won. And before you ask, I left before the dancing started. I wanted to be with you, Bridie. But I want one honest answer from you before I step inside. Why wouldn't you come?"

She looked up at him. The lamplight didn't reach this far. He was a barely lit moonlight shadow. She promised herself honesty with him, but still found the words hard to say.

"I admitted I left because I wanted to be with you," he said softly.

"I couldn't go. I didn't have a pretty gown to wear and I don't know how to dance and crowds of people make me tongue-tied."

The words were delivered in a rush with an underlying challenge. Kit merely shook his head. "Of all the things I thought of as reasons, it wasn't one of those. But you look mighty pretty to me. As for dancing, we'll remedy that right now. I don't know how I can make you comfortable in a crowd, but I'm not too fond of other company when I'm near you." He stepped inside and swept off his hat.

Bridie took it and set it on the small hall table. "I'm glad you came back."

"So am I, Bridie."

His voice was every bit as soft, but deeper somehow, and sent a delightful shiver running down her spine. She turned to the parlor but instead of following her, Kit walked back to the kitchen. When he joined her, he was minus one basket and his suit jacket. She watched wide-eyed as he pulled the string-tie free and tucked it into his pants pocket. Her brows lifted when first one, then two top buttons on his white shirt were undone.

"Make yourself comfortable," she managed to say.

"I am." Kit smiled. She did look pretty. And he was going to have his arms wrapped around that luscious body in a few minutes. Frustrating times were about to begin. But it would be worth it. A different kind of man would have taken advantage of Bridie and every situation he'd found her in. A different kind of man would be thinking far ahead to seducing her—with coaxing, gentle courtesy—right out of every stitch of clothes, and teach her to return the same.

Since he was standing there, tormenting himself, Kit took a few deep, steadying breaths. Bridie didn't know how lucky she was he wasn't a different kind of man.

"Come here, Bridie. We'll have your first dance lesson."

"We don't have any music." Her words sounded silly. He had music in his green eyes. She loved the way his thick midnight-black hair softly curled. His masculine features handsome enough to make her mouth go dry. The tall, rangy build. Shoulders, narrow hips and long muscled legs that showed to advantage in the hand-tailored clothes. No ready-mades for Kit. And there was the charm. The good Lord had given an extra large supply to him. And there was music inside her from the appreciative male grin, and the way his eyes lingered on her, as if she were the only woman in his world.

It was miserable to be shy and plain and not know what to do.

Kit took the decision from her. He hummed an old waltz tune and stepped close and bowed. "May I have this dance?"

"Kit, I truly don't know what to do."

"Trust me, you will." He placed one of her hands on his shoulder, one of his on her waist. Her free hand he held within his own. "I'm going to enjoy teaching you, Bridie."

She lifted heavy-lidded violet eyes to his. "I think it's long past time that I learned."

He hummed and counted the steps for her.

Bridie simply hummed, her body that is, she couldn't open her mouth busy as she was absorbing the heady scents of a woodsy soap and bay rum, the warmth of his hand holding hers, the heat of his touch at her waist. Her body felt fever flushed with every turn that brushed her breasts against his chest.

The chiming of the hour fell in a moment of silence. Bridie opened her eyes and found that they stood in the center of the parlor, no longer dancing, but swaying back and forth. Her head rested against Kit's chest where the racing beat of her heart played another music for her.

"Bridie," he whispered with his lips against the faint spicy scent of her hair, "the dance is over. Time to go home. You will allow me the pleasure of escorting you home, won't you?"

"Kit?"

"Hmmm."

"I am home."

"We'll pretend we took the buggy ride, and you invited me inside. I want to kiss you good night. And I'm trying to hold off as long as I can 'cause I don't want to leave you at all."

Something in his voice tripped a warning cord. Kit was asking for more. Bridie reluctantly lifted her head and tilted it back so she could look up at his face. The desire was in his eyes, but she knew a stab of fear. Could she face herself in the morning if she asked him to stay?

He slipped both arms around her. His forehead touched hers. Bridie licked her bottom lip. Kit's gaze went to her mouth. Her flesh seemed suddenly hot, then cold. Her heart was beating too fast. Shimmers of warmth spread inside her. Kit stroked her spine, lingering at the small of her back. His lips were slightly parted, hovering above her own. She closed her eyes. Her breath caught, feeling his warm mouth skim the shape of her ear. Shimmers turned to heated bursts with the slow slide of his lips down the side of her neck.

The small sounds were hers. She felt him over every inch

and nerve end of her body. He pressed a lingering kiss at her temple, then her eyes. She felt surrounded by him. His mouth touched the corner of hers. His hand crushed her hair. His murmurs filled her ears with accolades for her hair, her skin, her scent, and taste.

His lips touched hers, rich with masculine promise. His tongue, as arrogant as he could be, stole the moisture from her mouth. Desire rose, heady and hot, for the kiss to go on and on. She ached with pleasure. He deepened the kiss, his hand skimming her side, touching the curve of her breast. Bridie heard more strange sounds coming from her lips, but Kit seemed to approve, for he asked for more.

And when she couldn't stand, couldn't seem to draw breath, he nuzzled her cheek and eased away from her.

"Walk me to the door, Bridie. It's time for me to go."

"I . . ." She couldn't say another word, or look at him. But she knew what melted chocolate felt and tasted like. It described her insides too perfectly.

He drew her arm through his, but ended up sliding it around her waist as he went to fetch his jacket and hat.

"I'm real glad you didn't come tonight, Bridie. I had more pleasure this past hour than sharing you would have given me." He cupped her chin and kissed her again. "I don't know if I'll get much sleep tonight. But if I do, I'll be dreaming about you. Drive out with me Sunday."

"Sunday?" Her mouth tingled from his heat. She wanted to be in his arms, and knew she couldn't say it.

"If you're worried, I'll bring along a chaperon. Now lock up."

And he waited until he heard the turn of the key. But each time he looked back, he saw that the lamp remained lit. Regretfully, Kit kept going. And he wondered why he hadn't uttered one lie to Bridie.

❧ *Chapter 8* ❧

$\mathscr{S}$unday began in a flurry of activity for Bridie. She rushed through chores, all the while begging the Lord's forgiveness for not attending service. She knew Kit would. What she didn't know was what time he would call for her.

She spent an hour pinning her braided hair into a coil. She brushed out her black skirt and prayed no one would notice the patch near the hem. Her blue gingham was her best blouse, not that Kit would see it. The day was chilly enough for her to wear a cloak.

Should she make a picnic lunch? The debate with herself was settled with boiling eggs, a jar of pickled green tomatoes, and a loaf of bread she had baked yesterday. And there was the cake Kit had forgotten. And a good thing too, she thought. There was no way she could have hidden her shock at finding her cake in his basket. Then she settled down to wait.

Or tried to. She kept jumping up to peer out the window, paced the hall, the kitchen and parlor, ran upstairs four times to check her hair, pinch her cheeks and bite her lips for color, until she was so flushed, she needed no more.

As the clock ticked away, she tried not to worry who the chaperon would be.

Kit being Kit, he arrived when she was in the kitchen hoping a cup of tea would settle her nerves. After all, this was another first for her.

The teacup rattled as she set it on the saucer. A deep breath allowed her to greet him with a false measure of calm, that dissolved into surprise when she saw who he had brought.

"Laurel, say hello to Miss Delwin."

A smile touched rosebud lips, and was so close to Kit's that Bridie had to be forgiven for the quick beat of her pulse, and the butterflies that took up residence in her stomach. She invited them in, all the while thinking what it would be like to have a little girl like Laurel for her own. It was a reminder of loneliness she swiftly buried. Nothing was going to spoil her day.

"Alma didn't mind?" she asked.

"Mind? My sister was only too happy to have me take her. I hope it's you who doesn't mind. I thought this the best way to prove my honorable intentions." His breath caught seeing Bridie's smile, and Laurel tugged his hair. She wanted up, then for him to play horsey.

"We're going for a ride, lamb, that is, if Bridie's sure she wants to come."

"Bridie's sure." She slipped on her cloak, and went to open the door. Laurel surprised her by demanding up. Kit could barely hold his niece as she squirmed in his arms to get to Bridie.

And once she held the little girl, Kit took advantage to kiss her.

It was a brief meeting of lips, but gazes locked and spoke of warmer desires. Bridie felt so young and gay, she teased him about those honorable intentions. A tease she repeated when she saw his buggy. It was built for two. The leather hood was up making a cozy nook and a big-boned bay was harnessed to the carriage.

She was very aware of his strength when he lifted both of them onto the buggy seat and tucked a lap robe around her. Laurel, waving her arms as if she held the reins, kept urging him to go.

"On your order, imp."

He kissed the tip of his niece's nose as if it were the most natural thing in the world for a man to show affection. Bridie liked that about him, even as she tried to cope with the sudden smallness of the buggy's seat now that Kit sat next to her. She was very warm along the side that pressed against him. He set off at a spanking pace down the lane, then out to the open countryside.

Bridie found it a revealing ride. Kit had infinite patience with Laurel as she went from one lap to another unable to make up her mind. He talked of his plans to build a stud farm and Bridie listened with avid interest. She felt as if she had been given a special gift of seeing a side of Kit rarely shown. But the wind picked up, and Bridie most reluctantly suggested he turn for home.

Laurel was asleep when he pulled up by her front door. Bridie refused his invitation to return home with him for Sunday supper, an invitation that Alma seconded.

"Oh, but wait, Kit. Your cake."

He drew her close. "Keep it. I'd like to come back and share it with you."

"Yes, I'd like that, too."

Her lips were a little softer and trembling when he lifted his head. "Another kiss like that and I won't need to stoke the fires."

"Hold that thought. I'll collect on it later."

Kit held the thought, too, all the way home. Shy Bridie teased him, sassed him, too. He kept hearing her laugh and seeing her smile, her eyes glowing, cheeks flushed. Her scent stayed with him as did her taste. She had listened to his plans, asked intelligent questions and he couldn't remember another woman who had. Business talk bored Marylee. Sedalia only wanted to go where she'd be seen with him, and if he didn't have compliments waiting every time she looked at him, she'd pout.

He was so thoughtful that after supper, Alma took him aside in the kitchen.

"What's wrong, Kit? And don't tell me nothing's bothering you. You've been awfully quiet this afternoon."

"Alma, what's the worse thing that Tom could do to you?

I'm talking about killing any chance that you'd go on loving him.''

She stroked her brother's cheek. "Oh, Kit, what have you done?''

"Who said anything . . . ah, hell, Alma. I'm in a pickle barrel.''

"Can I help you?'' Her gaze filled with concern.

"Answer me.''

"I don't know how. I love Tom. I've loved him since we were children. I suppose it would strain our marriage if he betrayed my trust in him.'' Her voice became hopeful. "Is that what you wanted to know?''

"Just what I figured,'' he muttered. "I'm going out.''

"Kit, it's Bridie, isn't it? Laurel tried to tell me about a bird, but you've been seeing her, haven't you?''

"Why make a statement then ask a question? Women! Who needs them to complicate a man's life?''

"You wouldn't be here, Christopher Robert, if it weren't for a woman.''

Kit let her have the last word. He had enough on his mind.

Kit kept his horse to a sedate walk. He had a lot of thinking to do. He couldn't bear the thought of losing High Man to Jamie.

Bridie trusts you. You made her trust you.

And he told the bedeviling nag that at a darn high cost to himself. He hadn't suffered through nights of lost sleep since he'd come out of knee-length pants.

All because of Bridie. Innocent, shy Bridie, who kissed him with her heart in her eyes.

You could tell her the truth.

Guilt howled. Kit knew he couldn't. He'd hurt her. She would retreat and he didn't think he could stand that.

She was so sweet. Too sensitive. And kind. Different from any other woman he knew. She was prettier and more feminine than he had ever realized. She loved the puppy, and was patient as a saint with Laurel. He couldn't forget the longing he'd seen in her eyes while she held the little one.

Bridie need someone to protect her.

Mostly from you.

Shut up! I'm working through this. She was honest, and made him confront the nature of his bet. Who did he think he was, and Jamie, too, for that matter? Playing with someone's life? Who gave him that right?

She was strong and capable. Maybe she'd handle this.

And maybe she'd fall apart.

Maybe Alma was right. He'd done an awful lot of hell-raising these last ten years. And even his bedeviling nag couldn't stop the smile resulting from fond memories. Then Kit had the strangest thought that he could share some of the less colorful escapades with Bridie.

What was he thinking of? She had him so tied in knots he couldn't think straight.

Kit turned his horse across the open land to the lane. He could see the small glow of the lamp in the parlor window.

Bridie waited for him. Spice and heat. He ached with a need that chased every thought from his mind.

He thought he had plenty of time. When she opened the door for him, he knew time was against him.

Her smile lit up the darkness. "I thought you'd never get here. Come in, or all the heat will be gone."

Kit took a long look at her glorious chestnut hair. The coil gone, the braid free, and he remembered too well the feel of that thick silky hair crushed in his hand while he kissed her.

"What's wrong, Kit? Weren't you planning on—"

"Of course, I'm coming inside." He crossed to the table where he tossed his hat, gloves, and heavy jacket. And saw what she'd done to the parlor. The fire burned bright, but candles glowed on the mantel, on the side tables. A quilt was spread over the rug before the fire. He didn't have to guess it was her mamma's best china cups and plates on either side of the three-layer cake.

"I made coffee and cocoa to go with the cake," she whispered shyly behind him. And when he didn't answer she forced herself to speak. "Did I do something wrong? If I did, I'm sorry. I told you I've never had a man call on me and I wasn't—"

"Bridie." That was all he said as he turned and cupped her shoulders. "It's perfect. I'm flattered that you went to so much trouble for me."

"Oh, it was no—"

He stole the words with his lips. How could he think with the blood roaring in his head? With Bridie melting against him, soft and fragrant. His blood heated and pumped in response to the small sexy sounds she made in her throat. His body was tight with tension and steaming with heat. The touch of his tongue opened her lips. He plundered. Hard and impatient, he fought not to sweep her up into his arms and carry up the stairs.

Her eager, helpless sounds gave way to greed. She never wanted his kisses to end. She had the most handsome man in the county wanting her. And she wanted him to go on wanting her. She was afraid to name what she felt, afraid that it wasn't true, that dreams for women like her were just that—empty dreams.

"Bridie, I swear, you make all my good intentions jump out the door."

"Is that good or bad?" she asked with a hint of laughter.

"Good. Real good for me, Bridie. But innocent, it's bad for you. Not safe at all."

She chose safe over innocent. Bridie didn't want to be reminded of her ignorance that allowed no control over the wild, intense feelings sweeping through her. She leaned back against the support of his arms and looked up at him.

"Safe, Kit? That's a strange word to use. Are you a danger to me?"

He was drowning in the deep violet color of her eyes. Her silky hair teased his hands. He tried not to think of the mere inch separating lower bodies, or the lush curve of her breasts. He even tried stopping the image of soft flesh and wet cloth too sheer to protect her.

But what he saw in her eyes bucked building passion into wild, desperate need to claim her for his own.

"Bridie, if one of us is dangerous, it's you. You do things to me that no other woman has. Not ever."

"Oh, Kit." She closed her eyes briefly. "Thank you. Oh, thank you for saying that. This is all so new to me and I feel wonderful. Happy. More—"

"I don't know if you can believe this, Bridie, but this is new to me, too. And because I respect you, we are going to have coffee and cake."

He turned her within his arms and nudged her into the parlor. Eating would occupy his mouth and his hands until he caged this need. But he wasn't sure his mind was willing to cooperate in this attempt to protect Bridie's innocence.

Seated opposite each other, Kit's eyes fed the fire-gilded, glowing image of her until heat battered him inside and out.

He stared down at the cake. He loved sweets. Especially chocolate cake. Most especially this one. And due to need, he really looked at the cake. Something was missing. He had won and bribed his way to having a luscious four-layer.

Kit watched her cut the cake. He liked the smaller, feminine shape of her hands. Strong hands, capable. *Oh, yes, capable, all right. Capable of a touch that drove him wild.*

The knife slid down through moist layers just like desire sinking bone deep inside him. Sitting Indian style had seemed a good idea. He'd need a minute at least before he could move. A minute where he could think about what he was doing.

Now, he had to hunch over to hide from Bridie the shocking results of his thoughts. The thick slice of cake sat in the middle of the china floral plate she handed to him. He felt as if there was a far-off voice trying to tell him something. Something important. He couldn't hear it through the seductive whisperings that made him hang on to his honor with a slippery hand.

"Kit? Kit, don't you want the cake?"

"Yeah. Sure. I love chocolate cake. But I need to ask you . . ." He stopped and lifted his head to look at her. "Bridie, is this the one I brought here?"

Alarm bells rang. And quieted just as quickly. What difference could it make if Kit knew how she earned money? It was silly to hesitate, but there was a strange look on his face, one that made her think Kit was dangerous. She'd heard talk all her life about his hell-raising, even rumors of gun fights up in Indian territory. She couldn't imagine why she was remembering this now.

"Bridie, answer me."

"I . . ." That too-soft voice kept her silent. Then her practical nature took hold. "I'm being silly. No, this isn't the cake you won. Does that matter so much?"

Kit swallowed his disappointment. For a moment there he thought his search was at an end. He should've known better. The woman who baked such decadent cakes was a woman of passion.

Bridie's passionate.

Lusty, then, for every bite appealed to his senses after his eyes had feasted. His secret baker was a woman who took risks, one with a sensual nature. Pleasure-giving. And he had to stop. She was likely sixty years old, a plump grandmother with years of experience behind her. It could even be a man. *Lord, forbid.*

Bridie poured coffee.

Kit shunned his musings and took a bite. He closed his eyes. A soft moan of pleasure escaped his lips. Rich flavors exploded on his tongue. Damn! but the cake was almost as good as kissing Bridie. *Almost?*

She was smiling at him when he opened his eyes. "You really do love chocolate cake."

"This one. I've never denied having a sweet tooth, but this one cake is a taste of heaven. I've been haunting the Planters' House trying to find out who does the baking. It's a search—"

"Search?" Bridie rubbed her fingertips over the back of her hand. "Why are you searching for the baker?"

Now you've gone and done it. What are you going to say? I'm going to marry the woman—if it is a woman, and under thirty.

"I want to extend personal compliments for the delicious desserts I've enjoyed." *Smooth. See, you're back in control.*

Yeah, right. And Bridie looks mighty disappointed with your answer.

"Aren't you going to have any, Bridie?"

"It's a little too rich for me."

Kit worked his way through half the slice before her words hit him like a sun-fishing bronc dumped its rider. "I didn't know you'd been to the hotel. I thought you . . . well, most ladies don't go there alone."

"Well I do. Oh, not into the hotel dining room. But around back."

"The chef a friend of yours?" The jealous note made him push an extra large bite in his mouth. Bridie and that arrogant Frenchman who'd chased him out of the kitchen waving a knife that Jim Bowie'd be proud to own? No. No, not his Bridie.

"Jean-Paul likes to cook. We talk sometimes if he's not too busy."

Kit strained his eyes and knew that was a deeper flush on her cheeks. He'd embarrassed her with his question. Bridie must have been looking for work. He knew there were debts. No one lived in Denison who didn't know everyone else's business. But if Bridie was slowly paying off those debts, where was the money coming from?

Kit finished his cake. He emptied his coffee cup. He rose and went to her. Two seconds and he had her standing, a few more and he sat on the small settee with Bridie in his lap.

He cupped her chin when she would have turned away. "Oh no. Look at me. Answer one question. Did you make the cake?"

"Do women tell you that you have beautiful eyes and such thick lashes a woman would be dead not to envy them?"

"I don't care about other women. Are you telling me that?"

Her dreamy-eyed look and the gentle way she traced the shape of his brow was answer enough.

"Bridie, will you marry me?" And the only bet he was thinking of winning was the one he made with himself.

❧ *Chapter 9* ❧

*M*arriage? When she was just learning to enjoy the courting? When she was still afraid to name what she felt for Kit? Anger—unreasoning, she thought—but anger just the same began to build for his question. How could he spoil her newfound pleasure?

How dare he ask the most important question in a woman's life and spread kisses over her ear and neck that sent fire bursts inside her? How was a woman supposed to think? How could she think when aware of every masculine inch of his lean, hard-muscled body tense, and heated against her own?

He had the experience. She couldn't deny it. But she had instincts. Instincts that brought her hands up to cradle his face and hold him for a kiss.

Bridie poured passion into that kiss. All the passion he had brought to life. She, who had never shared herself with anyone, shared all the wild, glorious feelings flaming inside.

Kit took control. Her hands slipped down to grip his shoulders. She tasted her gifts coming back twofold. There was no gentleness, no soft coaxing of mouth to mouth. His kiss was raw, hungry, a prelude to mating. She wanted more. Kit arched his neck back, drawing her deeper into the kiss. She used the tip of her tongue in such a clever way, arrow shafts of need went straight to his loins. She held nothing back, and he took with a greed that in saner moments would astound him.

There were no thoughts of her innocence, only of hunger. He had taught her too well. She knew just how to angle her head and slant her lips to tease, torment, and spike need higher, deeper, and leave him wanting more. Soft flesh heated and melted against his. A second's parting for breath, to hear those sexy sounds she made, then plunder the rich, dark taste of chocolate-flavored passionate kisses.

"Lord, woman," he muttered, "you'd make a monk give up his vows."

"Kiss me again, Kit. You make my heart pound and my knees shake,—"

"Hush. You don't know what you're saying. What you're doing."

She leaned back against his arm and drew his head down. "Then show me the right way. But I don't think anything could be more wonderful."

Kit couldn't avoid the kisses she planted on his face and neck. His hands clenched around the tangled silk of her hair to keep himself from taking what she offered. "Stop, Bridie. You're making me crazy." His voice, husky with need, cracked with desperation as his body made opposite demands.

With more enthusiasm than finesse, she opened the top button of his shirt.

"Bridie," he warned.

She slipped the second button free and her fingertips trailed down, parting the cloth and setting his skin on fire.

"I wanted to touch you that night in the kitchen. I've never wanted to touch—"

"A damn good thing, too," he growled.

He had to get her off his lap. She weighed next to nothing, but the muscles in his arms were quivering from enforcing his will not to touch. She squirmed and pushed herself up. She bit his ear. Kit's knees went weak. What the devil had he unleashed?

He retaliated without thinking of the consequences. "Oh, Kit, do that again. I felt it—"

"Behave yourself. You don't need to tell me where. I know. Remember, I have the experience. And you're not the only one who wanted to touch. Do you have any idea of what you did to me that night? Draped in a flimsy excuse of cloth plastered to every lush curve? It's a wonder my heart didn't stop beating." He made the mistake of getting too close to her inviting mouth. Honorable intentions went the way of the good ones. The heat ran through him, torment and temptation. With a groan torn from deep inside he lost himself in her generous giving lips.

"Bridie." Her name was a plea. "I'm trying to be good. For your sake."

"You are. Good, that is. Kiss me again. I love the way you make me feel." Her fingers tugged on the neck of his shirt, then slipped beneath the cloth to touch his skin that was growing damp with sweat.

"Lord, help me." He was never more sincere. He moaned. "Have pity." He couldn't think straight. His breathing went off the ragged edge with the effort he made to keep himself from tearing off her clothes. And he discovered that Bridie had a wicked, dark side. The woman had no pity. No mercy. Not an ounce of sense to protect herself.

She nibbled his neck. "Do you really love—"

"Chocolate cake—"

"Me?" she whispered at the same moment.

Hands that caressed now pushed against him as she struggled to get up. "You're right. I don't know what I'm doing. I've made a fool of myself. I just didn't . . . oh, please, let me go." There was no place to look but at him. She closed her eyes. "Please."

Kit held her tight. "I can't let you go. I told you the truth. This is new to me. I've never asked another woman to marry me. And you never did answer me. You're very good at avoiding my questions." The heat in his blood hadn't cooled but he could think again.

"I shouldn't have asked."

He drew back so they were both sitting upright. "Bridie—"

"I'll answer you, but first I need to know if you just wanted me to say yes, or did you really want me?"

"Both." He gently brushed her hair back from her face. "Look at me. At me," he repeated softly. She lifted burnished lashes and he saw into the almost black depths of eyes that couldn't mask the desire that made her tremble. But there was more revealed to his gaze. Now he knew why she asked if he loved her.

Bridie loved him.

And he knew what he had to do.

"Bridie, there's something I need to tell you."

"We've both said enough."

"No. This is important. I want to be honest with you."

She looked down at her hands still pressed against his chest. "Some secrets are best when kept." *Don't tell me it's all a lie. I couldn't bear that.*

"Not this one. This is one of those that come back to haunt a man. And what I've found in you, with you, is too special to allow that to happen."

"Kit, will what you need to tell me change your mind about asking me to marry you?"

"No. But it might change yours."

She held his green gaze with a look so steady, direct and knowing that Kit held his breath. He was going to lose before he really had a chance of winning.

"Wanna bet on that, Kit?"

"What did you say?" None too gently, he hauled her arms up and around his neck. Added problems. He could feel her nipples pressing through his shirt to scald the skin beneath. And to his surprise, Bridie pressed closer.

"I said—"

"I heard it. Keep still, Bridie. This is serious."

"I know. I may faint if you don't get on with it." Her fingers tunneled upward into his hair. "I've wanted to do that for a long, long time."

"You asked if I wanted to bet. I don't. I know I don't.

"Oh, my. I'm very glad to hear that, Kit. A woman might reconsider a proposal if she had to worry about a man's gambling." She smiled and pressed a kiss on his chin, another on his cheek and, feeling his tension, drew back. "That is something you can bet on with anyone. Even Jamie."

"You knew? All this time . . . I ought to strangle you." But he kissed her, then kissed her again, putting all his frustration and all his need into it. And she met him more than halfway. When he managed to pull back, her eyes were heavy and dazed.

"Why didn't you chase me off?"

"I did. But you came back, remember?"

"Wild horse races couldn't have kept me away. Bridie, I want you to know that I never thought about hurting you."

"Kit, I don't want to know any more about it. I think it's time for you to share a secret of mine."

"I already figured out you're the woman I've been looking for, and not just for those delicious baked goods. You are more delicious. I could feast on your kisses the way I once could eat that whole cake by myself."

"You'd get an awful tummy ache if you did."

He nuzzled the soft skin behind her ear. "Would you rub it and make the ache go away?"

Her hand slid down his chest, leaving heat, and came between her hip and his belly. She made a slow circling motion. "Like this?"

"Lower." But when she started to follow his request, Kit swore. "Bridie, you stop throwing out my good intentions." He ached and throbbed and hurt. She slipped off his lap before he could stop her.

She tugged on his hand. "Come upstairs with me. I have something to show you."

Kit rose, but he swept her up into his arms. "I don't want you out of my sight."

She felt cherished, and fragile. Strong and desired from the hot gleam in his eyes, and the furious beating of his heart beneath her palm. She trembled when he reached the bottom of the steps. But it wasn't fear. She had yearned for him too long to be afraid.

"Bridie, if there's a 'no' left in you, say it now. I can't trust myself to say it for you."

"I can't say no. I'd be lying."

Minutes ago he was humbled by her forgiveness of his terribly reckless bet. But humble wasn't a suit that fit him well. Male arrogance did.

"I know."

She wanted to store every second. The taste of each kiss as he repeatedly stopped on the steps. Of the hunger that called and was answered. Of having someone like Kit want her. Dreams were no longer empty. Tender or rough, she didn't care as long as he didn't stop.

She tightened her arms around him, and her own greedy need brought her to savor the taste of his skin. And when she brought a groan from him, she laughed from sheer joy.

"The death of me," he muttered as he entered her room. But he was grinning as he tumbled to the bed with her. "Or better yet, I'll show you a little death."

"Kit, please, wait." She stretched her hand to reach beneath her pillow. He rolled to the side, one arm cradling her head, the other draped over her waist. "This is what you were looking for." She held the wooden valentine heart in the palm of her hand.

"All these years . . ." He touched the word he'd carved so long ago with his fingertip, then traced the heart.

"Miss Maples was right, you know," she whispered. "We all needed dreams. This was mine. You loving me."

"Never once. You never—" His eyes met hers. "Bridie, you make a wicked chocolate cake, but honey, right along with it comes powerful humble pie."

"I've loved you since I was a little girl. I want to love you as only a woman can." She touched his lips. "Can you love me, Kit?"

"Ask me if I can stop breathing."

She tilted her head back. She wanted to see his face, see

what came into his eyes. "I love you. I want to be your wife. I want to raise horses with you and—"

"And babies," he added, seeing through new eyes the love and beauty he held in his arms.

"And I'll bake you sweets every day. Chocolate cake and pecan pies, and lots of chocolate clouds."

He stretched out beside her and cupped her chin. "Bridie, speaking of clouds, let me take you to them. Let me love all the delights I've found in Miss Bridie Delwin."

"I've wanted that for so long. Show me, Kit. Show me what love is."

And he did.

THE TASTE OF
REMEMBRANCE

Alexis Harrington

❧ *Chapter 1* ❧

A chill February gust swept over Rebecca Baxter's ankles when her shop door opened and closed with a bang. Scraps of organdy and muslin fluttered, and then were still. Looking up, she was startled to find Aaron Monroe at the front of the dress shop. He had never once set foot in here. Indeed, in a rare joking moment he had said it was a place that even the bravest man dared not enter. But now there he stood, still wearing his shopkeeper's apron under his coat, and wringing his hat brim in his hands. The gesture was the only hint of his nervousness. His face betrayed none of it.

She rose from her chair at the sewing machine. "Why, Aaron, this is a surprise! What's the mat—"

"I'm here to say my piece, Rebecca." His tone was almost stern.

"Of course—" she began, baffled.

"I want you to marry me," he said abruptly. "Don't put me off this time."

She felt her face grow warm and her jaw dropped as she gazed at him. Thank heavens Mrs. Walker was visiting her sister in Denver. She probably would not appreciate Rebecca receiving a call like this during working hours. Laying aside the sleeve she had been basting, she walked toward him.

"Aaron, I haven't meant to put you off. I—surely you know that. The shop has been so busy—"

He waved his arm over the confines of the small place, over the bolts of fabric, and rolls of ribbon and trim. "Sarah Walker was looking for a dressmaker to help here when you rode in on the stage three years ago. She'll find another one. That's no call to put me off twice."

She nodded. Certainly, he was right; the shop was not a good reason. In fact, it wasn't the reason at all. "I'm sorry if it seemed that way," she repeated lamely.

"You ought to be sewing and doing for your own husband and children instead of strangers," he continued. "That's more important than anything else."

Ruddy from the bitter wind, Aaron's face was a good one, strong and honest. Not handsome, really, Rebecca supposed, not like— Beneath the pomade, his slicked-down hair was light brown, and his hazel eyes had flecks of gold in them. Serious and hard working, he had the town's respect. In fact, the citizens had thought enough of him to run him for mayor. He lost the election but he'd had his supporters.

He gave his hat another merciless twist. "It's time, Rebecca—for both of us. There's no use in pining away for a man long gone." She stiffened at this reference. "He's not here and I am, and a woman ought to be married. I'll give you a decent life and respectability. I won't be asking again, Rebecca, and I won't leave without an answer. If you mean to say no, then do it."

She glanced out the window at the dark winter day. Those things he mentioned, a husband and children, she had wanted all of her life. At twenty-nine years old, she knew that if she didn't begin soon it might be too late. She did not think she loved him, but was very fond of him and perhaps that was enough. And the reasons in her heart that had made her dither with an answer—they were from another place, another life. Aaron was right, it was no use to pine. And, yes, it was time.

Gage, I'm sorry, I'm sorry—

Drawing a quiet breath, she put her hand on his arm and

looked into his hazel eyes. "Yes, Aaron, I will marry you."

And that was that.

Though Rebecca tried to think otherwise, Aaron's proposal and her acceptance had had all of the romance of a horse trade.

Book work at his general store prevented him from staying longer, and as she made her way down the twilit street to Abigail Chatfield's house, she pondered her decision. One by one, store windows darkened as shades were drawn and doors locked for the night.

With each step on the planked sidewalk, she looked beyond the proposal and became more positive that her marriage to Aaron would be a good one, despite his unromantic courtship and proposals. Her cold, ascetic father had told her that romance was sentimental nonsense found mostly in books, and that women often learned to love *after* marriage. A dependable man who could plow a straight furrow was more useful than one who talked sugar and sweet words, he had pronounced. Apparently he did not believe that the two qualities could inhabit the same man.

But they could, she knew. Gage Bristol had proven it.

That evening Rebecca sat at Abbie's elegantly set dinner table and told her of Aaron's proposal.

"Well, it's about time," Abbie exclaimed, sitting up a bit straighter. "He's been buzzing around you for months and months."

A young widow, Abigail was Rebecca's closest friend. They met when Abbie came into the dress shop to have mourning dresses made. Her elderly husband had died shortly after Rebecca arrived, leaving Abbie a large house, three servants, and a lot of free time.

At Abbie's insistence, Rebecca often had dinner with her. After all, she asserted, it did not look right for a woman to dine by herself in a restaurant night after night. And her little room behind the dress shop did not provide cooking facilities. Rebecca suspected that eating alone was no more fun for Abbie than it was for herself.

"Actually, it was the third time he'd proposed."

"Third time!" Abbie exclaimed. "He's persistent, I'll give him that. I declare, Rebecca, what were you waiting for?"

She fiddled with the napkin on her lap. "I had—well, I wasn't quite ready to—" Gage was a tender subject, and she spoke of him gingerly, as one would press a careful tongue to an aching tooth.

Abbie stretched her slim white hand across the table. "Oh, dear, Rebecca, I'm sorry. I forgot about your fiancé." Her voice mirrored her distress.

Rebecca looked up and managed a wobbly smile. "I guess it's time that I do the same. I like to think that Gage would want me to carry on with my life."

"Of course he would, honey. He wouldn't expect you to become a spinster and live alone."

Rebecca shrugged and buttered a piece of hot bread. "You didn't marry young."

"No, I was twenty-five. But I didn't want to get married, and you do. Anyway, poor Ezra knew he wasn't bound to live long after our wedding, the old dear. I think he just married me to keep him company until he was gone, and that's what I did." She gave Rebecca an arch look. "Thank heavens widowhood gives me a good excuse to remain unmarried."

"Don't you think you'd like to have a husband again someday, Abbie?"

The woman shook her head and gave her a sly grin. "I adore men. I love cats, too, but I don't want one in the house, taking over. I just like to stroke their whiskers and then send them home."

Rebecca nearly choked on the bread from laughing.

"Good!" Abbie hooted. "I made you laugh again."

With her ink-black ringlets and blue eyes, Abbie was a beautiful, vivacious woman—too much so for a widow, Rebecca sometimes thought. Abbie spoke her mind and flirted with all men, young, old, bachelors, and husbands. She charmed them utterly. And she had scandalized the respectable churchgoers in town when she threw off her widow's weeds for more fashionable dress only a month after her husband's death. But she had befriended Rebecca when she came to Oregon from war-scarred Georgia with no plan other than to escape a broken heart. And sometimes Rebecca even secretly envied Abbie's free-thinking, outspoken ways.

"You should have a home so you can move out of that little rabbit hutch in the back of the shop," Abbie continued, pouring a drizzle of thick cream into her coffee. "Honestly, I'd think that Sarah Walker could provide better accommodations for her employee than that. You're living like a match girl."

"It's not so bad, really," Rebecca replied, but in truth, it was quite a change from the tidy home in which she had grown up. "Besides, that room is part of my pay. I can't afford to move anywhere else right now. You know I'm saving to open my own shop."

"Yes, I know. Does Aaron?"

"Well, no, I never mentioned it to him. I was afraid that if, oh, I don't know. I guess I thought that if I told too many people, it might be bad luck. So I only told you and a couple of others."

Abbie cut a slice from the tall chocolate cake sitting on the end of the table. "You know you'd get my business. You've made half of the gowns in my wardrobe."

Rebecca felt her enthusiasm bloom, as she always did when she thought about this. "Jim Sommers told me I could rent the space in his building. It's a good spot, between his land office and the express office. I just need to save a little more money."

"Then I wish you had agreed to come and live here. You could have paid me a token rent if it made you feel better, although I certainly wouldn't think to charge you otherwise."

Abbie had made this offer many times and Rebecca always turned it down, although she never revealed her true reason. As silly as she supposed it was, Rebecca had thought that somehow if Gage were not dead, if he were to search for her, it would be easier for him to find her in the back of a dress shop in town. That if she lived here with Abbie on this high bluff that overlooked Clackamas Falls, he might not be able to. It was a ridiculous daydream, she knew. Gage *was* dead, and he was not looking for her.

"Let's see, now, we'll have to think about your dress, and a guest list. You and Aaron are going to the Sweetheart's Dance tomorrow night, aren't you? I'm sure Martha Robbins will be there—you can talk to her about the cake. She's made every wedding cake in these parts since . . ."

Rebecca caught her breath and laughed again. "Slow down, Abbie!"

But Abbie charged ahead with her talent for organizing. She scrutinized Rebecca with a critical eye. "Hmm, too bad brides have to wear white."

"Abigail!" Rebecca gasped. Every time she believed she could not be shocked by Abbie's radical ideas, she was proven wrong. "Of course brides should wear white. It confirms their virtue, their . . . their . . ."

"Nonsense," Abbie snorted, "it does nothing of the kind. I've known several women who went to the altar in ten yards of white satin and then delivered healthy six- or seven-month babies. I'm just saying that with your chestnut hair and those green eyes, you'd look beautiful in blush pink satin, or maybe even dove gray. Speaking of hair, I hope you'll let me take it out of that bun for your wedding day. It will look better under the veil. Well, no matter. Of course, you must have the wedding here."

Abigail Chatfield prattled on with wedding plans until she called for Old Ben, the gardener, to drive Rebecca home.

The buggy arrived at the back of the dress shop just as it began to rain, and she hurried inside. When she lit the lamp, it revealed the plainly furnished room, and she looked around as if she had never seen it before. The worn settee, the little stove in the corner, the tiny curtained alcove that served as a bedroom. She had done what she could to make the place comfortable and homey, adding little touches where she could. But after living here for three years, it would not be hard to turn her back on it and go to her husband's home.

Husband. She would be Mrs. Aaron Monroe, not Mrs. Gage Bristol, as she had dreamed a lifetime ago.

She had found the western frontier to be a brash, alien borderland peopled with mountain men, Indians, homesteaders, cowboys, adventurers, and those like Rebecca herself, who sought forgetfulness or a new start. The price of a new start, though, had been unutterable homesickness.

She had come from a place of humid summer heat and soft-spoken voices, where the days passed slowly, and courtesy and decorum were as gravely important as they had been in the age of chivalry. But when she had left Georgia the South was struggling with Reconstruction, and she knew that the only way of life she had ever known had disappeared forever.

And now, in accepting Aaron's proposal, she felt as though she were truly bidding that life goodbye for the last time.

With steps like a sleepwalker's, Rebecca went to her trunk and opened the lid. Inside were memories from that other life: a lock of her father's hair wrapped in a scrap of tissue paper with her mother's wedding band, a silver-backed mirror, her own engagement ring. These few small keepsakes she had managed to hide from an invading army by burying them in the side yard at the home place.

Setting these aside, she reached deeper into the trunk for the last treasure, the sweetest remembrance of all. It was a heart-shaped box, decorated with yellowing lace and faded ribbon. Gage had given it to her the night he proposed.

It had been on Valentine's Day. There had been a ball that night too, like the Sweetheart's Dance that Abbie had mentioned at dinner. Gage had kissed her in the shadows when she accepted, and whispered how much he loved her. The memory of his soft, urgent kisses still had the power to bring heat to her cheeks.

During their brief stolen moments she had permitted liberties that no lady really could and still call herself a lady. But Gage had been like no other man of her acquaintance.

Elemental, she supposed, like fire and wind and cold, clear water, he had pulled her to him without even touching her. And he had drawn those feelings from her with his lips and hands. Sometimes he would drop by Daddy's store and she would feel his eyes on her. They were like blue fire and they conveyed what he did not need to say. *You're mine, Rebecca. I love you and don't you ever doubt it.*

Rebecca smiled slightly. Oh, Daddy had not liked Gage at all, despite the fact that he had known him since Gage was a boy. Or perhaps because of it. His relaxed, easygoing charm received no quarter from Phillip Baxter. Too wild and too damned handsome for his own good, Daddy had groused, he'd never earn an honest dollar. Probably couldn't plow a straight furrow, he'd speculated. But that hadn't mattered. Gage had not been a farmer, he'd been a saddle maker. The fact that he took over his father's saddlery down the street from Baxter's General Merchandise, and doubled the shop's income, had not improved Daddy's opinion.

When Gage had asked for Rebecca's hand her father had refused, and they made plans to elope. It had been a daring scheme, especially on Rebecca's part. She could not defy her father. But she could not deny Gage, her handsome, exciting fiancé.

Then the war came, and Gage had been in a hurry to join the army and make them all proud. Phillip Baxter reluctantly succumbed and gave his blessing. Gage had stopped by the house on his way to the train, glorious in his gray uniform, as blond as a wheat field, as tall as a pine. Rebecca had stood in the front yard, gripping her handkerchief and trying to be brave. No other soldier had ever looked as handsome, as heroic, and she loved him with all the ardor and heartbreak a young woman could possibly feel. He'd be back in a few weeks, he had promised. Two months at the most.

But the weeks and months had stretched into years, and he had not come back.

Now Gage and her father and mother were together somewhere in a land she could not reach.

Carefully she opened the lace and beribboned box, and

inhaled the faintest fragrance of chocolate that still lingered within. Once it had held the confection, dark and rich and bittersweet. Now it held the letters that he had sent her. There weren't many. Letters from the field had been hard to get. Some of them were grimy with dirt, a few nearly illegible from the rain that had fallen on them before she received them.

Beneath the letters lay Gage's gold pocket watch, sent to her by his commanding officer with a letter of condolence.

Regret to inform you ... Major Bristol fought valiantly ... a credit to his men and the Confederacy ...

Rebecca gripped the watch in her hand so tightly the stem dug into her palm. It saddened her to discover that his image in her mind had faded. She could no longer picture distinctly what shade of blue his eyes had been, or feature the precise shape of his mouth.

"Gage," she murmured aloud to him, as she sometimes did, "Aaron Monroe asked me to marry him. The first two times he asked I dilly-dallied because I still grieved for you." She took a deep breath. "Today he asked again and I said yes. It won't be the same with Aaron as with you, I don't think. No one could be like you. But I want a home and children, and he's a decent man." Tears edged her eyes and softened the harsh lamp flame to a blur. "I loved you with my whole heart ... my whole soul. You'll always have a place in me. But you're gone now, and I-I'm tired of being alone."

The tears that streamed down her cheeks were matched by the wind-driven rain on the window. Gently, she replaced the watch and closed the box, then put it in the bottom of her trunk.

"Goodbye, Gage."

❧ *Chapter 2* ❧

The next evening, Rebecca dressed with special care. Aaron was coming to escort her to the Sweetheart's Dance. The Ladies' Poetry Reading Circle sponsored the annual Valentine's event held at the armory, but she had never attended before and she was filled with excitement. There would be refreshments and decorations and music, a real party.

She had not danced since those final days before the war, when Gage had twirled her in his arms across the ballroom floor at a Christmas social. The gown she had worn—well, it had been . . . Slowly, she dropped her hands from her face as she considered her reflection. Rebecca could no longer remember what she had worn to that ball. She realized that over the course of the last few years the tiny details of those memories had begun to fade, slowly, imperceptibly, until only their outlines were left. She had thought that sleep might elude her last night after her farewell to Gage, that his face and touch and kisses would haunt her dreams, as they had for so long. There had been many nights when she awoke with a start, certain that she heard him knocking on her door, or talking to her. And she had known nights when sleep would not come at all and she watched the darkness until it faded with the sunrise.

But nothing had invaded her sleep last night. If she needed a sign to begin a new life with Aaron, perhaps that was it.

Rebecca stood at the mirror over her washstand, pinching

her cheeks and checking her hair. Abbie had teased her about her plain hairstyle, but it seemed suitable to her occupation and her life. Sometimes she wished she could be more like Abigail, more daring, more flamboyant. In fact, she had been freer as a young woman before the war. She had laughed and danced and been bold enough to plan an elopement with a man her father disliked. But time and events had matured her into a circumspect woman, and that was reflected in everything she did. She considered the dark blue wool gown she wore tonight. It had turned out beautifully, and the finely tatted lace trim around the neck and sleeves was just the right touch. Hesitantly, she reached for a small bottle that Abbie had given her, and removed its stopper to dab a bit of rose-water behind her ears. Her father had frowned on colognes for women; only women of questionable virtue used cosmetics or perfume. But this was a special night, she thought. Just a bit wouldn't hurt.

Following a quick glance out the window, she slipped a pair of small aquamarine earrings into her ears and was satisfied with her appearance. Thank heavens it had finally stopped raining. Rain fell for days at a time here in the Northwest, sometimes even for a week or two, a fact of the weather to which she still had not become accustomed. To see a half-moon rising in clearing skies was a relief; the puddles outside were already deep enough to ruin her dress.

She had stitched its seams in the evenings after shop hours, sometimes late into the night. A remark that Aaron had made yesterday drifted through her mind again, the one about sewing for her family rather than strangers. That was all she had intended to do with her skill. Never once had she imagined that her talent with a needle would earn her living. Now she squirreled away every penny she could with dreams of opening her own shop, and hoped that Aaron would understand. She could see it in her mind's eye—a larger, brighter location than Mrs. Walker's, with one or two other seamstresses, perhaps with ready-made gowns as well as custom—

A sharp knock on her door brought her out of her thoughts.

With a final hurried glimpse at the mirror, she plucked her cloak and fan from the settee.

Though the rain had stopped, it was still chilly and she could see Aaron's breath in the lamplight when she opened her door.

Stepping inside her tiny parlor, he hovered near the doorway, bringing the scent of rain-washed air with him. He wore a black suit, one that she recognized from a display in his store window. Aaron was a thrifty man, one of his qualities that her father would have approved of.

He gaped at her slack-jawed before recovering his usual reserve. "Rebecca—you look, I mean—your dress is very nice."

She smiled. "Thank you, Aaron." It was an awkward compliment, not like— She forced herself to halt the comparison. It wasn't fair to Aaron or to her. Then her eyes fell upon a small heart-shaped box that he extended to her and she forgot everything else. "For me?"

He shrugged self-consciously. "Well, I found—"

"Oh, Aaron," she murmured. She gripped the box in both hands and stared at it. The faint aroma of chocolate rose from it. Her gaze shifted from the package to his hazel eyes and back again. His courtship had been rather dry, but this—she felt her throat tighten a bit. Delight and budding affection ignited within her. "What a lovely gift. How did you know? I haven't tasted chocolate in ever so long." She beamed up at him. "Thank you very much." Impulsively, she reached up to peck his cheek.

His face reddened back to his ears and for a moment he seemed to melt under her admiration. "Um, I, well—you're welcome," he fumbled and jammed his hands into his pockets. "I hoped you might like it."

She looked fondly at the box again. Decorated with lace and a wide rose-colored ribbon, it was the first gift he had given her. Certainly a man's sincerity and intentions could not be determined by gifts alone—Rebecca had not expected a present from Aaron. But his thoughtfulness tonight went a long way to make her feel special, and to help her overcome any lingering doubts. How strange that this first gift should be the same one that Gage had given her. She placed it gently on the lamp table.

She turned the key to lock her door, and then Aaron helped her into his buggy waiting outside. "I've so looked forward to tonight, I can't wait to dance again."

Climbing in beside her, he said, "I've never done much dancing myself, I always thought it was a lot of foolishness. I usually go to these socials because it's good for business."

Rebecca took up the challenge as she tucked her skirts in. "Maybe dancing with me will be more fun than foolishness."

From the deep shadows of a nearby alley, a rain-soaked stranger watched the couple pull away in the buggy. He had waited and watched for days with the patience of a cat, hoping to see the woman without being seen himself. Always she had eluded him.

Now he emerged, holding his gaze on the horse as it splashed past his hiding place, through puddles and sucking mud. The wheels made a slick, wet noise as they rolled over the street, and he caught a glimpse of pink skirt in a rectangle of lamplight. Then the buggy turned the corner at the end of the block and was gone, lost under the timid light of a February half moon.

The stranger sighed and withdrew to the shadows once more.

The armory was a musty old barnlike building, and it smelled of damp wool wraps and a confusion of hair tonics and colognes. But as Rebecca watched Aaron head off toward the cloak room, she found all of it exciting.

Against one wall, long tables were covered with white cloths and laden with cakes and pies and other treats. Punch bowls were set up at strategic intervals, and a beer keg had been installed by the back door. At the end of the big room, the musicians were tuning up, and chairs and benches lined the other wall. Though flowers weren't available in February, the decorations included red bunting and paper lace.

Greetings were called back and forth, and the noise level began to rise as the room filled. Colorful gowns, many of which Rebecca had made, graced the women, although some ladies from the farming community wore less dressy clothes. The clothing of the men varied as well, ranging from suits on the businessmen, to clean work clothes worn by the homesteaders. She even saw a couple of trappers who lingered by the beer keg, dressed in buckskins and carrying their long rifles. They reminded her of the swamp men who used to come into her father's store.

Aaron had been gone several minutes when the music and dancing began. She scanned the hall hoping to find him on his way back. But when she spotted him he was in a conversation with the bank president and a few other merchants.

"Rebecca! How lovely you look!"

She turned and saw Abigail Chatfield approaching on the arm of Mobrey Dryden, who owned a very successful sawmill. Abbie looked stunning in the sapphire faille gown Rebecca had made for her. The color set off perfectly her cascade of jet curls. Her plump figure had been corseted into a flawless hourglass shape, emphasizing a waist that begged the span of a man's hands. Plainly, Mobrey was quite taken by his supremely feminine companion. He was a good fifteen years older than Abbie, and a lifetime of rich food and drink had given him the paunch of a middle-aged man, which was accentuated by the watch chain looped across it. But his face was as flushed as a schoolboy's in her presence. He squired her to Rebecca as if she were a queen in a sedan chair.

After the introductions were made, Abbie asked, "Where is Aaron?"

Rebecca inclined her head. "He went to the cloak room a few minutes ago with our wraps, but," he glanced briefly at Rebecca, "I think he's probably discussing drayage or the price of sugar with those gentlemen over there."

Abbie glanced at the group of men and her brows knitted just slightly. "Do be a dear, Mobrey, and fetch us some punch."

The man bowed—Rebecca expected to hear him click his heels—then he bent over Abbie's hand. "Certainly, ladies, it would be my pleasure. Miss Abigail, until I return . . ."

"Thank God!" Abbie exclaimed in a low voice as she watched Mobrey disappear into the crowd.

Amused, Rebecca said, "He's very attentive."

Abbie snapped open her fan and employed it with vigor. "Yes, he is, to the point of suffocation. I wish I'd devised a way to keep him busy longer. But, heavens, at least he didn't desert me for some boring old business meeting. He'd definitely hear about it if he did."

Rebecca shrugged and felt compelled to make an excuse for Aaron. "I'm sure Aaron will be right back. He told me he conducts a lot of business at these gatherings. Anyway, he said he doesn't much like to dance."

"Well, honey, he's your fiancé. He's supposed to at least *pretend* to like it. That man needs some training in the ways of courtship. Hmmm, we'll have to see about this. You remember the old saying about all work and no play—"

Abigail continued but her chatting faded to the back of Rebecca's mind. She became aware of the peculiar feeling that she was being watched. Glancing around, she saw no one in the armory who seemed to be paying her undue attention. But the feeling persisted, as if someone studied her from the shadows. Stranger than that, her senses were heightened; she felt her dress resting against her body, she smelled the rain-washed night.

She forgot about both Abbie and the odd sensation, though, when old Judge Malloy stepped up on the musicians' platform and brought the music and dancers to a halt in mid-song.

Smiling, he held up his hands for quiet. "Friends, I've just had a piece of news that is too good to keep to myself." This captured everyone's attention, and he appeared to relish the moment. "Now I might be letting the cat out of the bag with this, but I think everyone would like to know that our own Aaron Monroe is getting married to Miss Rebecca Baxter."

Rebecca felt her face flood with color before she thought to close her mouth. "How on earth did he find out—"

A murmuring buzz swept the guests, and heads craned to get a look at both her and Aaron on the other side of the hall. Those nearest Rebecca offered her best wishes, and then Judge Malloy motioned her forward.

"Come on up here, Miss Rebecca, and you, too, Aaron. Folks, let's drink a toast to the happy couple!"

"Go on, Rebecca," Abbie urged with a laugh. She stepped forward and joined the judge and Aaron on the platform.

Aaron grinned at her sheepishly, and quite charmingly too, Rebecca thought. It was a face that he had not shown her before, and her heart lightened as they stood together to accept the toasts and good wishes. Abbie offered a laughing, two-handed toast with the glasses that Mobrey had brought back to her.

"When is the wedding?" Martha Robbins asked. "I'll bake the cake."

"Miss Rebecca, if you give up the seamstress business my wife is going to be sorry, but you'll save me a passel of money," Frank Watson laughed, and earned a poke in the ribs from Ann Watson.

"Aaron, you two come to my store for your furniture. I'll give you a good price," Mr. Perlman called.

Until this moment, Rebecca had not realized how completely Willamette Springs had become her home, or how much a part of her life these people now were.

As her gaze wandered over the smiling faces in front of her she caught a glimpse of a stranger in the back doorway. The contact of her eyes with his was so brief, she wasn't even sure what she had seen before he slipped outside. He was dressed in old clothes and was as shaggy as one of the trappers, but he had seemed disturbingly familiar somehow. And the look in his eyes burned hauntingly.

Rebecca was positive she had never seen that man before in her life. And she was just as certain that she never wanted to see him again.

*　　　*　　　*

It was close to midnight when Aaron pulled the buggy to a stop at Rebecca's door. "Did you have a nice time?" he asked.

"Yes, and I'm glad that you finally decided to dance with me," she teased. The circumstances of their impromptu engagement party had forced Aaron into turning her on the dance floor a few times. She had not been surprised to discover that he had no particular talent for it. "Do you still think it's just foolishness?"

She saw his faint, brief smile in the glow of the lamp she'd left burning in her parlor window. "Well, maybe not. I'll have to practice if I'm going to dance with you at our wedding."

Tentatively, he reached for her gloved hand. "Rebecca, I'm not a man to talk about romance and stardust and such. I guess some women like that folderol, it just isn't—well, you won't be hearing it from me. But I want you to know that I'm glad you're going to be my wife. And I'll make sure that you never lack for anything. I'll put a good roof over your head and good food on the table. You'll never need to sew for pay again."

"Aaron . . ." she murmured, and tightened her fingers around his. Daddy would have approved, she thought. Aaron Monroe would feed and house her body; perhaps the nurturing of her heart and spirit would come from their children and her business. If she gathered the nerve to tell him about her plan for a shop.

He leaned a bit closer until his face was just inches from her own. She detected the yeasty scent of the one beer he had drunk, and then his lips pressed to hers, awkward and brief.

It was not the kiss she remembered from that long past Valentine's Day, demanding and powerful. But that had been years ago now, when the blood of youth had run higher and faster. Maybe this calm, steady betrothal with Aaron was more grown up.

He jumped down from the buggy and came around to her

side. Walking her to her door, he said, "Start thinking about a wedding date."

She nodded and looked up into his serious face. "Yes, I will. A Saturday in May might be nice, when the flowers are in bloom."

He lifted his hat to smooth his pomaded hair beneath, then replaced it. "No, a Sunday would be better. Saturdays are my biggest days at the store. And I don't trust either of the clerks to manage by themselves."

"But for your own wedding, couldn't you close for the day? Or maybe close a few hours early?" she asked.

He looked at her as though she had suggested giving away his inventory. "Well, Rebecca, that store will be our bread and butter. I'm not greedy, and I'd never cheat or lie to make money. But I sure won't turn it away when it comes to my own door."

A hint of disappointment nudged her. "Oh, I see. Of course not. We'll have a Sunday wedding, then."

He flapped the reins on his horse's back and the buggy pulled away. As Rebecca watched him go, it began to rain again.

✑ *Chapter 3* ✑

"*T*hat's just wonderful news about you and Mr. Monroe," Dolly Tull chattered in the shop late the next afternoon. She was there for her fourth dress fitting and expected Rebecca to perform the miracle of making Dolly's three-hundred-pound girth look half its size. The woman had complained that the garment made her "seem fat."

A mouthful of pins prevented Rebecca from doing more than making noncommittal noises, but that was all Dolly needed to continue.

"He's a real catch, if you ask me," she said, obviously admiring her own reflection in the full-length mirror. "He's the hardest worker I've ever seen. I think he'd keep that store open seven days a week if he could. My late husband, rest his soul, was a dear man but lazy, lazy, lazy. Give me a man who'll work and take care of his fam—oh, Rebecca, don't take that flounce away. It's so feminine. Can't we reduce the bulk somewhere else?"

It would help if you reduced your bulk, Mrs. Tull.

Oh, how Rebecca wished she could say it. It wasn't like her to be mean-spirited, but she was annoyed with Dolly and with Sarah Walker. Mrs. Walker had wired her this morning to say that she would be lingering in Denver another month while her sister recovered from a difficult childbirth. Rebecca had more work than she could handle alone, but lacked the authority or the means to hire help. Sarah took seventy-five percent of everything she made, so that didn't leave much for her dress shop fund.

After a few more adjustments, she managed to satisfy Dolly Tull, and edged her toward the door with secret relief. The day had been long and she was tired. She still had to sweep up before she could go up to Abigail's for her dinner.

"Well, I must be on my way, dear. I'll call for that dress, shall we say tomorrow at this time?" Dolly said.

"Oh, let's say day after tomorrow, Mrs. Tull," she replied, keeping a smile in her voice.

Dolly left smiling, too, and Rebecca hurried to close the door and pull the shades before the woman could change her mind and return. She had the tasseled pull in her hand to draw the last shade when a figure on the other side of the street caught her eye.

She stood in the window, mesmerized. A man with long dark blond hair and a shaggy beard stood in the doorway of a vacant storefront. He watched her for only a moment, then turned down an alley immediately next to the building. A ripple of fear rushed through her and then was still.

He was the same man she had seen the night before at the armory. And although the beard concealed the entire lower half of his face, and his hat the upper third, his eyes still burned with a haunted look. Again she was swamped with the feeling of familiarity.

She remained at the window until dusk began to gather, peeking around the edge of the green shade after she pulled it. The man did not return, and she finally decided it was safe to throw on her cloak and hurry to Abbie's for dinner.

When she arrived, she told her the story.

"What does he look like?" Abigail asked, leaning forward slightly as if secretly enjoying the mystery. Her fork, a green bean impaled on its tines, paused in its journey to her mouth.

"He looks . . . weary," she answered, realizing that aside from the stranger's physical features, his fatigue was most noticeable. She went on to describe the long hair and beard.

"Good heavens, Rebecca, that's frightening," Abigail said. "I swear I don't know where all these ruffians are coming from, but it seems as if Willamette Springs has more than its share. Have you told Aaron about this?''

Rebecca shook her head. ''I didn't mention it last night because I didn't think much of it. And I came up here right after I saw the man today.''

''And you have no idea who he could be?'' she asked, reaching for the salt.

''Not at all. I've never seen him before in my life.'' But why did she feel she had? she wondered as she toyed with the corner of her napkin.

''Well, promise me that you'll tell Aaron or the sheriff. They'll make short work of this man, whoever he is, and send him on his way.'' Abbie rose from her chair. ''Finish your dinner, honey, but I'm off to dress.''

Rebecca lifted her brows as she considered her. She already wore an afternoon gown so beautifully elaborate, she could have gone anywhere in it.

Abbie idly twisted a perfect black ringlet on her finger, looking like a cat with a pint of cream. ''Andrew Winters, that nice bank manager, is escorting me to the theater tonight.'' Willamette Springs, though perched on the edge of wilderness, was not without certain cosmopolitan features, Rebecca had discovered.

''Ah, and is Mr. Winters less suffocating than Mobrey Dryden?'' she teased.

''Why, yes he is. In fact, he has been quite shy, a quality that I find very appealing. It might amuse you to know that if Aaron hadn't set his sights on you, I would have enjoyed pursuing him for that exact reason.'' Rebecca's eyes flew open and she laughed. ''Oh, don't worry, he's all yours.''

''What will you do with Mr. Winters now that you have his attention?''

''Oh, nothing, honey. The fun is in the chase, not the capture. I have no interest in settling down again—I like my freedom too much. Now be sure to let Old Ben drive you home when you're ready to go. And have Aaron handle that stranger loitering around your shop.''

"I will," Rebecca promised as she watched Abbie climb her beautifully carved staircase.

But for no reason she could give herself, she knew it was a promise that she would not keep.

That night Rebecca tossed and turned with strange dreams. Sometimes she saw Aaron wearing the suit from his display window, and waiting for her at the bottom of Abbie's staircase with a parlor full of wedding guests standing behind him. Other times, she dreamed of her wedding night and felt his hands and lips moving feverishly over her bare skin, felt the tug of his mouth on her nipple. But when she wound her hands through his hair and he lifted his head to kiss her, she saw not Aaron's face but the stranger's. And the most frightening, most incomprehensible part of all was that she found the vivid dreams of the stranger to be indecently arousing. Only Gage had touched her so intimately, and that had been long ago.

The clock in her parlor was softly chiming three o'clock when she flung back the covers and sat up. Both her hair and her nightgown were twisted around her like ropes. She had too many thoughts whirling in her mind to sleep: the grueling workload, her plans for her own dress shop, and the nagging suspicion that Aaron would object to those plans.

Then there was the stranger with the haunted eyes. What in the world could there be about an unkempt drifter that made her feel as if she knew him, when she was thoroughly positive that she did not? Was he really following her?

The thought weighed on her mind until she stood and pushed aside the alcove curtain, and crept through her room to the front of the dark shop. The ghostly figure of the dressmaker's dummy lurked in the corner, draped in a swag of fabric, but she kept her gaze away from it. Pausing with her fingertips on the edge of the window shade, she hovered there for a moment. Apprehension made her heart pound like a drum in her chest, and her throat was dry as dust, as if she expected to see a face pressed to the glass, just inches from her own.

Finally she pulled aside the shade and looked. But the street was empty and quiet with the kind of desolate silence that only deep night could bring. She went back to bed and flopped onto the mattress. She worried for nothing, she told herself. Chance had probably put that drifter across the street from her shop a couple of times, and at the dance. He might have even moved on by now.

"Go to sleep," she ordered herself aloud, and clamped her eyes shut. But it was nearly dawn before she was able to comply.

Rebecca's sleeplessness told on her in the morning and she was late opening the shop. She awoke with a start just before nine o'clock and raced in five directions all at once.

After washing her face and pulling on her clothes, she hurried to the front of the shop to raise the shades. At least it looked like it would be a clear day for a change. The sun was bright in a clear blue sky that almost hinted at spring. She stopped at one of the fitting mirrors to rip her brush through her long tangled hair a couple of times. Then she grabbed the broom and unlocked the door to go outside and sweep the walk. But when she opened the door she tripped and nearly flew headlong over a paper-wrapped box that fell across the threshold.

Maybe it was her thread order from Chicago. She'd placed it weeks ago at Aaron's store, and the empty spools were beginning to mount up with the extra work. But there was no note on the package—it wasn't even addressed. Baffled, she picked it up and carried it inside.

When she snipped the twine and tore off the brown paper, though, she could only stare at the package beneath. She did not find thread. Instead, in her hands she held a lace and ribbon-covered heart-shaped box. It was very much like the one Aaron had brought her the other night. And within, she found chocolate, just as she had two nights earlier. Its heady fragrance drifted up to her nose and she inhaled it as if it were a bouquet of roses. Although she'd had no breakfast, she could not resist tasting one of the delectable morsels. She bit down on a piece and waves of flavor filled her mouth, rich and dark and bittersweet. She smiled to herself.

Aaron might have told her that he wasn't a romantic type, and on the surface she would believe it. After all, he had come into the shop and demanded an answer to his proposal, saying that he wanted to marry her, but he never said why. Did he love her, could he not live without her? Did he long to reach for her in the night and take her into his arms? Did he want her by his side for all time?

All right, she knew she was being fanciful and unrealistic. Aaron was never going to tell her those things. At least she had heard them once in her life, in that other life. Still, if leaving chocolate on her doorstep was not romantic, how else could it be described? Of course, it had to be from him— the package looked so much like the last one he had given her. And when she stopped to consider it, the lack of a note guaranteed he was responsible. He could bring her chocolate, but he could not bring himself to tell her how he felt.

Around lunchtime, Rebecca was struggling to put Dolly Tull's gown on the dressmaker's dummy. It stood in a corner that was too small; in fact, the whole shop was too small. Heaving a deep, exasperated sigh, she glanced up and saw the chocolate box again. It would be a good time to get out of here for a while, she thought.

Putting on her cloak, she locked the shop and walked down to Monroe's Mercantile. It was a prosperous and tidy place, almost painfully neat. Jars, bottles, cans and boxes lined the walls, and crates and barrels created displays on the floor. Aaron was just finishing the sale of a butter churn to a woman and her two young daughters when Rebecca came in.

"Oh, I don't know," the woman fretted a bit, and pointed to a churn. "This one is more money than I expected to spend."

"I know it is, Mrs. James, and if I thought the cheaper model was right for you, I'd recommend it in an instant. But I sincerely believe that this other one is what you need. Not only will it be easier for you to use, but your two assistants here won't have any trouble either." He leaned over the counter and smiled at the girls. "And the solid oak construction will last much longer."

He was so much different with customers, not as serious, Rebecca realized as she watched him from the pickle barrel. Outgoing and friendly, yet respectful and courteous, he charmed the mother and won over the girls by giving them each a peppermint stick.

After the transaction was concluded, Aaron took off his apron and smiled at Rebecca. "I'm glad you're here," he said, grabbing his coat, "and just in time for lunch. Let's go over to the café."

"That sounds wonderful," she replied, surprised by the offer. Aaron never left the store in the middle of the day. It wasn't that he didn't trust the young clerks who worked for him, she knew. Aaron simply didn't think anyone but he could handle a problem if one came up. But today he opened the door with only one backward glance at his clerk. Although the sun was bright, the street remained a treacherous slick of mud and he took her elbow to guide her across to the restaurant. He seemed to be in high spirits, as if he'd had good news.

"Bring us two bowls of corn chowder, Gladys," he called to the waitress. "Yours is the best in town." Then to Rebecca, "I hope chowder is all right with you."

"It's fine. I really came by to thank you for the chocolate. To get lunch too is a bonus."

He waved it off. "You already thanked me the other night, Rebecca."

"You're in a good mood," she commented with a smile.

"I had a good morning." Leaning forward, he grasped her hand. "I made a deal this morning with the owners of a logging camp just east of here. I'm going to provide all their staples—flour, sugar, salt, coffee—everything. It'll be worth a lot of money." He went on to explain the details, then stopped himself when Gladys delivered two steaming dishes of chowder. He chuckled. "Sorry, I guess I got carried away. You don't want to talk about my business. My wife won't need to know anything about that—you'll only need to know about taking care of my house and my children.''

Rebecca sat up straighter. If ever there was an opportunity— ''Oh, no, Aaron, I'm really interested in business. In fact, I'll want to keep sewing.''

He poked a spoonful of chowder into his mouth and nodded while he chewed. Swallowing the bite he said, ''I've been thinking about that. We'll build a house with a nice bright corner for your sewing room. You can make frocks for yourself and shirts for me. You'll have your pick from any fabric I carry in the store.''

She shook her head. ''No, I mean I want to keep working.''

''What—you mean for Sarah Walker? What for?''

''Not for Mrs. Walker. I'm saving money to open a shop of my own. That's been my dream for months and months. I've almost tripled Mrs. Walker's business but I know I could do better with a place of my own and more seamstresses. I have so many ideas—''

He looked dumbfounded. ''But you won't need to work. The world is a hard place, Rebecca, full of hard people.'' The drifter's image rose in her mind. ''Why would you want to be out in it when you belong at home?''

This was precisely the kind of response she expected, but hoped not to get. How could she make Aaron understand that while she disliked her present circumstances at Mrs. Walker's, she enjoyed what she did?

''But you like your work at the store, Aaron, it makes you . . . happy, doesn't it? You wouldn't want to give that up, would you?'' she reasoned.

''*That isn't—*'' he said, his voice climbing in volume. A couple of people at nearby tables turned to look. ''It isn't the same,'' he whispered just as emphatically. ''Married women aren't supposed to work. Not when they have a husband who can take care of them.''

''Well, let's not talk about it here,'' she urged, making a tactical retreat. God, she didn't want to argue about this in public. More heads were turning.

"I'm not sure I want to discuss it at all, Rebecca." Aaron put his napkin on the table, along with a dollar for the lunches. "I have to get back to the store."

They left the restaurant, and Aaron guided her back across the street, this time in silence.

"We'll talk later, all right?" he said, his tone softer.

She looked up at him, at the hazel eyes and the concerned expression. He *was* a good man, and she knew he had her best interests at heart. If only he understood what those best interests really were.

She nodded. "All right." She turned to go back to the shop under gathering clouds.

In fact, two days passed and although Rebecca saw Aaron, the subject of her shop did not come up again. She was too busy with her work to wrestle with it. They probably had several adjustments and understandings to come to but she still had lots of time for that until May.

One evening just at dusk she sat in her parlor hemming a petticoat for a new customer. Reaching over she adjusted the lamp flame on the table next to her to get a better look at the tiny white stitches. Her only company was the soft snap of wood in the stove and the tick of her clock. The lulling sounds combined with the repetitive flash of her needle, and her thoughts began to wander down old paths, to faces long gone, to desires and dreams now as dead as those she had lost. Sometimes she wondered where she had gotten the nerve to board a train to a strange land with only a few dollars more than her fare, and all of her possessions packed in a small trunk.

The uncertainty of the last few years had made her realize how fortunate she was to have her sewing skill. She had seen women who lacked respectable abilities forced into marriage to men with unsavory backgrounds. Some were reduced to polite poverty who lived on the dwindling charity of friends, falling back on the Southern tradition that required households to take in indigent females. But when the homes were gone, when there was no food left to feed all the mouths, what became of those women?

Realizing that her white spool was empty, she put aside the petticoat and went into the darkened shop to find another. Where *was* that thread order? she wondered again. If it didn't come in the next couple of days, Aaron would simply have to track it down to the manufacturer.

She was rummaging in a small cabinet when suddenly she heard a stirring outside the shop door. She stopped and listened for a moment. It must be the thin, gray-striped cat who had taken to coming to the front door. She usually didn't have anything to feed it, but tonight Abigail had sent a pot of beef stew home with her. She went to the door and without peeking around the shade, turned the key.

Opening the door, she began, "I'll bet you're hungry, aren't you, poor—"

But it wasn't the little cat. It was a man. With long, dark blond hair and a bushy beard, and he was in the process of putting a small, paper-wrapped package on her doorstep.

Startled, Rebecca gasped. He jumped back a step, apparently just as startled. He was taller than she had realized, and he stared at her with haunted blue eyes. He pulled his hat brim lower. Familiar . . . so familiar . . .

"I know you," she whispered, incredulous. She put her hand to her throat, as if she could slow the pulse that pounded like a hammer there and stole her breath. Her fingers on her skin were ice cold. Yes, she knew him, but from where?

"Becca, I—" he began, but then backed away, as if in fear of her. He turned and hurried away into the lowering darkness, a slight limp hampering his progress.

"Oh, God," she sobbed dryly, wracked with the tremors of one who had seen a ghost. She extended her shaking hand in his direction but he had already disappeared up the street. "Dear God!"

Gage Bristol was alive.

❧ *Chapter 4* ❧

*R*ebecca sat by the shop window that night, huddled in a quilt, and shaken to her very soul. Again and again she tried to assimilate those few moments with Gage. A hundred questions zigzagged through her mind, questions for which she had no answers.

At various turns she doubted her own sanity. Had that really been Gage, or had it been a ghost? No, it had to have been him. He looked different now, older and as tired as if he were seventy instead of thirty. But his voice was the same; she had heard it so many times in her dreams. Furthermore, tonight he had called her the nickname that he'd given her when she was just a girl. In fact it had been so long since she'd heard it, she had nearly forgotten it. *Becca.*

Obviously, some hideous error had been made when she was told of his death, but what had really happened to him? Where had he been all this time, and how had he tracked her to Willamette Springs?

And why, oh, why, after all these years, after the heartbreak of missing him and then losing him, why hadn't he stayed to talk to her?

She looked down at the unopened heart-shaped box on her lap. Had *Gage* been the one who left her the package yesterday? Suddenly she recalled something that Aaron had said to her when she thanked him for the anonymous chocolate she believed he had brought to her door. *You already thanked me the other night.* She felt too dazed to contemplate that on top of everything else.

Only one fact kept surfacing above the whirling confusion, and it was perhaps the most confounding truth of all: Gage Bristol was alive and Rebecca was engaged to marry Aaron Monroe.

"Good Lord, you look white and scared—are you sure it was him?" Abigail, tousled from sleep but beautifully so, stared at Rebecca across the marble-topped table in her bedroom. Rebecca had dressed and raced up here as soon as it was light. As she hurried along, she had peered into the face of every wagon driver she passed on the street, every horseman, every pedestrian. She had not seen Gage again.

Rebecca sprinkled sugar into her cup. Her breathless dawn arrival had put the entire household into a tizzy, and coffee and biscuits were brought up from the kitchen.

"At first I doubted it myself. How could it be Gage? The letter I received said he'd been killed." She went on to tell Abbie about the nickname. "No one else has ever called me that. Only he did. And now that I've had time to think about it, I realize why he seemed so familiar to me when I saw him in the shadows and at the dance." Rebecca closed her hands into tight fists on her lap. "But that's all I know. He's been watching me—I saw him. I don't know why, though, or why he never spoke to me."

Abbie shrugged. "If he was at the Sweetheart's Dance like you thought, he found out that you're engaged. Maybe that has something to do with it." She toyed with her spoon and then glanced up at Rebecca. "You're in a rather curious position, Rebecca, betrothed to two men."

"But I'm not, really," she protested. "I'm engaged only to Aaron."

"Are you going to tell Aaron about this?"

That was another one of the questions that she had asked herself during the long night by the window. She looked down at her hands. "I don't know."

"Well, Gage might be alive, but until he seeks you out

again—if he does—I don't suppose you have to do anything. For all you know, he could be married to someone else himself."

Rebecca's head came up. Married? The idea was impossible for her to accept. "No, no, I don't think so." She swallowed hard, and her voice dropped. "He looks as if no one in the world cares for him at all."

"Except you?"

Except her.

Rebecca left Abbie's house to open the shop, and she had no more answers than she'd had when she arrived. For the rest of the day, she was distracted and jumpy with her customers. When Dolly Tull arrived to collect her new dress, her high praise over Rebecca's alterations had no impact.

Aaron even ventured into the shop again at closing time and offered to buy her dinner at Gladys's café. Rebecca was tempted to plead a headache and refuse, but a vague guilty feeling forced her to accept. She picked at her food and made one-word responses to his conversation. She knew that Aaron thought her angry with him from the day before, but she could find no words to make him feel otherwise. Her own emotions and thoughts were in too much turmoil.

But after a couple of nights of fitful sleep, life for Rebecca began to return to normal. Gage made no more appearances, and she found no more chocolates at her doorstep. She still did not know what had happened to him in the war, or how he had found her in Oregon. But she feared she would become unhinged if she belabored the situation. None of her worrying or speculation had produced an explanation. Her only choice was to move on with her wedding and business plans as if she had not seen him.

If that were possible.

One gray afternoon a week later, Rebecca was sitting at her sewing machine trying to free the bobbin which had become hopelessly ensnared with thread. Muttering to herself and to the machine, she did not look up when she heard someone walk in.

"I'll be with you in just a moment," she called from the back of the shop.

"I have lots of time."

Rebecca dropped the bobbin and her head shot up. That voice—low and richly timbred, accented with the sound of home. He stood there amidst bolts of fabric and reels of lace, his hat in his hands. His dark blond hair was still long but had been cut to shoulder length. His face, now clean-shaven, still held the lean, angular lines that she remembered so well.

"Gage—" Rebecca's words sounded thin and far away to her own ears. She stood, letting the skirt she had been working on tumble to the floor, forgotten.

"Hello, Becca." A hint of a smile crossed his features, briefly crinkling the corners of his eyes.

She took a shaky step forward and then another, on legs that felt numb. Halting several feet from him, her breath was trapped in her chest. "It's—is it really you?"

He watched her expectantly, and held his arms wide, as if to permit her inspection. "Yeah, it's me."

Rebecca drew closer, letting her eyes take in every detail about him, almost expecting him to vanish in a puff of smoke. He wore better clothes than she had seen on him before, a pale blue-and-white- striped shirt with dungarees that looked as if they had been tailored just for him. Wide-shouldered and long legged, he was the same man—he was completely different. He had aged; war and nine years had seasoned him.

"Wh-what—why—" She could not seem to form a complete sentence.

"Can we talk for a few minutes?" he asked.

"Yes, yes, of course! I'm sorry, I don't know where my manners—" She hurried to the door and locked it, then pulled the shades. To close the shop in the middle of the day was unheard of—Mrs. Walker probably would not like it, but right now she could go jump in the river, as far as Rebecca was concerned. Everything, she wanted to know everything about Gage.

"This way," she murmured, and led him through the shop

to her room in the back. She heard the syncopation of boot heels on the hardwood floor behind her, emphasizing his limp.

"This is nice," he said, looking around the tiny parlor. He made the room seem even smaller.

"Well, it's not really like home," she replied nervously, pulling a chair around for him. She wished she were wearing something nicer than this plain green skirt and white blouse.

He shook his head. "Not much is," he said, more to himself. He sank awkwardly into the chair, favoring his stiff left knee. Rebecca perched across from him on the settee, her hands interlaced on her lap. They sat so close that her skirts brushed his pants legs.

In a gap of silence, she stared at him for a moment, taking in those details of face and form that had not changed, and those that had. He studied her with equal intensity.

"Gage, they told me you'd been killed," Rebecca said finally, her throat constricted. "Your commander—a colonel—he sent me a condolence letter with your watch." She struggled to keep the emotion out of her voice, but even now the memory of that day had the power to make it quiver. She gripped her hands more tightly. *"They told me you were dead."*

He nodded and sighed. "There were times when I wished I was, Becca." He shifted in the chair. "The battle to save Atlanta was a nightmare. Of all the engagements I fought in, I never saw as much death, or heroism, or butchery . . ." He paused, as if trying to decide how much to tell her. "A cannon ball landed on my horse and he landed on me. My knee was broken so I couldn't run, and I was captured. It probably would have healed better if the Yankees hadn't made me march on it for miles."

"March? Where?"

"To a prison camp in Ohio. Well, I didn't march all the way. There were wagons and a train ride too."

"But why did I get that letter? And your watch?" she demanded, a hot coal of anger growing within her. How could the army have told her that he was dead if he was alive? "I know it was yours, your initials are engraved on it."

He went on to explain to her the confusion of humanity, horses, mules, and equipment, and that he had supposed he might die so he gave his watch for safekeeping to another officer. If that officer lived, he was to send the watch to Rebecca. It was only in the last two years that he'd learned the man was also struck by cannon fire, and that so little was left of his head it was assumed he was Major Gage Bristol because his watch was found in the man's pocket. The Confederacy and her army were in a shambles by then, and apparently the error was one of many.

"When the war ended I was free to go, except that this knee hadn't healed yet. I guess I was lucky—a kind Yankee doctor was willing to try and save my leg instead of amputating it. And he let me stay in the hospital until I was well enough to leave. When I finally got back home, everything and everyone were gone—you, your father's store, the saddlery." He sighed and glanced at the floor. "Everything. The few people left told me you went to Oregon. I had money buried next to foundation stones so I dug it up and left too."

Rebecca wanted to hide from these memories. All of them were so painful to remember. She gazed at the chair leg. "I had no reason to stay and I wanted to get away from the heartache. Daddy died right after the Yankees set fire to the store. I think the loss killed him. That place meant more to him than Mama or I ever did. A-And I thought you weren't coming back." She looked at him. "How did you find me?"

Like so many men, he told her, after the war he knocked around the countryside, doing the odd jobs that his knee would permit and working his way west. Four years of fighting had left him with no purpose but one. To find her.

"I must have stopped in every town in Oregon along the way. But when I finally got to Willamette Springs, it wasn't hard to find you. Everyone I asked told me about the seamstress."

"Did you leave those chocolates for me?"

He nodded. "I remember how much you liked them."

"But why did you lurk around and scare ten years off my life?" she asked, her voice shaking again. "Why didn't you talk to me last week when I caught you outside?"

"I wanted to but I lost my nerve. At first I only intended to see you, to find out if you were married." He shrugged. "Then after I heard about your engagement, I thought it was too late. I meant to wish you well that night you caught me at the door, and then move on. I left town for a week." He leaned forward in the chair then and fixed his intense gaze on her face. "But Becca, I couldn't stay away. I had to come back."

Rebecca straightened a bit. "Why?"

He reached for her hand. His touch was firm and sure, not hesitant. "Because I never stopped loving you. You're mine—you have been since we were kids, and you always will be."

His frank avowal startled her and brought heat to her face. The lazy charm of Gage's youth was gone, but it had been replaced with something more vital. He was older now, and his step was a bit heavier, but his eyes still burned with that blue fire she remembered. In fact, this new Gage, weathered and rangy, was even more attractive than the young man who had courted her. And more dangerous. She withdrew her hand from his grip.

"But I've given my pledge to Aaron," she said, tormented by the turn of events. "I've promised to marry him."

Rebecca's statement felt like a knife blade twisting in Gage's chest. "You gave your pledge to me first, Becca." He had seen the stolid clerk at that Valentine's ball. He had even met him when he went into his store to buy these clothes he wore now. Rebecca Baxter was too much woman, too fine a woman, to be wasted on a man like that. Aaron Monroe would never understand what she wanted or needed, and so, would never give it to her.

Her chin jutted just a bit. "But Gage, I thought you were—I haven't seen you in years. Do you mean—Aaron is a good man, a decent man with a nice business. You can't mean you expect me to walk down to Aaron's store and tell him that the engagement is off just because you have suddenly appeared again.''

Deep down, that was exactly what Gage had hoped for. He'd lain in the barber chair with a hot towel on his face, imagining the moment of their reunion. In his daydream, Becca hadn't feared him, and he sensed now that she did. Instead she had thrown herself into his arms sobbing with relief that he was alive, and they had found a justice of the peace to marry them this very afternoon. But he couldn't admit that.

''I expect you to do what's right for you, Becca,'' he said. ''Not for Monroe or for me. For you.'' Stiffly he got to his feet. He did not think he could stay in the same room with her without either burying his head in her lap like a lost kid, or making advances that, after all this time, would scare her.

She rose too, and her skirts rustled with her movement. He liked the sound. ''Are you leaving? So soon?''

''Yeah, but I'll be around.'' He moved toward the door. ''I might even take a look at this town and see if it seems like a good place to open a saddle shop.''

Her green eyes widened. He would have chuckled at her expression if the situation weren't so damned depressing.

''Oh, well, then,'' and she put out her small hand. ''I'll probably see you from time to time. A-And I'm really glad that you're safe.''

Gage looked down at the proffered hand and almost felt insulted. He had traveled thousands of miles to get here, just to find her. He gripped her wrist and pulled her into his arms.

''Gage!'' she protested, but he couldn't let her go. Not just yet. Though her posture was stiff and resistant, she felt soft and smelled like rosewater, and her hair was silky against his cheek. When he relaxed his embrace she pulled back and looked up at him. He saw that fear again, and indignation, but something more flared in those green eyes. His gaze traveled down to her soft pink mouth, and before he could stop himself, his lips were consuming hers.

Stunned by this assault, Rebecca struggled briefly under the mouth that took hers so hungrily. But the sensations Gage evoked were powerful. Her heart beat like a bird's in her chest, and a kind of paralysis flowed through her limbs that made her stop fighting him.

He broke the kiss. "Is it so easy to forget what we had, Becca?" His voice was low and rough with emotion and heat. His eyes, blue and haunted, loomed before her face. "That spark is still burning in your heart. I can feel it."

"Gage, no," she choked, but her words lacked conviction.

He kissed her again, then held her away from himself.

"Can you honestly tell me that you don't feel anything for me?"

She felt weak and breathless. "No, I don't. Not anymore."

He frowned. "I said be honest, damn it!"

Rebecca looked away from his intense gaze. She couldn't answer. She repeated, "I'm engaged to marry Aaron."

He put on his hat and gripped the door knob. "Yeah, maybe you are today. I'll be around, Becca."

Rebecca watched the door close behind him, and saw him walk past her window toward town. The slight hitch in his gait seemed fitting on this new Gage Bristol. It had begun to rain, and he pulled his hat down lower.

"Oh, God," she whispered. She sank down on the chair he had vacated, taken with a paroxysm of trembling. Gage was alive and he was here—the hopeless dream that she had wished for night after night for so many years had actually come true.

But now that she had her wish, she didn't know what to do with it.

❧ *Chapter 5* ❧

"*T*his is fascinating!" Abigail said, obviously intrigued. "I've never known anyone in your spot." Pouring a cup of tea, she passed a plate of cookies to Rebecca, who waved them off.

"You sound amused," Rebecca snapped, and dabbed at her teary eyes. Her friend was perfectly coiffed and dressed in a lovely pale blue taffeta afternoon gown that showed the tiniest bit of cleavage. She always looked beautiful, Rebecca thought grumpily. Not like herself, with damp hair and red puffy eyes. "I'm in a terrible predicament. You probably think I'm a crybaby, running up here again."

Abbie leaned back against her red velvet chair. "No, I don't think it's amusing, Rebecca, and you're not a crybaby. Aren't friends supposed to take care of each other? But, honey, you're in a predicament only because you must care about both Gage and Aaron. If you didn't, you wouldn't have trouble with this at all."

Rebecca had let the shop remain closed and, running through the rain, had come to Abbie's after Gage left. Now she sat in her parlor, guilt-stricken and torn.

"Well, certainly I care about them." She sat forward and held her hands out as if the answer to her problem would fall into them. She spoke earnestly. "Abbie, I've never been wishy-washy in my life about anything. When I thought my father wasn't going to let me marry Gage, we made plans to elope. And I would have done it if not for the war. Then when the war ended and I realized I had nothing left in Georgia, I made up my mind to come west. I scraped my money together and I did it.'' Rebecca flopped back in the chair and looked at the opposite wall. ''I've always known what to do. Until now.''

Abbie selected a petit-fours from the tea cart. ''Then if you can't choose between these two men, they'll have to help you make up your mind.''

Rebecca glanced up. ''What? How?''

Abbie thought for a moment, and then an idea lit her face. ''I know! They'll have to prove themselves to you. I read a fable once, or maybe it was a fairy tale—a king had to find a husband for his only daughter. He had three suitors to choose from and to determine their worthiness, he tested each of them in some way. You know, one had to slay a dragon, another had to bring back a treasure that was guarded by serpents—''

''Abbie, for heaven's sake—'' Rebecca began, but the woman held up a hand to stop her.

''Now, wait, wait. This can work. Of course we won't send Gage and Aaron looking for dragons or buried treasure. But let's think about it—what three things would you want to know about a man?''

Her interest piqued by this idea, Rebecca thought for a moment. ''Well, I guess I'd want to know if he would be a good husband, what kind of father he'd make, and the kind of man he is.''

Abbie giggled. ''I might want to know two different things of your three, but I think you've got the idea.''

After some thought, Rebecca decided on three tests: the children test, the test of honor, and the kiss test. The last was Abbie's suggestion and although she rejected it at first, Rebecca succumbed.

''There are a lot of things you can tell about a man by the way he kisses,'' Abbie said.

''It seems frivolous and a bit, well, immoral,'' Rebecca replied primly, and took a cookie after all. ''It's one thing if a kiss happens spontaneously, but planning it makes it nasty somehow—''

''Oh, bosh!'' her friend retorted, and after more discussion, the kiss test remained.

Rebecca knew that the first thing she had to do was tell Aaron about Gage. If he wasn't going to leave Willamette Springs, word was bound to get around. How it happened she never understood, but this town was as gossipy as any she had ever known. She didn't want Aaron to hear such news from one of his customers.

In a chilly mist early the next morning, she walked to his store, hoping to talk to him before he opened for business. Although it was only seven o'clock, Rebecca knew she would find Aaron working. He rarely did anything else.

It took several moments of knocking before he came to the door, and while she waited Rebecca was tempted to give up and go back to the shop. She wasn't looking forward to this discussion at all. She heard the doorknob turn.

''We don't open until—'' Aaron began. Upon seeing her, he said, ''Rebecca! What are you doing here so early? Is something wrong?''

''Not exactly,'' she said. ''But I need a few minutes from you.'' Looking wary, he backed up to let her in. Mingled scents of the store waved over her—coffee, cured meat, soap. She couldn't help but notice his apron, and it occurred to her that except for the night of the dance, she had never seen him without it. She had never seen his hair without pomade in it, or ever really heard him laugh.

A case of nerves gave Rebecca the chills. The prospect of telling him that Gage was alive and in Willamette Springs was a daunting one. Wrapping her shawl more tightly around herself, she followed him inside.

He led her to a desk behind the counter. ''I guess we haven't seen much of each other in the last few days,'' he said. ''This place keeps me hopping, especially now that I'm provisioning the logging camp.''

She ventured a smile. ''I know how busy you are. That's

why I came down here early. I wanted a minute to talk to you before our work days start.''

''Well, I know I said we'd discuss your idea to open a dress shop. But really, Rebecca, I hope you've given up on that notion. I want us to have a quiet, peaceful home, and I just don't see how we can if you aren't there to take care of it. I work hard and I want a loving family to come home to at night.''

About to argue, Rebecca bit her tongue. The issue of the dress shop was not why she had come here, and it was best to keep to her original purpose.

She sat down in his desk chair and he pulled up a stool. A big, red-backed ledger lay open before her, its pages crowded with columns written in a neat, compact script. She gestured at the tall shelves and barrels. ''Maybe you should let Jim and Neddie help you more, Aaron. I know I wish I could hire help at the shop.''

He shook his head. ''I wouldn't let anyone touch those accounts except me.''

''Well, no, not the books, but what about other jobs like stock work and inventory? Aren't clerks supposed to take care of those kinds of things?''

''Nope. They can do the work, but I have to watch them every minute. If I don't, they'll start dawdling, or they'll do the work differently than the way I want it done. In fact, I ought to finish the accounts before they get here.''

Just like Daddy, she thought. He'd been unable to bear hiring anyone other than a boy to make deliveries and sweep the floors. That store was *his* and his alone, and he'd spent most of his time there.

She reached for his hand. ''I don't want to keep you, Aaron, but something has happened that I must tell you about.''

His serious expression grew downright solemn, and he gripped her hand. ''What is it?''

Rebecca drew a deep breath and told him about Gage, about the mix-up with his identity, and his trek to the West. She omitted the part about the gifts of chocolate on her doorstep, and Gage's kiss, which had left her breathless and rubber-legged.

Aaron pulled his hand from hers, and a deep frown creased his forehead. "Did you tell him that we're engaged to be married in May?"

"Yes, of course."

He rose from the stool and began straightening the already tidy shelves. "Then he should just do the gentlemanly thing and bow out!" Rebecca had never seen Aaron quite so angry. "Did you tell him to leave town?"

"I can't do that, Aaron. He's free to come or go as he chooses."

"Then I'll tell him if I see him. Oh, I know who he is," he said, his tone sly, knowing. "He came in here to buy clothes. And he asked about chocolates. I don't carry them, and I told him so."

Rebecca stared at him. "You don't sell those heart-shaped boxes?"

"No, none of my customers will buy that kind of thing. They're frivolous, a waste of shelf space. I suppose he wanted to give them to you."

"Aaron, where did you get the box *you* gave to me?"

The slow, quiet tick of the wall clock suddenly seemed very loud in the silence that fell between them. Aaron blanched, then turned as red as the binding on his ledger book.

"Well, it was—I found it—"

"It was on my doorstep that night?"

He nodded and looked away, tight-lipped and frowning. Then he said, "I thought that if you had another admirer who was leaving you presents, I didn't want you to know. I wanted you to think it came from me."

Rebecca didn't know whether to be flattered or annoyed. But one thing was certain in her mind. Whatever his motivation had been for lying about the candy, Aaron had just failed the test of honor.

*   *   *

"Say, there, mister—what'd you say your name was?" Juby Bushman asked. Juby was a grizzled little man in a bowler hat who owned the Juby's Springview Saloon.

"Gage Bristol."

"Well, Gage Bristol, these is pretty interestin' goin's-on you got into, bein' betrothed to our Miss Baxter when she done got herself promised to Aaron Monroe." He pushed a glass at Gage and went on polishing another one. The saloon carried the faint odor of stale beer and even staler cigar smoke.

Gage rested his left boot on the brass rail at his feet to take the weight off his knee. He had hoped to come in here for a couple of whiskeys and not suffer a lot of conversation. The elderly Juby put an end to that. Gage had forgotten how quickly news spread in a small town, and almost by magic. At least the saloon was fairly empty, with the exception of one drunk snoring at a corner table.

"First that little gal had no fee-ance, and now she's got two," the old man cackled.

"It's not a subject that's up for discussion, Juby," he warned lightly. "Just give me a bottle of whiskey."

Wearing a sly smile, the old man slid a bottle across the bar. "As you say, as you say. I'd be drinkin' too in your spot."

Gage threw some money on the gouged counter. Then grabbing the whiskey, he found a corner table far opposite the drunk. He looked around the place, at a painting of a bashful nymph hanging behind Juby, and at the huge, wicked-looking ax that was lodged in the wall over the door. This sure as hell wasn't where he wanted to be.

Pouring a drink for himself, he leaned back in his chair. He wanted to be with Becca. The hope of making her his wife was all that had gotten him through those months in prison, and led him like a beacon across the hundreds of miles to the West. He knew it had been a foolish, risky undertaking. The chances of finding her had been slim; that she would be single was even more unlikely. But he had come anyway. And he had been just days too late. He wished he had approached her as soon as he reached Willamette Springs, instead of hanging back to watch her. He hadn't realized what wheels of fate were turning while he got up the nerve to face her.

Now he was competing for her hand—the hand he had already won once—against a man who was almost exactly like her father, from what he could tell. Phillip Baxter had been cold and unemotional, and had seemed to live only to work. Rebecca deserved more than that.

Although her dress was more conservative now, and she wore her heavy chestnut hair in a plain bun, Gage knew that the fire he'd found in Becca's heart all those years ago still smoldered. He had felt it when he kissed her. The old memory of her smooth skin under his hands and lips had kept him awake part of last night. His imagination took over after that as he envisioned lying with her in a field of tall grass on a soft summer day, while a light breeze drifted over their bare limbs and rustled the grasstops around them. He had watched that scene play out on the hospital ceiling at night, and on the face of the night sky when he slept out in the open.

But then as he lay in the bed in the hotel room last night, the fear that she would never love him again had made his throat tight and his eyes burn, thereby stealing the rest of his sleep.

Someone had once told him that loss was what life was all about. Despite everything that had happened over the last nine or ten years, he had never really believed it.

Until now.

"Goodness, Miss Baxter, I heard the most astounding thing yesterday," Susannah Tremont said, watching while Rebecca put her new gown into a long box. "I don't have much taste for idle gossip, mind you, but I thought you'd be amused to know that I heard you're engaged to *two* men! Isn't that the most delicious thing you've heard this week?"

Rebecca felt her face grow hot as she wrapped a length of string around the box and tied it. "Delicious? What an odd way to put it, Mrs. Tremont, especially since you don't have much 'taste' for gossip.'' She put the box in her arms.

Oblivious, the woman laughed and walked to the door with her package. "Oh, there's no accounting for rumors. They're just like colds; we catch them and pass them on. Well, goodbye, my dear. I'll be back next week for another fitting.''

Rebecca was just about to close the door when she glanced down the street and saw Gage. He was sitting on the edge of the high sidewalk outside the bakery, and two boys were crowded around him.

What a perfect opportunity to observe him with children. She was too far away to hear what they were talking about, but she thought she might be able to slip in behind them to listen. Grabbing her shawl, she flapped the ends around herself and hurried down the sidewalk. When she neared Gage and the boys, she slowed and pretended to look in the bakery window behind them. Luckily, he was busy enough not to notice her back there.

"... one heck of a frog, I agree. But you'd better not take him into the bakery or the ladies there will get pretty upset.''

Keeping to the shadowed wall of the building, Rebecca chanced a peek over her shoulder and Gage's to get a look at the topic of their conversation. One of the boys held up an enormous bullfrog—the thing must have weighed four or five pounds in her estimation. Her gaze then drifted over Gage's shoulders and down to his forearms, muscled and dusted with blond hair. She moved to his right slightly, so she could see part of his clean profile.

"Aw, dang,'' one of the boys moaned. "It's just a frog. He won't hurt no one.''

"Well, shoot, we was gonna get a doughnut,'' the other youngster added. "Our ma gave us two pennies. If they won't let us in with him . . .''

"You could turn the frog loose,'' Gage suggested. This was met with protest.

"No, it took all morning to catch this son. He's big but he's fast.''

"Or I could hold him out here for a minute so you could get your doughnuts," Gage offered.

"Really, mister? Would you?" one boy asked.

"I don't know," the skeptical brother said. "He's pretty valuable. How do we know you won't run off with him yourself?"

Gage nodded with apparent understanding. "Tell you what, I'll pay you rent for him," he said and stretched his torso to reach his pocket. "Here's a quarter. If I'm not sitting on this step with the frog when you come out, at least you'll have the quarter. Then you can buy twenty-five more doughnuts. Does that sound like a fair deal to you?"

"Yes *sir!*"

"Ohh, wow."

"Um, you probably ought to wipe your hands on your pants legs before you touch the doughnut," he advised them.

Rebecca cringed but smiled broadly to herself.

"We'll be right back," the younger one said, and thrust the frog into Gage's hands. This was followed by a vigorous slapping of denim pants legs. Then they scampered past Rebecca into the bakery.

Rebecca took advantage of the opportunity to slip back to the dress shop without being seen. She risked one last glance at Gage as she stole away, and saw him sitting patiently on the sidewalk step, holding that big bullfrog and watching the street traffic pass.

She smiled again.

❧ Chapter 6 ❧

"Aaron, I really need my thread order. I'm getting close to using twine." Rebecca stood at his back counter and surveyed the scissors in the display case while he searched his back room for the missing package. "I placed the order weeks ago."

"I think I remember it," he said, reappearing in the doorway, empty-handed. "I'll look in the order book."

Rebecca kept her eyes on the scissors while she struggled with rising annoyance over the situation. This was the third time she had asked him about that thread, and he never quite followed through with it.

"Hey, you boys," he barked at two youngsters looking in one of the glass cases. Rebecca didn't think they were much older than six or seven. "Haven't I told you to stop lollygagging in here? This is a place of business—"

"Gee, Mr. Monroe, we were just lookin' at the pocket knives. I been savin' up to buy one." The boy had an earnest face, still tinted with a sweetness of childhood.

Aaron waved them off with a shooing motion. "That's fine, you come back when you're ready to buy. Until then, stay out of here, or I'll tell your pa."

The boys scurried off, and Rebecca turned to stare at him. "For heaven's sake, Aaron, they weren't hurting anyone. They weren't noisy or disruptive. They weren't even touching the merchandise. They were only looking."

"Oh, they get underfoot," he said irritably. "I run this store for customers who want to buy, not for boys with a penny or two." He ran a finger down a long column in his order book. The writing was cramped and looking at it upside down, Rebecca couldn't read it. "When did you say you asked for that thread?"

"It was two months ago. I don't remember the exact date, except it was right after Mrs. Walker left for Denver."

Neddie Gordon, one of the young clerks, passed Rebecca on his way back from the store room. "How do, Miss Baxter. That sure was a pretty dress you made for my ma."

"Why, thank you, Neddie," she said, and smiled. "Your mother is one of my favorite customers."

Aaron continued his search, then closed the book with a soft *clap*. "Well, it's in the book, but I don't know what to tell you, Rebecca. The thread just isn't here."

Neddie stopped in his tracks. "Oh, if you're talking about Miss Baxter's order, I sent it back just like you told me to, Mr. Monroe."

"What?"

"Don't those cans of beans need to go on the shelf, Ned?" Aaron mumbled, his face flushing.

Rebecca gaped at him, and a red-hot fury burned behind her eyes. "Wait, Neddie. When did you send that thread back?" she asked, keeping her gaze on Aaron.

"Oh, I guess it must have been the day after you two had lunch over at the café. Mr. Monroe said the factory sent the wrong colors."

"Thank you. Don't let me keep you from your work." Neddie went back to the other counter, and Rebecca said, "What about this Aaron?"

"Now I remember. The thread did come, but not in the colors you asked for, just like Ned told you. I had him send it all back."

"Aaron," she said, struggling to keep her voice low. "I don't think you're telling me the truth. Now, what's going on? First you lie to me about the chocolate, and today the thread."

Aaron glanced around the store, which had a few customers in it. "Jim," he called to the other clerk, "watch things here for a minute." Then he came around the counter and took Rebecca's hand to lead her to the store room and closed the door.

Nervously, he pulled out a crate for her to sit on. "I'd rather stand," she said.

He ran a hand through his pomaded hair, making it stand up stiffly on the ends. If Rebecca hadn't been so angry, she would have laughed at the picture he made.

He reached for her hand, but she was in no mood for that and she pulled away. "Rebecca, I didn't mean to lie to you. The chocolate, well, I told you why I did that. As for the thread, you got that notion about opening your own shop, and I just thought how much time that would take away from us and a family, when we have one. I know it was wrong of me, all wrong."

Exasperated, she felt only a little charity for his tragic expression. "Aaron, good lord, you know that thread was for Mrs. Walker's business, not mine! I need it to finish the work I have right now."

"I know, I know! I haven't been thinking straight. And now Bristol is here, and you've been preoccupied and distant—I was just afraid that I'd lost you." He reached for her hand again, and this time she let him take it. "Maybe he knew you a long time ago, but I've been courting you for two years, and I worked hard to get your acceptance. I was afraid that either your idea about a business or Bristol would take you away."

"But Aaron, I have to stay with you because I want to. Not because you've tricked me into it. Don't you understand that?"

He nodded. "I just did what I thought I had to. After we're married, everything will be better."

After we're married. Her future was all very clear now, and what she saw frightened her. If she married Aaron, she would be trapped in a sewing room in the corner of their house, while he spent all of his time here at the store, perhaps even grousing about men who could keep a plow straight in a furrow, just as her father had. She would not have the companion she sought or the partner who would share her life. She would be subservient to Aaron.

God, she would rather remain alone than let that happen.

She would much rather be married to the man who had proposed to her more than nine years earlier. The man who was intended to be her husband.

Rebecca pulled her hand away. "Aaron, I'm sorry. I can't marry you."

"Rebecca, no—"

She shook her head and continued. "It's not your fault or mine, Aaron. We simply are not meant for each other. I can't be what you want, and I would be lonely in that life. You see that, don't you?"

He stared at the floor between them and nodded. "I should have realized when you put me off the first time I proposed. I'm sorry, Rebecca, for everything."

Feeling enormously relieved, she grabbed the store room door knob and said, "Don't be sorry, Aaron. I really am honored that you asked me to be your wife. I'm just glad we found out now what a mistake we almost made."

He saw her to the sidewalk in front of his store. "I'll reorder that thread for you." She nodded. Then suddenly he took her into his arms and gave her the first full hug she'd ever had from him. That was followed by a kiss that made pedestrians look twice and teamsters in the street howl with appreciation.

Then Aaron went back inside.

From a table by the window at the saloon, Gage Bristol watched his fiancée embracing and kissing another man, in full view of witnesses. Even a blind man could feel the emotion that passed between them at that moment. Gage sighed and knocked back his drink in one gulp.

Then he left the saloon to go pack his gear.

*　　*　　*

"I'm looking for Mr. Gage Bristol, please," Rebecca told the hotel desk clerk. The clerk eyed her askance; after all, what respectable woman went into a hotel asking for a man who was not a relative? But at the moment, she had to talk to Gage and she was willing to risk her entire reputation to do it.

This was an important occasion—it would be the night she became engaged again. She had even gone back to her room to comb her hair and put on her nice navy wool dress.

"I'm sorry, ma'am, but Mr. Bristol checked out of the hotel about an hour ago."

Panic filled her. "Checked out! Do you know where he went?"

"No, ma'am, only that he was headed upriver. I thought I heard something about Seattle."

Seattle. Nearly two hundred miles away. "I see. Thank you."

Rebecca dragged back to the shop in the waning light. So many things in her history with Gage involved missed opportunities and cruel whims of fate. Perhaps this final episode just completed their story.

As she approached her door in the half-light of dusk, she saw something on the doorstep, a small, plain-wrapped package that now looked very familiar. The difference was that this one had her name written on it in heavy strokes. *Becca.*

Hurrying inside, she opened the paper with hands that shook. Within were more chocolates, but this time a note was enclosed with them.

Beloved Becca,
 Sometimes there is no going back, no matter how much we might want to. Be happy in your new life, and know that I have always loved you.
 Gage

He didn't know that her engagement with Aaron was broken. He didn't know how much she loved him. "Oh, Gage. I never got the chance to tell you any of it."

Rebecca put her head down on the settee and cried.

*   *   *

The next morning Rebecca went through the motions of
work but her heart wasn't in it. In some ways she felt as sick
with grief as she had when she received the condolence letter
and Gage's watch. Yes, she knew he was alive this time, but
he was as beyond her reach as he had been before. Now she
had another letter to add to the ones in the heart-shaped box
in her trunk.

No one came into the shop for most of the morning, and
she was grateful for that. But just as she began pinning a
ruffle to a hem, a sharp March gust swept over her ankles
when her shop door opened and closed with a bang.

A man stood in the front of the shop. He filled the small
place with a presence that was at once quiet and yet very
powerful. She had forgotten that about him, the vibrant, magnetic pull he'd had on her, and in some ways still did. In the
confines of this feminine establishment his maleness was
even more obvious.

"Hi, Becca." He took off his hat, revealing the crown of
his long hair.

"Gage!" She took two steps forward and stopped. She
wanted to blurt out that she and Aaron were no longer engaged, but something in his deadly serious expression
stopped her. Still, his very presence lightened her heart.

Outside, the noise of the street traffic faded away while
she listened to the sound of his voice. "An opportunity has
come up that I could take advantage of. I want you to tell
me what you think I should do."

"Me?"

He nodded, and she directed him to a chair, then sat down
next to him.

He crossed his ankle over his good knee, and tipped the
chair back against the wall. The action made his lean torso
stretch out, and Rebecca was fascinated by the display of
taut shirt and snug dungarees.

"There's some vacant space I've been looking at down-
river in Portland. It would be good for a saddlery and I'm
going to rent it."

Rebecca looked at him. "I-In Portland?" Saddlery. *Seattle?* "There's a space next to the express office here in Willamette Springs. That's the one I had wanted to rent."

"Really? What for?"

"Oh, I was hoping to open my own dressmaking shop someday. I'm mostly running this place by myself," she gestured at the walls, "but I'm not being paid very well. I know I could do better with my own business in a good location, and I've been saving for a long time. It's all just a dream anyway."

"Rebecca, I'm getting tired and I'd like to settle down someplace." He reached over and intertwined his fingers with hers. "Don't marry Aaron Monroe. Come with me. I'm not the same man I was in Georgia, but I still feel the same about you. If you want a dress shop, that's fine, too."

She risked a glance at his lean, handsome face. "Oh, Gage," she whispered. "Yes, yes, yes, I will marry you. Today, this morning, whenever you want."

He let the chair legs hit the floor. "You will? Just like that?" He looked surprised.

She told him what had happened the evening before, about breaking her engagement with Aaron, about looking for him at the hotel. "When I got home and found your note, I thought I would die," she said, her voice beginning to tremble. "It was like hearing you were dead all over again."

He pulled her into his arms. "Honey, I'm sorry. I saw you all lovey-dovey with Monroe in front of his store, and I figured that was the end of the road for me. But then today I realized that as long as you weren't married to him yet, I still had a chance. I had to try one more time. Thank God I came back."

A second chance. Finally, they were getting a second chance. The man she agreed to take as her husband had finally come back to her.

"Becca." The single word, her nickname, he spoke in low, rich tones, like the chocolate he had left for her. He lifted her hand to his mouth and kissed it. His hair brushed her wrist, and his lips were warm, soft. The chills he raised made her shiver.

"I've been waiting to make love with you all of my life."

Rebecca reached behind to grab the pulls on the window shades. The dress shop was closed for the day. She stood up and reached for his hand.

"And I've been waiting for *you*, Gage. Welcome home."

Alexis Harrington loves to hear from her readers: P.O. Box 30176, Portland, OR 97294.

SWEET CREATIONS

Sue Rich

✎ *Chapter 1* ✎

"*I*s he dead?"

"Nope."

"Sick?"

"Nope."

"Then exactly what is he?"

"Asleep."

Wade Carlisle stared in disbelief at the comatose youngster sprawled beneath an elm tree. His hat was cocked down over his eyes, his feet crossed at the ankles. He'd gathered his vest and holster beneath his mop of thick blond curls like a pillow. The kid had been with Wade for the better part of a year, and he'd done his best to outshine the older, more experienced, ranch hands. Until now.

"What the hell's going on, Lefty?" Wade demanded. "Why am I suddenly finding my hands asleep beneath trees, or in bed complaining of sickness, or fighting, or staring off into space with stupid grins on their faces?"

"Can't rightly say."

"Any suspicions?"

Lefty shoved the brim of his hat back with his thumb, revealing intelligent blue eyes, thick sideburns, and frizzy red hair. " 'Pears to me they been visitin' Hank's Saloon."

Wade had considered that several times over the last

weeks, but he hadn't seen any of them with a bottle, and short of searching their gear, he couldn't prove they were drinking at all. The only thing different was the pink bags they'd all taken to carrying—miniature draw-string flour sacks from a new candy shop in town called Sweet Creations.

How could the boys let him down like this? And now, when he needed them most.

His eyes narrowed against the bright spring sun as a thought hit him. Sweet Creations was across the street from Hank's Saloon. Was it possible that Hank was selling miniature bottles the hands could carry in their pockets?

Wade nodded toward the kid. "Take him to the bunk house and dock him a day's pay, then set down hard on the others and have them start that new corral next to the barn. I'll see you when I get back."

Leather creaked as Lefty dismounted. "Where you goin'?"

To hell if he had to. "Laramie." Reining his horse around, Wade nudged the animal into a trot.

He tried to dispel a feeling of doom as he rode along a trail that meandered down a hillside overlooking Laramie. Sunlight glinted off the Laramie River as it wound its way through town. Gleaming Union Pacific railroad tracks dissected the landscape. Acres of flatlands bordered the town on three sides. Only his side, the Pole Mountain side, had any height.

He loved the miles of open spaces, the wide blue sky, and lumbering herds of antelope. He'd been struck by Wyoming the first time he saw it when he was twelve years old, and now, even at thirty, he was still awed.

It was God's country.

And it was his.

He and his pa, Daniel Carlisle, had started the Bar C Ranch eighteen years ago with four heifers and a bull, and a dream of raising the best beef in the country. Although his father hadn't lived to see their goal fulfilled, Wade would.

He'd spent years crossbreeding the heartiest herefords with sturdy Indian stock he'd located near the Black Hills. Yes, he'd fulfill their dream—*if* he got his cattle ready in time for the meeting with the representatives from the Stock Association.

For the hundredth time, he thanked the Almighty that Wilber Crawford, the man who could make or break him, had gone to North Dakota to speak with stock growers about expanding the organization. Wilber was a meticulous man who insisted on inspecting Wade's herd, and Wade, himself, before he'd even consider recommending Wade's new breed.

But, if he got their recommendation, the price of his beeves would produce enough money that he could afford the track of land adjoining his, and with that land, he'd be able to double the size of his operation—just as his father had envisioned.

A wave of grief swept Wade when he thought of his father—and of the woman who had caused his death.

His hands tightened on the reins. Charlotte Murphy Carlisle had killed his father as surely as if she'd put the barrel of a shotgun to his chest.

No! He wasn't going to think about his traitorous stepmother who would—and did—do anything for money.

Sweat trickled down his jaw, and he swiped it away with the back of his hand, then nudged his horse into a faster gait. Damn, it was hot for May.

When he reached the foot of the hill, he studied the small community that had once been a booming railroad town. But the workers had moved on, leaving only a handful of folks to settle the new city. All the Union Pacific left behind were tracks and a wood frame depot that now needed painting.

Wade's gaze drifted to a big red sign that announced the location of Hank's Saloon. The sign was at least five feet tall, and it had been repaired or repainted four times in as many months. The town's womenfolk who'd gotten fired up in the temperance movement had done their best to demolish it, from painting it over with black, to smearing it with tar, to bombarding it with eggs, to shooting holes through it with buckshot. Hell, Hank even had to board up his front window after the women shattered it so many times.

He smiled, thinking of the hot-tempered gals who were determined to rid Laramie of spirits. They were a feisty bunch, but their leader, Miss Emma Whitehall, was downright vicious.

Glad he'd never had a run-in with that particular female, he guided his horse toward Main Street.

The boarded-up front window of Hank's kept the interior of the saloon cool, and Wade savored the momentary relief as ambled over to the bar. Sawdust shifted under his feet, and the smell of tobacco and liquor hung in the musky air. He wasn't a drinking man and never had been, so he didn't spend much time in saloons. The odors didn't agree with him any more than the liquor did. But he was thirsty.

Hank Pollack, a hefty man with mutton-chop sideburns and a drooping mustache, looked up as Wade placed a hand on the counter. "Surprised to see you here on a week day," he said in a gravelly voice. "What's the occasion?"

"Wanted something to cool down."

"Sarsaparilla?" the bartender asked knowingly.

"That'll do."

As he reached under the bar for a bottle, Wade braced his forearms on the scarred counter. "Seen many of my hands in here lately?"

Hank set the Sarsaparilla on the bar and uncorked the top. "Nope. Ain't seen a one."

Wade closed his fingers around the green bottle with a paper label and took a swallow. The tangy flavor made his mouth tingle. "You sure?"

"You bet, I'm sure. My cash box is as empty as Emma Whitehall's bed."

Wade nearly choked on the soda. Hank never had been one for tact. When Wade could breathe again, he set the Sarsaparilla aside and stared dead on into the bartender's watery blue eyes. "Hank, my ranch hands are getting liquor from somewhere, and I want it to stop. I've talked to several of them, and they all swear on their mothers that they haven't been to a saloon. So if they're not getting it from you, where are they buying booze?"

Hank's heavy jowls wobbled. "I ain't got no idea. But I *do* know since that gal and her sis opened that chocolate shop across the street, I ain't seen half my regular customers."

"Do you think she's selling spirits on the side?" It would sure explain the pink bags that had suddenly become a part of his ranchhands' gear.

"Naw. It's just that the town males are getting so fired up over that Danielle woman that they're too busy courting to spend time in here."

"She's a looker, huh?"

"She's a damned sight more than that."

Wade arched a brow. It wasn't like Hank to go on about a female. He was as confirmed a bachelor as a man could get. "Maybe I'd better see if something's going on over there." *And maybe that little chocolate shop was dealing in more than just sweets.*

Hank sighed and wiped an imaginary spot off the counter. "Sure, go on. Get in line with the rest of them tongue-lolling idiots."

Checking a smile, Wade tossed two bits on the bar. "Don't take it too hard. With all the courting going on, she'll probably get married and close up shop before long."

"Couldn't be soon enough for me."

Unable to contain his smile, Wade concealed it under the pretense of straightening his hat as he headed out the door. From the boardwalk, he studied the establishment across the street with its large window bordered by lacy curtains. The building was pink, just like the bags, and frilly red letters that he'd seen stitched on the small sacks were displayed again in larger script on a swinging sign hanging from the roof of a covered boardwalk. It read: Sweet Creations.

He wondered just how "sweet" her creations were. Small clouds of dust rose from the dirt street as he crossed to the other side and pushed open a pair of red, swinging doors to the chocolate shop.

He hadn't been in the building since Marty Whitcomb sold

out his hardware store and went back east to work in a factory.

It had changed. Where there used to be shelves of whitewash, hammers, saws, and barrels of nails, were now clean pink walls and small tables with checkered cloths.

Where rolls of barbed wire and hog wire had been stacked on a long table there was now a glass counter with plates of chocolate clustered at one end. The aroma of vanilla and bubbling sugar filled the small room, giving it a homey, welcome feeling.

A young girl who looked as if she should still be in school was standing behind the counter. In front of her stood at least a half dozen men. Even the sheriff was there.

Hank hadn't been joking when he said Wade could get in line.

He cocked his head to the side so he could get a better look at what they were selling. He studied the tray of chocolates at the end of the counter. Some were decorated with frosting, others resembled small beehives, and some looked suspiciously like rabbit droppings. He scanned the contents in a glass case below the counter. Those he recognized. Peppermint sticks, fudge, gum drops, licorice, and horehound candy.

The display was appealing, and he almost wished he liked the stuff.

"Give me a bag of them Chocolate Towers, Janie," Clem Michaels, the owner of the mercantile, ordered.

The girl flipped a long blond lock of hair over her shoulder and smiled, crinkling the corners of her wide blue eyes. "Sure thing, Clem. Want a bag for Willy, too?"

"Hell no," Clem mumbled. "That lazy good-for-nothing nephew of mine can get his own candy. I pay him enough to buy the whole blamed store—thanks to my wife."

The girl tried not to smile, but she wasn't very successful. "In that case, I'll make sure to charge him double next time."

Clem chuckled. "You do that, darlin'. Yeah, you do that."

Stuffing a pink bag in his vest pocket, he nodded to the others as he ambled out the door.

"She's a sweetheart, isn't she?" Sheriff O'Brien said as he nudged Wade's arm. "And she's going to be a damned fine looking woman when she grows up—just like her sister."

"Since I've never seen the woman who has half the town males stepping on their tongues, I don't know what to say. But I do agree with you that the young one's going to be pretty enough when she's gained a few years."

O'Brien whipped his head around, causing a long lock of straw-colored hair to catch in his beard. "You ain't never seen Dani?"

Wade assumed that was the girl's older sister. "Nope. Haven't had the pleasure."

"Pleasure's the right word, that's for sure." The sheriff's gaze drifted to the side. "And hold onto your gunbelt, boy. You're about to have that pleasure right now."

Wade followed the direction of the sheriff's gaze and fixed on a small, dark-haired woman coming out of a curtained doorway. Something slammed into his chest. It felt like a fist. God a'mighty, he'd never seen a woman that lovely.

He had to remind himself to breathe as he watched her set a plate on the counter, then stick her finger in her mouth to suck off a glob of white frosting. Even though he didn't like sweets, in that instant, he'd have given most anything he owned to help her lick the goo off her finger.

Mesmerized, he watched the gentle sucking motion of her lips. He could almost feel the moistness. The softness.

Desire moved through his lower body, and he shifted his attention. Critically, he tried to find a flaw in that exquisite face. Maybe her cheeks were too pale.

No, there was a healthy peaches and cream glow that looked like satin.

The nose then. Surely it had a flaw.

He doggedly inspected the small, uptilted flesh. The damned thing was perfect. And the eyes, ah hell, those shimmering green pools were deep enough to drown a man.

"Get a grip on yourself, boy. You're starting to drool."

A flush crept up Wade's neck as he glared at the sheriff. "I wasn't drooling, damn it. I was just trying to see what all the hoopaloo was about." Determinedly, he kept his gaze from drifting back to the woman.

O'Brien smiled. "So, what's the verdict?"

"I've seen better."

The sheriff threw his head back and laughed, a deep, full-bellied rumble. Then he thumped Wade on the shoulder. "Boy, you'd better go to church Sunday and make your peace. The Almighty don't cotton to lying."

If Wade's neck got any hotter, he was going to set his shirt on fire.

"Sheriff O'Brien, it's good to see you," a soft, husky voice drifted from behind them.

Leave. Get the hell out of here while you still can, some crucial, desperate part of him warned. The urge to heed that warning was strong enough to make him take a step toward the front doors. But, manners had been instilled in Wade since infancy. No matter how much he wanted to, he couldn't just walk out.

"Dani, girl. If you get any prettier, I'm gonna run away with you."

A musical chuckle floated over Wade like a soft summer breeze.

"Oh, sheriff. If it weren't for that lovely wife of yours, I'd be mighty tempted."

"I'll shoot her."

Wade turned, and his eyes collided with shimmering green ones.

For a heartbeat, hers widened, then lowered in sudden shyness.

"Dani," O'Brien said, clearing his throat. "This here is Wade Carlisle, owner of the Bar C Ranch. Wade, this is Miss Danielle Jordan, proprietress of this here shop."

Her gaze fluttered back up to his. "I'm pleased to meet you, Mr. Carlisle."

Wade could only stare. Her mouth was so soft, so deliciously pink, and she was so close, he caught her scent. She smelled like vanilla sunshine. Trying to ignore the pangs of lust clamoring through his body, he forced himself to respond. "The pleasure's mine, ma'am."

O'Brien snickered at Wade's word choice, then nodded toward the counter where the younger girl was waiting on the banker's son, Toby, and his friend, Pete. "Got any of them Chocolate Towers left, Dani?"

"I'm sure we do. Janie made up several trays this morning."

"Then give me half a dozen."

A wing-shaped brow lifted in surprise. "That's quite a bit even for you, sheriff."

"Ain't all for me. Got a U.S. Marshal coming through today and thought I'd give him a treat."

Wade was glad to focus on something besides the woman, and he saw right through O'Brien's remark. It wasn't any secret around town that O'Brien was bucking for a better-paying job. Deputy Marshal would be a good start.

"Would you like to try our Chocolate Towers, too, Mr. Carlisle?"

Wade slid his gaze back to the woman. The way she said his name made his skin tighten. "Um, sure. Same as the sheriff." Now why'd he go and say that? He hadn't planned on buying anything.

Disgusted with himself for allowing her to sidetrack him, he determinedly got to his purpose for coming here in the first place. "By the way, you got any liquor for sale?"

O'Brien made a choked sound.

A flicker of disappointment touched Danielle's eyes, then she clamped her mouth into an angry line. "No, Mr. Carlisle. We don't offer spirits. Nor do we allow them on the premises. However, if you're in desperate need, I'm sure the gentleman across the street would be more than happy to accommodate you."

Wade knew her words couldn't have been any colder if they'd blown off a block of ice—and he felt like a damned fool. "Chocolate's fine."

She stepped away from him and mechanically went about placing six beehive-shaped candies in each of the two pink bags.

Wade winced at the thought of carrying one of those on his person, and knew as soon as he got home he was going to give the thing to Eula, his new cook.

"Here you are, sheriff." She handed him his order. "That'll be two bits."

O'Brien gave her the money, then tipped his hat. "See you later, sweetie." He nodded. "Wade." Looking as if he was about to explode with news to tell someone, he hurried out the door.

"That'll be two bits from you, too, Mr. Carlisle."

Wade glanced down to see her holding a bag toward him. Her expression wasn't in the least friendly, and it made something inside him draw into a knot. "Listen, Miss Jordan. I don't know what I said that made you angry, but I apologize."

"I'm not angry, Mr. Carlisle. What you do is no concern of mine." She gestured to her outstretched hand. "Two bits, please."

He dropped a silver dollar in her palm. "Keep the change." Snatching the bag, he gave her a sharp nod, then strode out.

Danielle watched his broad back disappear through the swinging doors and sighed. Without a doubt, he was the best-looking man she'd ever seen. No one she knew had hair that gleaming black, or eyes that steely gray color, or a mouth that beautifully shaped, or looked so magnificent in snug jeans.

Stop it, Danielle, she mentally scolded. *You spent your life with one drunk. Wasn't that enough?*

It was more than enough.

At thoughts of her uncle, Stanley Jordan, she felt a familiar wave of nausea. She couldn't count the times he'd staggered in the door in the wee hours of the morning. Or the times he'd slobbered all over her and Janie in an attempt to show affection while in a drunken stupor. In the mornings, though, she never knew whether she'd wake up to a hug or a slap. His alcohol-numbed temperament was as unpredictable as the Wyoming wind.

Because of his disgusting habit, there'd never been enough food to eat or decent clothes for her and Janie to wear to school. Even now, she could hear the other children's taunts about the shabby Jordan sisters, *poor relations of the town drunk.*

The only good thing in her life after her parents died in a buckboard accident had been her baby sister. Janie was a bright, beautiful child, and if there was any way possible, Danielle would see that she had a decent life. They wouldn't be rich, but they'd have plenty of food and clothes, a real bed instead of a mat on the floor, and a roof over their heads that didn't leak. And they'd never be ashamed to walk down the street again.

Her gaze drifted around the chocolate shop, and she again said a prayer of thanks for their neighbor in Medicine Bow, Mrs. Liebermann. If it hadn't been for her gift of the recipes and molds for the chocolates when Uncle Stanley died, Danielle and Janie would probably be scrubbing floors or doing laundry for pennies rather than owning their own business.

She smiled fondly at her little sister. Janie was the heart of Sweet Creations. If it wasn't for her, they would have closed their doors after the first weeks. There hadn't been many customers then, only an occasional ranch hand.

Janie had saved the day with a new recipe she guarded like the crown jewels of England. She said Mrs. Liebermann had given it to her right before they left, and made her promise not to show it to anyone. But, whatever was in the recipe, it was worth its weight in gold. Ninety percent of their sales were Chocolate Towers.

Danielle almost wished she could taste one of Janie's creations, but she couldn't. She was allergic to chocolate. Even the smallest portion made her break out in hives.

Her gaze drifted back to the swinging doors, and she felt a twinge of regret that, like chocolate, Mr. Carlisle was good to look at, but would be very unhealthy for her fragile new peace and happiness.

At that moment, the doors swung open, and Emma Whitehall strolled in.

She wore a black wool dress, with a high, tight collar that went clear up to her pointed chin. Her pumpkin-seed eyes squinted as she scanned the room, then settled on Danielle. "Ah, Miss Jordan. I was hoping you would be here."

"What can I do for you, Miss Whitehall?" She tried to keep the distaste from her voice. Emma Whitehall reminded her of a woman in Medicine Bow who'd looked down on Danielle and her sister like they were muck-covered animals.

"Plenty, my dear. Plenty. I would like for you to join our movement. The good ladies of Laramie will put a stop to the sale of intoxicants and bring our menfolk home where they belong. You, dear, would be an asset to that cause."

As much as Danielle detested alcohol, she disliked confrontations even more. "I sympathize with your cause, Miss Whitehall, but don't have time to participate in your marches and demonstrations. When the shop is closed, we're cooking into the late hours, preparing candy for the next day. We barely have enough time to sleep." It wasn't exactly the truth, but Danielle wasn't going to mention that, except for making Chocolate Towers, which Janie made in the mornings, she and Janie took turns making the candies at night, so each had a little free time. Still, she wasn't about to spend that precious time spreading tar on the sign above Hank's Saloon.

Miss Whitehall sniffed and slapped her gloves against the palm of her rail-thin hand. "Surely a small loss of sleep is worth the morality of our community."

Danielle refused to back down. She'd done enough of that in her life. "I'm sure it is, but if one of us should become ill from lack of rest, our very livelihood would be in jeopardy. Surely you understand that."

Miss Whitehall's features tightened into a skeletal frown. "Oh, I understand perfectly, Missy. You have sided with the heathens!" Whirling around she stalked out of the shop, slamming her hand against the doors as she went.

Danielle sighed. There was just no reasoning with the woman.

"What did the old biddy want?" Janie asked, walking up behind Danielle.

"Janie, how many times have I told you not to speak that way about your elders?"

"About a million."

"Then please try to remember."

Janie grinned, showing adorable dimples in her cheeks.

"I'll give it my best effort. By the way, who was that gorgeous man with the sheriff?"

"Wade Carlisle."

"And?"

"And what?"

"Did he ask you to a social or anything?"

"Of course not. Why on earth would you think that?"

Janie watched the last of the customers go out the door, then untied her apron and walked behind the counter. "Because of the way he was looking at you like an ice cream on a hot summer day. I think he wanted to eat you up."

A queer flutter moved through Danielle's middle. "He didn't."

"Yes he did. His eyes were all over you. I'm surprised you didn't *feel* them."

Heat raced to Danielle's cheeks. "Don't talk like that."

"Why? You always told me to tell the truth."

What could she say? No, I want you to lie this time? "Well, I'd rather not talk about Mr. Carlisle anymore. What do you want for supper?" It was Janie's night to make candy and her night to cook. "I'll start it while you close up."

"There's plenty of chicken left from last night. Let's just have that."

"Fine, I'll put on some greens and potatoes to go with it." Tugging on one of her sister's shiny blond curls in an affectionate gesture, Danielle headed upstairs.

Their tiny overhead apartment only had one large room but it was homey, and it was theirs. No empty bottles of whiskey lined the sideboard. Wet stains didn't mar either of the two narrow cots. No fist slammed down on the warped wooden table, and no drunken form was sprawled in one of the ladder-back chairs.

For the first time since she was ten years old, she had a real home.

She glanced at a three-legged cook stove that sat near the sideboard and would serve as heat in the winter . . . if they were still here. Which she hoped they wouldn't be. As much as she loved their little place, she knew if the profits kept coming in as they had been for the last couple of weeks, by winter, they could afford a real house. With a fireplace.

Mentally keeping her fingers crossed, she pulled a pan from the bottom of the sideboard and began pumping water in it for the turnip greens. Once she had a fire going and the vegetables on, she sat at the table to peel potatoes.

As she worked, her thoughts drifted to Wade Carlisle. She pictured him again, standing next to Sheriff O'Brien in his snug jeans, black vest, and gray shirt that had been partially unbuttoned. She had caught a glimpse of soft, curling black hair on his chest, and by the deep tan in that particular area, she figured he probably spent a lot of time without his shirt.

Those wretched flutters started up again.

In her mind's eye, she saw the gun he wore. The tooled leather holster hung low on one side and was tied with a leather strip around his muscular thigh. The pearl handle had looked as if it had been made to fit his hand.

But most of all, she remembered his soft gray eyes. They had looked into her very soul . . . and touched her.

Suddenly, inexplicably, she hoped she never saw him again.

৯ *Chapter 2* ৯

*W*ade leaned his shovel against an upright post and wiped the sweat from his face with his handkerchief. Even the wind didn't help. The Wyoming sun was brutal. Stuffing the cloth into his back pocket, he reached for a canteen lying on a stack of log posts yet to be set.

He'd been working since sunup, but he hadn't been able to drive Danielle Jordan out of his thoughts. He could still see her sweet curves in that calico dress . . . and the disappointment in those heart-stopping green eyes.

The image didn't set well.

Damn it. What was the matter with him? He didn't owe her anything. He didn't owe any woman. After the lessons he'd learned from Charlotte, he'd kept his distance from women. Oh, not that he didn't visit Betsy Hawker once in a while. He did. But only when he needed to—and there were no ties with his sultry blond lady friend, and with the way his body had started acting up lately, he knew he'd have to pay her another visit . . . real soon.

"Cook says dinner'll be ready in ten minutes—if you're still alive by then."

Wade turned to see Lefty sidestep a pile of manure as he strolled toward him. "What are you talking about?"

The foreman propped a foot on the stack of posts. "The pace you've been settin' since dawn. Keep it up, and you'll be ready for a coffin come nightfall."

"The representatives will be here in less than two weeks. You know that."

"This ain't got nothin' to do with the Stock Association. It's got to do with that gal you're tryin' to forget."

Wade wished he'd kept his mouth shut and never told Lefty about Danielle. "She's already forgotten."

The foreman thumbed his hat back. "Boy, if your pa was still alive, he'd take a strap to you for lyin' like that. And, I don't know why you're tryin' to deny your feelin's for the gal. The banker's boy told me how struck you were."

Ah, hell. Had he been that obvious? Damn Toby, anyway. "Okay, so I did take a liking to her. It doesn't matter. She took to me about as much as a hog does to a butcher."

Lefty fingered a sideburn. "Because she thinks you're a drinkin' man. 'Pears to me that you oughta set her straight."

"Why bother? I don't want to get involved with her. I don't want to get involved with any female."

"You still compare all gals to Charlotte, don't you?"

"They're all the same."

Lefty snorted. "No, they ain't. Charlotte was a money-hungry bitch. Hellfire, boy, she isn't even in the same class with Dani Jordan. That little gal has an honest business, and only so she can keep her and her sis fed. Charlotte wanted money for them fancy clothes and hats and stinkin' toilet water. She wanted folks to think she was some highfalutin lady who was better'n others, not just some lowly rancher's wife."

Wade studied his friend. Lefty wasn't one to praise anyone, especially a woman. "You fancy Danielle, too, don't you?"

Lefty grinned, showing a gaping hole where his front tooth used to be. "Hellfire, boy. I'm too old for the likes of that one. But, shave twenty years off my age, and I'd give everyone of you young bucks a tussle." His expression turned serious. "Go on, Wade. Talk to her. You'll see she ain't like Charlotte."

"Can I have my dinner first?"

He rolled his eyes. "Anything to waste time."

Chuckling, they headed for the house.

Eula, a thin woman in her middle years, was standing by the kitchen door with her arms crossed when Wade walked past her and took a seat opposite Lefty at the table. "Mmm. This smells good."

She sniffed and tucked a loose strand of brownish gray hair back into the tight bun at the nape of her neck. "It's better when it's hot."

Wade winced. She reminded him of the housekeeper he'd had when he was growing up. Like Eula, Marybeth never had to scold him. A simple remark would make him feel like a heel. He tried to soothe Eula's ruffled feathers. "How was the candy I gave you last night?"

She turned away. "I haven't sampled it yet. And reminding me of your kindness doesn't change the fact that you were late for dinner."

"It was Lefty's fault," he lied baldly.

The foreman cackled out loud. "Sure, boy. Blame it on me. Get Eula all fired up so I'll have to eat burnt steak for a week."

"I never burn food," Eula countered indignantly.

Lefty had the good sense to keep his mouth shut.

Wade had to agree with Eula. In the two months she'd been here, she hadn't once set an overcooked meal on the table. In fact, she was a very good cook.

At the reminder of her culinary skills, Wade's thoughts drifted to another woman's expertise. He shoved a bite of stew in his mouth. He had to stop thinking about Danielle Jordan.

Maybe Lefty was right. Maybe he should talk to her again. Over the last twenty-four hours, he'd built her up in his mind to be some ethereal, divine creature. A second look was bound to bring him back to earth.

Danielle folded her apron and set it on a shelf near the chocolate molds. It was Janie's night to make candy, and her night to relax. Tomorrow, too, since it was the Sabbath.

Placing a hand on the small of her back, she twisted, trying to relieve a kink she'd gotten from bending over the stove for the last two hours. Mercy, she was tired. And hot. The temperature in the kitchen must be thirty degrees hotter than outside, and it was murderous in the street.

She hadn't finished the batch of confections for today's sale until nearly two this morning, and she'd opened the shop at eight, then most of the day, she'd been running between customers and making her specialty, small white cake squares with lemon frosting.

Knowing how hot it would be in their upstairs room in the heat of the afternoon, she entertained the idea of taking a nap under a tree.

"Dani? Miss Whitehall came in while you were frosting the little cakes, and she wanted to talk to you. She said she'd be back at four."

Danielle glanced at the clock on the rear counter. It was fifteen till. If there was any way she could avoid it, she wasn't going to wait around for another quarter hour. "Did she say what she wanted?"

A blond curl slipped over Janie's shoulder, and she brushed it back, then wiped her hands on a chocolate-stained apron that shielded her skirt. "I think she wants you to supply treats for a temperance meeting since you—and I quote—'*cannot seem to find time to participate.*'"

Danielle sought patience from the ceiling. The woman never gave up. "Fine. Tell her to leave the date and time of the next meeting, and I'll send over a batch of chocolates." Maybe she'd break out in hives.

Withdrawing some pins from her pocket, Danielle coiled her hair on top of her head and secured it, then looped her reticule over her wrist and headed for the door. Even if she didn't take a nap under a tree, she needed fresh air. Hot, but fresh.

Main Street was deserted, except for a lone horseman riding in at the opposite end of town. Dust curled up in little puffs as the fetid wind gusted across the road. A corner of Hank's newly painted sign had come loose and knocked against a back support.

Somewhere down the street, a dog barked. A child laughed.

Staying in the shade of the boardwalk, Danielle lifted the hem of her skirt and walked toward the mercantile. Maybe Mr. Michaels had received her Sears Roebuck catalog order for a heart-shaped candy mold.

As she walked, she felt again the pride at being able to walk down the street with her head held high. No pitying eyes followed her progress. No mothers shuffled their children out of her path as if she had some disease. She wasn't the niece of the town drunk anymore. She was a respectable member of the community.

Smiling to herself, she passed an old man sitting in a rocker in front of Tulley's eatery. His gnarled hands held a small knife and a stick. Wood shavings littered the boardwalk between his feet.

"Afternoon, Miss Jordan. Right hot, ain't it?"

"It certainly is." She nodded to the gentleman, trying to remember who he was. Then it hit her. He was Emery Whitehall, Emma's father. Giving him a half-smile, she hurried past, wanting to avoid any discussion about his daughter.

The rider drew closer, and she had a sense of familiarity about him. She shaded her eyes from the sun and squinted, trying to focus. Fluttery wings beat against the walls of her chest. Wade Carlisle.

She didn't want to see him. She detested the things he made her feel. Stepping into the first door she came to, she quickly closed it behind her.

"May I help you?"

Danielle turned at the sound of a man's voice, then closed her eyes in resignation. The barber shop. "Um, good day, Mr. Bramble. How are you?"

Neatly trimmed gray brows drew together. "I'm fine, Miss Jordan." He glanced at the scissors in his hand, then back to her. "You need a haircut?"

The mere thought horrified her. She'd never even had as much as a trim. Her hair was past her waist, and it was going to stay there. "No, no thank you. I, er, just wanted . . . a . . . bottle of hair tonic."

"You do?"

"Er, yes. It's for . . . one of my customers," she lied. "He lives a ways out of town and asked me to pick him up a bottle." She'd never made a very good liar—and now was no exception. For goodness sake, she could feel her cheeks turning red.

Mr. Bramble scratched his round belly, then shrugged and ambled over to a shelf lined with bottles and shaving brushes and combs. He retrieved a brown bottle that read: Dr. Miracle's Sweet-Smelling Tonic, and handed it to her. "That'll be one dollar, Miss."

Danielle nearly groaned out loud. A whole dollar just to avoid Wade Carlisle—and after she made her purchase what was she supposed to do? Tell Mr. Bramble she wanted to stay out of the heat for a few minutes when it was even hotter in there than outside?

She stared at the bottle in her hand. What on earth was she going to do with gentlemen's tonic?

Taking a silver dollar out of her reticule, she handed it to the proprietor, then prayed that Mr. Carlisle had already ridden past as she opened the door.

Steel gray eyes slammed into hers.

She drew in a sharp breath. Wade Carlisle was standing right in front of her—so close she could smell leather and dust and an intriguing scent she couldn't put a name to. She opened her mouth to speak but no words came out.

He appeared to be as speechless as she. Finally, he collected himself and took her arm. "Miss Jordan, I saw you come in here, and I wanted to speak to you." He glanced toward the eatery two doors down. "May I buy you a lemonade?"

She'd rather drink from a horse trough than share anything with him. "Thank you, Mr. Carlisle, I'd like that." Okay, so she never had been very assertive.

Inside Tulley's eatery, he held a chair for her as she sat

down at a small round table covered with a red-and-white-checkered cloth.

When two tall glasses of iced lemonade were in front of them, he lifted his toward her. "This, Miss Jordan, is what I wanted to talk to you about." He studied the pale yellow liquid. "Since I was sixteen, I haven't had anything stronger than this to drink." Those mesmerizing eyes met hers. "Yesterday, I asked you if you sold liquor because my ranch hands have taken to carrying your pink bags and showing up for work . . . not in their best condition."

If Danielle had been speechless earlier, now she was completely mute. He didn't imbibe. Her voice finally found its way up her throat. "They're coming to work drunk?"

"When they show up."

"And you thought I was selling it to them?"

"Not really. I was just covering all bases."

That appeased her somewhat. "Then I owe you an apology, Mr. Carlisle. I jumped to a conclusion without being aware of all the facts."

His eyes crinkled at the corners. "There's another fact you're apparently unaware of."

"What's that?"

"My name is Wade."

The rough velvet of his voice slid over her flesh like a gentle hand. Tingles skittered up her arms. He was asking for an intimacy she wasn't sure she was ready to give. Then her eyes melted into his, and she felt her better judgment crumbling. "Mine is Danielle."

"I know."

She swallowed. "Was that all . . . Wade?"

"No." He reached across the table and took her hand. For several seconds, he stared at her fingers, so pale wrapped in his own. She was sure he could feel the pulse pounding wildly at her wrist.

"I'd like to start over by taking you to church tomorrow, and to the spring social afterwards."

Curse her racing pulse and those blasted wings that kept flapping around in her chest. "Why?"

His eyes held hers as his thumb traced her knuckles. "Because there's something about you that calls out to me. Something I can't identify, and I can't explain. But I know you feel it, too."

She wanted to deny his words, but she couldn't. She knew exactly what he meant. Still, she wasn't sure she was ready to explore those unsettling feelings. For the first time in her life, she was free and independent. She didn't have someone to order her around and make decisions for her. She was her own woman.

Still, her emotions countered. What harm could there be in going to church? "I believe services begin at ten—and my sister will want to go, too."

His mouth spread into a beautiful smile. "I'll pick you both up at a quarter till."

The sermon was long and boring, and most of the reverend's biblical sayings went right over Wade's head, but sitting next to Danielle, inhaling her delicate lavender scent, and admiring the way her pretty yellow dress clung to her curves, made it all worthwhile.

He still wasn't able to believe she was so lovely. Yesterday, he'd been certain she couldn't possibly have been as beautiful as he remembered, but when he saw her up close again, the image he'd built of her in his mind hadn't even done her justice. But, why had she gone into the barber shop?

His gaze drifted to Janie who was seated on the other side of her sister. With her blond curls and pink dress, she had turned several boys' heads when she had walked down the aisle to take her seat.

Danielle had turned more.

"Let's bow our heads and say a prayer for the widow Martin." Reverend Larson's voice broke into his thoughts. "She needs God's guidance in her hour of sorrow."

Wade tried to think about the widow who'd lost her husband last week in a hunting accident, but he couldn't stay focused. His attention strayed to Danielle as she lowered her head. A dark curl brushed against her jaw. Her thick lashes fanned out on her porcelain cheeks. He was in the house of the Lord, and he couldn't think about anything but her. It had to be sacrilegious.

But no matter how hard he tried, he couldn't stop his gaze from roaming to her full lips, or the slender column of her throat that disappeared into her high, lacy collar.

He explored the sweet, full curve of her breasts and felt himself stir. Embarrassment heated his neck. God a'mighty. This had to stop. He was in *church*.

Fixing his attention on the white-haired reverend in austere black, Wade listened intently to the rest of the sermon about lust and greed that seemed focused on him. When it was over, he escorted Danielle and Janie outside, shaking the reverend's hand as he passed through the door.

A blast of warm wind hit them as they walked down the steps, lifting the hem of Danielle's dress. Wade smiled at her attempts to keep it in place and enjoyed a brief glimpse of trim ankle.

"Toby and Pete set up tables out back," Danielle's younger sister announced, drawing his attention. He glanced at the budding blonde as they entered a grove of cottonwood trees that ran along the banks of the river, and he knew that before long Janie was going to have a line of boys at her front door. Like her sister must have had.

The shade of the cottonwoods was a welcome relief, and he was glad the picnic would take place near the water— anything that would help dispel the heat.

"Miss Whitehall said they were up half the night hauling benches and tables and they even made a platform for the twins to play music."

Searching for the two in question, he saw them standing next to a rough-hewn table covered in white linen and stacked high with food, and a various assortment of pies and cakes. Crocks of lemonade and cider were in the shade of the table at one end.

The twins, Harley and Lawrence Thompson, were a pair of lanky, good-looking lads with reddish brown hair and blue eyes that no one could tell apart. Probably not even their folks. One played a banjo, the other a mouth organ, but he'd never figured out which did which.

"Well, Miss Jordan, I see you did find time to attend the picnic."

Wade felt Danielle stiffen, and they both turned to see Emma Whitehall standing behind them, her arms crossed over her flat chest, her mouth set in a tight line.

"My, my, how convenient that you can find the time to attend a picnic, yet you are unable to pull yourself away from that little sweet shop long enough to spend one hour at a meeting for the betterment of our community."

Danielle didn't flinch. "Is the meeting held on the Sabbath, Miss Whitehall?"

"Of course not."

"Well, I'm afraid that's the only day I can call my own. So, unless you plan to change the day of the meetings, you'll simply have to carry on without me." She smiled up at Wade, and he felt his heart trip over itself. "I'm terribly thirsty, how about you?"

He tried his best to contain a grin. "Absolutely parched."

Danielle returned her attention to Miss Whitehall. "You will excuse us, won't you?" Without waiting for a response, she tugged on Wade's arm and urged him toward the tables.

"I take it you and the spinster don't get along."

The corner of Danielle's mouth twitched. "Her cause is righteous enough, but I don't care for pushy people."

When they reached the table where the refreshments were, Danielle dipped lemonade from a crock and handed a cup to him before filling her own mug.

As he sipped the cool liquid, he surveyed the serving dishes on the table. There were several cheeses, bowls of baked beans, greens, salads, fried chicken, ham, ribs, and plates of fruit.

He filched a chicken leg that was covered in sauce and took a bite. A sweet yet tangy seasoning rippled over his tongue. "Mmm. That's good."

"Thank you."

So that's what had been in the basket she'd set at the side

of the building before services. "You made these? They're delicious."

Danielle smiled. "Actually it was my mother's recipe. She used to make them for her ladies social club every week in Richmond. After she died, I tucked the recipe away in an old cook book and forgot about it until we opened Sweet Creations."

A wave of sympathy moved through him. His father had died two years ago, and he still felt the ache. "How'd she die?"

A flicker of old pain darkened her eyes. "Both my parents were killed when their buckboard overturned and rolled down a cliff, ten years ago."

"I'm so sorry."

"So am I."

"Dani! Come on. Harley's going to play!" Janie's shrill voice sang across the distance separating them.

Danielle studied her sister. "She doesn't even realize she said Harley instead of 'the twins.' "

"She's sweet on him, huh?"

"I'm afraid so. She has been since the day he first walked into the shop to order a plate of fudge for his mother's birthday. At least I think it was Harley."

"Can she tell them apart?"

"Without any problem at all."

"How?"

Danielle's mouth drew into a soft pink bow. "She says Harley's eyes are bluer, and his voice is deeper."

Wade had listened to the boys since they were six years old, and he'd never heard a difference in their voices, and he'd damn sure never seen a difference in their eye color. "She sees a lot more than I do."

"Most girls in the throes of first love do."

"You sound like an authority on the subject."

Her musical laugh moved through him like a caress. "Not hardly. I've never been in love, 'first' or otherwise."

"Why not?"

She popped a grape into her mouth. "Aside from the fact

that there was never much time to spare when I was looking after my uncle, I guess I just never met the right fella. What about you?''

He swallowed a mouthful of lemonade. "I've never met a woman I wanted to give my name to." *Until now.* He nearly choked as the liquid went down the wrong way. Where the hell had that come from?

"Are you all right?"

Wade could only nod.

"Dani!" Janie called again. "Come on!"

Wade cleared his throat and gestured to the platform. "Guess we'd better go." He gave her a flirty wink. "Besides, I want to dance with the loveliest woman here."

Her eyes twinkled with humor. "Then you'll have to wait until Miss Whitehall gets back from the privy." Trying unsuccessfully to hide a smile, she sauntered toward her sister.

Wade started choking again.

Danielle was still chuckling when she reached Janie's side.

Janie frowned. "What's so funny?"

"Nothing. Be quiet now, they're starting to play."

Eagerly, Janie turned back to watch the twin playing the banjo, the one Danielle assumed was Harley. She studied the boy's thick-lashed blue eyes, then the other one's. There was no difference in color whatsoever.

The twins burst into a lively rendition of the "Virginia Reel," and folks gathered in a clearing in front of the platform. Ladies' skirts swirled, gentlemen's feet shuffled, and Danielle couldn't help tapping her toes to the frolicking beat.

Warm hands closed over her shoulders, and Wade's velvet voice murmured in her ear. "It's more fun when you have a partner . . . and Miss Whitehall's still in the privy."

She burst into laughter as he led her into the throng of gyrating dancers.

For such a big man, Wade was an excellent dancer, his movements graceful and smooth, not in the least awkward like one might expect from a man well over six feet. But it was his smile that caught her attention and held it. She'd never seen a man with teeth that straight or that dazzling white. Out of nowhere, she was assailed with the urge to touch her lips to that beautiful mouth.

Horrified by her thoughts, she stumbled, and only Wade's quick reaction kept her from falling.

When she was righted again, she gave him a weak smile, then took his hand and continued the dance as if nothing had happened, but inside, she was a jumble of nerves. What on earth was the matter with her? She didn't want to get involved with him.

The rest of the afternoon passed with Danielle dodging the advances of several gentlemen, and flinching at the evil eye their wives kept giving her. And watching Wade scowl. She didn't dance with Wade again. In fact, she kept her distance from him as much as possible without appearing obvious.

Near evening, Janie and one of the twins went for a walk along the river, and Danielle found a large stump to sit on in the shade of a cottonwood, where she could enjoy the cool breeze coming off the water until her sister returned.

As time went by, folks drifted off, and soon Danielle found that she and Wade alone were left to wait for Janie and the twin.

Wade lounged on the grass at her feet, looking magnificent in his snug black britches, white shirt, and silver brocade vest. Even the string tie at his throat looked better on him than most.

"I haven't been to a church social in years," he said, chewing on a blade of sweet grass. "I'd forgotten how much fun they were."

Danielle drew her gaze from his handsome profile and stared out over the water. It had been fun until she'd become painfully aware of him. "They are nice. By the way, was that the beautiful Miss Whitehall I saw drooling on you a few minutes ago?"

He glanced over a broad shoulder at her, his eyes bright with amusement. A lock of midnight hair toppled onto his brow, making him look younger. More approachable. "Sure was. She'd hinted at dancing with me a dozen times today, so I finally made the offer."

"That must have made her day." Danielle hated the wasp-ishness in her voice, but she couldn't help it. Emma White-hall set her teeth on edge.

"Actually, Danielle, she's not as bad as folks think she is. I think she's just a little overzealous about what she believes in."

Even though it was Emma he was defending, Danielle was touched by his compassion for others. He took the time to look beyond the surface, something she, herself, often forgot to do. Shame colored her cheeks. "I've grown hateful in my old age."

"Old?" A black brow arched. "What are you, eighteen?"

"Nearly twenty."

He placed a hand over his heart. "My God. You're ancient."

"And an old maid."

He came up on his knees and faced her at eye-level. "Why haven't you married? With your looks, I know, even though you didn't have much time, you must have had plenty of offers—unless every man in Medicine Bow was blind."

He was such a kind man, and he couldn't know that folks there steered clear of kin of the town drunk. "I told you, I just never met the right man."

He leaned closer, so close, she could feel the warmth of his breath on her lips, and when he spoke, his voice came out husky and very, very warm. "Maybe you haven't been looking in the right places."

❧ *Chapter 3* ❧

*D*anielle's heart jumped into her throat. What was he saying? She couldn't think with him that close. "I . . . haven't been looking at all."

He took her hands in his big ones. "Why not?"

Her lungs constricted. He was so handsome, so close, he was making it hard for her to breathe. "I told you, I was taking care of my ailing uncle. When he died, four months ago, Janie and I had to find some means to survive."

Those gray eyes softened. "That must have been tough on both of you." He rubbed his thumbs over the backs of her hands, and tingles wiggled through her belly. "What made you think of a chocolate shop?"

She swallowed, trying to suppress sensations she'd never experienced. "I didn't. Our neighbor, Mrs. Liebermann, did. She was from Switzerland, and she had a whole collection of candy recipes. Mostly chocolate. She encouraged us to leave Medicine Bow for a larger town and open a shop."

Amusement lightened his eyes. "Laramie isn't much bigger."

There was no way she'd tell him she'd moved to escape the label the townsfolk had bestowed on her and Janie because of their uncle. "It's big enough to make a living."

"With all the pink bags I've seen lately, you oughta be doing a booming business."

"So far," she admitted. "What about you? I hear you have a ranch."

"The Bar C."

"Where is it?"

He gestured toward Pole Mountain. "Up there."

"Do you raise cattle?"

"Sure do. I've been crossbreeding for years, trying to develop a prime breed. I've finally succeeded, but I need a recommendation from the Stock Association to assure a market for them." He rose and stared out over the water. "Eighteen years ago, before the town was even settled, the handful of ranchers in the area branded us no accounts because we started with only one bull and four heifers. It took years for them to accept us, and even longer for us to gain their respect."

She felt a well of sympathy for him. She knew how he must have felt.

He fingered a curl that brushed his collar. "I'm having a cookout Saturday after next for the representative. I want him to taste the beef, and if he likes it—which I'm betting my future he will—word'll spread faster than a grass fire. I'll not only get top money for my beeves, but ranchers will want the services of my bulls—" he stopped abruptly, then started again just as suddenly "—I mean . . . uh . . . with the prospects, I'll be able to buy the Simpsons' place that adjoins mine."

She pretended not to notice his embarrassment. "How many acres do you have now?"

"Eight hundred. But, with their thousand-acre tract added to mine, and the water rights to the creek that runs through their place, I'll be able to build the Bar C into the kind of ranch my father always dreamed of."

"Is your father there?"

"No." He lifted his chin, and she saw his throat work as if words were hard for him. "His heart gave out on him two years ago." There was a bitterness in his tone that she didn't quite understand.

Still, she could tell how much it bothered him to talk about his father, so she quickly changed the subject. "Have you ever been married?"

"No."

The same question he'd asked came to mind. "Why not?"

"Bad examples."

She was dying to know what he meant by that but the frown on his face kept her from asking. She glanced toward the path that led beside the river. "I wonder what's taking Janie and Harley so long?"

Wade seemed to shake himself from his disturbing thoughts, then he again knelt in front of her. "I have a pretty good idea."

"What?"

He studied her for a few moments, his eyes filled with a warmth like she'd never seen. The sudden, soul-shaking intensity was almost frightening, and she had the strongest urge to run. Then slowly, gently, he framed her face with his hands. "This." He lowered his head and tenderly brushed his lips over hers.

Surprise held her frozen in place. She'd never felt anything so shocking . . . so wonderful. His lips were soft, yet firm, and so deliciously warm. She could have drowned in the slow, lazy kiss.

A sigh left her, and she pressed closer, sinking into him.

His fingers slid to the nape of her neck, and he pressed her closer, touching her lower lip with the tip of his tongue.

Warmth spread to her lower body.

A distant giggle tinkled through the trees, and he pulled back. "Damn."

Too embarrassed to look at him, she focused on the river path, knowing it was Janie's giggle she'd heard. Only a second passed before she saw her sister and Harley come into view. They were holding hands and smiling at each other.

Wade shifted, and she reluctantly glanced in his direction.

He was staring at her like he'd never seen her before.

Forgetting her embarrassment, she touched his arm. "Is something wrong?"

Those silver eyes met hers, and she could see something

deep and troubling in their depths. "Yes, beautiful. There's a lot wrong. With me." He stepped out of her reach and picked up the blanket they'd shared during dinner. Folding it over his arm, he held it while he waited for Janie and Harley to join them.

"Oh, Dani, you should have seen the herd of antelope we saw. There must have been a hundred of them."

"About thirty," Harley corrected in a voice that started low and broke into a soprano pitch.

Danielle wasn't fooled. Janie's lips were as swollen as Danielle's felt. "You've seen antelope a thousand times. Now what took you so long?"

Her sister blushed, and Harley shuffled his feet, looking anywhere but at her.

Wade came to his feet and stood beside her. "I thought I already explained that to you."

Heat rushed to Danielle's cheeks. If he said anything in front of her sister, she'd die on the spot.

"Explained what?" Janie asked.

"What you and Harley were doing that took you so long."

Janie's blond curls bounced as her chin came up. "And exactly what was that, Mr. Carlisle?"

"Kissing."

Her sister looked as if she was about to swoon.

Harley started sputtering.

Danielle was too shocked to speak for several seconds, then at last, she regained control of her tongue. "Um, Janie, you and Harley take the blanket and plate of chicken and lemon cakes home. I want to have a word with Mr. Carlisle, then I'll join you."

As soon as her sister and the twin were out of earshot, she turned on Wade. "How dare you embarrass my sister like that." She poked his chest. "If I were a man, I'd punch you."

"We both know it's the truth. They're young, they're attracted to each other, and their instinct to kiss is as natural as breathing. I was only stating the obvious."

"Did it ever occur to you that my sister may not be like

that? That she and that boy may have done nothing more than hold hands?''

''No.''

She jammed her hands on her hips. ''Why not?''

''Because she's like you.'' His gaze touched her lips as if he was remembering their kiss. ''She's too passionate for her own good.''

Danielle knew she was going to sink through the ground. Passionate? She wasn't passionate, for goodness sakes, she was . . . well, she didn't know, but it certainly wasn't that. ''Excuse me, Mr. Carlisle, but it's getting late, and I have to go.''

''What's wrong? Afraid to face the truth?''

Walk away, her common sense told her. Just go. Don't argue. She marched right up to him and stared him in the eye. ''The truth? Exactly what is the truth? That you took advantage of me? That you kissed me without an invitation, then accused my baby sister of the same infraction?''

''I didn't take advantage of you,'' he said in a quiet tone. ''You could have pulled away at any time.''

He had her there. ''I was too stunned to react the way I should have,'' she only half-lied. ''A true gentleman never would have—''

''I've never claimed to be a gentleman. But I know damn well you felt the same attraction I did the first time we met. You wanted to be kissed as much as I wanted to kiss you.''

She opened her mouth to deny his words, but clamped it shut again. There was no arguing with the man. ''Goodbye, Mr. Carlisle.'' She turned to walk away, but he caught her arm.

''When is it Janie's turn to make the candy?''

What did that have to do with anything? ''Tomorrow.''

He gave her a very male smile. ''Go for a ride with me then.''

''Have you lost your mind?''

''No. Only my heart.''

The flush that stole up her cheeks nearly singed her eyelashes. ''I . . . I . . .''

"Just say yes," he urged as he lowered his head and brushed his lips over hers.

Danielle couldn't think. The feel of his mouth on hers was enough to melt her brain.

He slipped his arm around her waist. "I'm not going to let go of you until you agree." He kissed her again, longer, deeper, his tongue tracing the edge of her lips.

If that was a threat, he was failing miserably. She would be content to stay in his arms the rest of her life. Of course, she was supposed to be angry with him, so she had to do something without appearing obvious. Leaning back, keeping her lips just out of his reach, she nodded. "If that's the only way you'll release me, then I guess I'll have to agree."

He chuckled. "Five o'clock?"

"Fine." If she lived that long. Her heart was trying to pound through the walls of her chest.

Easing his hands from her waist, lingering for a moment before he released her completely, he smiled, then sauntered toward the horses.

Danielle's legs folded, and she sank back down on the stump.

Wade slammed the shovel into the post hole he'd started and then stomped it with his boot. He'd been working since dawn, trying to drive the demons away. Ever since he'd left Danielle yesterday, he hadn't been able to stop thinking about Charlotte.

In his mind's eyes, he pictured the last time he saw her, the day before she left the ranch. She had been in the bunkhouse, in bed with one of the drovers, a stack of silver lying on her discarded dress.

His stomach knotted at the memory. For months before that, his father had wondered where she was getting the fancy material for the dresses she made. Although she'd claimed her friend who owned the dressmaking shop gave her the cloth, his father hadn't believed her. His suspicions had been confirmed that day.

He'd fired every hand but Lefty.

Wade dumped another mound of earth onto the pile beside the post hole, remembering when the sheriff came several weeks later, telling them that Charlotte had been killed when she took up with an outlaw.

His father had buried his wife, and two weeks later, died of heart failure. It was then that Wade realized that his father had loved Charlotte so much it killed him.

After that, Wade had become gun-shy. To love a woman that much was scary. He'd refused to get involved with any female . . . until Danielle. He smiled. At least she was an honest business woman, not some tramp who would go to *any* extreme to earn money—and not care who she hurt.

Five o'clock. He'd see her then, and they'd go for a nice, long ride. His smile widened. Maybe he'd show her the old gold mine.

Danielle wished she'd never agreed to go with Wade. She was so tired, every bone in her body ached. The picnic yesterday had been nice, but last night, it was her turn to make the candy, and she hadn't finished until after three o'clock that morning.

And Mondays were always their busiest days.

Running a brush through her hair, she was too tired to even put it up, so she simply drew it back with a ribbon and tied it at the nape of her neck.

Giving her appearance one last glance, she straightened a fold on her blue gingham dress, then picked up a matching bonnet and settled it on top of her head. Leaving the ties dangling, she retrieved her reticule and headed downstairs.

The line of customers hadn't diminished. You'd think they could go one day without candy. Shaking her head, she made for the doors, intending to wait for Wade on the boardwalk.

He pushed through the opening before she even reached it, then smiled when he saw her coming toward him. "Woman," he murmured, "you are breathtaking." Looping her arm through his, he led her out the doors.

Her insides were going all funny again. Every time she got near the man, her senses acted up, and the feel of his hard muscles beneath her hand made her warm all over.

Apparently unaware of her turmoil, he led her to a pair of buckskins. A gelding and a mare. "This is Firefly," he said, reaching up to stroke the mare's sleek neck. "She's as gentle as a new calf."

He rubbed the other horse's nose. "This fella, on the other hand, is more trouble than he's worth. Sandstone, say hello to Danielle."

The gelding nickered and bobbed its head as if in greeting.

Wade smiled, those heavy-lashed eyes crinkling at the corners in the shade of his stetson. "All set?"

Extremely grateful for Pastor Davenport at her church in Medicine Bow, who'd taught her and Janie how to ride, she nodded, then moved beside the horse and waited for him to help her mount.

She expected him to cup his hands for her to use as a foothold. Instead, he caught her by the waist and set her atop the sidesaddle.

For a heartbeat, his hands remained on her waist, and their eyes met. There was such warmth in his, her toes curled. Several breathless seconds passed before he stepped away.

As she watched him swing up onto the back of his horse, chills ran along her arms, even though the day was hot. Caused by exhaustion, she told herself determinedly, *not* a reaction to the way his jeans molded so well to his firm rear end. She always got chills when she was tired. *Always*.

The wind gusted and lifted her skirt, and she quickly brushed it down, then securing her leg around the saddle horn, she reined her horse around to trot alongside Wade.

"There's an old gold mine a few miles from here I thought you might like to see." He gestured toward Pole Mountain. "It's near the eastern boundary of the ranch."

"I thought most of the mines were in the Medicine Bow Mountains."

"They are, but a few hopeful miners spread out. One located a small vein on the Bar C, long before my pa bought it. When the gold ran out, the miner abandoned his claim."

"Is it in a cave or above ground?"

He sent her a quirky grin. "I don't want to give it all away before you get there, beautiful."

The endearment made her blush, and she fixed on the scenery ahead so she wouldn't have to look at that mischievous twinkle in his eyes. Sage brush and range grass. That was all that covered the flat plains and sloping hill up to Pole Mountain.

The wind had died down some, but she knew it wouldn't last long. If the wind wasn't blowing in Wyoming, just give it a minute.

The terrain lifted into a gentle slope, and she tightened her fingers around the saddle horn. "How does the grass stay so tall with all the cattle and sheep around here?"

Leather creaked as Wade turned in the saddle to answer her. "There's a lot more land than there is livestock. By the time they get to this grass, other areas will have grown as tall."

"With the open range laws, don't the herds get mixed up?"

"Sometimes. That's why we have brands and why we formed the Stock Association to oversee branding, roundups, and quarantines. They even hire brand inspectors to check the herds." His gaze drifted to a lone cow ahead of them. "We have trouble with rustlers, though. That's why I fenced my range." He gestured to a long stand of log posts farther ahead of them. "I use barbed wire to keep the stock from breaking the fence down."

"That's your land?"

"Yes. See where the fence ends over there on the right? That's my eastern boundary. The Simpsons' place I was telling you about is on the other side."

"The meeting with the Stock Association's representative is really important to you, isn't it?"

His gaze drifted over the area beyond his fence, then he lowered his gaze to his hands on the pommel. "My father's dying wish was for me to finish what he started. Without the approval of the Stock Association, that isn't going to happen. They're becoming a powerful force, and the cattlemen listen to them. If they recommend my breed, I'll fulfill my father's dream.''

Compassion touched her, and she could almost feel his pain—the same pain she'd experienced when her parents died. ''You loved him very much, didn't you.''

He couldn't meet her eyes. He couldn't even speak. Instead, he avoided her gaze and nodded.

She was so touched, tears stung her eyes. How rare it was to find a person who cared so deeply for others. She blinked rapidly and surveyed the fence. ''Will we go by the ranch house?''

He appeared grateful for the change of topic. ''Not this time. The ranch is in the west section. We're going northeast.''

They both fell silent as they rode up the slope that grew gradually steeper until it reached the mountainous top. The wind had kicked up again, tousling the tops of limber and lodge pole pines. The trees clustered in one area, while towering granite boulders and meadows of spring grass and wild flowers filled others. It was a wonderful mixture of rugged beauty.

''See that mountain of granite over there?'' He pointed to the rocks. ''The mine's in there.'' He reined his buckskin toward a stone wall at least two hundred feet high.

Numbly, Danielle wondered if they were going to have to climb. As tired as she was, she knew she'd never make it.

When the horses began the ascent up to the base of the rock mountain, Wade veered to the left, then guided his mount into a crevice between a huge rock and the sheer granite wall. ''This is the only way in or out.''

She hadn't even seen the opening until he went into it. ''How far is the mine?''

''A couple hundred yards, but it's slow going because the trail's so narrow.''

It was cooler inside the passageway and out of the wind, yet the walls were so close, she could stretch out her hands and touch both sides at the same time. But the worst part, or maybe it was the best, was her view of Wade's broad back and firm rear end. She was entranced by the way his thighs flexed and tightened with the movement of the buckskin, the perfect shape of his spine as it turned when he pulled the reins in the winding passageway, the way his shoulders bunched and relaxed.

She was getting those chills again.

"This is the place," he called out, motioning for her to enter a wide area just ahead. His eyes gleamed bright silver as he dismounted and came to help her down. When his hands closed around her waist, he smiled up at her. "This used to be my favorite hideaway when I first came to the ranch. I would come here to get away from my step—my problems." He took her hand. "Come on, it's this way."

Danielle couldn't help smiling at his enthusiasm as he pulled her up a small trail that led to a flat, round granite plateau about twenty feet in diameter. Off to the right was an opening in the rock wall. "A cave?"

"Yes and no. Come on, I'll show you." He ducked his head under the opening, then walked a few steps and stopped. "Whatever you do, don't let go of my hand."

That sounded awfully ominous. It was dark in the cavern, and she couldn't see anything beyond the beam of sunlight from the opening that stopped within a few feet.

Once they moved beyond the light, he stationed her against the wall of the cave, but didn't release her hand. "Hug the rock with your back, and keep your heels against it as you step sideways to the left."

A tingle of fear moved through her, and she gripped his big hand as hard as she could.

"Relax, beautiful. I'm not going to let anything happen to you."

She almost did, until she felt the ridge of a cliff in the center of her left foot. "Wade? What's in front of us?"

"A shaft that leads down to a second mine."

Every muscle in her body tightened. "How deep?"

"About sixty feet."

Fear clawed up her middle, and she had to swallow several

times to keep from being sick. "I . . . don't think this is a good idea."

Instead of answering her, he gave her hand a swift yank. "There. We're past the mine shaft." Still holding her hand, he fumbled in his vest pocket for a moment then lit a sulfur match. He held it high, illuminating a small ledge. "Good. The candle's right where I left it thirteen years ago." Lighting the wick, he then took off his hat and laced his fingers through his hair and grinned. "I brought a young lady here when I was seventeen, and she was so frightened, she refused to go in. After I took her home, she politely but firmly informed me she wouldn't be seeing me again."

"What made you think I wouldn't react in the same way?"

He gently ran a finger down her cheek. "Because you're courageous. No woman would take on the responsibility of caring for an ailing uncle, running a business, and raising a thirteen-year-old sister unless she was either damned stupid or damned brave. And, there's nothing stupid about you."

His ability to read people was amazing—and she wasn't about to tell him she'd been scared out of her skin when he told her what was in front of her. "Thank you, Mr. Carlisle. That was a nice thing to say."

He pulled her against him. "Oh, no you don't. You're not going all prim on me again. We passed far beyond that yesterday."

She felt her cheeks warm, and she felt something else, too; the hard contours of his body pressed to her own. For goodness sakes, he was so close, she could feel his heart beating against her breasts. She could smell his clean, leathery scent. The tips of her breasts began to tingle, then tighten.

"Did you hear me, Danielle?"

She swallowed. "Yes."

"Yes what?"

"Yes, Wade. Now please let go of me."

He immediately released her and stepped away, then his gaze drifted over her, lingering at the bodice of her dress for a heartbeat before he lifted the candle from the ledge and motioned her toward a second opening. "There's another room over there."

The next chamber was a circular room, with a high, rounded ceiling, and a floor thick with sand. Gouges intermingled with veins of bright colored rock formations that dissected the granite walls. Specks of what she assumed was pyrite, or fool's gold, glistened overhead like a thousand twinkling stars. "It's lovely."

He fingered a strand of her hair that had slipped over her shoulder. "I've seen better." He was looking at her.

Those cursed chills shimmered through places in her body she didn't even know she had. But no matter how shocked she was by her reaction to him, she couldn't pull away. She was mesmerized by his magnificent features. She wanted to run her hands along that hard, hair-roughened jaw and slide her fingers into those thick, silky black strands. But most of all, she wanted to feel his mouth on hers again.

"Jesus, Danielle. The look in your eyes is enough to set me on fire."

His eyes were shadowed by the darkness in the cave, but she could see the sensual message he couldn't hide. And she was beyond caring.

The thought had barely formed before his mouth was on hers.

Her whole world careened, then spun. There was such a sensual vitality about him, such fierce passion. Unable to stop herself, she opened her mouth for him, and almost swooned at the feel of his tongue brushing against hers. It was so shocking. So wickedly wonderful.

He drew her fully against him, and she again experienced the hard contours of his body, his manly scent, his heat.

Every moral fiber cried out for her to stop, but she couldn't. She wanted this more than she wanted to breathe. She pressed closer, and slid her arms around his neck.

A low groan rippled across her tongue, and his fingers began massaging the curve of her waist, her spine, the sensitive place at the back of her neck. A trembling sensation tightened her breasts, and she pressed closer still, needing . . . what?

He knew. Oh yes, he did. He covered her breast with his palm.

Streaks of fire shot to her very core, and she gasped against his mouth.

The sound brought him to his senses.

He pulled away from her, his chest rising and falling as if he'd been running. "No," he said on a ragged whisper. "Not like this. Damn it, you deserve better."

"What?"

"Never mind." He grabbed her hand. "Come on, let's get the hell out of here."

⅀ Chapter 4 ⅀

Wade slammed his hand against the jamb of his bedroom door. After what had nearly happened at the mine, he was so angry with himself he could put his fist through a wall.

What was the matter with him? He *knew* if he made love to Danielle, he'd have to marry her. Jesus, he wasn't ready for a step like that. He doubted if he'd ever be—not after the lessons he learned from his beloved stepmother. Charlotte had been everything his father had ever dreamed of, too, at first.

But Danielle is not like Charlotte, his heart argued. *She's as genuine and beautiful inside as she is outside.*

He wanted to believe that more than anything in the world. The idea of waking up next to Danielle every morning, seeing the way she smiled, hearing her laughter, and watching her eyes light with pleasure, seemed so right.

Was that love? The thought scared him more than just a little. Pa's love for Charlotte had killed him.

Ah, hell. He didn't have time for this. He had a cart load of work to do.

He glanced at the bureau where the bottle of hair tonic she'd given him last evening sat. When he'd taken her back to the shop, she'd asked him to wait while she ran inside for something. He smiled, thinking of how she told him about going into the barber shop to avoid him and buying the tonic as an excuse for being there.

Shaking his head, he picked up his hat and headed for the corral.

The next week, he divided his time between the ranch and Danielle, and each day, he made a little progress with the homestead, and great strides toward falling in love with the owner of Sweet Creations. He was rapidly approaching the point where he couldn't imagine life without her.

"Wade, we got a problem," Lefty called out as he came around the side of the barn. "Jack was supposed to have mended the west fence yesterday, but he was feelin' poorly and went to bed. At least fifty head escaped. I've got the boys roundin' them up now, but they're probably scattered from here to Canada."

"Damn it!" Wade roared. "If one more hand complains with sickness, I'm going to fire the lot of them." Tossing down his shovel, he headed for his horse.

It was near midnight before they finally corralled the last bull, and Wade was so tired, he didn't think he'd make it to the house. But, before he went to bed, he was going to put a stop to whatever was going on once and for all. He couldn't afford another setback. The representative was going to be here in two days.

God a'mighty, he'd had enough trouble this last week to last him ten years. Between the men's shenanigans and his cook's strange behavior in the last couple days, he'd considered firing the lot of them. He cringed, recalling the supper Eula had served last night. The potatoes had been scorched and the steak so tough it would have taken a saw to cut it.

And she'd claimed sickness, just like his drovers.

He glared at the bunk house as he stepped up onto the porch and shoved open the door. "What the hell's going on around here?" he asked without preamble. "Why am I finding half of you asleep under trees when you're supposed to be working?" He glared at Jack, an older hand who'd never been ill a day in his life, until today. "And claiming sickness." He turned on Willie. "And what about you? Hammering on a post that doesn't even have a nail." He eyed every man in the room. "Something's going on, and I want to know what it is. Right this second."

No one moved. No one spoke.

Wade's eyes narrowed. "You've got five seconds to start talking . . . or start packing."

Henry, a quiet, older man with a thick bushy beard, stood up. "I need my job too much to cover for anyone." He kept his gaze directed at Wade, ignoring the heated looks of the other hands. "It's the candy."

Several curses erupted.

"What are you talking about?"

Henry pulled a pink bag from his vest pocket and tossed it to Wade. "These. The Chocolate Towers are filled with bourbon—and a helluva lot cheaper than a shot at Hank's."

Bourbon? Candy? *Bourbon in the candy.* Pain robbed Wade of breath for several seconds. She couldn't have done this to him. Damn it, she *couldn't* have.

But she had.

Turning abruptly, he headed for the stables. All remnants of fatigue had been replaced by blood-pumping rage. Damn her! *Damn her to an eternal hell with Charlotte!*

Clutching the bag in a white-knuckled hand, he saddled his horse and rode toward Laramie. Danielle Jordan would pay for this. By God, she would.

Danielle couldn't sleep. The day had been long and grueling, and she was too keyed up to relax. It had been her day to make the candy, and Janie had been gone most of the afternoon with Harley. Their stock had gotten so low, Danielle had to make a new batch of practically every item they served. She'd been so rushed, she hadn't even had time to make the cakes for the temperance meeting, so she'd sent over a plate of Chocolate Towers for tomorrow's meeting.

Stirring sugar into a cup of coffee near midnight, she slumped over the table and sipped the steaming brew.

A loud pounding on the back door nearly made her jump out of her skin.

"Open up, Danielle, or I'll break the door down!" A fist slammed against the wood again.

"Wade?" She jumped to her feet and raced to open the door before he woke Janie.

Anxiously, she shoved the bolt back, then turned the key. Seeing Wade standing on the step, she opened her mouth to ask what was wrong, but the furious look on his face froze the words in her throat.

A muscle ticked in his jaw, his nostrils flared, and his eyes fairly shot sparks of silver fire.

She took a step back and cleared her throat. "W-What's wrong?"

"Why don't you tell me," he snapped, then stepped inside and kicked the door shut behind him.

"Wade, you're frightening me."

She thought she saw a flicker of regret, but it was gone so quickly she couldn't be sure.

He gripped her upper arms. "I'd like to do a helluva lot more than that." He jerked his hands away as if he was afraid he might strangle her. With an angry movement, he yanked a pink bag from his pocket and shoved it into her hands. "And I'd damn sure like to hear your explanation for this."

Dumbfounded, she stared at the bag. What was she supposed to do with it? Her fearful gaze slid back to his. "What—"

"Taste it."

"But, I'm allerg—"

"*I said, taste it.*"

"Wade, please."

"*Now, damn you!*"

His voice was so hard, so threatening, she was afraid if she didn't do what he said, he'd shove it down her throat. Knowing she was going to suffer the consequences, she opened the bag and withdrew a beehive-shaped cone of candy. Taking a breath, she watched him warily as she bit into the chocolate.

Alcohol squirted into her mouth, and her eyes flew open.

She coughed and sputtered, trying to spit the stuff out, but she swallowed most of it. Struggling to catch her breath, she glared at him through watery eyes. With all the anger she could muster, she threw the bag in his face and croaked, "Very funny."

He caught her wrist. "I don't think your selling booze to my drovers is a bit funny."

"What," she coughed, "are you talking about?"

His grip tightened. "You know damn well. You laced the candy so you'd make more profit." His eyes blazed, and she was afraid he'd strike her.

"Wade, I didn't—"

He shoved her away from him as if her touch repulsed him, then he strode to the rear entrance. With his hand on the latch, he looked back. "I thought you were different, but now I see you're just another money-hungry bitch like all the rest."

Wrenching open the door, he stalked out.

Danielle crumpled into a kitchen chair. Someone had put liquor in the candy, and he blamed her. But who? She dropped her head down onto her folded arms.

Janie. Who else?

Not knowing whether to laugh or cry, she massaged her temples and tried to think what to do. Then it hit her, the most horrifying thought of all. She'd sent bourbon-laced chocolates to the temperance meeting.

Oh, God. What was she going to do?

Get them back.

Bolting to her feet, she grabbed a shawl and a plate of fudge. She'd have to switch the plates.

Cool night air sent chills racing along her spine as she crept along the field behind the rows of establishments bordering Main Street. Emma's house was the last one.

Not a single light shone in the windows of the small, white frame house with green shutters.

Creeping slowly toward the back door, Danielle tried to turn the rusty door knob. It was locked. Very quietly, she tiptoed through the flower beds below the kitchen window.

It, too, was locked. So were all the others on the back side of the house.

Danielle was just thinking about quietly going around front when she heard the back door open.

"Whoever is out there, I have a gun," Emma's thin voice announced. "Get out of here, right this minute, or I will blow a hole in you as big as Texas."

Danielle froze, then went wild with panic. Frantically, she whipped her head from side to side, looking for some means of escape. The trees!

Clutching the plate of fudge close to her chest, she lunged for the cottonwoods.

A gun blast exploded. Buckshot peppered the leaves overhead.

Danielle broke into a full run—and didn't stop until she was safely inside her shop.

Leaning against the door, gasping for breath, she closed her eyes, listening to the voices and running feet outside, and thanking God that Emma couldn't hit the side of a barn if the barrel of her shotgun was against it.

"Janie," Danielle groaned from the bed the next morning. Her eyes were swollen almost shut. Large red whelps covered her face and arms and legs. Like so many times before, she'd taken fever and had trouble getting out of bed because of the dizziness. "Janie!" she called louder.

"What?" her sister grumbled as she opened the door, then started in shock. "Holy cow, Dani! What happened to your face?"

She narrowed a puffy eye on her younger sibling. "It seems someone has been lacing the Chocolate Towers with spirits. I wouldn't have believed it if Mr. Carlisle hadn't made me taste one."

A red flush stole up Janie's cheeks, and she lowered her gaze to the floor, her fingers twisting the hem of her apron. "I didn't mean no harm. It's just that we were so broke, and I knew if something didn't happen right quick, we'd have to leave Laramie to find work in a bigger town. I didn't mean to do nothing bad. I was just trying to help."

"Well, you helped a great deal. You've single-handedly ruined everything we've fought for over the last months." Danielle knew she was being hard on the child, but she couldn't help it. Because of Janie's antics, they were right back where they started from when they were in Medicine Bow. In fact, once Emma Whitehall tasted the candy, they'd be in even worse shape. "Janie, there's something you have to do."

She sniffed. "What?"

"There's a temperance meeting at Emma Whitehall's today, and I sent over a plate of Chocolate Towers yesterday."

Her sister's eyes sprang wide. "Oh, no!"

Ignoring Janie's horrified expression, Danielle went on. "You're going to have to try and get them back." She scratched a red bump on her jaw. "I tried to sneak into her house last night, but—"

"The *gunshot*!" Janie screeched. "Oh, God."

"Never mind. Just see if you can get them." The fever was making her brain fuzzy. She couldn't think. "I don't know how, but you've got to try."

Janie stared at Danielle for several seconds with concern, then suddenly brightened. "I'll get Harley to help." Like a whirlwind of pink gingham, she spun out of the room.

Danielle closed her eyes and prayed.

"I quit," Lefty groused.

"You can't quit, there's too much work to do before the representative gets here tomorrow," Wade countered.

"Well, I am. I've had all the badgerin' I'm goin' to take. I didn't have nothin' to do with that dadgum candy, and I'm tired of bein' punished for it. Hell, I never even tasted the stuff."

Wade sighed and set his hammer aside. "I'm sorry, Lefty. I guess I've been a little edgy today."

"Edgy, my aunt Bertha. You've been downright nasty. Every one of the boys is ready to walk out."

Taking off his hat to wipe his brow, Wade nodded. "I

know, and I apologize. I'll apologize to them, too."

"Ain't gonna help if you don't stop. What's got your dander up, anyway? I know it ain't just because the boys was nippin' on the side—though you've worked 'em hard enough to make up for all the days they messed up and then some."

Wade stared at his oldest and closest friend. "No. It's more than that."

"Well, spit it out, son. What's the problem?"

"Money-hungry women."

Lefty fingered a frizzy red clump of hair. "You ain't thinkin' that Dani gal is like Charlotte, are you?"

"She's just like her."

Lefty's craggy brows rose. "I see. So you caught her in bed with one of the drovers."

"No."

"Oh, she sold some of the silver, then, for one of them fancy hats."

"No."

"Did she steal money from your pants while you was sleepin'? Or trade a rifle for a sparkly necklace?"

"No."

The foreman crossed his big arms. "Then how can you say she's like Charlotte?"

"Like my beloved stepmother, Danielle will do anything for money, no matter who it hurts. She knew how important it was for me to have everything ready for the Stock Association, but she sold liquor to my hands anyway. Nothing mattered to her but the money." Wade tried to control the tightness in his chest without much success. The pain was unbearable.

"She didn't do it."

"What?"

"The little one did. Young Joe told me. He seen that Harley come out of Hank's Saloon and give a bottle to the young'un. Hell, Joe even helped her once when she got behind on orders and her sis was out riding with you. From what Joe says, Dani didn't know nothing about the bourbon."

"Are you sure?"

"Positive."

Wade felt as if someone had kicked him in the stomach. Because of Charlotte, he'd assumed Danielle was guilty without even asking for an explanation. "Son-of-a-bitch," he groaned. "What have I done?"

"I don't know, boy. But you'd better *undo* it right quick."

"We were too late," Janie said in a subdued voice as she stood at the foot of Danielle's bed. "The temperance meeting had already started." Her small hand held tightly to Harley's slightly bigger one. "What are we going to do now?"

Danielle dragged her legs over the side of the bed and sat up. Unconcerned that Harley could see her nightgown, she laced her fingers through her hair and tried to think. All morning, her brain would only stay focused on Wade . . . and his anger.

She forced herself to return to the subject at hand. "We're going to have to face Emma and her friends. As soon as the candy is served, they'll be here." She glanced up through blurry eyes. "Close the shop and lock the doors, then hide everything breakable in the cupboards. I'll be down in a minute."

When Janie and Harley left, Danielle forced herself to stand. Her legs wobbled, and she gripped the washstand for support. When the room stopped rocking, she edged toward the wall where her clothes were draped over pegs.

It was a trial getting out of her nightgown and into a white blouse and dark blue skirt, but she managed after several stops to rest. She couldn't wait until tomorrow when most of the swelling and fever would be gone.

Finally, fully clothed, and her hair tied back, she staggered downstairs.

"They're coming!" Janie cried, just as Danielle reached the lower level.

"Get away from the window," Danielle ordered. "Harley, go out the back way and fetch the sheriff."

Janie started crying as Harley ran through the kitchen. "Dani, I'm so sorry. So very sorry."

"Don't think about it now. Let's just get through this." Danielle took a deep breath and leaned against the counter . . . and waited.

She didn't have to wait long.

"Won't do any good to try and lock us out," Emma Whitehall's tinny voice rang from outside. "We know you're in there, and we know what we have to do to rid our town of heathens like you!"

A rock crashed through the front window, and an explosion of glass ripped across the room.

Janie cried out, and turned her face to the wall, her slim shoulders shaking with fear.

Danielle ignored the stings that struck her arms and marched toward the shattered window. "Get out of here, or so help me, I'll tear your hair out, Emma Whitehall!"

The back door flew open and several women she recognized from church marched into the room wielding axes and boards.

Emma stepped over the jagged window ledge and motioned to the others. "Destroy this den of Satan."

"No!" Janie screamed as one of the women raised an axe and smashed the glass case beside her.

Danielle raced to her sister's side and shoved her behind her. She tried to stop the destruction while still protecting Janie, but the gesture was useless. Emma threatened to strike her with an axe every time she moved. Helplessly, she watched the women open the cupboards and break the candy plates and dishes, destroy the pots and candy molds with their vicious weapons, and set fire to the recipes, ignoring her threats and curses.

Then they went upstairs. Except Emma, who continued to swing an axe like a madwoman.

It was all Danielle could do to stay where she was and not dive in the middle of her, but she wasn't about to leave Janie.

The horrible crashing sounds seemed to go on forever and

Danielle, like Janie, felt the tears slide down her cheeks.

Suddenly a voice roared above the chaos. "What the hell's going on here?"

Danielle turned to see Wade stepping over the window ledge, and relief made her sag against her sister.

Emma ignored him and raised her axe to a picture of a gingerbread house on the wall.

Wade caught her wrist and yanked the axe out of her hand, then roughly shoved her back. "Get your pack of wolves out of here, Emma, or so help me, I'll have every one of you witches locked up for vandalism."

"You won't have to," the sheriff's hard voice announced as he and Harley came from the kitchen. "Emma Whitehall, you're under arrest. Sarah, Elizabeth, Constance, and Virginia, get down here this instant!"

Harley rushed to Janie, and drew her into his arms.

Danielle didn't know which shocked her more, Harley's forwardness or the quartet of women who came solemnly down the stairs, dragging their weapons behind them.

The sheriff glared at each one. "I've had my fill of your righteousness," he spat. "Now march your holier-than-thou butts over to the jail and figure out how you're going to pay Miss Jordan for all the damage you did." His eyes narrowed. "And you will pay for it or spend the next six months in a cell."

Several gasps echoed around the room.

Danielle was too numb to respond. Everything they'd worked for was gone. Everything. Another tear trailed down her cheek.

A gentle hand wiped it away. "Are you all right?"

The last thing she wanted was Wade Carlisle's concern. Angrily she pushed his hand away. "Don't touch me. Don't even come near me."

Dragging Janie away from Harley, she gripped her arm and marched upstairs. She was going to see what they could salvage from their clothes and leave this godforsaken place.

But when she saw the destruction in her room, she nearly burst into tears. She had one dress left, and she was wearing it. All of her clothes, and Janie's, had been torn to shreds. Their brushes were broken, their shoes chopped up by axes, and their toiletries shattered into millions of pieces.

"Oh, Dani, look what they've done," Janie said with such anguish that Danielle whirled around.

Her sister was holding the tattered remains of the doll she'd had since she was two years old.

"Oh, Emily. What am I going to do without you." She hugged the unrecognizable cloth body, then sank to the floor and cried.

Danielle swallowed and lifted her chin to control her own urge to weep.

Another sound alerted her, and she turned to see Wade standing in the doorway, his mouth set in a grim line as he shifted his gaze between her and Janie and the tumbled room. When he spoke, his voice was sharp enough to cut metal. "Gather whatever you can salvage. I'm taking you and Janie to the ranch."

She'd been through too much in the last twenty-four hours. She couldn't take any more. "I'd rather sleep on a bed of cow paddies than go anywhere with you. Get out of my life, Wade. And *stay* out of it."

"Danielle, I was wrong."

"So was I. About you." Shoving past him, she stumbled down the stairs. She had to get some fresh air.

Wade felt as if his soul had been ripped out as he watched her go. Then he turned to Janie. "What happened to her face?"

The little blonde sniffed, then rose to her feet. For several seconds, she held onto the cloth in her hands, then finally let it fall to the floor. "*You're* what happened."

"What's that supposed to mean?"

The imp jammed her hands onto her narrow hips. "It means, Mr. Carlisle, that you made Dani eat chocolate, when she's allergic to it. She's been sick all night, and running a fever—not that it matters to you." Like her sister, Janie pushed past him and tromped down the stairs.

Wade knew he'd never felt more like a heel than he did

in that moment. And there wasn't a damned thing he could do about it.

Or was there?

"Harley said you wanted to see me, sheriff," Danielle announced as she walked into the office. "What about?" Curiously, she noticed that all the cells were empty. So much for Emma and her clan's punishment.

The sheriff went to a wall safe behind his desk and opened it. "This is what I wanted to see you about." He held up a thick stack of bills, then tossed them on the desk. "Emma and her friends have each paid a hundred dollars for the repair of your shop. There's five hundred dollars there."

Danielle stared at the money. "I'm not going to open the shop again."

Genuine sadness filled the lawman's eyes. "I'm sorry to hear that. But the money's still yours. Do with it as you wish."

At any other time, Danielle might have thrown the money in those wretched women's faces, but she couldn't now. She and Janie had no place to live, no clothes, and very little money to buy food. She had no choice but to take it.

"As much as it galls me, I will. If you need me for anything else, I'll be at the boarding house until tomorrow morning. After that, I'll be on a train headed west."

"Where to?"

"It doesn't matter as long as it's away from here."

The older man's features softened with compassion. "Honey, don't judge all of us by the likes of Emma Whitehall and her snooty friends. Most folks around here are decent, and God-fearing . . . and understanding."

She touched the back of his weathered hand. "I wish I could stay, sheriff, but there's more to it than just Emma."

"Wade?"

She turned away to keep from saying something she might regret.

But the sheriff was wiser than she gave him credit for. "Ah, honey. Wade Carlisle is crazy about you. Hellfire, girl,

I haven't seen him so starry-eyed since he was a young buck in the first throes of lust.''

Danielle couldn't picture Wade as a "young buck." But it didn't matter, nor did it change the fact that she never wanted to see him again. "Laramie isn't the place for me or Janie." *Especially since they'd never be able to hold their heads up in town. It was Medicine Bow all over again.* She squeezed the sheriff's hand, then reluctantly picked up the money and headed for Lowell's Boarding House, where she'd left her sister. Danielle had gone there to rent a room when the sheriff sent for her.

Janie joined her as she approached the desk. "What'd the sheriff want?"

"I'll tell you later."

"Howdy, Miss Jordan. Janie," Parker Lowell, the owner, greeted.

"Mr. Lowell," Danielle acknowledged. "I'm sure you heard what happened at my shop today, so if it wouldn't be too much of an inconvenience, we'd like a room for the night."

The gray-haired man's thin lips tightened with anger. "Someone oughta take a strap to Emma Whitehall's backside, if you ask me." He opened a drawer and withdrew a key and handed it to her. "Room six."

"How much do I owe you?"

"Nothing. The room's already been paid for."

"By whom?"

"Wade Carlisle."

She clenched her teeth. "I will pay my own way, thank you. Now how much do I owe you?"

"But, Dani?"

"Shut up, Janie." She turned back to the proprietor. "Well?"

"But—"

"No buts. Either I pay for the room, or I'll find accommodations elsewhere." It was a bluff and they both knew it. There *were* no other accommodations.

Mr. Lowell sighed. "That'll be one dollar, miss."

Laying a bill on the counter, she nodded then headed for room six.

Janie trudged up the stairs behind her. "I wish you'd tell me what's going on. Why are we going on a train? And where'd you get the money?"

"The sheriff made those women pay for the damage to our shop, and we're going on a train because we're leaving Laramie."

"No."

Danielle arched a brow at her younger sister. "You don't have a say in the matter. In case you've forgotten, *you* caused this."

"I'm sorry," Janie whined, "but we can't leave. We just can't!"

"Throw a tantrum all you want, Janie. It won't matter. You'll be on that train in the morning if I have to drag you by the ear."

Mutinously, she crossed her arms and glared.

Danielle had been handling her sister since Janie was three years old. She knew ignoring her was the best solution when Janie pouted.

Sticking the key into the lock, she opened the door to their room. But as she started across the threshold, she stopped. This couldn't be the right room. Boxes from the mercantile and dressmaker's shop were stacked on the bed.

Even some from the shoemaker's.

She glanced up at the number on the door. It was room six, all right. "Wait here, Janie. Mr. Lowell apparently gave us the wrong room."

"No, he didn't," a voice drawled from inside. "The boxes are for you." Wade stepped away from the window and walked toward her.

He looked so handsome standing there in his tight jeans and gray shirt, his hair all mussed as if he'd been raking his fingers through it. But she refused to let him get under her skin again. "I don't want them."

"Ah, hell, Danielle, be reasonable. If not for yourself, at least for Janie. Neither of you has any clothes or all the other things ladies need. Clem, down at the mercantile, got his wife to fix you up with some woman things she thought you'd need. And Helen at the dress shop picked out clothes that would fit.''

''Who paid for it?''

''I did, beautiful. It's my way of saying I'm sorry for last night.''

''What happened last night?'' Janie asked, apparently forgetting their argument for the moment.

''Nothing,'' they both answered in unison.

Her sister's brows shot up. ''Oh, I see. Well, that's good.'' Her gaze drifted to the boxes from the dressmaker. ''Can I open those?''

''Yes,'' Wade answered.

''No,'' Danielle countered. ''He's taking them back.''

''No I'm not.''

Danielle clenched her fists. ''Then I'll pay you for them.''

''Like hell you will.''

''I won't keep them, otherwise.''

He threw up his hands. ''Throw the damned things out the window for all I care. *I'm not taking your money.*'' In a huff, he stormed out of the room and slammed the door.

Danielle kicked a chair and sent it crashing across the room.

Janie just sat on the edge of the bed, grinning.

❧ *Chapter 5* ❧

*W*ade stood staring out his bedroom window, watching the pink glow of dawn silhouette the upper ridges of Pole Mountain.

He hadn't been able to sleep all night. Guilt and anger took turns twisting his nerves. He'd wronged Danielle, and those women had hurt her. Oh, not physically, but inside, they'd wounded her beyond repair. Just as he had. All because he was so sure Danielle was like Charlotte. Because he'd accused her instead of trusting her.

His gaze moved over the grounds beyond his window. Everything he could see was in perfect shape. The rail on the breeding pen had been repaired. The pen had been raked. The barn had a coat of paint and a new corral. Lumber that had been dumped into a pile by the door was now stacked neatly against the barn wall and covered with canvas. The lawns were mowed and the latch on the back fence gate had been fixed. Hell, even the tables that were stationed around the open fire pit had been polished.

His hands had done a good job—once their heads had cleared.

He glanced at the clock above his fireplace. The Stock Association representative would be here at eleven, and it was only a few minutes till six. He had time to bathe, and shave . . . and see if he couldn't convince Danielle to forgive him.

He mentally went over the amount of time it took to ride into town and back. Thirty minutes each way. He'd need at least an hour to talk to her. It would take him an hour and a half to heat water and bathe, then another half hour to dress and shine his boots.

Calculating the amounts of time, he knew he'd have at least an hour and a half to spare before the representative arrived. Plenty of time. Smiling, he headed downstairs to start the morning fire and put water on.

Two and a half hours later, and right on schedule, Wade rode into Laramie and headed for Lowell's Boarding House.

All night, he'd been going over what he wanted to say to her, but nothing he'd come up with sounded right. Only the truth; he'd learned his lesson once and for all about jumping to the wrong conclusion before getting all the facts. And he loved her.

Now if only she'd give him a chance to tell her.

Drawing in a fortifying breath, he dismounted and crossed the boardwalk, then opened the door to the boarding house.

Parker Lowell looked up from his desk. " 'Mornin', Wade. What can I do for you?"

"Nothing, I just came to see how the ladies fared last night."

"They looked all right a half hour ago, when they left."

"Left for where?"

Parker shrugged. "Didn't say. Just took off for the depot in time to catch the eight o'clock train."

If Parker had picked up a .44 and blown a hole through Wade, he couldn't have been more stunned. He opened his mouth to say something, but nothing came out. Every muscle in his body was paralyzed.

Danielle was gone.

Several seconds passed before he finally found his voice. "Where," he swallowed, "was the train headed?"

"California, most likely. Course, the ladies could get off at just about any stop between here and there. Oh, that reminds me. Danielle left all them boxes you brought in yesterday. She said to give them back to you."

Wade felt like his heart had been chopped into kindling. Anger and devastation clawed through his guts. He had to get out of there. "Burn the sons-of-a-bitch."

Without waiting for Parker's reaction, Wade yanked the door open and stalked out onto the boardwalk. He stood there for a moment, gathering his composure, and willing the ache in his chest to ease.

It didn't.

His gaze swung toward the depot at the other end of town. With all his heart, he wanted to go after her, but to do so would mean giving up his father's dream. If he wasn't there to meet the representative, he wouldn't get the Stock Association's recommendation. Wilber Crawford had asked specifically for Wade's presence, and if he didn't show, Crawford would think Wade was irresponsible. Damn it, he couldn't go.

Another wave of pain washed over him.

Clenching his teeth, he threw himself into the saddle, then guided his horse toward the ranch. He wasn't going to do this to himself. He'd turn to stone before he let a woman destroy his dreams.

Kicking the gelding into a gallop, he headed for Pole Mountain.

The ache in his chest became so fierce, he began to sweat. His stomach rolled, and he knew if he didn't stop the horse, he was going to be sick. Pulling hard on the reins, he brought the animal to a halt.

The buckskin snorted and sidestepped, tossing his head.

Wade steadied him with a soothing hand, then took off his hat and wiped his damp brow. His gaze shifted between the mountain and the railroad tracks leading out of town. Indecision tore at him. In one direction lay his dreams. In the other, his heart.

He closed his eyes and felt a burning sensation behind his lashes. No matter which direction he chose, he'd lose.

Danielle leaned her head back against the seat and lowered her lashes. The incessant rattle, and jerky, swaying motion

of the train, was beginning to grate on her nerves. Oh, why
had she chosen the car next to the caboose? She'd always
heard it was the worst place to ride. Now she knew that to
be true.

And Janie hadn't spoken to her since they boarded. In fact,
she wouldn't even sit beside her.

Opening her eyes, she scanned the rows of seats until she
found her sister. She was four rows up, sitting by herself,
staring blankly out the window.

Danielle could still hear her last words before she lapsed
into angry silence. "I'll never forgive you if you take me
away from Harley. Do you hear me? *Never.*"

No matter how hard she'd tried, Danielle hadn't been able
to convince Janie that they didn't belong in Laramie. Like
in Medicine Bow, they'd never be able to live down their
ugly reputation.

Her thoughts drifted again to Wade as they had throughout
the night and morning. She could picture the way he smiled
and laughed, the way his eyes twinkled, and how his big
hands gestured when he spoke. And no matter how hard she
tried to forget, she could remember vividly how very gentle
those hands could be.

Stop thinking about him, her logic warned. You're only
torturing yourself for no reason. It's over. Accept it. No, her
heart countered. You love him. Don't do this to yourself.
Don't do this to Janie.

Her head felt like a battleground, and she massaged her
temples, trying to still the voices. Suddenly, out of nowhere,
her mother's favorite saying came to her. *Your logic will
always lead you in a safe direction, but your heart will guide
you down the risky road to paradise.*

She leaned her cheek against the window and stared out
at the passing scenery. Is that what life with Wade would be
like? Paradise? If she dared reach for it.

She thought of his compassion for others, of his intelli-
gence and wit. His volatile anger. The gentle way he held
her. The way his body felt against hers. That was as close
to paradise as she'd ever been.

Then she remembered his angry accusations. Had he truly been wrong to blame her? The spirits had come from her business, and she *was* in charge. She was the one who let it happen by not demanding to know what ingredients were in the ever-so-popular Chocolate Towers.

Wade was right to blame her.

Still, the thought of going back terrified her. The streets would buzz with gossip about her and Janie. They'd be shunned and ignored. Ladies would cross the street to keep from passing them. She'd been through it all before. But worst of all, Wade would suffer. They'd blame him for keeping her around.

He didn't deserve that. He'd worked too long and too hard to gain folks' respect for her to destroy it for him.

"Oh, no," a woman in front of her cried. "I think we're going to be robbed."

"Do you see something?" a man seated directly behind Danielle asked quickly. The older woman with shaky, gnarled hands nodded and pointed out the window. "There's a man out there, chasing the train."

Danielle swung her gaze to the window, and nearly choked on a gasp. Wade was almost to the caboose. This time, she knew her heart had taken flight.

The man behind her rose.

"Call the conductor," the old woman yelled.

"No," Danielle blurted.

A sea of faces turned toward her, and she wanted to sink through the floor. "H-He's not an outlaw. We had an argument, and he's trying to catch the train so he can talk to me."

Janie let out a delighted squeal.

Danielle glared.

The other passengers eyed her for a few seconds, then returned to what they were doing before the interruption.

The man behind her remained standing.

Danielle's gaze drifted back to the window. Wade was riding hellbent-for-leather, trying to close in on the caboose.

Her heart was beating as fast as his horse's hooves. He'd

come for her. No matter what he thought she'd done, no matter what the townsfolk said, he was coming for her.

"Oh, no!" Janie wailed.

Danielle jerked her gaze to her sister. "What's wrong?"

"Mr. Carlisle. He's hanging from the railing of the train."

"*What*?" Danielle nearly knocked herself out when she slammed her head against the window so she could see.

The pain in her head was nothing compared to the terror that squeezed her chest when she saw Wade hanging onto the caboose rail by one hand and fighting desperately to grab with the other hand. The speed of the train was so fast, it had him flapping like a flag in a wind storm.

"Oh, God!" Danielle bolted from her seat, tripping over feet and baggage as she raced toward the back of the train.

The last door was stuck, and she fought wildly to get it open. Suddenly, strong hands set her aside and hauled the heavy door inward.

The clatter of metal wheels against the tracks was deafening as she stepped out onto the platform and saw the tracks shooting from beneath the train at an alarming speed.

"Grab my hand," the man who'd opened the door yelled to Wade.

Wade shook his head. He couldn't reach it.

"Damn," the other man spat. "Lady, hold onto my coat, and whatever you do, don't let go. I'm going over the rail after him."

Danielle was absolutely horrified. She'd never be able to hold on to such a big man. "Janie! Get out here and help me!"

"Grab the coat, lady, before your friend falls."

Danielle caught the wool material with both hands, and held on with all her might as the stranger leaned over the rail.

Janie burst through the door. Assessing the situation, she immediately dropped down to the floor and wrapped her arms around the man's leg.

If the situation hadn't been so serious, Danielle would

have burst into laughter. But it wasn't a laughing matter. Wade's life was in danger.

The man's coat ripped out of her fingers so suddenly, she almost fell.

Janie let out a scream and clung to the man for dear life. Danielle lunged and caught the wool again.

Suddenly more hands were there, more men. They were all around her, grabbing for Wade and the stranger who was helping him.

"We got him," a man crowed.

Danielle went weak with relief, and the minute Wade set foot on the platform, she wanted to throw herself into his arms, but she was too afraid to release the stranger's coat.

She closed her eyes and said a prayer of thanks to the Almighty.

"You can let go now, beautiful. I'm right here."

Her eyes sprang open, and she saw him standing beside her, his hair tousled wildly, his vest ripped, and his shirt covered in dirt, but he was the most magnificent being she'd ever seen.

His mouth curved into a smile. "The marshal can't move until you let go of his coat."

Startled, Danielle glanced down at her hands to see both fists filled with black wool. Heat rushed to her cheeks, and she dropped the material.

The man straightened and faced her, his eyes bright with humor. He was tall and rugged-looking, and he wore a metal badge that read: U.S. Marshal. "You did a good job, miss. I don't think your friend would have made it without yours," he glanced down at Janie who was still sitting on the floor, "and this little gal's help."

"For that," Wade injected, "I'm eternally grateful. I would have hated to die before I could ask the lady to marry me."

Chuckles erupted from the group of men.

Danielle grabbed the marshal's coat again to keep from falling. "What did you say?"

The marshal cleared his throat. "Gentlemen, I believe

these two would like to be alone. Why don't we go back inside?'' He gently removed Danielle's fingers, then helped Janie up. ''You, too, miss.''

Danielle was barely aware of the others' departure. She was staring at Wade. ''Did you just ask me to marry you?''

''Yes.''

''Why?''

''Well, it damned sure wasn't because you wouldn't listen to the apology I've been trying to make for two days, or because you ran out on me, or because you saved my life— even though I am grateful.''

The flutters in her chest were so bad, she figured her heart had taken flight. ''Then what is the reason?''

''You know damn well what it is. I'm in love with you, woman, and I have been since the day I walked into your chocolate shop.''

That rough velvet voice was so steady, she didn't doubt for a second that he meant it. Her heart exploded into frantic beats. Then another thought hit her, one that should have occurred to her the minute she saw him. Anxiously, she snatched the pocket watch out of his vest. ''Eleven thirty! Wade, you missed your appointment with the representative!''

''I know.'' He took her hands in his big strong ones, and those heart-stopping, mercury eyes sank into hers. ''But, something more important came up.'' He brought the palm of her hand to his lips and gently kissed it. ''You. And I'm still waiting for an answer.''

She'd never known such pure joy as she did in that moment. She was more important to him than his ranch. Than *anything*. Love filled her, and a smile tugged at her mouth. ''What was the question?''

''I can't remember, but I think it had something to do with you becoming Mrs. Wade Carlisle.''

''No.''

''*What*?''

As much as she wanted to be with him, she knew she

couldn't. "The folks in Laramie will never accept me or Janie after what happened, and if I was your wife, they wouldn't accept you either. The respect you and your pa worked so hard to gain wouldn't be worth two bits."

"I don't give a damn what people think about me, and as far as that disaster at the chocolate shop, there's not a person in town, Emma Whitehall aside, that would blame you for what Janie did. They wouldn't even blame her. She's a child. Folks overlook children's mistakes—and if that's the only thing holding you up from marrying me, then I'll sell the damned ranch and move somewhere else."

Tears welled in her eyes, and her chest expanded with love for this remarkable man who was willing to give up everything for her. It humbled her. "I don't want you to leave your home, and I don't deserve someone as wonderful as you."

"Then you'd better grab me while you can." His smile was so adorable, it was all she could do not to kiss him. "You wouldn't want me to get away, would you?"

"Well . . . I suppose not."

He threw his head back and laughed. It was a beautiful sound that she would treasure every day for the rest of her life.

Then he kissed her, a long, slow, devastating kiss that told her far better than any words just how much he loved her.

Turn the page for an exciting sneak preview of a wonderful historical romance from St. Martin's Paperbacks

DEEP AS THE RIVERS

By Shirl Henke

A MARYLAND POST ROAD, 1811

$\mathcal{T}$he air was redolent with a hint of spring. Samuel looked around the low marshy countryside, still sere and brown from winter's cold. Tall patches of marsh grass grew in thick clumps off to the east side of the wide rutted road. Two gulls circled in the distance and the bare branches of a willow tree rustled softly in the brisk breeze.

By the time he reached St. Louis the weather should be breaking. The thought heartened him, as did the fact that he would be leaving Tish and her whole family behind. He threw back his head and took a deep breath of air. The slight movement saved his life as a bullet whistled a fraction of an inch from his temple.

Years of conditioning took over as he responded with pure reflexive action. He swung low to the right side of his mount, but before he could turn the horse and kick it into a gallop, another shot rang out. His horse stumbled to its knees. Samuel kicked free of the stirrups and threw himself away from the dying animal. He landed hard, thrown onto his right shoulder, striking his head a glancing blow against the hard rocky earth. The gelding nearly fell on top of him as it convulsed in its death throes, then lay still. A third shot grazed his cheek before he could flatten himself behind the fallen horse. Quickly he studied the terrain, trying to locate better cover. There was a dense copse of pampas grass in a slight swale to the east of the road. His eyes swept the rest of his surroundings, searching for a way to cover his retreat even as his hands pried desperately at the stock of his Bartlett Flint Lock, which was wedged firmly in its scabbard beneath the dead horse.

No help there, and his Martia I pistols were not accurate enough at the range from which the assassin fired. Mercifully there seemed only to be one man, but he was damnably proficient at reloading and firing. Cocking a pistol, Samuel futilely returned a shot where he saw faint movement in the brush. Cursing, he pulled out the second pistol.

Quiet. For several moments Samuel heard nothing. Then another shot rang out, this time burning through his jacket sleeve and slicing a furrow across his left bicep. The killer had circled around to his left. Soon Samuel would be without cover. He surveyed the clearing in which he lay and decided his only chance was to make a run for the tall grass at the opposite end from which the last shot had come. If only his foe had not again circled back, waiting for him to do precisely that.

Samuel shook his throbbing head to clear it, ignoring the raw burn of his arm. Just as he tensed his muscles, preparing to make the deadly dash, the drumming of hoofbeats broke the deceptively bucolic quiet. A faint rattling of harness grew louder as the tempo of the hoofbeats accelerated. A vehicle was coming around the bend in the road, the galloping horses headed straight for him.

The driver, hidden in the shadowy interior of the small phaeton, slowed the team as they neared Samuel's position. A high clear voice yelled out, "Jump aboard!" as the wheels narrowly missed the fallen horse.

Samuel tumbled onto the seat, sprawling half on the floor of the small carriage as another shot rang out, whizzing past his head. The driver whipped the well-matched team of bays into a gallop with a sudden lurch. Dazed, he hung onto the side of the phaeton and struggled into the seat. Another shot whistled harmlessly over the top of the carriage as they hurtled toward the capital.

"You're bleeding all over Uncle Emory's new velvet upholstery," a soft feminine voice said in lightly accented English.

"So, we meet again," Samuel replied, arching one black eyebrow at his rescuer.

"We never *met* in the first place," Olivia said sharply, recalling the cool way he had cut her, turning his back and stalking across the ballroom floor.

"We've not been introduced, no." He could see that she was piqued at his dismissal last night. The spoiled little cat wasn't used to having men ignore her. "Given that a beautiful young lady has just saved my life, the very least I must do is offer my name. Colonel Samuel Sheridan Shelby, at your service, my dear." He grinned as her cheeks pinkehed at the suggestive tone of his voice.

"I am not your 'dear,'" she snapped, giving the reins a sharp slap although the horses were already galloping. "Use my scarf to bind up your arm. I can't have you passing out and falling beneath the carriage wheels before we make good our escape."

He pulled a heavy woolen scarf from her neck and wrapped the cloth securely around his throbbing arm. The roadside moved by them in a blur. When the phaeton took a curve on two wheels, then righted itself with a swaying bounce, he cautioned, "Careful or you'll overturn us."

"I've driven some of the finest and the worst carriages ever made as fast as they can go and I've never overturned one yet, 'my dear,'" Olivia replied smugly.

"Beautiful and modest, too," Shelby said dryly, his eyes assessing her delicate profile with amusement. Damn but she was a stubborn beauty with her chin jutting pugnaciously and her pink lips pursed in concentration. He was forced to admit that she handled the reins with considerable expertise. "Am I not to receive the favor of your name, at least? After all, according to custom, when one person saves another's life, it belongs to the rescuer from that day forward."

"I've never heard of such a custom," she said, curious in spite of herself. She pulled on the reins and slowed the lathered team to a trot.

" 'Tis a common belief among certain of the Indians of the far West."

"You've been West?" she asked, turning to look him full in the face for the first time. A slight bruise had begun to discolor his left temple and his face was smeared with dust and sweat in spite of the chilly air. For all that, he was still so devastatingly beautiful and disturbingly male that her breath caught in her throat. Then he smiled, and Olivia was lost. The brilliance of that smile outshone all the candles on the biggest chandelier in the White House.

"Yes, I've been West. I've spent some time among the various tribes on the Great Plains, even those living in the vast mountain ranges that cross sect the continent."

"You sound as if you've traveled with Lewis and Clark," she said, her eyes alight with curiosity.

Samuel realized he had already revealed more of his background than he normally ever did to a strange female, no matter how beautiful or plucky she might be. "No, I was not privileged to make that journey. I've had other assignments across the Mississippi. You still have not told me your name. I know you're French." He cocked his head, studying her with blue eyes so piercing that she looked away.

Olivia could feel his gaze on her and knew her body was responding most unsuitably, making her face an unbecoming shade of pink that clashed with her hair. *Merde*! Why did he have to fluster her so? "I'm Olivia Patrice St. Etienne. Also, it would seem, at *your* service for this afternoon's work." There, dare him head on! If only she could muster the nerve to return his stare. Olivia forced herself to meet those penetrating dark blue eyes, which at the mention of her surname seemed to grow an infinitesimal bit wintry. Then he smiled again and she was not certain if she had imagined it.

"Charmed, Mademoiselle St. Etienne."

"How did you know I was French?" she blurted out, cu-

rious about his reaction—or her imagining of his reaction—
to her name.

"Although your English is fluent, there is a faint trace of
an accent," he hedged. He had no desire whatsoever to discuss his mother with the beauteous Mademoiselle St.
Etienne.

"Have you some aversion to my countrymen, Monsieur
Colonel?"

"Certainly not to the lovely young lady who has just saved
my life," he replied gallantly.

Olivia recognized evasion when she heard it, having been
raised by Julian St. Etienne, a luckless gambler who had been
more expert in his choice of words than his choice of cards.
She chose a frontal assault to test how much Samuel would
reveal—or conceal. "Why was someone trying to kill you
back there? Do you know who it was?"

Samuel shrugged. "I have no idea. Probably a simple rob-
bery. My horse was quite valuable."

"But of course! Precisely why the assassin shot it out from
under you, so he could lug it off to the meat market," she
responded scornfully, meeting his eyes with a dare.

"Maybe it was an unlucky shot," he said smoothly. "His
first shot nearly took off my head. I was turning the horse
suddenly, trying to reach cover when it went down. Lucky
for me the brigand was something amiss as a marksman."

"He was not all that bad a marksman or you would not
be dripping blood like that," she replied with asperity. The
woolen scarf was soaked dark red now in vivid contrast to
the colonel's face which was growing decidedly pale beneath
his sun-bronzed tan.

"Don't worry. I won't pitch over the side and spook your
horses," he said in grim amusement. "I've suffered far
worse. It's just a scratch."

"That *scratch* is bleeding profusely," she countered.
"How can you remain so calm while your lifeblood just
seeps away?"

"Practice." He swore beneath his breath. Between the
burning nuisance of his arm and the throbbing misery of his

skull all he wanted was to lie down, preferably on some surface not bouncing wildly up and down.

Olivia reined in the team as they neared a farmhouse situated on the outskirts of the capital. There was a well by the roadside with a bucket beside it. "Maybe you'd better clean up your wounds. We must stop the bleeding before you ruin the upholstery. We could see if the people here have some fresh bandages. If not," she fluffed her voluminous skirts and added boldly, "I can always use one of my petticoats."

He grinned at her cheerful voice, noting that she turned a bit green around the gills when she looked at his blood-soaked arm. "Now you must promise not to faint and fall beneath the horse's hooves," he teased.

Olivia gave an indelicate snort as she jumped from the phaeton, scanning the farmhouse door for signs of occupancy. A mangy old yellow dog eyed them suspiciously from the rickety porch and bared his gums in a toothless growl. "No one seems to be about," she said with a sigh, turning back to Samuel who by now had climbed out of the carriage.

He walked determinedly to the well and lowered the bucket, then cranked it back up with his uninjured arm. Lifting the moldy oak container, he leaned forward and poured it over his head, then let it drop by its rope once more into the depths below with a splash.

Olivia watched as he shook his head to clear it and combed his finger through his glossy black hair. Brilliant droplets of water sprayed around him in a rainbow arc of color. She felt her heartbeat accelerate when she observed a fine sheen of droplets forming on his face and rolling slowly over his boldly masculine jaw and down his throat to vanish beneath the collar of his uniform. This was not wise, not wise at all. Other than the fact that he was devastatingly handsome and charming, what did she really know about Colonel Shelby? He seemed to be involved in some mysterious intrigue and people most certainly were trying to kill him. She was altogether too attracted to this stranger.

"Damn. I lost my hat when I fell. It was brand new. This

whole uniform is ruined," he grumbled, inspecting his bloody, torn and dirt-smeared clothing.

"You . . . you had better see about that wound, else more than your uniform will be ruined," she said, moistening her suddenly dry lips with the tip of her tongue.

"Not out here," he replied distractedly as he pulled up the bucket and unfastened it from its rope. "It's a bit cool now that the sun's setting . . . and it's too exposed."

After a quick glance back down the road, she watched him stride toward the front door of the log cabin. "What if no one is at home?"

He turned at the uncertainty in her voice and raised one eyebrow. "Then we just go in. I don't plan to rob them, just use the shelter long enough to change this dressing . . . that is if the offer of your petticoat still stands good?" He waited, watching her to see what she would do.

She walked up to him as if taking the dare, but then as he turned to open the door she said, "It really isn't proper for us to be alone—indoors, that is."

Samuel threw back his head and laughed heartily. "You are a caution, *ma petite*. It is a bit late for the proprieties now. First you come thundering wildly to my rescue out of nowhere, alone and unchaperoned. Then you drive like a London hackney and nearly kill us both on the road. Now you suddenly turn vaporing belle."

Olivia felt like stomping her foot at his mocking laughter. "For a man who owes me his life, you are very rude, Monsieur Colonel." Anger thickened her accent.

Samuel noticed the shift in cadence as well as the blaze of emerald fire in her eyes. "My apologies, mademoiselle, but you still have not explained why you were driving alone in the middle of nowhere," he could not resist adding as he turned and entered the obviously deserted house. The hound on the porch raised its head once, then thought better of the exertion of further protest and instead slunk inside the shelter of the cabin behind Shelby.

Olivia stood alone in the yard for a moment. The impulse to dash to the phaeton and take off, leaving the arrogant colonel stranded, was tempting. But he was injured, and she was more attracted to him than she had ever been to a man before in her life. *Fool,* she berated herself.

Olivia reluctantly followed him into the dark interior of the cabin and watched as he unwrapped the soaked scarf from his upper arm. In spite of a slight wince of pain, his hands remained steady. Then he began to unbutton the heavy uniform jacket. As he slipped it easily off his good arm and began to work it carefully free of the injured one, Olivia stood rooted to the floor of the deserted cabin. The sheer white lawn shirt beneath his jacket stretched across his broad shoulders and clung lovingly to every inch of his lean muscular torso. Then he started to remove the shirt, too!

"What are you doing?" Her voice cracked on the last word.

"If I'm going to wrap this wound to stop the bleeding, I first have to bare the skin," he replied reasonably, continuing to pull the ruined shirt off.

She had thought his chest and shoulders were revealed through the sheer lawn covering. Now she could see how mistaken that assumption had been! Darkly bronzed skin rippled with sleek muscles as he tossed his shirt onto the crude wooden bench beside the table. A heavy pelt of black hair covered his chest, then tapered into an enticing vee that arrowed down to disappear beneath the belt buckle at his narrow waist. Her eyes would have strayed scandalously lower but a bitten-back groan distracted her.

Samuel cursed as he tried to flex his injured arm. "The bleeding's grown worse. If I don't get it stopped, I might pass out and bleed to death before you can summon help. I'm afraid I'm going to need those petticoats."

"M-My p-petticoats," she stammered, then instantly felt like a fool.

"You're not going to faint now that the shooting's done, are you?" His voice was light but a sheen of perspiration glistened on his forehead in spite of the chilly evening air. "I'd search around here for some cloth for bandages but somehow I suspect that any to be found in here would blood-poison a possum,'' he added wryly as Olivia came out of her trance.

His whole arm was soaked with blood and here she had been gawking at his naked chest as if she had never seen one before! Well, come to think of it, she *had* never seen a grown man's bare chest before. With clumsy fingers she began to tear at the top layer of her petticoats but the heavy linen would not give.

"Here, allow me," he said with mock gallantry as he knelt in front of her and reached for the snowy slip with his uninjured hand. In the other one a wicked-looking knife gleamed. He sliced through the hem of the undergarment, then let her tear it until she had a little over a yard of cloth with which to wrap his arm.

"Tear another piece about the same length," he commanded as he lowered his injured arm into the bucket of cool water he had placed on the table. A small hiss of pain escaped his clenched jaw but he made no further sound as he bathed the injury until the water ran red between his fingers.

Olivia stood holding the makeshift bandages, feeling utterly useless and somewhat queasy as she watched. An ugly furrow marred the perfection of his upper arm, slicing in a nasty angle across his bicep. She swallowed and moved closer as he raised his arm out of the water. "I'll wrap it," she said.

He held out his arm and let her cover it with the linen. He could feel the tremors that wracked her body vibrating through her hands as she worked. "Pull it tight so the bleeding stops. Aargh! Yes," he rasped as he pressed the end of the linen against the wound to hold it in place.

"I'm hurting you!" she gasped, dropping the bandage.

"No! I mean yes, but it can't be helped. Just get the damn thing wrapped around my arm and tie it off good and tight." He began to wrap the bandage himself. Suddenly Olivia's fingers, soft and cool, brushed his hand as she once more took over the task, pulling on the wrapping the way he had instructed her.

As they worked, their hands continued to touch each other.

Her skin felt silken and she smelled of jasmine. He watched her bite her lower lip in concentration as she tied off the bandage. Her mouth was soft, pale pink, utterly kissable. And he was utterly insane. He was still a married man and he knew nothing about her except that she was young, French and spoiled. That should have been enough to deter him but somehow it was not. Her hair had come loose from its pins during the wild carriage ride and a fat bouncy curl of pure flame brushed against the sensitive inside of his wrist.

Without thinking Samuel cupped his hand around the back of her slender neck and lowered his face to hers as he drew her against him. "Such good work deserves a reward," he murmured as his mouth tasted the soft pink lips that had beckoned him.

Olivia felt herself melting toward the hardness and heat of his chest. Her palms pressed against the crisp hair and her fingers kneaded in it as her lips tilted upward to meet his descending mouth. The kiss was fierce and hungry yet oddly delicate and exploratory at the same time. His lips brushed, then pressed hers and his tongue lightly rimmed the edges of her mouth until she emitted a tiny gasp of delight, allowing him entry to taste the virgin territory within.

She'd had the adulation of legions of lovesick young swains but she had never been kissed like this. Olivia could feel the pounding of his heartbeat against her palms and the answering acceleration of her own wayward heart. The exotic texture of crisp chest hair delighted her questing fingers but it was her mouth that felt the full drugging persuasion of Samuel's sensual coaxing. The tip of his tongue dipped and glided inside her lips, then danced a duel with her tongue and retreated only to plunge in for another jolting foray. She heard a low mewling sound like a lost kitten crying, without realizing that it was her own voice.

She was pliant and willing yet there was an inexplicable sense of surprise and wonder in her responses that did not befit a belle of her apparent experience. Yet the hunger that he felt left no time for further consideration or caution. It had been far, far too long since he had lain with a woman.

As the enmity between him and Tish had grown, their physical hunger for each other had waned. Two years ago he had quit her bed when he learned that she had visited a notorious abortionist in Maryland. Sickened and desolate, he had never touched her since. When his physical needs became unbearable he betrayed his marriage vows with carefully chosen professionals. The encounters always left him with such bitter, sordid regrets that he seldom succumbed. Instead he buried himself in his dangerous work.

His compelling attraction to Olivia St. Etienne was utter madness. She was obviously from a good family, gently reared with the expectation of a proper marriage even if she did behave irresponsibly. There was no place for such a female in his life. Then why was he drawn to her with such an inexplicable longing? His hand, deft and sure, had found the small sweet enticement of her breast, cupping it through the soft linen of her jacket. When he rubbed his thumb against the hard bud of her nipple she cried out against his mouth and pressed closer to him in the mindless desire they shared. His fingers tangled in her thick, lustrous hair and he twined the curls around his fists like scarlet ribbons.

If he did not stop at once he would take her here in this filthy deserted cabin on the crude plank floor, rutting like the cur dog that lay quietly in the corner of the crude bare room watching them. This was insanity born of simple deprivation. Surely it couldn't be anything more. With an oath he pulled away, supporting the breathless, dazed girl by holding her shoulders. He could feel a shudder of surprise rippling through her. She raised her head and their eyes met. Hers were wide and dazed, turned the deep green of a tree-shrouded forest pool.

The pull of her mute entreaty frightened him with its intensity. Without words she asked him why he had ended the passionate interlude. Without thinking he replied, "I've wanted to do that since the first moment I laid eyes on you. Don't deny that you wanted it, too," he added, stung by her wounded expression and his own guilt.

Shame washed over her in waves. Feeling her face flame,

she raised her hands and pressed them to her cheeks, backing away from him. Dear merciful lord, what had she almost done—allowed him to do? "No, I am scarcely in a position to deny anything." Her voice was hoarse, soft as if coming from a great distance. She could still feel his heat, the virile magnetic presence that held her in thrall. His eyes pierced to her very soul. She felt naked as he was, defenseless.

Samuel could feel her vulnerability and the pain of it hit him like a slap. He turned to pick up his discarded clothing. The shirt was a blood-soaked mess which he quickly abandoned, attempting instead to slip his injured arm through the sleeve of the heavy uniform jacket.

Olivia watched him struggle with the stiff coat then stepped closer and pulled the blood-caked sleeve straight, helping him ease it over his bandaged arm. He shrugged the other arm into the uniform, then began to button it. She stepped back yet their gazes locked and held. When Samuel had completed the task, his arms dropped to his sides.

He continued to study her with those unnerving blue eyes. "I'm truly sorry," he said stiffly. "You saved my life and I behaved abominably."

"You dared nothing I did not allow," she replied with candor, meeting his gaze unflinchingly.

"There is something between us, Mademoiselle St. Etienne, something quite remarkable . . . disturbing . . . and dangerous," he said, groping for a way to express his tumultuous emotions without revealing too much.

She smiled wistfully. "Yes, I believe you are right." Then appearing thoughtful she added, "Since I've already been as bold as any hussy, I may as well be even bolder. Don't you think after all that has happened, you might call me Olivia?" Her bones melted when his face, so harsh and austere a moment earlier, split into a heart-stopping smile.

Olivia. How classically lovely. It fit her perfectly. "Hussy you are not. Bold you definitely are. My name is Samuel, Olivia." The sound of her name rolled off his tongue like song. Damn, he was bewitched! "We had better return to the city before you are missed by your family."

She returned his earlier smile. He was clever at extracting information without revealing himself. "I have only my guardian, Samuel. Emory Wescott, a St. Louis merchant who is currently in the capital to attend to business matters."

"St. Louis?" he questioned, caught off guard.

Olivia picked up on the surprised note in his voice and turned to him as they approached the phaeton. "Yes, that is where we reside, unless Uncle Emory takes me traveling with him."

"Even a guardian so remiss as to allow his charge to go careening about the countryside unescorted will be upset if she's not at home by dark," he ventured as he helped her into the carriage.

"Not tonight he won't. He is yet in Maryland . . . collecting some bills owed him," she said with a mysterious smile. "As long as I present myself all packed and ready to sail for home on Friday he will not note my absence. Anyway, 'tis I who must see you home since I am the driver and you are the passenger. Now, let's hurry so *I* get *you* home by dark."

A smile hovered about his lips. "Such solicitude for my reputation! How can I refuse so generous an offer?"

Dusk had settled over the city with a glittering cloak of frost when Olivia's phaeton pulled up in front of the elegant three-story Georgian brick house that had been Senator Worthington Soames's wedding gift to his beloved "Tisha-Belle." Samuel hated the looming monstrosity.

Olivia eyed it with amazement. "Your house is as grand as any I've seen, even in London," she murmured, wondering how Samuel could afford it on a colonel's pay.

He could see the questions looming: Mercenary speculation? Or mere curiosity? As the daughter of French émigrés she had grown up living with the grating reality of champagne taste and gin swill income. Although it had always bothered him to admit the house and its lavish furnishings were a gift, he especially did not want to confess such to Olivia St. Etienne. Nor in their long and earnest conversation on the ride into the capital had he confessed that he was married. *But what if he were free?* Free to do what? Become involved with a wild young French hoyden who drew him like a wet hound to a warm fire?

"It's just a house. I don't even own it," he replied dismissively, raising her hand for a chaste salute. Somehow once he had pressed his lips to the jasmine-scented silk of her skin, he could not release her.

Olivia's fingers curled around his wrist while their eyes communicated in eloquent silence. He surprised himself by saying, "I'll be posted to St. Louis within the month. Perhaps we'll meet again."

Her smile was dazzling. "St. Louis is not so large a city that you could hide from me. I shall delight in tracking you down!"

Letitia Soames Shelby stood behind a Brussels lace curtain at an upstairs window watching Samuel and Olivia say their farewells. Her eyes narrowed to pale golden slits as the sound of their laughter drifted up to her. "Such tendresse. Who is the red-haired tart?"

Her companion peered out in the gloom and swore as Olivia's flame-colored hair danced in the light from the torch held by a servant who had come out to greet Samuel. "That's the rig that rescued him! An expensive lightweight phaeton with those superb matched bays."

Tish turned to face him with a scornful expression hardening her patrician features, robbing them of the doll-like beauty that always turned heads.

"Forget the worthless little nobody driving that carriage. Tell me why you failed to kill my husband."

DEEP AS THE RIVERS — a March 1997
St. Martin's Paperbacks bestseller!

If you crave romance and can't resist chocolate, you'll adore this tantalizing assortment of unexpected encounters, witty flirtation, forbidden love, and tender rediscovered passion...

MARGARET BROWNLEY's straight-laced gray-suited insurance detective is a bull in a whimsical Los Angeles chocolate shop and its beautiful, nutty owner wants him out—until she discovers his surprisingly soft center.

RAINE CANTRELL carries you back to the Old West, where men were men and candy was scarce...and a cowboy with the devil's own good looks succumbs to a sassy and sensual lady's special confectionary.

In **NADINE CRENSHAW**'s London of 1660, a reckless Puritan maid's life is changed forever by a decadent brew of frothy hot chocolate and the dashing owner of a sweetshop.

SANDRA KITT follows a Chicago child's search for a box of Sweet Dreams that brings together a tall, handsome engineer and a tough single mother with eyes like chocolate drops.

For The Love of Chocolate

YOU CAN'T RESIST IT!

Against the backdrop of an elegant Cornwall mansion before World War II and a vast continent-spanning canvas during the turbulent war years, Rosamunde Pilcher's most eagerly-awaited novel is the story of an extraordinary young woman's coming of age, coming to grips with love and sadness, and in every sense of the term, coming home...

Rosamunde Pilcher

The #1 *New York Times* Bestselling Author of *The Shell Seekers* and *September*

COMING HOME

"Rosamunde Pilcher's most satisfying story since *The Shell Seekers*."

—*Chicago Tribune*

"Captivating...The best sort of book to come home to...Readers will undoubtedly hope Pilcher comes home to the typewriter again soon."

—*New York Daily News*

COMING HOME
Rosamunde Pilcher
_____ 95812-9 $7.99 U.S./$9.99 CAN.

No one believes in ghosts anymore, not even in Salem, Massachusetts. And especially not sensible Helen Evett, a widow who lives for her two teenaged kids and who runs the best preschool in town. But when little Katie Byrne enters her school, strange things begin to happen. Katie's widowed father, Nat, begins to awaken feelings in Helen that she had counted as dead. But why does Helen get the feeling that Linda, Katie's mother, is reaching beyond the grave to tell her something?

As Helen and Nat each explore the pain of their losses and the joy of their newfound love, Linda Byrne's ghost plays a bold hand, beseeching Helen to uncover the mystery of her death. But what Helen finds could make her the target of a jealous killer and a modern Salem witch-hunt that threatens her, her family...and the magical second-time-around love that's taking her and Nat by storm.

BESTSELLING, AWARD-WINNING AUTHOR

ANTOINETTE STOCKENBERG

Beyond Midnight

Once upon a time...

A lovely lady fell asleep in a charmed ring of flowers and dreamed of Comlan, king of the fairy realm. She spent a few magical hours by his side, enjoying the company of the handsome king whose golden hair and green eyes could turn the head of any mortal maid...and whose charming attentions captured her heart.

But the year is 1850, and Amy Danton knows better than to believe in fairy tales. However wonderful Comlan seems, he is nothing but a figment of her imagination.

But then, across a crowded ballroom, she sees him— the man of her dreams...

"An exciting romance...this novel has everything a romance reader desires...a beautifully poignant fairy tale."—*Affaire de Coeur*

Once Upon a Time
Marylyle Rogers